DEATH & CO.

Also by David Brierley

Big Bear, Little Bear

The Cody Series
Cold War
Blood Group O
Skorpion's Death
Snowline
Death & Co.

DEATH & CO.

DAVID BRIERLEY

BRASH
BOOKS

Copyright © 1999 by David Brierley

The characters and events portrayed in this book are fictitious. Any similarity to real persons, living or dead, is coincidental and not intended by the author. No part of this book may be reproduced, or stored in a retrieval system, or transmitted in any form or by any means, electronic, mechanical, photocopying, recording, or otherwise, without express written permission of the publisher.

ISBN: 978-1-954841-72-7

Published by
Brash Books
PO Box 8212
Calabasas, CA 91372
www.brash-books.com

This is for John
May your fish always swim in wine

PROLOGUE

Though if Agnès Ledru had known how the police were going to be misled, at least initially, she might have worn a bra that day. Then again, if Agnès had had an inkling of what would happen, she'd have stayed at home, chained the gate, locked and bolted the front door, gone upstairs to the bedroom and locked that door too. She wouldn't have so much as stuck her little snub nose outside.

'Come on, Rina, time we were going.'

But she paused in the hall to look in the full-length mirror. 'Why do we need a mirror like that downstairs?' her husband André had asked. 'For functional narcissism,' she'd replied. He had looked baffled, as anyone might. Why come out with a phrase like *functional narcissism* instead of saying So I *can check my make-up*? The baffled look had turned to a frown. What had become of the pretty girl with the snub nose who had giggled the first time they made love because she said he tickled her inside? Where had the fun and laughter gone?

Agnès Ledru inspected her face: too many lines, skin too dry, too many spider's legs round the eyes from the bright Midi sun. That button of a nose, which was fine on a girl, looked ridiculous on a mature woman. She should get it changed. Once upon a time André used to grin and press her nose as if it were a doorbell. *Anyone home? Can I come in?* When the Muppets had been a brief fashion, he'd called her Miss Piggy. But on a woman past thirty, the snub nose was an embarrassment.

'Rina, Ecaterina Ledru...'

She stooped suddenly and swept up the three-year-old who had been squatting on the carpet. The girl had dark eyes and dark hair while Agnes's own eyes were grey and her hair light brown. André had similar light hair but it didn't matter that the girl was dark. That wasn't important at all. Agnès gave her a kiss.

'Come on Rina-nearly-Ledru, why are we wasting time? We're going to buy you lots of pretty things and a doll and a cuddly rabbit and an ice-cream ... Do you understand?'

The girl stared. Agnès gave her a hug. 'I am your *maman* now. I'll teach you French in no time at all. Say *Bonjour, Maman*.'

The girl stared. The smile, or part of it, remained on Agnes's face. They'd always known the beginning would be difficult, the first days or weeks. They'd talked it over and decided that was another thing that didn't matter. What did matter was that they were able to discuss things now rather than shout or, worse, keep silent. André had so much wanted a family and after they'd had all the tests he'd said, 'See, it's not my fault. Don't blame me.' Fault! And blame! As if she'd been caught out in some marital infidelity.

'Come on, my precious.'

Rina was strapped into the back of the car. Absolutely the first thing they'd bought was a child's seat. When Agnès was behind the steering wheel she turned round and put on a bright face.

'Okay, all ready to go.'

The girl stared. Despite herself Agnès sighed. She wanted to see a smile, though the man had warned her that Ecaterina had gone through traumatic experiences and would need patience before she came to life again. Agnès pressed the radio-control button, the gates swung open and closed automatically after she drove out. She turned left and began the slow, winding descent from the chic converted farmhouse surrounded by high wire and security lighting up in the hills between Nîmes and Alès.

'See, there's a tree, lots of trees, we call them olive trees ... There, that tall dark one is a cypress ... In the fields there are vines. Do you like grapes? See the birds hopping between the rows, those black birds, those are called crows...' She wasn't at all certain they were crows, but it was important to use a lot of words with the little girl so that she got accustomed to hearing French and eventually to speaking it. So far she hadn't opened her mouth at all except to eat. She hadn't even cried, which Agnès found unnerving. It wasn't natural she should be so silent and withdrawn. 'Look, there's a car behind us. A sort of dusty white car. It's the kind of white that people call ivory, like the big tusks of elephants in Africa.' She scowled a bit at the car in the mirror then gave her attention back to the road. 'We mustn't be too long with our shopping. Papa said he would come home for lunch.'

There was a minor miracle. Yesterday, instead of eating at the office canteen where the sinuous black waitress from Martinique had a special smile for him, André had come home at midday, surprising Agnès in half a bikini by their swimming pool. He had stared at little Rina in her playpen for some time, then turned to Agnès and brushed his fingers across a breast. 'Come inside a few minutes. She'll be safe in the playpen.' They had made love on the settee, which they hadn't done for a very long time. It had seemed to Agnès that her husband had been punishing her for not being able to have a child by refusing to touch her. Now, miraculously, a child was there and he'd come back to her.

'Ah, some drivers are so impatient.'

The car was crowding them from behind, giving a sharp blare on its horn.

Agnès said, 'He's in a hurry to get to his own funeral. And on such a lovely day. Look at the blue sky, Rina, no clouds anywhere. Doesn't it make you happy? Can't you feel a smile bubbling up inside?'

Again the horn blared. Agnès took a long curve and came out into a straight stretch. She lifted her foot from the accelerator.

'Go on then. Leave us in peace.'

The dusty white car drew level and as it went past Agnès had a glimpse of two people who seemed to be muffled in scarves. On a hot day like this. Maybe they were Arabs who—

The car had swerved in front and she had to brake sharply. Then she saw the car's red lights pop on and she had to stamp harder on her brakes and haul the steering wheel over and come to a grinding halt, thinking *Merde*, but not saying it out loud to further Rina's education.

Her mouth was open and she was panting from shock, hands gripping the wheel. Two figures got out of the car in front and ran back, and she was so stunned at the sight she didn't even try to get the car into reverse. They wore Balaclavas to mask their faces, check shirts and jeans. One was a woman. The man was holding a pistol. He wasn't aiming at Agnès in particular, the gun was weaving all over the place as he charged up on her side of the car.

God, muggers, she thought, *muggers ride round in cars now.*

The woman, on the far side, had opened the rear door. The man, on Agnès's side, flung her door open. Now the pistol was pointing at her.

'What do you want? Don't point that thing at me. Is it loaded? You want money? I have some money...' She gestured at the handbag on the seat beside her. Then, looking over her shoulder she shouted out, 'What are you doing? *No!* Leave her alone.'

The woman with the masked face was unclipping the twin belts that held Rina secure in the child's seat. Agnès jerked upright to reach back and was caught by her own seatbelt. She snapped it open and made to grab the little girl. A hand gripped her arm and she found herself dragged out of the car and sent sprawling across the road.

'Don't you dare touch her. Help!' she yelled. 'Help!' Her voice died away among the olive trees on the hillside. There was nobody to help.

She scrambled to her feet and tried to get round the car to snatch Rina back from the woman who was now holding the child in her arms. The man was in her way. She started to dodge past him, the pistol never entering her head as a danger, and he grabbed hold of her blouse, took a fistful of it and swung her so hard the material ripped and the blouse fell open to her waist. She staggered back and came forward again. She was desperate. She was stronger than him, filled with a mother's strength. She would tear him apart and wade through his broken body to get her Rina back. The man stood right in her way. The pistol was between them but she didn't see that. All she saw were dark eyes glaring through holes in the Balaclava. She reached out to scratch the eyes, blind him, but what she got was a handful of the Balaclava. She tugged as hard as she could, thinking to unbalance him, and the material ripped, coming clear of his face.

Agnès stopped, her arm outstretched, petrified. She'd wanted to scratch his eyes out, but now that the Balaclava was freed from his face she stood like rock. She saw the man's features, suddenly with a shine of sweat, but overlaid with other images. So the present seemed to dissolve, mixing with the past, and confusion gripped her.

She opened her mouth and took a deep breath, but all that came out was a whisper. 'You.'

The man raised the pistol a little higher and shot her between her naked breasts. She staggered, dropping on hands and knees while her blood spurted on to the tarmac. The man stood above her and shot her in the back. She shuddered. He shot her a third time and she toppled sideways on the road beside her car. She was dead.

The woman holding the child said nothing. Little Rina, as always, stared…

CHAPTER ONE

It was his eyes I was watching because they would signal his attack. It would be no more than a flashed warning, a twitch of facial muscles, a blink, a fractional shift in focus. Such a tiny thing to alert me to his onslaught. He was bigger than me, stronger, his body honed by training. His reach was greater, both his arms and his legs. The legs, in particular, were lethal. I knew he'd spent time in the Far East, trained there. A foot under my chin, the instep angled just right, could snap my neck. It would come so fast, which is why I watched his eyes, needing that fraction of a second's warning.

I decided I had to draw him. I couldn't wait for him to choose his moment. I would tire, my reactions slow.

Hold his eyes, I warned myself. Don't let your concentration go. Not for an instant.

I moved. I was aware of increased tautness in his body but there was no other response. We were both crouching slightly, knees bent. I extended my left arm, fist clenched, wrist turned a degree. Go on, take it. It's my gift to you. Aren't you tempted? Don't you think you could use that arm, twist it, break it? Don't you think you'd have me at your mercy?

Now he was moving. Not his eyes. They held mine, trying to read my motive. His right hand extended towards my left hand. Would he make a simple grab? A chop? Would he try to come inside my gift of a limb? I was prepared.

With infinite caution his hand approached mine. His fingers tensed, making a blade. Then the thumb separated, making a hook. I could see this at the edge of my vision as I held his eyes. He was considering the possibilities of my gift, sifting, rejecting. He was undecided. His knowledge of *savate* and *tae kwon do* was of no help because he didn't know my intentions.

I saw the sweat begin on his face. He was well-muscled, fit, and it wasn't the sweat of a man out of condition. It was warm in here but it wasn't jungle-hot. I had manoeuvred him, while we were taking each other's measure, until he had the sun on his face, shining in his eyes. No woman takes on an attacker half her weight again without every scrap of help she can get. But it wasn't the sun that made him sweat either. It was nerves.

At any moment his nerves would snap.

We were very close.

Once more he was moving, waving away my offer of a limb now, almost batting my hand, again and again. He was tense and the rhythm of his hand reaching out and striking at mine was building the tension in him, until very soon it would become unbearable. I don't think there was any warning in my face: I simply did a backward roll and jumped up to face him once more. His eyes were wide in surprise and then narrowed again. I saw the bob of his Adam's apple: forehead wet, throat dry, that's how it was taking him. To attack me now would need three strides, maybe four. I had to make him do it, I had to make him take the risk, I had to force him into error.

I turned my back on him.

I stood at my full height, shoulders straight, head at a slight angle to improve my hearing. But I didn't look at him, my eyes no longer held his. I would get no warning from the flicker of his glance. I relied on another older sense, inherited from the wild. We have no name for it. We call it the sixth sense, which means nothing.

In the *corrida* at Valencia I had seen Luis Herrero turn his back on the bull. That was when Herrero was at his peak. It was to show his confidence, his complete mastery over the animal. Five minutes later the bull was being dragged from the arena. In my case it was more of a confidence trick. In five minutes time it could be me—

Now. He was on the attack.

I did a forward roll, jumping up, spinning to face him as he completed his action. It had been a jumping kick, left leg extended, right foot bracing left calf. I didn't know the name of that move, nor of the swinging kick that was aimed at the back of my neck. I ducked, feeling the rush of air, and dropped to all fours. His kick, missing me, unbalanced him. But he was prepared for that and stamped his foot on the boards to give himself impetus; he jumped back to confront me, legs apart, hands protecting his stomach and his throat, hands like claws, vicious and dangerous claws, frustration and anger darkening his face, the pressure of blood rising until his vision would be darkened and his hearing dulled and his brain flooded with the single thought: Kill her.

The move they call *le petit chat* has nothing to do with martial arts. It is a simple survival technique. And if you want to survive you have to be fast. *Le petit chat* is diving between your opponent's open legs, tunnelling, squirming, scrambling, whatever it takes. For a second or two he is disoriented, and in his confusion he doesn't know whether an attack will come from in front or behind. If he's male, there is the added fear that the attack could come from underneath. Even the possibility unnerves him, unmans him. The panic factor stops any rational counter.

I shot upright behind him. Now I had him, now while his nerves were shooting out distress signals, flooding his brain. I simply climbed his body, knees gripping his waist, fists to either side of his head, thumbs pressing into his neck under his ears.

'Don't move,' I said, my voice urgent.

There'd been no words until now. I could feel his body weight shifting under me.

'Don't try a counter,' I warned. 'Don't think you can throw me. I can kill you. It would take two seconds, three seconds, finish. There'd be no way back for you. I've had the training, you haven't. You've learnt a sport, I've learnt how to survive. And if my survival means the other person's death, that's tough.'

It was a long speech when you're gripping like a monkey and you're poised to end someone's life.

'You're beaten,' I said. 'You've lost. Admit it. Just say "Yes".'

I felt his lungs expand. He wanted to shout, to express his anger, but it came out a harsh whisper. 'Goddamn you, Cody.'

He could have said worse. I dropped on to the balls of my feet and for a moment was wary. Al Richards was a friend, but a friend can look for revenge.

We had lunch. That was when he evened the score. The male ego is a tender thing and I had bruised his too much for that day. No man likes to admit defeat at the hands of a woman. I would have been happy with a *casse-croûte* from a Tunisian café but Richards wouldn't.

Richards was one of those people who can live on the fringe of your life for years, more than an acquaintance but never a bosom pal. We'd first met at a mutual friend's studio. Erica Fawcett was holding a *vernissage* of her latest and most daring. 'I call it post-bullshit art,' she said. 'The critics call it dirty pictures.' The canvases were of nudes, very explicit, with jokey titles. A close-up of a woman's genitalia was entitled 'The hole in the O-zone'. Another showed a male erection and Richards had materialized at my shoulder. 'How does she get her model to hold his pose?' he asked, before we had even swopped names. 'Volunteer,' I told him. 'Who knows what she does with a paintbrush.' Our eyes had locked together at that first meeting but somehow nothing had come of it. We'd seen the occasional film, had dinner, but nothing serious. Just once he'd run a finger across my lips when we said goodnight. It was sexier than a kiss. Possibilities, but Al was romancing elsewhere at the time and it went no further.

Then one day we'd met by chance in the Champs-Elysées. There was an exhibition of Botero's statues, great bold bulging nudes set among the trees. 'Like Erica Fawcett on steroids,' Richards said. 'Your type?' I asked. For an answer Al had smiled and linked his arm through mine. So our on-off relationship was on again, and a little closer. Not the ultimate closeness but I could see that idea hovering in his mind. I could feel my way into his male thought processes: Yes, make the challenge to this woman with the rather special past, one-to-one combat, use superior strength and a longer reach to pin her to the floor, body pressing down body, until she is helpless and has to cry out *I submit.* Which was the reason for today's session, and now lunch.

'I'm buying, I'm choosing,' he said. 'Do you know the Kwan Dinh?'

'I trust you, Al.'

His full name is F Albert Richards. I don't know what the initial F stands for, never considered it until now. Why choose to be known by your middle name? That's not the American way. Perhaps the F is for Francis. He would be Francis Albert, like Sinatra. But he didn't want to be Frank. And why had I said I *trust you?*

Richards could choose the restaurant, I could choose the table. We sat outside where three tables crouched behind some tubs of greenery. The Kwan Dinh was a Vietnamese restaurant in a side-street off rue Monge. Paris was in the grip of the tourist season but not in this backwater.

So if I chose the table, it was his turn again and he chose the food. And the wine. 'Is the Muscadet sur *lie?*' he asked the waiter. The waiter had to fetch the bottle and Richards scrutinised the label before he was satisfied.

'Taste it,' Richards said.

I tasted it. 'Nice,' I said. 'Perfect for a hot July day.'

'Nice?' He pretended outrage. He was still riled at the defeat and that was working its way through his system. 'Can't you taste more than that, Co? A good grower in the Sèvre-et-Maine leaves the wine on the lees until Easter. Bottle it straight after Christmas

and it's like, oh, picking strawberries when they're half white, you're missing the full flavour. The patient *vigneron* lets the yeast decompose and the wine picks up all sorts of subtle flavours. You get a salty yeasty tang. Sometimes you taste a hint of greengages or peaches or apples, or even grass. There should be a *zing*—'

'Grass, did you say?' I sipped again, pursing my lips, rolling the wine round my tongue, casting my eyes towards heaven, the whole show. 'I've never drunk grass before. Smoked a bit…'

He stared and stared. I held his eyes in the same routine we'd gone through only an hour before. 'Okay,' he said, 'so I'm a wine bore.'

That was better. It wasn't that Al Richards was a wine bore but that he'd learnt too much too fast. I remembered an earlier meal, one of those inconclusive evenings. He'd said, 'I'm just a farm boy from the boondocks, Co. Can you imagine what a revelation this city was? The food and wine in Paris, hell, they're like meat and drink to me.' I can forgive a lot in a man who pulls up short and gives himself a swift kick in the pants.

So why didn't I relax and simply enjoy the lunch? Al was a friend, so why not laugh and let my hair down and maybe flirt a little? I had the sense of something incomplete. Al had been trying to move deeper into my life in the past few weeks. It gave me the feeling of a hand wriggling to fit into a glove, and this glove was not certain it wanted those fingers stretching and flexing as they eased themselves inside. I had bettered him in unarmed combat. I had mocked his dedication as a gourmet. Now I attacked his integrity in his work. That's a terrible thing to do to a man. It's how he defines himself. He can say: 'I'm a bricklayer, I'm a doctor, I'm President of General Motors, I'm President of Venezuela, I'm a journalist.' That is the core of his being, the heart. I was about to stab him there. Perhaps he would never speak to me again. How was I to know it would end up in less than a fortnight with us close, so close, yes, almost that close? You can't see the future. You can only make a mess of the present.

This is what I did. This is how it happened.

We had eaten crab on skewers of sugar cane and were waiting for the next dish, a fish called pomfret 'specially flown in, crisp-fried, with a sauce of ginger and *nuoc mam*'. *That* was the foodie side of Richards speaking again.

He'd used a spare chair to hang his jacket on, and laid a couple of newspapers on the seat. One was the *American Journal*, published right here in Paris. Al was a staff reporter on the *AJ*. The other paper was *Libération*. I picked them both up. The *AJ*'s lead story was about the big Berlin conference. There'd been a photo-call with half a dozen men looking grave but satisfied with themselves. They were important fellows, weren't they, presidents and chancellors and such, and they were going to put the world right. The world had been screwed up by their predecessors, other important fellows who'd looked equally solemn and smug. But *Libération* gave only a paragraph to the Berlin Summit down at the bottom of the page. The big black headlines shouted: MOTHER KILLED, GIRL KIDNAPPED. The daughter had just been adopted. There had been no witnesses. There was no ransom demand. The husband was distraught. There was a thumbnail picture of him but the big spread was of the woman's corpse on the road beside her car. The newspaper hadn't airbrushed out the blood, as they used to do. This was a shocker and meant to be.

I stared at the photo. I was glad the deep-fried pomfret hadn't been brought. I wasn't feeling hungry.

The photo showed a woman a year or so older than me, blonde hair, with her shirt torn open. She lay on her side, her legs drawn up. She could have been on her knees praying when she was shot and simply keeled over. Agnès Ledru was the woman's name. I don't think her prayers had been granted. She wore no bra and blood stained her breasts. Goddamnit, why didn't they have the decency to cover her nakedness? A police spokesman was quoted as saying: 'Because of the condition of the clothing and because the victim was an attractive woman who was not wearing a bra, we initially thought this was a rape that had gone wrong.'

Jesus Christ. Jesus *Christ.*

A rush of anger blotted out every other thing I felt.

'Tell me,' I said to Richards, though it was no fault of his, 'what is a rape that goes right? The rapist succeeds and walks off smiling?'

His eyes were switching between my face and the lurid photo spread. He said, 'We don't print that kind of stuff. You know, sex 'n' violence—'

'Huh.' I wouldn't let him go on. I was filled with rage at the woman's fate, the police spokesman, the lottery of pain we call life. My anger was spreading in all directions and now I focused it on the man sharing a table with me. I held both papers up side by side. It was like some cheap lawyer's trick in court. *Members of the jury, you see the evidence before your own eyes...* It's not a moment I'm proud of.

'Al, tell me, what kind of rag do you work for? This dominates the front pages of all the papers in France and you don't give it even one miserable paragraph. Not a sentence. Nothing. So far as you're concerned she might never have lived.'

Richards took a sip of Muscadet. He didn't seem to be tasting greengages or grass. From his expression he'd put his lips to the specimen bottle.

I could have stopped right there. I could have pulled a grin: Only kidding, Al, just putting on a floor show until the pomfret arrives. But the fate of Agnès Ledru, the callousness of the press in printing that disgusting photo, the attitude of the police – I was boiling. Also... also... my thinking was affected by the situation with Al Richards. If I'm honest, I have to admit that. I'd won once today and I wanted to win again. Cody always has to win. The will to win has saved my life in the past. Some day, somewhere, I'll be up against someone with a stronger will to win. I don't think about that day.

He put his glass down and opened his mouth to reply. I wouldn't let him.

'I know what you're going to say: a newspaper selects. Every newspaper does it, selects what it judges important for its readers. There are a million stories a day you don't run and the Ledru murder and kidnapping is one of them. Right?'

He was going to agree. I didn't need it.

'Sure, you'll say, it is devastating for the people concerned but on the Richter scale of global human suffering it doesn't score a blip. It is not significant to the readers of the *American Journal*. Well, it's time your readers joined the human race and if you printed a story like that, showing human suffering and not just politics and wars and the three-month forward rate for the Deutschmark…'

I ran out of steam. I couldn't even think how to finish the sentence. Part of me was needling him, part of me believed it. The readers of the *AJ* were resident Americans in Europe, businessmen, military brass, embassy and airline people. Plus tourists from the States, middle-aged guys from Milwaukee and Pittsburgh with pouchy faces like German bishops. Plus the new Euro-élite who'd done a spell in the States, financiers and marketing executives and men who packaged big deals.

'And you,' he said. 'You read my rag.'

He was adding me to the list of people I'd thought of but hadn't spoken out loud. It was as if he was keeping pace with what I was thinking. Goddamnit, get out of my mind, keep your distance, stop making a take-over bid.

'Don't you even care? As a reporter, don't you think you should dig out the story? As a human being, doesn't it concern you?'

He said, 'I had a phone call yesterday evening. It was early, around seven, before the paper was put to bed. I'd finished my think-piece on the Berlin conference and the editor was skimming through it. Phone call for Mr Richards.'

I already had a chill feeling up my spine. I'd been provoking Al and when someone is so calm in responding you know it's because he's holding all the aces.

'It was André Ledru on the line. I know him, you see, Co. I care. I've known him a long time. We go back to my Far East days. The French were in Vietnam long before we Americans fucked it up, but they had the sense to get out. I was in Ho Chi Minh, aka Saigon, and there weren't many roundeyes about and I guess only one Frenchman, André. I don't know what he did during the day but we had a couple of nights out together. Later on, when I was based in Bangkok, I ran into him again. Bangkok is quite a city for men on their own and we went on the town together. Then when I got the job in Paris on the *AJ*, he read my by-line and got in touch. He'd just got the job with Systel down near Nîmes.'

The waiter arrived with the next dishes. The fish was still sizzling on a big platter, swimming in a puddle of pale brown sauce. There was rice that was fragrant, with nuggets of smoked pork. There was a basket of fresh herbs: basil, coriander, mint. The waiter filleted the fish and served us, bowed his head and left. But we couldn't eat yet. We had unfinished business.

'So, the phone call last night. Are you listening, Co?'

'I'm listening.'

'André asked me for two things. The one was a favour. Would I keep the story and the photos out of the *AJ*? Hell, I'm a reporter, I'm not the editor. I told him I couldn't make that kind of decision, not even for old times' sake. In any case, I said, even if I did, the other papers will all run it. He said he didn't know people on the other papers or he'd call them too. But the *AJ* was important because a lot of top businessmen he dealt with read it and he didn't want his personal tragedy paraded in front of them. Then he came out with a more persuasive argument, something my editor would buy. This is where you make your entrance on stage, Co.'

He started to eat then. He was just making me wait, building the suspense. I *knew* that was what he was doing. He was making himself part of my life. I took a bite of food and said, 'The pomfret is fan-bloody-tastic.' That was an Erica Fawcett word but it got no response. I looked away, turned my attention to the street.

From rue Monge, a block away, came a sudden growl as a wave of cars was released by traffic lights. Two young men stopped to inspect the menu. Students from Germany, I decided, short shorts and no socks. The sun was almost directly overhead and in half an hour the table I'd chosen was going to be impossibly hot. Across the street the shutters of an upper window were thrown open and a woman in a dressing-gown leant out to inspect the day. Why was she just getting up? Paris is a city with a million mysteries.

'André said to me, on the phone, my editor standing at my shoulder and tapping his pen at something in my think-piece he didn't like, André said: "Tell your editor if he keeps me out of his paper, he can have an exclusive on future developments." I said: "How can it be exclusive when you've got the police PR guy holding press conferences?" This brought him on to the second thing he wanted from me: the name of an investigator, someone good from Paris. He said that for a lot of reasons he didn't want to go into he couldn't hire someone locally and the cops were dead on their feet and—'

'Hey, whoa, hold it.' I smacked the table and made the glasses jump. 'Are you leading up to what I think you are? I am not a private detective. I am not going to the South of France to tangle with an official police investigation. So you weren't so dumb as to give him my name. Al? Al, look at me.'

'André said to me: "Don't give me his name over the phone because even now the police are probably listening in." I said: "It's not a him, it's a her." '

'Richards, I do not believe what I'm hearing.'

'André said: "A *woman?* If she gets in a tight corner, I have to hold her hand?" '

'I've heard enough. I'm getting up and getting out. I am not Marlowe or Peter Wimsey.'

Not Marlowe, not Lord Peter, not Sherlock Holmes. That's true. However. There's always a however in life. I earn my living, I do certain jobs, track people down, carry parcels, find out what's going on, whatever's necessary. But the big but is this: I'm not for hire to everybody, I am the one who chooses, not some reporter helping out an old carousing pal.

Al laid his knife and fork down to give his full attention to me. 'But you find out the score, you ask questions, you dig deep, you don't accept defeat. Plus you've got the training, you're a survivor.' He put a hand up to touch his neck where it was sore. 'My editor is a stubborn old mule but I persuaded him. Which is why the *AJ* doesn't mention the *affaire Ledru*. He said, my editor, that if you cracked the case and came up with an exclusive you'd be paid top dollar and he'd give you a by-line. You'd be a star. Your name up in lights. How does that grab you?'

Grab me? Like a pit-bull terrier. I was horrified. I hate personal publicity. I won't have people prying into my life, what I've done in the past, what I'm doing now. There are too many psychopaths out there in the jungle and I don't want them beating at my door. Richards knew that.

'You bastard.'

'That's my girl.' For the first time that day he looked happy. Medium happy, I'd say. He reached his hand out and covered mine. The skin of his hand was rougher than you'd expect for a journalist but not for someone who worked out in the gym for an hour most days. To my mind a man who does that is punishing his body for past sins.

'Okay, you're not a pro. You come up with something, I'll help you knock it into shape, give it a touch of colour. You know the kind of thing, how the birds no longer sing along the road of death…' He paused and his open farmer's boy face went into a frown. 'Of course if you think it's too much to handle…'

If I'm not a private eye, I'm not a reporter either, never have been, never could be. He was just issuing a different kind of challenge. He was being cynical about it, trying to establish his authority and my inferiority. I *knew* that. Everything was so clear, his motives so transparent. Then why didn't I simply tell him to get lost? Or stand up and run away down the sunny side of the street after the two German students? I can pretend it was because of a murdered woman and a kidnapped child and arrogant police. True, all true, but not the whole truth.

Damn Al Richards. A challenge is a challenge. Like the challenge to fight him had been. Like so many challenges in the past. You're the kind of person who backs off from a challenge or the kind of person who rises and takes it. Even when it's stupid and dangerous and carries a big red sticker on it saying: *Keep off – your life is at risk.* Or should that be: *Even because?* Perhaps I should ask Richards. He seems to understand me so well.

CHAPTER TWO

It was the heat that made it almost unbearable. It was heat that had been building for months, never quite going away at night. Two pairs of tall windows stood open to a balcony but it was afternoon and no breath of fresh air came in.

Dr Fignon said, 'They promised an air-conditioning unit years ago. I forget, seven years, nine years ago. The air-conditioner is agreed in principle. It is a question solely of money. The budget has been cut, they say, or spent or promised elsewhere. I thought now that Chirac was President there would be more money but...' He shrugged his shoulders. 'Maybe next year, they say. Though they say that every year.'

The smell in the room was appalling.

'It's difficult to get to grips with bureaucrats,' I said.

'Exactly, madame. If there was a principle to argue with, it would not be so frustrating. But if there is no money...' A shrug finished his sentence again.

'It is necessary to think like a bureaucrat,' I said. 'Burrow into their thought processes. They say it is a question of priorities. Yes? Then may I suggest that priorities can be a matter of principle.'

The French adore a bout of logic-chopping. I've played these games before but never in such conditions. I could scarcely breathe.

Dr Fignon went quite still. His head was half-turned so he kept one eye on me. He was short, tubby, balding and brown from the sun. 'You know,' he said, 'that approach might have possibilities. I shall draft a memorandum on the principle of priorities. Yes, yes, yes.'

He turned away towards a bank of drawers. My eyes were watering now, the rasping stink of formaldehyde catching at my throat. Dr Fignon was used to it. Perhaps he felt ordinary fresh air lacked a certain bite. I thought we were at last getting down to business but he turned back to me.

'Those windows are the problem,' he said. He pointed an accusing finger. 'They give on to the courtyard. If they gave on to the street I could not have them open because there would be complaints. But I leave them open for the hottest months, so why do I need an air-conditioner?'

'Security?' I suggested. 'Is there an entrance into the courtyard from the street? A burglar could climb through the open windows.'

Dr Fignon thought about this. I failed with my suggestion this time. 'Who'd want to steal a corpse? People want to lose corpses. That is common. A corpse is left in the boot of a car or tucked into a dustbin. But who would think: Ah, what my house needs…'

Come to that, who wanted to view a corpse? It was necessary, I told myself. I'd come to Nîmes and made the mortuary my first call. Get it over with. Also, get the impact of it. You think a photo in a newspaper is shocking until you see the real thing. The reality of the broken body is like a punch in the solar plexus. You feel the pain of the murder, not just think about it.

Finally he pulled open one of the drawers and pulled out a metal-framed stretcher on rollers. A pale green sheet covered the body. Fignon twitched back the cloth from feet that looked marbled and dull. He tipped his head to one side to read from the tag tied to a big toe.

'Ledru, Agnès. Date of birth. Identity number. Autopsy reference. Body identified by husband. So forth. A summary of life when it is over.' Fignon dug a piece of paper from his pocket to refresh his memory. 'Is Chief Inspector Crevecoeur interested in such details?'

'Crevecoeur. I detest the man. Don't get me started on the dead end jobs he's pushed me into. 'In due course.' I'd used Crevecoeur's name to bluff my way in. Call it payback time.

'Sûreté Nationale,' he said, wondering. 'Well, I don't know what Agnès Ledru's death has to do with the security of France.'

'Nor should you know,' I told him. I used my no-nonsense-from-you-my-man voice. 'When there are reasons of state concerned...'

It was my turn to leave a sentence dangling. Not that it needed finishing. You can do what you like in the name of France – blow up a Greenpeace boat, hand millions of francs over to terrorists, send in the *paras* to prop up some Neanderthal dictator in Africa. Nobody argues if it is in the interests of France.

Dr Fignon considered what I'd said. 'Certainly this death is somewhat out of the ordinary. My usual customers are male, Arab, with stab wounds. An argument over a woman, an unpaid debt, a family feud carried over from their *bled* back in Algeria. So Ledru, Agnès, time to show your face.'

He peeled the sheet back from her face, her shoulders, her chest, as far as the bottom of her ribcage.

I thought I was going to vomit or faint. It's just the smell of formaldehyde, I told myself. Think of El Salvador. Think of anything rather than this life cut short. Look at her, note details, but set the brain another task to blunt the shock.

Al Richards could never come here. He can't stand blood or doctors or needles. He confessed he has to have a general anaesthetic before the dentist can use a drill. You'd never think that of a man who trains so hard and devotes himself to martial arts.

Her lips had been sewn together, Agnès Ledru's lips. Her nose had been wiped clean except for a tiny smear of black blood in one nostril. One eye was closed tight, the other open a fraction as if she was peeping out at a nightmarish world. She'd been right: the nightmare had overwhelmed her.

In a corridor outside, a man was whistling. Why is it only men whistle? Think about that fascinating fact and not Agnès's sewn lips. Is a man's whistle a form of territorial marking? Construct a whole sociological theory about that.

'Her assailant shot her three times,' Dr Fignon pointed out. 'First here towards the centre of the chest, the edge of the mammary, through the lung. She was at a slight angle to the assailant, possibly looking over her shoulder at something, but that is a conjecture. There is no exit hole for the bullet. It lodged against the spine. The ballistics people have it now.'

There was an area of cold round my feet and ankles. It was coming from the open chiller drawer. There were smells too. Formaldehyde was the dominant one but there were floral notes I caught. The body was washed after the autopsy. It could be the soap I was smelling. It could be that she'd been wearing perfume that hadn't faded or been lathered off.

What perfume would she wear? I wear *Joy de Patou*. Not all the time. Not when I'm in the gym facing a man who's determined to subdue me. Not on a visit to a mortuary. But there are other times, the theatre, a special dinner. I wear it behind the ears, between the breasts, in bed. And you, Agnès, did you like *Joy de Patou*?

Fignon was continuing, 'She was shot twice in the back. Note, these are not entry wounds but exit wounds. You understand, madame?' Did he think I was blind? Stupid? 'She was on her hands and knees and the assailant was standing above her.'

Assailant. Dr Fignon liked that word. He used it in its masculine form, assuming it was a man who shot her. I asked, 'How do you know he was above her?'

Fignon seemed surprised at the question. 'Grit from the road on the knees of her slacks. Also embedded in her palms. See the marks in the skin.'

> *Marjolaine, t'es si jolie*
> *Marjolaine, le printemps est fleuri…*

The man in the corridor burst into song. He ran out of words and went on to *la-da-da-da*.

There were three or four shallow indentations in one of Agnes's palms. They looked like the tiny craters left by adolescent acne. Fignon let the hand fall back.

'Here – this one – is the third shot. The exit hole after it passed through the ventricle. So, cause of death, heart failure.'

The clinical cause of death. A lot of people die of heart failure but not in the way Agnès Ledru had. No, Richards would definitely not have been able to stomach a visit here. Instead he'd flown to the conference in Berlin. That was more his style. The politicians were clearing up after the last bout of hostilities but at least the corpses were fifty years dead and decently buried.

> *Tu m'avais dit*
> *Que tu m'attendrais…*

Another cheerful burst of deceived love from the corridor.

'Do you want to see the entrance wounds on the back? You'll have to help me turn her.'

'That won't be necessary.'

The skin of her breasts had been cleaned but the bruised flesh was dark purple against ghost white.

'She hadn't been drinking?'

'No,' Dr Fignon said, then added, 'except breakfast coffee with milk.'

'No drugs?'

'No.'

'No sign of sexual interference?"

'There you are. That just shows how the police blunder about without really thinking. Her blouse was ripped open before she was shot. The police originally had the idea she was resisting rape but they seem to have dropped that notion. There is no sign of recent intercourse or other sexual use.'

I gave myself a few seconds rest, looking round the mortuary room instead, at the white ceramic shades on the lights, at the tiled floor, the tiled walls. Easy to scrub down. In El Salvador, at the army base outside Pulapeque, I'd rescued a man from the room where they interrogated guerillas, or the cousins of guerillas, or anybody whose face they took a dislike to on a slow day. That room had had walls draped with polythene sheeting: easy to wipe away the blood and gore. The smell had lingered, though, because they couldn't scrub the air.

I looked back a last time at Agnès. There were lines at the corners of her eyes as if she screwed her eyes up too much at the sun. Her hair was pale brown and the blonde streaks in it could have been natural. I felt she'd lived a lot of her life out of doors, going topless in her own garden. Her torso didn't show the marks of a bikini top. Her snub nose and the half-open eye gave her the look of a girl pretending to be asleep but watching all the same. And the lips sewn together as if she had something to tell and the only way to stop her was to close her mouth permanently. What did she want to confide in me? A name? A dark secret from her past? A description of what Dr Fignon called her *assailant*?

'Tell me,' I said, 'was there anything else you noticed not strictly to do with the cause of her death?'

'You're referring to the fibres under her fingernails?'

'Cody,' the inspector said, to himself more than to me. He was standing at the open double windows. There was no air-conditioning here either and he had his jacket off. 'Miss Cody, sit down please.' He spoke these few words in English to show he wasn't your average truncheon-wielding thicko, then switched. 'But you understand French well enough, so I've heard.'

'I speak French.' Heard from whom? It was a typical cop's trick, getting you worried that every secret of your life was known.

'I am Inspector Gaudet.'

He held my *carte de séjour* in his right hand. He had no left hand. His shirt sleeve was pinned up above the elbow. A bullet, a butcher's cleaver, a concrete slab, a speeding car – how had he lost the limb? Wasn't there some regulation against being a one-armed police inspector?

'I have telephoned the Sûreté Nationale in Paris.'

'Of course,' I said.

'Sit down,' he told me again. 'You're not going anywhere.'

He was running his thumbnail across my *carte.* You get one of those mailing shots and scratch away at the grey panel until you uncover the news that yes, your name has been entered for the big draw. If the residence card turned out to be fake, I would be the grand prize.

'I spoke to Chief Inspector Crevecoeur. The Chief Inspector appeared ... agitated at my questions. Indeed he was acquainted with a woman called Cody but she did not work for the Sûreté, he had given her no authorization to act in any capacity in this matter, nor to use his name.'

Inspector Gaudet fixed his eyes on mine. I had been picked up when I left the mortuary and brought to the police headquarters. He was waiting to see what I confessed to.

'Chief Inspector Crevecoeur is a friend.' I crossed my fingers at the lie. 'Does a woman need more authorization than that?'

I surprised myself. It just slipped out without planning. Gaudet lowered himself into a chair and was transfixed. He sat rigid, not a blink or a breath or a twitch, simply staring. He had a small office and I was aware of sounds coming through the opaque glass partition: a telephone ringing, a typewriter, a radio tuned to a foreign station that played classical music.

'Well,' Gaudet said at length. 'Well now.' He was baffled about the relationship and lit himself another cigarette.

I said, 'I've been able to perform one or two services for him in the past. Services for the security of France, I mean.'

Crevecoeur confused his own needs with the security of the state. He had made use of me, bribed me, threatened me, coerced me into doing things. He had ways of hinting that my residence permit would be cancelled or my tax affairs investigated. At least once he hoped what I got into would end my life. He is a bastard. He is good at his job. He would say the two things go together.

'So your visit to the morgue,' he said, 'had nothing to do with the Sûreté Nationale?'

'No.'

'Nor had it anything to do with Chief Inspector Crevecoeur?'

'No. When I said he was a friend, I really meant that he's made use of me before. Leant on me. Imposed himself. So in my turn I made use of his name. There you are. Now you are in possession of the facts.'

Gaudet changed. He slumped back in the chair, cigarette in his mouth, one eye closed against the spiral of smoke. He put a hand behind his head. His stump of an arm moved in sympathy and he'd have put his left hand behind his head if he could.

'Good,' he said. 'Very good. I hate them. The people up in Paris. The smooth types, the snobs, the phonies, the know-it-alls, the empire builders ... Have I left anybody out?'

'The double-crossers, the blackmailers, the dealers, the thug—'

'We have thugs here.'

'Official thugs who cheat and kill for the good of the state?'

'Oh yes.' He sat straight in his chair, extending his stump of an arm. 'I was left-handed until 1987. March that year, the middle of the month.'

'The ides of March.'

'That's right.' He smiled. You don't often get a smile from a French cop. 'We had a tip-off about a suspected drugs factory. Strictly it was in the *gendarmerie's* territory, out in the country.

But the tip-off had come our way and we do have something of a drug problem so we felt justified in acting. Afterwards, of course, all the smart alecs said it served us right for poaching, but at least we were bloody *doing* something...' For a moment the memory of old turf wars brought colour to his face. He shrugged. 'Go to this isolated farmhouse, we were told, and you'll find it's where they're cooking the opium to make heroin. I went with two carloads of men after dark. There were no lights showing in the building. So, being young and hot and foolish, I went in with three men, the rest hiding out in some bushes. The first room, nothing, nobody. The second room we went into – the kitchen in fact – was bare except for a table. I mean, no pots and pans, no food, no bottles. Just the table and on the table this wooden crate. I remember it was a moonlit night and the shutters were open and there this crate sat, waiting. It was stamped in big letters even a child or an idiot policeman could see: *Motori a scoppio*. Now our anonymous phone call had said it was Turkish truck drivers bringing in the opium base.'

'*Motori a scoppio* is Italian?' I was pretty certain though I only have tourist Italian.

'Correct. After they came through Yugoslavia – this was in the days when there was a Yugoslavia – the Turkish trucks used to pass through Trieste, Verona, Milan, that route. I thought the opium could have been repacked somewhere in Italy. Actually I didn't think. What I did was lift the lid of the packing case. They'd made it easy, it wasn't even nailed down. Boom! It had been booby-trapped. I lost my hand. That explosion was the signal and the windows were smashed in and the doors flung open and about a dozen men with guns were screaming: "Freeze, don't move or you're dead." My men had their guns out and there was a certain amount of shooting, couple of people were winged, then my reinforcements came to the rescue, screaming: "Freeze, don't move," et cetera. So it all stopped and we all glowered at each other. These men with guns weren't Turks. And they realized we weren't Lebanese. They'd been trying to do a sting, entrapping these Lebanese arms dealers, and they never bloody told any of us. Can you believe it? These high-powered Paris types never told the hick cops what they were doing. The sound of laughter very far off – if you could have heard it – was some Middle Eastern arms king enjoying his joke of setting the police to fight the police.'

You don't often have a tête-à-tête like that in a police station. But the right button had been pressed and the bitterness in him had flooded out. I said, 'Crevecoeur wasn't there by any chance?'

It wasn't Crevecoeur's style. Crevecoeur was a loner. What might have been his style was setting the confrontation up, but what would be the point? Gaudet was busy lighting himself a fresh cigarette. He was frowning at my question or at his memories.

I went on, 'You'd remember Crevecoeur because he's very thin. Everything seems squeezed out of him. Narrow body, no chest to boast of, compressed face. His lips are like two playing cards…'

I came to a stop. Gaudet was eyeing me as I went on about Crevecoeur's physical looks.

'These were the usual Paris fat cats. Too many lunches, not enough exercise.'

The door opened without a warning knock. A man in uniform glanced at me first, then at Gaudet. He said, 'We've got a preliminary on the fibres.'

Inspector Gaudet did the flickering eyes routine as well: first the uniformed cop, then me, then the cop again.

Agnès Ledru had fibres under her fingernails but I wasn't meant to know anything about that. I was in Copland, a state of mind that is the same the world over. The men all wear uniforms. The men who wear plainclothes all wear suits that look like uniforms. The men in deep disguise all wear designer denim that looks like a uniform. The women are all men really. It is a giant masonic brotherhood and the sign they recognize each other by is toughness. Even when they hate each other's guts, they give a nod to each other's toughness. Theirs is a code of conduct that excludes ordinary citizens. And every scrap of information is a secret. I had broken one taboo by viewing the corpse. Fibres under the fingernails? I almost yawned at such talk. Count me out, fellers. I'll just sit here and look decorative. I'm the raw material for one of your future investigations waiting for disaster to knock me down.

The new policeman was waiting for Gaudet to finish his talk with me. And Gaudet, who'd opened up so out of character because of his dislike of metropolitan types, remembered he'd found out nothing about me. He put on a show in front of his subordinate.

'So why are you here? Why are you asking questions, bluffing your way in to view the corpse?'

I wasn't a journalist but what else could I say that was plausible? Richards had manoeuvred me into this, challenged me. I'd use him.

'I'm doing a piece for a newspaper.'

'Crevecoeur didn't say you were a reporter.'

'Not what you'd call a career journalist. A special project.'

He frowned. Papers are bad news for the police. They may report the arrests but they also report the bungles and the corruption and the brutality.

'About the murder and the kidnapping?'

'Yes.'

'Which newspaper?'

'The *American Journal.*'

His face had frozen over. He gazed at me and then his look went inward. I could follow his thought processes: What have I said? What have I given away to this woman? Nothing was the answer. I was a rotten reporter who didn't even ask questions. Here was one question it was too late to ask: Why did Gaudet imagine the Sûreté Nationale might be interested in this obscure provincial tragedy?

Gaudet said to the uniformed man who still stood near the door. 'How many journalists are out at the house?'

'Less than half a dozen, last I heard.'

'Has Monsieur Ledru spoken to them, given an interview, answered questions, posed for photographs?'

'No to all of that.'

Gaudet turned his attention back to me. 'What point is there in staying here? The professionals are getting nowhere so you're not likely to learn anything. Go back to Paris is my advice. There's an overnight train. Be on it.' He nodded in the direction of the window. The station was a stroll away.

But Agnes's corpse was very fresh in my mind. I felt for her. She had been wounded and while she crouched on all fours with her lungs filling with blood, her murderer had shot her twice more. Her face might show lines of wear but her body was still youthful and firm. A lot more fun in life had lain ahead of her but now she was just so much carrion. To the police she was a statistic, almost a bore, a nuisance who attracted the hated media. She'd had a terrible death and deserved better than this cynical inspector.

I said, 'Why is Agnès Ledru's murder and the kidnapping the responsibility of the Nîmes police? Wasn't the crime committed out in the country? Isn't it the business of the *gendarmerie?*'

He took a moment to think about his answer. 'The kidnapper or kidnappers are very likely hiding out in the city. It is natural we should take a deep interest in the affair. Cooperation between the branches of law and order is strong.'

That was a lie. The police and the *gendarmerie* hated each other's guts. Inspector Gaudet hated the Sûreté Nationale. The Sûreté loathed all the secret networks. And the secret networks, whatever titles they were known by this year, held everybody else in contempt.

I tried a long shot. 'Could it be you already had an interest in the Ledrus before this murder?'

He leant his fist on the desk to help push himself upright. 'You're just another one of the Paris types. Nosy, arrogant, lying. You lied your way into the morgue. You lied about working for the Sûreté. Maybe you lie about working for the *American Journal*. You waste my time with your false pretences and irregularities. I've had enough.' He turned away. But like everybody who protests they've had enough, Gaudet had an appetite for more. He swung back and jabbed out a finger. 'I might have to pursue your case more rigorously. And enquiries, once they are launched, not only take a long time to reach their conclusion, they have a habit of turning up other information which may need to be acted on. Do you understand what I am telling you? Get back to Paris, madame – that's what I'm telling you.' Gaudet kept his eyes on me but spoke to the uniformed cop. 'Escort this woman downstairs. See that she leaves the building. Do not answer any questions she may put to you. Do not open your mouth. Do not even say goodbye. And do not smile back if she smiles at you, because if you smile at a Paris whore she thinks she's in business.'

CHAPTER THREE

In the mirror I saw, not the Roman arena, but tall blocks of apartments. What else? Late afternoon traffic. The dark blue Renault, one of the larger models, was still there. I could have had it on a tow rope. It was a hundred and fifty metres behind as I left the *route nationale* and took a minor road through scrub-covered hills. Then I lost it in a village and I was on my own. At a twist in the road I caught a glimpse of flat vineyards stretching out towards Montpellier. I stopped the car once and got out to listen: sound of a tractor somewhere, a peeping bird, a cicada or ten – how can you count them? A car came towards me and swept past, the driver not stopping to ask whether I needed help or, if I was doing nothing, how about going for a drink? He sneaked a quick look and drove on. Didn't so much as lift his foot off the pedal. So I'm twenty-eight, I'm not a bimbo. But at twenty-eight you shouldn't be invisible. At twenty-eight you should be able to stand at the side of the road and stop a tank. The driver must have picked up negative vibrations, so put a smile on. At twenty-eight you have a smile that means something. It means I've been there and come back and perhaps I can show you the way too. Whatever.

An aircraft was in the sky too high to see, making a noise like cloth tearing. It was heading towards Nice. ATC there would re-route it on to Rome or Athens or Vienna. There was no clatter of a helicopter. Why should there be? The police had no reason to follow me. I'd done nothing except look at a corpse and pretend a close acquaintanceship with a security cop.

I got going again.

The Ledru property was called a *mas* though you'd wonder what people had farmed round here. Goats? A few olive trees? There were pockets of soil that could be ploughed but nothing much. So the farmhouse had been abandoned until the new wave of immigrants came: northerners looking for the sun, foreigners, retired couples, businessmen from the science parks, other businessmen whose business you kept your nose out of.

I was on a straight stretch of road when I caught the white paintmarks on the tarmac. I'd already passed them by the time I braked so I reversed back. I was no better than the ghouls who stare at the prison gate when an execution is scheduled. This was the spot where Agnès had been shot to death. The blood had been washed away but the paint marked the position of her body and the car. She had been right by the driver's door, made no attempt to run.

Once again I got out of the car. Whoever shot her must have been blocking the road. Why then had she got out? Why hadn't she reversed when she saw danger? It could have been someone she knew well, a *crime passionel*. And the rejected lover shoots her and makes off with a three-year-old adopted child. Crazy theory.

I looked round. No houses overlooked the road. No witnesses. I listened. Insects. Nothing else. No birds sang along the road of death...

Al, you were damn right. Dust down some more purple passages.

I tried for a mental picture of what had happened at this spot. Perhaps it had been some everyday driving incident that turned violent. I looked round for the glitter of broken glass. As a motive, a bump on the road was a non-starter but I looked anyway. You stupid cow, look what you've done to my shiny new virility symbol. Fiery southern temper. Bang, bang, bang, you're dead. Oh, and take the kid as a souvenir. Another crazy theory.

Why this spot?

The road was straight so the assailant's (thanks, Dr Fignon) car could have come from behind, overtaken and forced Agnès to stop.

Been following her.

Why choose a public place to kill her?

I tried another theory. Her death hadn't been intended. This meant that the abduction was the primary aim. The little girl was the reason, though I had no idea why. Agnès had simply tried to stop it. Or – since she'd been shot three times – she had to be killed because she saw the kidnappers face. One or two bad guys? There was no telling.

I kept coming back to the little girl. To shoot Agnès was one thing. To take the child was a different thing altogether.

Inspiration ran dry and I gave up.

It was another couple of kilometres to the *mas*. I passed some ruined farm buildings, dirt tracks, olive terraces, a crumbling stone wall, up a gentle hill, a final curve and there it was. No mistaking it. A police van and four cars were parked outside a closed gate. The gate was modern and set between sturdy gateposts. I drove in second gear along the length of a stone wall topped with barbed wire. Looking into the grounds I could see floodlights. Ledru took security seriously. But if you're in an isolated patch of country within burglars' commuting distance of Marseille, you have to.

All the precautions explained why the crimes had taken place on the road.

There was no point in joining the crowd at the gate. No one was getting inside. Eight or nine pairs of eyes swivelled as I drove past and a camera was raised, just in case. For fifteen seconds I was famous. I breasted a rise and disappeared from sight.

I turned into what I thought was a dirt farm track that soon degenerated into a dried-up streambed and I had to stop. I parked in the shelter of some rocks. Far enough off the road, I decided.

Standing beside the car I stretched. That was the animal in me, waking up for physical action.

I worked my way up the slope of the land, feeling exposed and vulnerable. But I was out of everybody's sight. Why did I feel I was being watched? A lizard had its eye on me before it vanished with a flick of its tail. I looked round and could see no other living thing.

When I reached the fence, the top of the house was in sight over a band of trees. They weren't olives; the leaves were darker green and the growth was thicker. All I could see of the house was the faded pink of the roof tiles and a stone chimney. The front gate and the waiting cars were out of sight. Nobody was watching.

The fence here was two metres high, links to above my head, then strands of barbed wire. I could have gone back to my rented car and got one of the floormats, tossed it over the barbed wire and climbed in. But when you're up in the air, with one leg either side of the barbs, you feel so naked.

I turned right and went along the fence. El Salvador was in my mind a lot today. Partly it was the heat, though the South of France didn't have that tropical intensity. Partly it was the sniff of violence, the hacks gathered to report the latest deaths. In El Salvador I'd asked if the local girls got inside the army camp near Pulapeque. Of course, because the young men were all conscripted into the army. If the girls get in, how do I get in? I asked Dinora whose son had been tortured and murdered. What do I do, Dinora?

I did what I'd done then: I found a place where a storm drain had been laid under the wire. In the winter the storms here can be torrential and the run-off would be carried down to the streambed where I'd left the car. The drain was a pipe as big as a culvert under the road. It's still a squeeze and you dirty your clothes but that's how you get in. You crawl through on your hands and knees if you can, or wriggle on your belly like a snake, then make your way up to the house and introduce yourself to

Ledru: *Salut,* I'm the person you've hired to find your wife's killer and get your little adopted girl back. The locked gate? The cops? The barbed wire? No problem. Still think I need my hand held in a tight corner?

A nice introduction.

Which is why, when I clambered like a spider out of the other end of the drain, I felt so stupid. A pair of shoes was waiting for me. Above the shoes, tan slacks. Above that, a mid-blue shirt and a hand pointing a pistol between my eyes.

'Cody, you say?'

'That's right.'

'Proof? Papers?'

Ledru was dressed all in white: white polo shirt, white slacks, white espadrilles. The only sombre note was the black band round his right arm. The man in blue and tan who'd marched me up to the house stood against a wall. The pistol had disappeared into a pouch that was hung around his waist. I was puzzled by this man but I turned my attention to Ledru.

'My *carte de séjour* is in my bag. The bag is in my car. Do you want me to go and get it? A woman called Cody is coming to see you. A woman crawls out of a drainpipe and announces she is Cody. Why don't we just accept that for now? Are you André Ledru? How about showing me your identity card.'

The man with the pouch stirred and was still. Ledru stared at me, the muscles in his jaw clenching. He raised a glass to his lips and took a big bite out of the whisky in it. He held the whisky in his mouth a moment before swallowing.

'You come on strong.'

'It's not been the most relaxing day.' I thought of the mortuary and the corpse, the police interview, crawling through the drain, the man pointing a gun in my face. I decided against telling Ledru any of it. He'd think I wanted my hand holding.

'Do you want a drink?'

A bottle of Macallan single malt stood on the table. It was half empty. I shook my head.

'Take a seat.'

We were outside on the terrace. Huge Provençal urns foamed pink geraniums. A free-form swimming pool was fed by a waterfall. The late afternoon light had that faded quality that makes white garden furniture glow. I sat facing Ledru with the other man at the edge of my vision. He wasn't included in the invitation to sit. His pouch had a large Naf Naf logo on it and he could have strolled along the boulevard St-Germain and looked in fashion. What he reminded me of was the man who shadows the American President and carries the bag with that day's codes, which the President would use to unleash World War Three.

'Shouldn't he be patrolling the fence?'

'His colleague is inside watching the monitors.'

I hadn't even spotted the cameras. I was out of training, soft, slow. I could get the better of Richards in the gym, but out in the real world I was a loser. There is an extra edge, a fine tuning, that means the difference between success and failure, life and death, and I was going to have to get it back fast.

'You take your security seriously. Cameras, floodlights, barbed wire.'

He shrugged. I'd made an obvious comment that needed no reply.

'And armed guards.' They were what worried me. You don't have private armies in France. It was not the United States with its rent-a-cops. Nor – it was in my mind again – nor was it El Salvador. In the capital there I'd seen two men armed with rifles guarding the entrance to McDonald's. The Beethoven supermarket – a peaceful civilized name – had a sign by the door warning that all guns had to be left outside. Guns had been everywhere. But here in France?

'They seem a necessary precaution.'

'Have you always had them?'

'No. They came yesterday.'

The day after Agnès was murdered. Stable door, bolting horse. It seemed he knew where to hire armed men.

He said, 'Al told me you were good. He said you had training and experience. He said you found things out. He also said you kept your mouth shut.'

Ledru came to the end of my good qualities. He found his glass was empty and spent a little time refilling it. He used a squat heavy tumbler and he filled it halfway. He waved the bottle at me.

'Change your mind?'

I shook my head. The level in the bottle was now well down the label. I didn't know if it was the first bottle today. He took another mouthful and once more held it before swallowing. He liked the taste or it gave him the chance to collect his thoughts before speaking. He was a man who was finding it difficult to decide whether to say something.

Had he made up his mind about me? Had I made up my mind about him? I do jobs, but not everything that is pushed my way.

'Also, Al said you were a survivor.'

Why didn't I get up and walk away? Just that one remark should have warned me. Instead I said, 'But since I walked straight into the sights of your security guard, you don't know whether to believe him.'

Ledru shrugged as if to say, It can happen. He didn't know a damn thing about tight corners. To walk in front of someone's pistol once is once too often.

'The point is, you survived.'

Again I had the impulse: make an excuse and leave. There was something not right about Monsieur Ledru. I don't mean his film-star looks, the white clothes, the rumpled hair, the crossed leg with an espadrille hanging loose from his toe. I didn't like his security arrangements. He was Chief Executive of Systel, a computer installation company, and you don't expect armed guards with them.

'You've known Al for some years?'

'Sure,' Ledru said, then looked at the security guard. 'Max, leave us,' he said. 'Wait with Jacques.'

I watched the guard go. He stepped inside, leaving the double doors open. Listening, I heard no sounds from inside. Smelling, I caught no cooking odours. The house had died too.

'They're good boys,' he said. 'Toughish but good at what they do. And what they do is pretty much what you've experienced: keep the property safe. And me, of course. Though not –' he took his mouthful of Scotch, held it, swallowed, '– not Agnès. Because I didn't know I needed them until after it happened. How could I know? I blame myself and then I say: How could I have known? Doesn't do any good. It's my fault. I don't know why or how exactly but it's my fault. It doesn't matter how much of this I do…' He waved a hand towards the bottle. 'I can't get it out of my head that I'm alive and she's dead.'

He stopped. I suppose I could have reassured him, said it was not his fault. I doubt it would have had much impact. What I did instead, I reached over and lifted the glass from his hand.

'I think I will after all.'

I drank from his own glass while his eyes focused on me. To use his glass was a gesture. It was more intimate than patting his shoulder, it was saying we're in this together. I didn't trust him, didn't like him, didn't know if I would work for him, but he was in need of human comfort.

'One thing you can set your mind at rest about,' I said. 'She won't have felt anything.'

'You crazy? She didn't die like that…' He snapped his fingers. 'It took three bullets.'

'To be shot where she was, the first bullet is such a shock it knocks out the whole nervous system. Believe me, she felt no pain.'

I put all I had into it, trying to ease his guilt feelings.

'I had to identify her body,' he said. 'If you'd seen her—'

'I have seen her body. Before I drove up here I went to the mortuary in Nîmes.'

He took his glass back. This time he swallowed without the business of holding it in his mouth.

'You've seen what was done to her and you still want the job?'

'I won't know until you tell me precisely what the job is.'

'I want you to find the bastards that did it,' Ledru said, 'and then I'm going to kill them.'

He opened his hands in front of me and then clenched them until they were tight fists.

We sat out there as the dusk gathered. I had my own glass now and kept him company with the Scotch. After a hot day I'd have preferred wine, but wine was off the menu. It wasn't a coherent evening. Nothing to do with the Macallan. Or maybe it was, maybe all the alcohol he'd been using as an anaesthetic had finally got through to him.

He wanted to talk about a whole lot of different things and he'd start a subject, side-track, and come back.

'I loved her. We had our rough patches like everybody else but we stuck together. Even when I was in the Far East and we were separated, I used to telephone her.'

From Al Richards' hints, Agnès had been a light weight on Ledru's conscience. But that's the Far East for you. Also men.

'Have you ever killed anybody?' he asked.

There's a question to break the ice at parties. I took my time, not particularly wanting to talk about it. But he had said he would kill Agnes's murderers and maybe he needed to confront that possibility.

'Yes. Twice.'

'How did you feel?'

Diminished. My own life had shrunk as the life went out of their bodies. How to explain? 'I'm not a killer. That's not my trade. I won't do it for you.'

'I don't want you to.'

'Both times it was self-defence. I'm positive it was.' My voice had risen. To my ears it sounded as if I was justifying myself. 'The first time, I'd been tied to a bed and he came in, unbuckling his belt. He was going to rape me and then he was going to kill me. No doubt about it.'

But Ledru's mind jumped to Agnès.

'She wasn't raped or abused. No sign of it. Her shirt was torn but I guess she was fighting for her life.'

'Are there ... ' I couldn't think of an easy way to phrase it. 'Do the police know of any child molesters round here?'

He looked at me as if I was insane to have such an idea. And maybe I was. Your average sexual pervert doesn't cruise deserted country roads, spot a little girl in a car and think: Hello, I'll just take my handy gun out of the glove compartment, murder the mother and make off with the tot.

Ledru said, 'You find out who it is or who they are, and I'll deal with them myself. If they've hurt Ecaterina, I'll make it twice as bad for them.'

'Have you any thoughts who it might be?'

He shrugged. A shrug can mean no idea or not important. It can also mean: I'm not saying.

I tried again. 'Do you have any enemies? Okay, we all have quarrels with somebody. I mean dangerous enemies.'

'Well,' he said, 'well now.' He took a mouthful of Scotch to help put his brain together. He swallowed. 'At first I thought it might be something from my past. You know how it is, young man in a hurry, cutting corners. Something, you know, from ... '

He nodded his head towards the darkening east. He could have been referring to something just down the road. Marseille, for instance, a couple of hours' drive away. But his concern wasn't local.

'In the Far East you make a profit, you make an enemy. That's why I got the tough boys in fast. In case it was somebody I'd crossed when I was out there. Asked Systel's normal security firm if they knew of people at the shady end of the trade... But it doesn't make sense, does it?'

'Nothing makes sense. Why kidnap the girl?'

He shrugged.

'Have you had any ransom demand? They might have warned you against telling the police. No? No letter using cut-out newspaper headlines?'

'No.'

'No phone call?'

'Nothing.' He looked away into the sky where a bird was winging its way to a tree. 'And be careful when you speak to me, the police are tapping my telephone.'

'Did they ask you or tell you?'

'Neither, but they are. They want to know the moment there's any ransom demand. They want to get involved. You know what cops are like. Cops everywhere.'

'What progress have they made? Have they any theories? Have they searched the district?'

'Bloody questions.' He drank and came back to me. 'The police... I answer their questions but they're out of their depth. They're small-town thinkers. Give them a clear-cut motive – jealousy, ransom, robbery – and they follow their noses. This?' He shook his head. 'It's *you* I want to find the killers, point your finger at them.' He clenched his hands again, hugging the fists against his chest.

Ledru's experience of police was not happy. He set off on a rambling story about police corruption in the Far East and I watched him. Some men tell stories against themselves but Ledru wasn't one of them. He was the star. That's the sum of him. He acted for the camera. I was the camera.

He was in Thailand, in his anecdote, driving up north to conduct some bit of business. But then he interrupted himself as he remembered he'd spent the evening before in Bangkok with our mutual friend Al Richards and as a result had been feeling fragile. Ah, those Bangkok nights. So I was told the story about that nightclub down Pat Pong Road where the girls shoot ping-pong balls.

'You know what I mean? They're totally nude and they just open their knees and shoot balls into the audience. Hey, do you think that's why it's called Pat Pong Road?'

He gave a look to see how I reacted. I thought: He's making a play for me. His wife is still in the chiller drawer in the mortuary and he's already making his moves. I kept a neutral expression on my face and said nothing.

'Anyway...' Then we were back driving north-west, beyond Chiang Mai, on the road to Mae Hong Son towards the Burmese border, the police stopping him...

I listened to his voice, not his words. He was playing with his voice, up and down, emotions, reactions. You can do that in French without sounding a fruitfly. I listened to him putting on his one-man show. For now Agnès had been written out of the script. The little girl Ecaterina might never have had a part. I was going to have to pump him for information. How did the adoption take place? Can I see the papers? Can I have photos of Agnès and the child?

A movement in the shadows. The security guard Max with his Naf Naf pouch came on to the terrace.

'Monsieur Ledru.'

Ledru held up a hand to silence him.

'So I'd beaten this cop down to one thousand baht. That's peanuts but it was the principle of the thing. On-the-spot fine he called it. Huh! So I said to him, I said, "I don't know anything about a test certificate. It's the rental company's responsibility, not mine. So give me a receipt for the thousand baht and I'll pass it on to Hertz." The look on that Thai cop's face! He just got on his big bike and rode away.'

He was grinning, waiting for me to show my appreciation. André Ledru outwits the wily orientals. He turned to Max and said, 'Yes?'

'It's time to go.'

For a moment Ledru looked nonplussed. What was the man talking about? Understanding dawned and he turned to me.

'We're going to have to continue this interesting talk some other time. Tomorrow. Max just reminded me. I may be widowed but I have a business to run. New clients…'

He shrugged.

'But,' it was my turn to be nonplussed, 'we've hardly started. I need information about your late wife, names of her friends, her interests, places she visited, her habits—'

His charm left him. 'I'm not paying you to dig up dirt on her, I'm paying you to find her killers.'

'I'm not sure you're paying me at all.'

'You'll get what those two are getting. I mean the two of them together. Plus a performance bonus when you find the killers. You want a contract, my administrative secretary will deal with it.'

How about the little girl? Didn't he care? No. About the dead Agnès he cared, because the murder of his wife was an insult to him. An adopted daughter didn't rate.

He was turning to Max. 'Give me your gun.' He stood with his legs apart, knees kinked. He slipped the safety off and held the pistol in the classic grip, two-handed, the way the Agency taught me. See *that target, Cody,* the army sergeant had breathed in my ear, *I want to see you hit that bull right in the balls.*

I watched as he aimed. I saw his knuckle whiten as he squeezed the trigger. The bang is never as loud as you're expecting. But it echoes in your head longer than you think possible.

In a tree halfway down the garden there was an explosion of black feathers. It was the sheerest fluke. Nobody with a skinful of whisky could shoot fifty metres and hit a cow, let alone a crow. Not in semi-darkness. And then, and then, he blew into the muzzle of the pistol. It was straight out of some ancient *film noir.*

'Just point out the killers to me.' He handed the pistol back to Max. 'Okay, where can I give you a lift?'

'My car's on the road,' I said. 'I'll see myself out.' I could use the tradesmen's entrance, the way I'd come in, and avoid the hungry eyes at the gate.

'Tomorrow afternoon,' he said. 'All the details you want.'

Did I even want the job? He was a bastard.

I got the engine going, switched on the headlights, reversed out of the streamed on to the road.

There were enough police in France to track down the killers. That's what the police are there for. That's why we pay taxes.

I drove back the way I'd come. There were just one car and the police van still parked outside the gate of the *mas*. Their orders must be to guard the property, not follow Ledru to his meeting. It was late to be seeing clients. This was the new thrusting France, computers, after-dinner business talks, guards with guns.

Blinking, I flicked the anti-dazzle switch on the mirror.

Nobody gave a thought for the little girl. I had learnt nothing about her from Ledru. So far as he was concerned she hadn't been family. All I knew was what I had seen in the newspaper.

The car behind had caught up with me. It flashed its lights. The new thrusting France was impatient.

Who was going to help the girl if I didn't?

Where did I start?

He was flashing again. My beams showed the road straightening ahead. He was pulling out and began overtaking. I held the wheel steady, my eyes caught by the daubs of white paint on the road where Agnès's body had lain. The car was past me now, a dark saloon, man driving, no passenger. Then he slowed, positioning his car on the crown of the road, blocking the way. His hazard-warning lights began flashing and I saw the glow of his brake lights.

It was a replay. The tightness in my chest told me. It was a replay in exactly the same place and maybe with the same man.

I did what Agnès must have done. What else could anyone do? I stamped on the brake, hearing loose grit under the tyres, seeing the car in front drift away to the right as my car pulled left, correcting, slowing, leaving no room to squeeze past. Now I had to do what Agnès failed to do: move it, get out fast. Had she stayed to argue, remonstrate, talk to someone she knew, protect her new child? Nothing would hold me.

My wheels stopped and I had the door open while the car in front was still rolling. It wasn't totally dark. He was going to see me as I ran.

Over there. Shapes of rocks, could be another dry streambed. Make for that.

I'd taken a dozen steps, like a sprinter kicking out of the starting block, trying to get out of pistol range. I heard a shot. No, his car door slamming. Then a loose stone under my foot turned and I was flung forward on to the ground, my head striking hard earth, the wind knocked out of me. I tasted whisky in my mouth as if I'd thrown up. Get on your feet. Run for it. No chance, I'd hobble. I'd be a big slow target against the glow of the western horizon. I squirmed round to face the road, scraping a handful of earth. If he got close enough, even dirt can be a weapon.

I was still dazed, the world swaying in front of me. In the side-glow from the headlights I saw him. He was standing with an arm stretched above his head to the sky. He looked like a man swinging at the end of a rope. I screwed my eyes closed to force the image away. I heard a shout and looked again. He'd lowered his arm and now he was just a silhouette, like someone seen at the end of a city alley at night. He started to come towards me.

CHAPTER FOUR

He was in no hurry. Why should he be? He'd witnessed my headlong tumble and groggy recovery and knew I was running no further. He was outlined against a scrap of moon which made him bigger. He had his arms held wide of his sides, his hands idling by his hips. I knew what he looked like: the gunslinger advancing down the dusty deserted street.

What did I look like to him? A log. I shouldn't be a log, I should be an Apache. Not a Paris *apache,* but an Apache brave who could throw himself to the ground and be swallowed up. He'd be racing towards you one minute, and the next he'd take a dive and disappear.

'I can see you,' he said. Something like that. My head was clearing but there was still blood pounding in my ears and his voice was fogged.

It's said you could pass within ten paces of an Apache and never pick him out. Skin colour helped, the colour of the dry prairie. But the secret had to lie under the skin: the Apache willed himself to be invisible.

'Are we going to shout at each other?'

He wasn't shouting. He was only half a dozen metres away. I hadn't said a thing. I was willing myself to be invisible and it wasn't working. I was failing, just like I'd failed at everything today. No more. I found a bit of pride and kept hold of it.

'Cody, are you hurt?'

I got to my feet and tested the ankle. It wasn't serious. I couldn't sprint but it wasn't a bad sprain. The earth was sticky in my hand so I chucked it away.

'Getting agricultural, were we?'

'Can't shake,' I said. 'My hand's all dirty.'

'So?'

So he came forward the last steps, I held my wrist out and he shook that. I wiped the sweaty earth from my palm down the side of my slacks.

'You drove past the *mas*. I said to myself: Can it be? The one and only Cody? Here? Then this must be serious.'

'I didn't see you.'

'I was disguised behind a camera.' He raised his hands in front of his face, looking straight at me, and gave a double click with his tongue.

Pelletier, given name Lucien. A crime reporter, a true heavyweight, been on one of the Paris dailies until he had a fight with the management. He said they tried to curb his activities. Others said it was his expenses they wanted to keep in check. In a profession notorious for its expenses, Pelletier's were a legend. *Camels 12,400 francs,* some petty accounts clerk queried, *Why do you need camels in Clermont-Ferrand?* Pelletier put his knuckles under the unfortunate's chin and tilted it until they looked eyeball to eyeball. *You toad, don't you know camels is a euphemism? You snivelling ignoramus, don't expect me to undertake your education.* It was agreed such creativity needn't be explained further, but the editor ruled that Pelletier might find life more congenial as a freelance.

A car came round the corner and at once slowed. It was confronted by our cars on the crown of the road, at night, abandoned, headlights blazing. If he chanced the soft shoulder, the driver might squeeze past with the right-side wheels in the rough. No one in his right mind stops in the dark to find out what's going on – except this driver. He halted so there were now three cars on the lonely stretch of road where Agnès Ledru had been murdered. A spotlight was switched on and its beam swept the open country until it settled on us.

'You two,' a voice was raised, 'come here.'

In case you were stupid enough to dispute this order, a touch on the siren sent a low howl through the night.

'Knuckle-draggers,' Pelletier muttered. 'You'd think we looked like *clandestins*.' France was going through one of its periodic witch-hunts of the illegal immigrants that were supposed to be swamping the country. We picked our way through scratchy grass and stones, up that shining moon-path of a spotlight to the side of the car. A pair of unlovely *gendarmes* gave us the cop stare, cold and disbelieving.

'Why have you abandoned your vehicles in the middle of the road?'

Pelletier, perplexed, peered at the men. 'Because we couldn't drive them over there. Too rough, you see.'

There was a pause while this unhelpful answer was chewed over and spat out.

'Monsieur,' with sarcastic politeness, 'please be good enough to explain why you wanted to go down there.'

'Monsieur,' with Pelletier's deadpan expression, 'to answer a call of nature.'

'The two of you together?'

Pelletier draped an arm round my shoulder. 'Monsieur, it was that kind of call of nature.'

If anyone else had made that reply, the *gendarmes* would have got out and set to work: stomach, kidneys, anywhere that hurts but doesn't show a bruise. But Pelletier projects a kind of confidence that he alone has straightened out the loopiness of the world.

The second *gendarme* had kept silent until now. He made a noise in his throat, perhaps clearing it, perhaps a chuckle. 'My friend, in cases of such urgency, at least pull over to the side of the road. It is a courtesy to other drivers. Also it stops a crowd collecting to offer encouragement.'

'Sound, very sound.' Lucien Pelletier nodded his thanks for this piece of advice and squeezed my shoulder as a signal to move. 'It must be something in the air,' he said. 'Negative ions, ozone, electricity. Supercharges one's system, short-circuits the brain, sparks fly, the metabolism goes into overdrive.' He mumbled this gibberish to cover our retreat. He knew how to make an exit, before the others had second thoughts. He escorted me to my car and leant in through the window. 'The hormones grab each other.' He winked.

Everyone knows him as Lulu.

'At first glance, one of Ledru's bits of fancy stuff. At second glance, hello, he's got himself a bit of class with this one. At third glance I see it is you.'

'Thank you,' I said. 'Such gallantry.'

'What were you doing there?'

'Lulu, tell me first, does he have a lot of women on the side?'

'You can see them off, Cody.'

'Seriously.'

Pelletier looked at me, looked at my eyes.

'André Maxime Ledru is known to have had many extra-marital adventures,' was his prim answer, 'but this is held to be perfectly normal for a man in his position. It is expected that the boss of a dynamic company should have a mistress or two, which implies constancy or at least regularity. Then he might pick up the odd girl to suit the hour, a bright sunny blonde, a dusky brunette...' He eyed my hair which is dark brown, perfect for the time of my arrival. I would be a sundowner. 'But you are not truly contemplating...' He broke off to shake his head, no.

The night was warm though a breeze plucked at the tablecloth. The breeze was in a playful mood unless it decided to grow up into a howling gale. We were still in the mistral belt and that is a wind that does funny and not so funny things to people. Treat winds that have names with respect. That is a golden rule. The real restaurants in Nîmes were closing so we sat outside a place called Pizz' Ritz. Treat eating places with apostrophes in their name without respect. That is another golden rule.

'Why are you interested in him?' I asked.

'A murder, a kidnapping, a mourning chief executive, why do you think?'

'I think Lulu Pelletier wouldn't cross the road for a story like that, let alone drive seven hundred kilometres from Paris.'

Pelletier and Richards were both journalists, but they were out of different boxes in my life. Lulu had been covering the gang scene in Paris which was in one of its violent convulsions. He was like a war correspondent, one of the Vietnam groupies doing a body count, three dead on one side, four on the other, cars written off, blood on the zinc counter of a café, terrified peasants of the 10th *arrondissement* huddling in doorways. The Corsicos versus the Marsiales was the name of the game, as they fought over turf and the police chiefs smiled and let them shoot each other down. There had been a truce which was broken when Fonza, the *capo* of the Corsicos, was killed. I'd had a reason to visit him in his grand house and a week later Pelletier had nosed me out, wanting to know my business. No business of yours, I'd told him, I'd had no part in Fonza's death, I was not one of either gang, I was just trying to find the killer of a friend. So you went and asked the *capo*? Yes. What did he say? That I was very foolish or very brave or very ignorant. Or all three, Pelletier said and left. Looking from my window down on to rue St-André-des-Arts I watched him walk away, still shaking his head.

'Agnès Ledru was stopped on the road and murdered just where we stopped.' Pelletier was suddenly talking, taking a sip of wine and making a face, talking again. 'Her money wasn't taken but her newly adopted daughter was. Why? What's the motive? Of course someone has already claimed it was a motiveless crime, just a symbol of the crisis of bourgeois morality, blah blah. Another profound philosopher analysed it as a consumer-society killing, picking a victim at will like one picks a packet of soap powder from a supermarket shelf. A spokesman for the Police Judiciaire says no ransom demand has been made to the widower Ledru. To which I would add: Not yet.'

A waiter like a rugby player gone to fat brought the Pizz' Ritz speciality to our table. Pelletier poked at it with distrust.

'Is that tinned pineapple?'

'Morning gathered at the Intermarché,' the waiter said amiably and shambled away.

Pelletier gouged out the offending pieces. 'We are witnesses at the deathbed of French civilization. What has tinned pineapple to do with our cooking? If I were the Ritz Hotel, I'd sue this dump for taking my name in vain.

For a moment I was dislocated. It could have been Al Richards talking. Two journalists, both passionate about food. I was a disappointment to them both. I ate Pelletier's rejected pineapple chunks. The breeze was sharpening my appetite.

'The ransom demand will come, you'll see.' He picked up the thread of what he'd been saying. 'Ledru is the boss of a small but rich company. The kidnappers have done their research, they know he'll pay. That's point one.' He held up one finger then aimed it at me. 'You asked why I was interested. So point one, a murder and a child-snatch is a good story. Will Daddy pay up straight away or will he wait until he gets the little girl's thumb in the post? Point two,' he aimed two fingers at me, 'and on this I was advised by a local informant, is that Ledru has hired himself a pair of crooks as bodyguards.' Now the versatile fingers tapped his nose. 'And I smell not just a sob story but a real Lulu Pelletier tale of corruption and intrigue. I don't know what yet, but wait till the action starts, wait till the ransom demand is made.'

'Lulu,' I said, 'the kidnappers must have done their research damn fast because the child had only been there a couple of days.'

He looked at me, looked at his pizza, then pushed the plate away. 'I can't eat any more of this.' He was frowning at what I'd said. 'Good point. Then they must have had advance knowledge of the adoption,' he decided.

'Tell me about the little girl.'

'You don't know?' The scowl disappeared from his face as if the wind had changed. 'She is an orphan, a Romanian orphan. There has always been a special – um – special affinity between the French and the Romanians. You see, the Romanians are actually a Latin people, they just have the misfortune to live on the wrong side of a lot of Slavs. The last Romanian king left his queen for his mistress who was French. Now, thanks to the deranged Ceausescu, there is a good supply of Romanian orphans. And generous French people take these orphans into their homes and hearts. Sorry to sound as if I'm quoting but I am. Read my piece in tomorrow's paper.'

A Romanian orphan? I couldn't quite get my brain round this. Significant? Irrelevant?

'Does your paper have a photo of her?'

'No. Of the house, of the distraught man being driven in a car, of the Systel office, but not of orphan Ecaterina. But she'll be small, have dark hair and dark eyes. That's what Romanian three-year-olds look like.'

'The official authorities must have one. Whoever they are.'

'The Council for French-Romanian Friendship, the International Red Cross, the United Nations Foundation all say no. Little Rina was not adopted through them. A piece of private initiative? The police spokesman was suddenly shy. And Monsieur Ledru had locked his gate on us. There we sat, the cops and us, ignoring each other like the bride and groom's relations on the wedding day. The cops were in their van with all its listening gear, itching to defend peace, social justice and profits with their batons. And us, the esteemed members of the press, desperate for an interview, a photo opportunity, a drink. And who should dawdle past and disappear from sight but Little Red Riding Hood.'

He bowed his head in my honour. I only knew Lulu as the hard-hitting crime reporter. I should have guessed he had a fanciful side. He sneered at the pizza again and sipped some wine.

'What were you doing? The truth now, Cody. Assuming you really weren't signing on as his *petite amie*. How did you get in? Fly? Swim? You vanished and didn't reappear for an hour and a half. You did go in, I take it?'

'I crawled in like a sewer rat. There was a storm drain under the wire and I used that.'

'The truth?' He beamed then went serious. 'Tomorrow, that drain will have barbed wire across it. You can't repeat your sewer-rat performance. Obviously he didn't send for you or you'd have gone in the front gate. So I ask myself: Why did you go?'

Ledru had sent for me but I had wanted to show off. Pelletier was interested in me now, intrigued. He knew the kind of thing I did because he was a reporter who had his sources. Cody does little jobs, Cody takes risks, Cody will walk on the shady side of the street after consulting her own private moral code. But this was something else. Ledru wanted me to track down his killer. Suppose I did find the killer. Suppose I told Ledru. Suppose Ledru carried out his threat and shot the man. That made me an accessory before the fact. It's not a thing you start boasting about. But I had my other story ready-made.

'I'm doing a piece on the crime.'

'A piece?'

'Lulu, don't be thick.' He raised an eyebrow. 'An article, a feature, a story.'

'A journalist? You?'

He seemed to come to a complete stop. I could hear the breeze playing with dry leaves in the gutter as if it was autumn already. A bullfight poster had been slapped on a tree trunk and a corner of it fluttered and caught my eye.

'The *American Journal* say they'll publish it if I get something good.'

I shut my mouth and smiled at him. Lulu peered at me through narrowed eyes. He didn't believe me. And then he did. He laughed and slapped the table hard enough to tip the bottle over. A small puddle of red ink seeped into the paper tablecloth.

'Bloody marvellous. I sit here telling a rival everything I know, which is not much. While you tell me bugger-all about actually seeing Ledru. You'll make a reporter, I tell you. You've got quick wits and a pretty face, Cody. You'll do.'

He half-rose to lean over the table and kiss me on both cheeks.

He was wrong. I would never make a reporter. How would I learn to fill in my expenses claim? For tonight Lulu would probably write: *Sewer rat 8,100 francs.*

'I can find my own way,' I said.

'You're sure?' His hand clutched my elbow, so caring for my safety, but the fingers were restless, edging upwards.

'I'm sure. I'm a sewer rat, remember?'

I left Pelletier because if he walked me to my hotel that was halfway to my room. I didn't think of him like that. I tried to work out how I did think of him. He was a friend, nothing special, though he was something special to himself. He was one of those journalists with the conceit that they know the *real* story, even when they don't. They know the dirt that cannot be printed because of libel laws or heavy threats or national security or because the owner of the rag is a friend of a friend of…

There were footsteps close behind me, male, one pair. They'd only just arrived. Whoever he was had been standing in some assassin's alley. But my hotel was on the corner ahead and the street was well lit.

'*Vos papiers.*'

The curt tone, the demand for documents in the plural as if one piece of paper could never satisfy his appetite, typical cop. I stopped and he stopped, just past my shoulder. At the edge of my vision I could see he had a hand outstretched, a beggar's hand, though no French cop ever begs. Normally they ask for ID only from people they can bully: destitutes, North Africans, whores. I didn't look like the first two.

I reached for my shoulderbag and as I touched it I realized my *carte de séjour* wasn't there. Inspector Gaudet had never given it back. Turning to explain this, I found Gaudet himself confronting me, my residence card now grasped in his hand. His face was dark and the blackness seemed to come from inside him.

'You haven't told me the truth,' he said, as if I'd betrayed him in love.

It wasn't a question. I answered nothing. Some men came out of the bar of my hotel and began cheery alcoholic farewells. Gaudet turned and beckoned me. We went back a few steps and stopped under a neon sign that said SEXY SHOW. It flashed red over us.

'You're no journalist. That was a lie. I know a lot more about you now.'

'My file,' I suggested helpfully.

'Oh, there'll be files gathering dust in various offices. I'm talking of the computer in Paris, the Big Boss computer in rue des Saussaies. Heard about it, have you? It knows all your worst secrets, like a priest. It can send you to hell, like the devil. And it definitely does not exist, like God.'

He was being very French, high-flying and furious both at once. The livid red light from the sign cut him in half, leaving one side in darkness. He'd begun without a left arm. Now he had no left cheek, no left eye, no left side at all to his body.

'I found out all your personal details, place of birth, names of parents and grandparents, sexual history, and so on. Your tax position, which has been the subject of some enquiry.'

I had Crevecoeur to thank for that.

'Did you have a driving licence? A pilot's licence? Any traffic offences? Been the subject of police investigations? What researches were carried out before you were granted residence status? A lot of stuff is on record.'

At the door of the Sexy Show a man with large shoulders appeared. He said, 'If you're coming in, shut up. If you're not coming in, piss off and argue somewhere else.'

Gaudet never took his eyes off me but he lifted his chin so that he spoke over his shoulder. 'What are you offering? Underage girls? Drugs? Which jail did you just get out of? I can get you back in so quick you'll wet your pants.' He finished and began immediately on me. He couldn't wait to let it all pour out. 'Recruited by the British Secret Service, I discovered. Sent for training in the United States. Four years in the hands of the CIA. And now you're here, poking your nose into something that's none of your business, lying to me.'

'Here you, what do you mean?' The bouncer was coming out of the entrance, rolling his shoulders.

Gaudet at last looked at him. 'Police.'

The doorman stopped and a smile struggled for life on his face. 'But monsieur, why didn't you say? Come in please, and the little lady. Charming. For a policeman of your standing, monsieur, there is no charge. Relax, enjoy the show, a little naughty here and there but it will take your minds off whatever is bothering you. Drinks, of course, are with the courtesy of the house.'

'Go,' Gaudet said. 'Just leave us in peace. I said, get away from us.'

The bouncer backed into the entrance to the club. I don't know how far down the corridor he went or whether he made sense of anything we said. A thumping disco beat was the background noise to our talk.

'It was a bad time for the British spy establishment,' I began. A couple of men walked past us into the Sexy Show. I started again. 'This was a few years ago. It's probably always a bad time, but then there had been so many scandals, defections, moles, fourth and fifth men, Reds under and in the bed, that the American cousins were losing faith. So a small group of us was sent to the States for training by the CIA. That way we couldn't be contaminated by pinkos in Britain. If any of us turned out to be Moscow's men – or woman, I was the only one – it would be the Yanks' fault.'

'You admit all this?'

'Didn't the computer admit it? It's known.'

'We don't let admitted spies live in France.'

'I'm not a spy. I quit.'

'There are sections of your computer file that are blocked. Anyone who wants to find out the secrets has to have the password. Without the password it is necessary to consult – guess who?'

I nodded. The long leg of Crevecoeur trips me up, the long arm taps me on the shoulder, the long shadow falls across my life.

'You have a whole history that is secret. There are names of deceased persons – consult Chief Inspector Crevecoeur, Sûreté Nationale. There are enquiries into a Luxembourg bank account in your name – consult Crevecoeur. There are entries that are like chapter headings. Blood Group O – consult Crevecoeur. Skorpion – consult Crevecoeur. Snowline – consult Crevecoeur. But they are not chapter headings. They are the code names those glamorous fixers in Paris give to operations. And you were involved in them. You are Crevecoeur's creature.'

I turned abruptly and began to walk away. Then the fury boiled in me and I went back to him.

'You have a filthy mind,' I told him. 'Go in and enjoy the show.'

For a moment he was stunned, as if I'd slapped his face.

'You're angry,' he said, 'because you've been found out.'

'Never say I work for Crevecoeur. I don't.' That is the truth. But ... but ... it is also true that in the past our lives have been twisted together like bindweed. Crevecoeur is the one who has done the twisting.

'I advise you to get back to Paris. This is a local crime. If the Sûreté Nationale wish to involve themselves for some reason, they should liaise through the normal channels.'

'I am not—'

'Listen to me. There is a police presence at Ledru's *mas*. They reported a car driving slowly past and the sound of its engine cutting out as it was hidden off the road. The car was parked there for an hour or longer and then came back again. The licence number was of a car rented from Hertz. The person who rented it was you.'

His anger matched mine. Carried on the tide of it, he raised his left arm, accusing. He pointed at me with the stump that was left after the Sûreté Nationale bomb blew off his hand.

'So don't lie to me that you aren't involved.'

My day wasn't finished yet.

My hotel was of the old-fashioned kind, rare in France now. The room had floral wallpaper, dark furniture, a bidet but no bath. The bed was big enough for two people on very good terms. I lay on my back feeling more drained than I had for a long time. With my eyes closed I could hear the wind kicking up a fuss. The telephone was held to my ear as I waited for him to answer.

'Hello?'

'And how is Berlin? I've not broken in during a tender moment, have I?'

'Co! How did you know where I was staying?'

'Knowing what creatures journalists are, I started at the most expensive hotel, intending to work down. I didn't have to go very far down. Al, I've met your friend and I don't know that I like him.'

Meaning, in my opinion he was a turd, but Richards could work that out for himself. I wiped moisture off my hand where I'd been gripping the phone.

'Well, not so much a bosom pal, just someone I knew a long time ago and from a different life. Out in the East you make your friends for fun and don't dig deep into all their activities.'

'I didn't have to do any digging, he came straight out with it. He wants me to find his wife's killers so he can kill them.'

Silence.

'Did you hear? I can't write that. I can't write a story for the *AJ* that he asked me to track them down so that he could have revenge. He'd more than deny it, he'd sue the *AJ* into bankruptcy. He sent the only witness away before saying it.'

'Oh boy,' Al said, 'have I landed you in the shit.'

I closed my eyes again, wishing I'd never got involved. It was the fate of little Rina, the orphan, that held me, nothing else. I wished I was anywhere else, even Berlin.

'How is Berlin?' I asked. 'Last time I was there they still had the Wall. Used to be rabbits that hopped round the grassy strip on the People's Democratic side. They were too light to trigger the mines. Hippety-hippety-hop they went, nibbling at daisies. What's happened to the bunnies? Are they the unmourned victims of the collapse of the Soviet empire?'

'Co, what the hell are you on about?'

'Just trying to get a little colour into your news story.'

It was the small hours of the night.

A little girl with dark hair was running towards me down a deserted road. She ran the way a toddler does, clumsy feet, threatening a tumble with every step. I had my arms stretched wide to gather her up and hug her. Just as she was reaching out for me there was the sound of a shot, close by. She staggered as if struck by a bullet, fell into my arms and fell right through me. She wasn't flesh and blood. She was a ghost.

I struggled awake to find the shutter had blown loose. I fastened it again before its banging forced its way into any more dreams.

And in the morning I woke to find the sky blue and the wind died away. It was going to be a beautiful day.

CHAPTER FIVE

Two men, two pairs of eyes looking at me.

Being a woman adds an extra angle to the kind of work I do. Are they showing an interest in me because of their male hormones? Do they start to wonder what I look like with the clothes off and feel a stirring? Or are they staring for another reason?

I had a lot of telephoning to do this morning and I wasn't going to do it on an empty stomach.

There was a café across the street from my hotel and I aimed for that. But I showed perfect kerb drill before I crossed. Left-right-left. That settled the doubts. My appeal was nothing to do with my tight jeans and sexy Thai silk shirt. The second time I looked left the two men had their faces hidden, one with a newspaper, the other by tilting his head down.

Hot chocolate, rolls with a crunch to them, butter. I sat at a table outside to enjoy the morning and to watch the two men in the car watching me – the number 30 on the licence plate, so it was a car from round here.

So who were they? They smoked Gitanes with yellow maize paper. The man with the newspaper peeped and retreated. The other man had pulled down his sun visor, as if that made a damn bit of difference. They were low-grade talent with no professional training. They were a couple of *mecs* from a local gang who believed that sitting in a car made them invisible.

I had a sudden thought. Beyond the hotel was the Sexy Show, its red neon light switched off. In the morning the club slept, exhausted after faking so much passion. The two in the car could be waiting to collect their weekly insurance pay-off. The probability of that was next to zero, but I would keep the faint chance at the back of my mind while I did my telephoning. I had been too long out of training and it felt good to be making a move. It was the same desire that drove me under the fence yesterday like a sewer rat. I went inside the café.

The barman was a short man, balding, with a white apron tied round his pot belly. He doubled as the waiter and had brought my breakfast out to me. A newspaper was spread over the counter, AGNÈS, the headline screamed, POLICE EXPECT EARLY ARREST.

That stopped me.

'Do they know who killed her?'

'Who?'

'The police. Do they know who killed the woman?'

He shrugged. 'Cops know everything. They know who the underworld kings are, who the drug barons are, who run the *maisons closes* and the gambling dens, who the arms dealers are, who the Arab terrorists are, who the Israeli agents are, who the millionaire tax swindlers are – but those fine gentlemen are all at liberty, even though the cops know every detail about them down to the size of their underpants. However, picture a cop coming in here and seeing an ashtray on the bar counter – well, that is illegal, a crime, five years in a pig pen.' He flapped a smooth white hand at the paper. 'At this moment the police expect an early arrest, in two days' time they will be eagerly following a new lead, next week fresh evidence will mean the net is closing, the week after that people will say Agnès, who was Agnès?'

Glad I asked. 'Use your telephone?'

'Sure. Help yourself.' He jerked his head towards the back of the room. Over his shoulder in the mirror I could make out the car and the two men staring at the café. They'd think I'd gone for a pee or to pay the bill.

I dug out my *télécarte* and got to work. The only other customers that morning were two teenage girls eating pink ice-cream from tall fluted glasses. I hunched away from them.

'American Journal.'

'I want to speak to Soraya Kachik.'

'Connecting you.'

Soraya was a colleague of Al Richards, born in Tehran and missing it and her family. Soraya came from Iran, Richards was born in Oklahoma, I was born in England, the missing Rina was born in Romania. You can see why the French are edgy about a foreign invasion.

'Soraya Kachik,' the husky voice came down the line.

How could she ever return to Iran? *Me wear a chuddar?* she'd joked, covering her face with her hands. Only her eyes were visible, dark and full of infinite promise. Then she dropped her hands to cup her breasts *I don't even wear a bra.*

'This is Cody, remember?'

Also, she'd written something rude about the Ayatollah after he'd died and the *AJ* had had a police guard for several weeks. We'd met a couple of times when she'd been with Richards.

'As if I could forget someone who beat up Al. Good to hear from you.'

'Was he mad at me?'

'El Al? He was mad at *me* when I asked how it had gone.'

So that was what he was known as round the office. 'Has El Al filed from Berlin today?'

'Too early for him.'

'Soraya, when he does, see if he writes about the rabbits which used to run on the far side of the Wall being the unmourned victims of the collapse of communism.'

She wanted to know what that was all about and she laughed and then I got down to business. I wanted information, the kind of information I had no way of digging up for myself: who are the backers for Systel, who put the money up?

'I mean,' I told her, 'Systel wasn't found under a gooseberry bush. It had to have parents, or at least a midwife. And Ledru isn't a computer man, he isn't your average French businessman, his experience has been out in the East, so how did he land the boss's job?'

So far as I knew it wasn't relevant to finding out the killers of Agnès and the kidnappers of Rina, but it was relevant to whether I agreed to work for Ledru. I gave her the telephone number of the café.

'Would half an hour be over-generous?'

I held the receiver away from my ear a moment. Iranians are good screamers. At the edge of my vision I could see someone on the pavement peering in through the plate-glass window. It was one of the men from the car, checking I hadn't slipped out the back door.

'It's just that I'm in a fix and I don't have much time.'

With Soraya's protests still in my ear, I rang Ledru's home number. A man answered. He didn't have the tone of a servant. Perhaps it was Max or the one I hadn't met yet. Ledru wasn't there. I rang Systel's office and got through to Ledru's secretary. He wasn't there either. Out on business, not known where he'd gone or when he'd be back. I was supposed to be meeting him today for a fuller briefing and he'd disappeared.

'Can I help you?' the secretary asked.

She sounded young. Was she a bright sunny blonde or a dusky brunette? No, she couldn't help me.

I walked to the window. Both back in the car, smoking. What did they want of me? Was I to be followed, questioned? Who ordered them here? There was no logic to it. A woman was killed, a girl kidnapped, so why show interest in me who'd arrived from Paris just the day before? The only answer was this: what I was interested in was a part of something bigger. But what, I had no idea, no information.

I returned to the bar and ordered coffee.

'May I?'

I turned the barman's paper round and read the main story. There was a photo taken through mud of Inspector Gaudet who believed an arrest was imminent. 'The police are working twenty-four hours a day on this tragedy.' Apart from the time taken to lie in wait and be rude to me, that was. 'The murderer left several clues behind.' Clues unspecified. Fingerprints, bullets, ejected casings? These would all point to a known criminal with a police record. Hey, how about —'

'Dr Fignon, please.' Who else could I call? I was in luck; he'd just finished an autopsy.

'It was fascinating. The woman had been killed by a bite to the throat that had severed the windpipe. The deceased was discovered in the gardens of the Palais des Congrès. The police officer who found the corpse thought it could have been done by a Doberman. But the configuration was wrong for a dog. Human teeth caused the wound. You should see the markings. A lovebite in the extremes of passion, what do you say?'

'Engrossing.' I was gripping the telephone tight. I relaxed my fingers and filled my lungs. 'Dr Fignon, have you further information about the fibres under Madame Ledru's fingernails?'

'That is a matter for the Identité Judiciaire.'

'Chief Inspector Crevecoeur has instructed me that for reasons of state his interest in this death must not be spread to unnecessary persons. Since you already know of it and the Identité people do not, I must request your cooperation.'

It was a longshot, because of course analysing fibres would not be his speciality. But he'd struck me as a man of boundless curiosity, a busybody who would poke his nose everywhere. So I was patient while he protested – not his position, betrayal of professional ethics, and so forth – and then he said: 'The fibres under the victim's nails were based on terephthalic acid. You're familiar with its derivatives, of course.'

'Refresh my memory.'

'A polyester. Polyesters can vary in quality as much as cottons or silks. This, for instance, was definitely not US Dacron. In fact it was of such abysmally low quality that the forensic experts immediately sought comparisons among East European fibres. Are you interested in the nature of the tests carried out?'

'Later, doctor. But the results?'

'The fibres were Romanian. Obvious when you think about it.'

Dr Fignon left me on that chiding note. Obvious, yes. New mother, adopted Romanian child, dressing her, hugging her. Blindingly obvious, Dr Fignon, when you think about it.

The phone rang and I picked it up before the barman had taken a step. He stood watching me, curious.

'Co?'

'Yes.'

'Soraya here. It was easier than I thought, getting the information you wanted, and more difficult. The money for Systel came from – are you ready – Exrilgor SA, registered in the Dutch Antilles. Someone in our financial section had already found that out. My next question was: who are Exrilgor SA? That my colleague couldn't help with. Did I know how many banks there were in the Dutch Antilles? Did I know how close Aruba and Bonaire and Curaçao were to the coast of South America? Did I know how easy it was to fly there from Colombia? Had I any idea how many shell companies had their nameplates up there and how secretive they were about their activities? By the way, they're known as the ABC islands,' she ended, 'in case you're doing a travel article.'

'And Ledru?'

'Not in our morgue.'

Newspaperspeak for their files.

'Thanks, Soraya.'

'Now you take care.'

Sure, I look both ways before I cross the road and see the bad men waiting in their car. I left the phone to drink my coffee. Cold. In the mirror I could see the men still waiting. Time to shift them.

'Busy morning,' I told the barman. 'One last call.'

It was a man who answered. My accent is good. I used to affect an Alsatian throatiness when I was going with Michel. I had lost that accent when I lost Michel and now the words slur in the Parisian fashion, chasing each other out of my mouth. Slow down to a provincial speed. Put in a hint of the Midi. Don't be too smart.

'You know the Inspector who's investigating that murder and kidnapping?'

'Inspector Gaudet,' said this man at the Police Judiciaire headquarters.

'You tell him there's a couple of prime suspects sitting in a car outside the Sexy Show. They look real villains. They could be waiting for another victim. You know the Sexy Show?'

'Madame, who is calling.'

'A concerned citizen.'

Back again to the bar. I drank another cup of coffee, hot this time. I believe in caffeine, like I believe in champagne and skiing and cats and Van Gogh and little three-year-old girls and skinny-dipping when the moon is gibbous and making love on the beach afterwards. In five minutes the police arrived, great restraint, no siren. They went one each side of the parked car. They made the watchers get out and put their hands flat against a wall and patted them down. No gun, no knife, big disappointment. Vos *papiers*. The questions, why are you here, what are you waiting for, where were you last Tuesday, what is your occupation? You could tell the injured innocence from the way the watchers' eyebrows and shoulders and hands flew up. Us – we're just waiting for a little old lady to help across the street. But one of the cops gestured with his thumb: *Filez*.

Me too. When the street was clear I paid the barman and left.

The sun was high overhead and the cicadas had woken up. They were calling for mates in all the trees except this one. My presence silenced them. The trunk of the olive tree had forked and was twisted with age. Old fellow, you're good for another few centuries provided the bulldozers don't get you.

I was crouching behind the trunk for shelter and that wasn't sensible. I kicked my legs out behind me and lay flat on the ground, then worked my way forward to the edge of the terracing. The whole side of this hill was terraced, which meant I could peep over the edge, with the profile of my head broken by a bush of wild rosemary that had taken root between the stones. One shoulder was exposed, but the silk shirt had a pattern of muted blue and pale green which wasn't eye-catching. I checked the angle of the sun one final time because the binoculars I'd bought didn't have anti-flare on the lenses.

I focused on Ledru's property. There was a patch of scrub-covered *garigue* at the foot of my hill, with his converted farmhouse on a gentle incline opposite. It formed three sides of a square with the swimming pool and the terrace where we'd sat yesterday in the middle. There was a separate stone outbuilding, a barn which had been converted to a three-car garage. Two cars had been abandoned in front of the garage. I could see the front gate, a police van, only two press cars today. The streamed I had parked in was masked by shrubs. The wall ran alongside the road, the rest of the boundary being marked by fencing. Floodlights were obvious but not cameras. I set to work with the binoculars looking for cables and the sharp, dark outlines of cameras among branches. I spotted three, two covering stretches of fencing, one aimed at a door. On the side of the house nearest me there were six casement windows, two with their shutters closed.

No sounds except, close by, the cicadas.

There were no people in sight. All inside. If I had a mobile phone and rang the *mas,* would I be told Ledru was away on business?

I heard a door bang shut, a sound thinned by distance, and a man came into view round the corner of the house. It was a gardener aiming towards a bed of red cannas. I switched to watching the camera nearest him, focusing tightly, and the camera never moved, didn't swing to keep pace with him. It was static, not infra-red activated. Yesterday they'd got on to me because I'd walked into their sights like the rawest young recruit.

The gardener picked up a hoe and got to work on the weeds. He wore a straw hat. I didn't and I had to wipe the sweat that trickled into my eyes.

So what is the verdict?

I'd come here not for logical reasons but for personal ones. Let me look at the *mas,* try to understand Ledru the man and his lifestyle, then decide whether I would in any way consent to do what he asked. More than understand, *feel* Ledru. Feel him right here where my belly was pressed against the earth. We say we are rational beings, but that is where we make our vital decisions, not in our heads. He wanted to pay me but I'd already decided I wasn't going to be hired. I might *give* him the kidnapper of Rina, assuming I got to the man before the police. Or I might not. The choice was mine and in the end it was going to be a gut reaction: emotionally I would align myself with Ledru or against him.

Then my choice was made.

A car came down the road, another reporter, maybe Lulu. No, it stopped at the gate and a man got out to speak into the entryphone. The gate was as solid as the one that used to bar the way at Checkpoint Charlie. It lifted and the car drove through and slewed to a halt by the other vehicles. I was frowning at the number plate and then at the men who got out: the two who'd kept watch outside the café. They walked towards the house, one flicking away the butt of a yellow cigarette, then disappeared from sight.

So that was it. My gut clenched with anger. That was the end so far as doing anything for Ledru. One day he's hot to use me. The next he has low-grade local hoods check on my movements. Ledru was a – I turned the words over in my head, the naughty ones, the taboo ones, and they seemed overblown, overused. There was no shock in calling someone a shit, no moral judgement in saying he was a bastard. There was something rotten about Ledru, a bad egg, stinking in my nostrils. I didn't know how Agnès had stuck him. Of course they'd gone through 'rough patches', and he'd lived a freewheeling life in the Far East. A lot of wives stand by vicious husbands without a spark of poetry in their souls. And in his own way he had loved her. Love for him meant male possession and that had been taken from him and he wanted—

I stopped thinking about it, shut Ledru right out of my brain because something more urgent was clamouring for attention.

It had grown quiet on my right, the cicadas had stopped shrilling, fallen silent as they had when I had sheltered behind this olive tree.

Turn your head, find out why. Easy command. You want to do it quickly to confirm something's there. You have to do it infinitely slowly so that no movement registers at the edge of vision.

Thirty seconds maybe, I wasn't timing myself. I had the wreck of the old rosemary as a partial shield. Maybe a whole minute.

The man was not as much as fifty metres away, standing behind a gnarled trunk with his eyes fixed on the farmhouse below. He was dressed in chinos, a check shirt and a cap. He cradled a rifle against his chest.

Half-thoughts tumbled through my mind in no particular order. Holy Mary, we've gone from handguns to rifles. Must be one of Ledru's security guards patrolling the outer perimeter. Or another tough from a local gang. Or a hunter. Or the murderer going to blast the windows. Or a local vigilante. Or some sort of *garde champêtre*.

I wasn't badly concealed. Tufts of grass, thistles and the rosemary lay between us. If he looked directly my way I'd be seen and challenged. Sooner or later he was likely to turn, but for the moment his attention was locked on the house. I couldn't simply get up and sprint for the car round the side of the hill because he'd see me and yell to a colleague or loose off a shot. I waited for a chance.

Finally he let his eyes wander from the farmhouse round to a field to his right. Next it would be in my direction. But he patted his pocket, got out a crumpled pack of Gitanes, then dug for his lighter, flicked for a flame with his head ducked down, maybe flicked a second time with a hand cupped to shield the flame.

That is what he must have done, but the moment he got the cigarette into his mouth I moved and trusted in the goddess of luck for the rest. I swung my legs through one hundred and eighty degrees and slithered over the edge of the terrace. He could no longer see me, though if the gardener looked up from the weeds I was in full view. Crouching, I moved along in the shelter of the terrace wall, round the curve of the hillside, until it was safe to stand up and run for the car.

Where had he sprung from? No vehicle, no farmhouse, no building of any kind except what looked like a stone shelter for sheep up on top of the hill.

I slowed as I got close to my Peugeot 205, the hot hatch version. It was dusty from the back road I'd come on but the windows were clear enough to see it was empty. It was home, safety. I longed to grip the wheel and hear the rasp of its engine. I longed to put distance between myself and the *mas,* Ledru and every breed of tough. But longing isn't enough.

It was clever having that man with a rifle flush me out. No noise, no fuss. It made me eager to get away, hasty, until I saw the smoke. I can remember a flash of irrelevant thought: It's like a Red Indian war signal in the hills. The grey smoke drifted up in a cloud, there was a pause, then another puff of smoke. I actually had the key out to slip in the lock, but I put it away. I had to go round to the other side of the car. My feet dragged. I knew in my belly – where I'd known that Ledru was no good – who was waiting for me. The cigarette smoke was deliberate. It signalled to me: Don't even think of driving off, Cody, we've got business to attend to. We have a castle to storm, a flag to rally to, a battle to win.

The sun and running had made me lightheaded. I was too high-flown. It could just be that we had a score to settle and debts to be paid.

He squatted on the ground, his back against a wheel, which is what had hidden him as I drew near. His knees were drawn up and he rested his chin on them. What he looked like to me was a jack-knife, sharp and lethal, carve your life up in the blink of an eye.

Chief Inspector Crevecoeur rose to his feet in one abrupt movement and turned the full force of his bitterness on me. He was all vertical lines, his face narrow, his chest cramped, his legs and arms thin.

'This time, Cody,' he said, 'you are truly in the shit.'

CHAPTER SIX

'Up there,' Crevecoeur said, pointing like an old revolutionary to the glorious future, to the stars, to inspiration.

'Where to?'

'Just up. Bloody get going. Follow the track.'

The track was slashed by run-offs from winter storms and sudden ridges of rock. I kept my foot on the accelerator and fought with the wheel to steer past pot-holes. Crevecoeur gripped the grab-handle with one hand, the fascia with the other. I saw what looked like a shortcut, maybe just a path the flocks were driven along, and I swung on to that.

'Jesus Christ, what are you trying to prove?'

Not a thing. Not my driving skills, not my toughness, not my death wish. I was letting my anger out. Some people hammer on the wall or kick the furniture. I hauled on the wheel and felt the harshness of the terrain and showed I was in command. Showed who?

'Stop,' Crevecoeur yelled in my ear. He'd hunched round to look back through the rear window. 'Stop the car.' He straightened up and leant across my legs to get at the ignition key. I slammed on the brakes.

'Don't you touch me.'

I brought my knee up and caught his fingers against the fascia. He snatched his hand back, flexing the fingers. There was a time of glaring, of vague lip movements as if he was trying out what name to call me. I hadn't used the mirror while I was dodging the rocks but I looked now. A corner of the *mas* had come into view.

'I told you to take the track,' he said.

The track had disappeared round the side of the hill, out of sight of the farmhouse. We sat in silence getting our breath back, listening to ticks from the cooling engine.

'I thought you were in Paris,' I said. What a dumb thing to say, like a wife catching out a cheating husband.

'I was in Paris. Paris is where I should be, not on some hillside in Languedoc sitting in a roasting pan.'

He hung an elbow out of the window and stared into space. He was as moody as a teenager.

'You fucked it up for me.'

Crevecoeur spoke that in English to remind me he wasn't a French bloody intellectual but had done a stint at the Washington Embassy and could deal with people who thought they were street-smart. I wound down the window fully to stare out my side. Now we weren't moody teenagers, more a long-married couple having a row. It happened every time I ran into the man. A blazing, bruising row. When a marriage is on the rocks, you can get a divorce. But you have to be married first. To Crevecoeur? Imagine waking up in the honeymoon suite and finding that you had tied yourself for better or for worse to... No, my imagination wasn't bold enough.

'Crevecoeur, I have no idea what you are talking about.'

Staring at the top of the hill, I caught a flicker of movement inside the animal shelter. If Crevecoeur had left Paris to come here, there was a reason. If he flushed me out from the olive terrace overlooking Ledru's house, there was a reason. If he said I'd caused chaos, gave him sleepless nights, the reason was he wanted me to do something. I got out of the car. Crevecoeur was quick on my heels.

Take the track. Go round the side of the hill.'

We reached the track and followed that, climbing out of sight of the *mas*. Animals had cropped the grass short. Even the bushes had been stripped. Goats do that, not sheep. Bare branches prodding out of rocks provided the only cover. I looked again at the shelter ahead and made out half a face in a gap in the stones.

'Are you bringing me here to kill me?'

The other half of the face was hidden by a rifle.

'If that's how it goes,' Crevecoeur said.

His tone was indifferent. He wasn't trying to throw a scare into me. He meant it.

The animal shelter was just below the top of the low hill. The track led to a gap in the stone wall on the side away from the *mas*. Inside was parked a 4WD Renault Espace with number plates of the Bouches-du-Rhône. There were a couple of two-person pup tents, a camping stove, collapsible table and folding stools, remains of a picnic lunch, a crate of beer bottles, a radio transceiver, binoculars mounted on a tripod for zero handshake, ditto a camera with a voyeur's long lens, four men with the bristled chins and wide-spaced eyes of people who've been living rough on a stake-out. Two of the men carried rifles. All of them wore hats against the sun.

Four pairs of eyes watched my entrance into the animal shelter, switched to check with Crevecoeur, then looked at me again. Their eyes said we could never be bosom friends. There was a tension in the set of their jaws which said that if we were enemies they would tear me to pieces, chew me over and spit me out.

I looked at Crevecoeur. He nodded to me: Yes, these are my men and they do whatever I order. He raised a hand and flicked a finger towards the binoculars. One of the men moved, keeping his eyes on me until the last moment.

'This is Mademoiselle Cody,' Crevecoeur said. 'She is English but the Americans trained her and now she hunts on her own. Whoever pays her—'

'Not whoever. I would never be hired by you.'

'She has done jobs in many parts of the world. El Salvador, Holland, Tunisia, Turkey. Not much in France because we take an interest in her, cramp her style. Remember her pretty face.'

Even the one who was bowed over the binoculars straightened. They all stared in my direction again. 'She is skilled and quick-witted and resourceful and stubborn. She thinks she could take all of you. No problem.'

I experienced the massed willpower of these men directed against me. Their suspicion and resentment were a weight I could feel. I truly wondered if Crevecoeur was in his right mind. A deep anger was driving him and his control might snap and he would order his men to attack like so many dogs. Four of them, plus Crevecoeur. Two of them, yes. Not more, not with rifles. I heard a pebble grate behind me and when I turned round it was to find the man from the olive terrace with his rifle at hip height but pointed at me.

'She has got in my way before,' Crevecoeur said, 'but she has also proved to have her uses.'

The men hadn't spoken or let any expression pass over their faces. Just their eyes showed what they thought.

'A week now in this bloody place,' Crevecoeur said. 'They've got licence plates and candid-camera shots of everybody who's gone in, including you. In the Espace they've got crates of sophisticated listening gear, laser stuff for picking up vibrations off the windows. But if they're discussing anything significant, they must do it in the rooms with the shutters closed. You don't know what the hell I'm on about. Or maybe you do.'

'No.'

'Imagine sweating it out for seven days and seven nights in this goat pen. Not Jean-Louis,' nodding to the beater from the olive terrace, 'he came from Paris with me. Do you need a sun-hat? Speak nicely and one of the boys will lend you his.'

We sat at the collapsible table in the heat of the afternoon sun. Sweat made a trickle down one cheek. I could feel the clamminess of it on my body, how it moulded my shirt to my breasts.

'I'd like something to drink.'

What did I say wrong? It must have been my tone that acted on Crevecoeur like a drug, swinging his mood. He scrambled to his feet, driven by his demon, acting a little charade. He folded a waiter's imaginary napkin over his arm and gave an obsequious bow. 'Mademoiselle, the Café les Deux Merdes is honoured to serve you. A glass of champagne? Alas, the Krug is just finished, but if I might recommend the Taittinger or—'

'For God's sake, Crevecoeur.'

I pushed past him and helped myself to a bottle of Kronenbourg. There was no opener in sight so I banged the cap off on a rock and came back to my stool.

'Chief.' The man at the binoculars beckoned.

Crevecoeur stooped to the eyepieces, frowning with concentration. He sniffed. 'Journalist,' he said. 'They like the afternoon watch. They park outside and sleep their lunch off.'

'What are they hoping to see?'

'That is a mystery.' Crevecoeur sat opposite me. For a moment he was genuine, shaking his head, perplexed. 'They hope for an arrest, a confession, an interview, the return of the little girl.' He frowned. 'Or they've heard a whisper of another story.' He was steeling himself to tell me something and finding it difficult. 'A different story altogether, more interesting.' He was a security cop and they are not as ordinary people who thrill to pass on a secret. It was costing Crevecoeur blood. 'Something more important,' he brought out.

I took a swallow of beer from the bottle, thinking: I could try walking out, see if they stop me. Or clamber on top of the wall and wave and shout to the farmhouse below. Or wait and see what's gnawing at Crevecoeur's guts. Funny, even then I thought I had a choice.

He said, 'What are you doing here?'

Here was not an animal shelter at the brow of a hillside in Languedoc. *Here* was Nîmes, the *mas*, Ledru, the double crime. *Here* was getting in the way of Crevecoeur in his self-appointed role as God. *Here* was my mule-like stubbornness in behaving as a free person. I took another swig of beer. Crevecoeur was made up of a lot of different pieces and this was a prime example of colonial expropriation: he was convinced he owned my life, could boss me around.

'In two minutes I'm going to get up and walk away. You've got two minutes to make your pitch, Crevecoeur.'

He sat rigid on his rickety little stool. His face has never had much colour, not in summer, not in Central America, not on the fringes of the Sahara. But I had never seen it so pale. The blood had left his cheeks. He seemed to have stopped breathing. The lungs pump air automatically but he had sent commands to his chest to be still. His eyes bored into mine. I forget what colour his eyes are. In normal times, I mean. Could be grey or blue or green. Now they had no colour. They were as empty as space. Looking into them was like staring into the eye sockets of a skull.

There was a bitter taste in my mouth, maybe from the beer, and I swallowed. Behind me was a metallic click, such as a weapon being cocked makes. Speech had died in Crevecoeur. I had killed it.

Ten seconds, ten minutes, I had no understanding of the flow of time. But the two minutes I'd given him were certainly up and I had to move. With an effort of will I reached out to place the bottle on the table. Beer had been a mistake. It was coming out of the sweat glands all over my body. It took a greater effort of will to push myself up on my feet. I felt I should say something before I left. Goodbye. Good hunting. You look as though you need a holiday.

Why should I be concerned about Crevecoeur? We weren't friends, we weren't lovers. He was a bastard. He must have been ruthless and self-centred and uncaring and deceitful in the first place. Then doing the job had given a couple of extra turns to tighten up any slack in his character. There was nothing I could do for him. He should see a doctor or a psychiatrist or a priest.

I turned and hesitated a beat. Jean-Louis held his rifle down by his hip, pointed at my stomach. At that distance there was no need to aim. I began to walk, slow careful steps, towards him, towards the gap in the wall, the track, my car.

'Where do you think you're going? You think you can walk out?'

Crevecoeur's voice had risen, indignant, like a frustrated teenager. I kept walking. When he spoke again he'd switched to the tone I remembered from the past, a little weary, cynical, knowing. He'd recovered himself.

'Are you planning on going back to Paris?'

I didn't answer. None of his damn business. I'd taken another couple of steps when he went on.

'I'm curious, that's all. Because Yildirim is there. Just thought you'd like to know.'

I stopped. I stopped dead. *Yildirim is there.* His name was Bayezit, but everyone referred to him as Yildirim, just as everyone knew Pelletier as Lulu. But there the similarity ceased.

'Yildirim must mean something in Turkish,' Crevecoeur said. As if he didn't know.

'Thunderbolt.'

'Speak the language, do you? Picked it up when you were there in – let me see, when was it?'

'Goddamn you.' I swung round on him. He was playing me like a fish. I'd taken the bait. He'd got the hook into me and now he was watching me twist and squirm. There are people who take pleasure in that.

You know about Bayezit, someone had warned me, know about the original one. A sultan five or six hundred years ago. Always at war. He was known as Yildirim. He even had his own brother strangled. This one, the modern Yildirim, went one better: he shot his own mother when she said he was a bad boy, the things he did. Yildirim, the Thunderbolt, a member of the Grey Wolves.

'Why is he in Paris?'

'He's looking for you, Cody.'

By trade Yildirim is a professional killer. If the price is right, he'll accept anyone as a target. But he specializes in political kills. His normal theatre of operation is the Middle East: Jordan, Lebanon, Cyprus, Turkey. Mubarak escaped by a sheer fluke, but it is said Yildirim has sworn to get him sooner or later 'as a matter of honour'. Now he'd come to Paris, looking for me.

'Why?'

'Don't be naive.'

In the sky beyond Crevecoeur's head a raptor of some kind was drifting in long lazy circles. Not even the tiniest fieldmouse would escape its eye.

'How do you know?'

'Because he's been asking around.' Nodding his head to one side Crevecoeur said, 'Jean-Louis, give me a cigarette.'

His own man from Paris offered a cigarette.

'The whole packet.'

'You said

Crevecoeur's look silenced the man. To me he said, 'He keeps my cigarettes for me. I'm giving up smoking.'

'Not like that you're not.'

'Another bloody one. Nag, nag, nag.' He blew a plume of smoke in the air, then rubbed it out with a couple of waves of his hand in case there were watchers down below watching the watchers up here. 'The thing about Yildirim is that he's a hired gun and the people who hire him are terrorists, so when he comes to Paris those are the names he knows. An Iranian, some Palestinians, Libyans, exactly the people I keep my ear tuned to. Which is how I know he wants your address. "The bitch who put me away for the Americans."'

I shook my head. I had been tricked into it. I was younger, more innocent in those days. Duraine was running the CIA show in Turkey and I'd not long quit the spy game. Perfect for Duraine. I was operationally trained, I was expendable, I was deniable. Yildirim was setting up a kill...I don't like to think of it any more. But it became apparent that I was on one side, Yildirim on the other, and that only one of us could come through. When push came to shove – pure Duraine, that expression – I was on the morning flight out of Istanbul for Paris, while Yildirim was helping the Turkish police with their enquiries.

'What else did I hear he was saying?' Crevecoeur thought I needed prodding. 'He said, "The four walls of a secret police cell concentrate the mind wonderfully on what to do to her." So he wants to know where you live.'

Bastard. He didn't put it in words. He just let it grow in my mind.

'You're saying you might just push my address his way.'

Crevecoeur raised an eyebrow. '*You're* saying it, not me.'

'But that's what you mean.'

'Cody, *you* mean it.'

Crevecoeur lies, Crevecoeur bluffs, but not this time. He might be blackmailing me but he was telling the truth: in Paris there was a Thunderbolt ready to strike me.

'All right, a deal.'

Crevecoeur shook his head. 'I don't make deals.'

Ah, there he was lying. Or perhaps he deluded himself.

'Look,' I said, '*soixante-neuf* is a deal. Think of it like that.'

Crevecoeur blinked and went still. This is the way I could always hook him: the sexual innuendo. You kiss mine and I'll kiss yours. 'Okay, Yildirim will be expelled from France when you've done this little thing for me.'

'What little thing?' I wanted to know. 'It's to do with the murder? The kidnapping?'

I'd swear that Crevecoeur had forgotten about that. His conviction is that people should not have areas of their private lives that interfered with his interests.

'Of course not. That is nothing to do with the security of France. It really could not have come at a worse time. Unfortunate for the persons concerned, without question, but a distraction.'

Crevecoeur drew and drew on his cigarette, more smoke than his little lungs could ever hold. His face clenched just like a fist does. He was going to have to open the door a little on his secret world and that pained him.

'Once upon a time...' He drew on the cigarette again before grinding the butt under his heel. He had more resolve about him. He would treat it as a fairy story, easier to tell that way. 'Once upon a time there was a silly young fellow who didn't seem to know what to do with his life. He drifted from job to job: clerk in an estate agency, salesman for a design and printing firm, something to do with the installation of swimming pools. I suspect it was that job which turned his head. It's only people with big houses and big gardens who want to have a pool installed. He must have said to himself: I want some of that for myself. He must have looked at the sprinkler keeping the lawn green during the dry months, the drinks on the table under the parasol, the ladies who were careless about wearing their bikini tops when the pool was installed – and maybe their bikini bottoms when André Ledru called to check everything was in order. He ran into a bit of trouble with his employers – cheque altered, maybe a cash payment mislaid, I don't know the boring details. But the result was that Ledru left his wife behind in France while he went abroad to improve his fortune.'

'Chief.'

Crevecoeur hustled over to the binoculars, the man who'd called him standing to one side.

'Who's with him?'

'Vanderaerden.'

'Sure. Get back to bloody Belgium.' Crevecoeur returned to his stool. 'Our mutual friend has appeared. Taking the afternoon sun by his pool. Plus a bottle. Plus a business associate.'

'From Systel? From Exrilgor?'

I might not have spoken. Crevecoeur carried on. 'Anyway when Ledru left these shores he went first to the Côte d'Ivoire. He needed to collect his breath and take stock of his life. Also, when he fled it was the middle of the night and the Abidjan flight was just about the only one out of the country at that hour from Nice. Then he hopped along the coast to Benin, which to my ear has an unfortunate echo to it. I preferred it when it was Dahomey. There he kept company with certain people who at that time drank at the bar of the Hotel Central in Porto Novo, which is how we first got interested in him. As you are aware, there is a spirit of deep co-operation between France and her former colonies in Africa so we naturally learnt of the connection between a French citizen and certain gentlemen with international experience. We were able to identify very quickly Ladoin, ex-Captain in the *paras*; Schuyler and Black, ex-Foreign Legion; Elaouf, who had access to Syrian arms. Another one of those tedious African *coups* in the making. Most of them committed suicide while awaiting trial, shooting themselves a dozen or twenty times to make certain. Don't ask me where the guns were supposed to have come from in their prison cells.'

Crevecoeur lit himself another Gitane to celebrate this happy outcome. As he blew out the smoke, his expression soured to a scowl.

'Ledru, however, escaped before interrogation. Few are capable of escaping afterwards. A bribe, I suppose. Wisely he smuggled himself out of West Africa and we think he smuggled himself into France, to enjoy visiting rights with his wife and to call in at his bank. Certainly records show a surprising sum of dollars deposited. Also we have information that he made contact with a Marseille *clan*.'

The French use the word *clan* where the Americans speak of a *family,* in the Mafia sense. I looked away from Crevecoeur at the other men. No one watched the house. Their eyes were on their

Chief. I'm sure they were appalled to hear their secrets spilled to an outsider, a woman at that.

'How many dollars did he deposit?'

'Forty-eight thousand and some. Paid off his debt to his old employer.'

'Forty-eight in cash?'

'In cash. In some of those countries that's enough to buy half the army, though if there's a French military adviser you'd have to shoot him.'

'Who put the money up?'

Crevecoeur looked taken aback. He recovered and said, 'I hardly think that's relevant. The point is he now had a bankroll and shady connections.'

But I had the beginning of an idea. 'Washington provide the dollars? Moscow? The Cubans? The Libyans? What year was this?'

Crevecoeur was drumming his fingers on the table.

'I think,' I said, letting my idea grow, 'it was the French who provided the money. Here is how it might go. Chirac was Prime Minister, Mitterand was President, the time of cohabitation of socialists and conservatives, otherwise known as kicking the other party in the shins. Someone in the conservative government thought to bankroll the *coup,* someone on the President's staff torpedoed it. You used to be on call to Mitterand, didn't you? I think you dropped them in the cesspit. Just a possibility. But I like it.'

He stopped drumming his fingers. There is a bit of de Gaulle in Crevecoeur: he serves a certain lofty idea of France. It is the people of France, alas, who are not worthy enough.

'You get some crazy notions in that pretty little head of yours.'

So I was right. He was only using sexist language to get me angry.

I'd thrown him off balance, scored a point in a minor skirmish. It's good to do that with Crevecoeur, remind him you can't be walked over.

I had an idea and pointed to the Renault Espace. The 13 number plate is Bouches-du-Rhône and Marseille is in that department. 'The Marseille connection with the *clan*. Your local men have been playing a very long game.'

Crevecoeur didn't think that needed a response. He said, 'Ledru left France again, assuming he'd ever been here, and went east. Bits and pieces mentioning him were filed from all the usual hotspots – Bangkok, Ho Chi Minh, Hong Kong, Manila, Chiang Mai. Plus some of the less obvious places – Hat Yai, Medan, I forget. He was doing business by day and enjoying himself at night. So we heard. There was no way he could be followed twenty-four hours a day, no real justification either. But his file grew with hearsay and one or two informers' reports. Illegal immigrants from Vietnam, passports to the Macau Chinese, smuggling twelfth-century artefacts from northern Thailand, drugs from all the major sources. He'd come a long way from the man who used to call to measure up for a swimming pool, and enjoy a little bit on the side. Now he was shipping under-age Filipina girls to Tokyo and enjoying service all along the way.

'Then last year he returned to France. He put some of his profits into this *mas*, the rest into a Zurich bank. And he had a serious talk with the Gabizzi *clan* he'd been helping with supplies of opium.'

Abruptly Crevecoeur stopped. He was staring. All six men were staring at me. He'd given me history and background but nothing to do with why the Sûreté was on a hillside at this moment keeping watch on a farmhouse.

I said, 'Don't look at me. I've nothing to do with Ledru.'

'Nothing to do with him! You spent nearly an hour and a half with him. You're spying on his house. Nothing to do with him?'

'I'm not in the drugs trade. You know that.'

'The gangs use their drugs profits to expand into other areas. Sometimes they are legitimate. They go into real estate, into manufacturing, into supermarkets, into entertainment. Then they don't live so much in the shadows, politicians can be photographed shaking hands, they pay taxes, their wives get to wear their diamonds at charity dinners, their daughters go to Swiss schools. But sometimes one of these big bosses sees an opportunity to invest in a new area of crime that he finds irresistible. The challenge of something new. Progress. If you like you can see it as a form of evolution. You start by banging someone over the head and stealing his wallet, and you end up with…' He jerked a thumb over his shoulder towards the *mas*.

That was all. I wasn't going to be told the what and the how and the who. I was an outsider, not trusted.

'What the hell do you want with me, Crevecoeur?'

He wasn't quite ready for that yet. He pursed his lips. 'Why did you mention my name at the morgue? Why did you bring in the Sûreté?'

'It was my best access. I had to start somewhere with the murder and kidnapping.'

'Why?'

'Ledru wanted to hire me.'

'You work for Ledru?'

I heard one of the men letting out a hissing breath. *'Quelle chiotte.'*

'He wanted to find out who was responsible for his wife's murder. I wanted to save the little girl. Also…'

I frowned. I'd been needled into accepting Al Richards' challenge, and now that seemed frivolous. But Crevecoeur already knew.

'Also you've become a star reporter, or so I've heard. Is that true?'

'If I get a good story, the *American Journal* will print it.'

'Of course. You're seeing the journalist Richards. I've heard that too.'

'You keep your nose out of my private life, Crevecoeur.'

'Well, well.' He raised an eyebrow at me. 'I seem to have touched a tender spot there. Never mind. So at present you are working for both Ledru and the newspaper.'

'No. No, I'm not. Yesterday morning I knew nothing about Ledru. Now I know more than enough. I couldn't work for Ledru.'

Crevecoeur got to his feet and stretched the muscles of his shoulders. 'On the contrary, Cody, you could most certainly work for Ledru. In fact I think you must.'

He had a quiet, confident tone. There were no threats. He'd made those already.

'You are ideally suited. You have just the qualifications we lack. Firstly, Ledru wants to hire you. Secondly, you have no ostensible connection with the Sûreté. But thirdly, above all, you are a woman.'

I wiped the sweat that was trickling down my neck. The beer, the sun.

CHAPTER SEVEN

Broken.

Put it down to the sun. I lay on the terracing under the twisted branches of an olive tree. Where the leaf cover was broken, the sun powered through. My mind wandered.

Broken. It must be the most desolate word in the language. Broken health, broken promises, broken marriage, broken home, broken back, broken down. What else? Broken heart, broken spirit.

Also, 'I want the room with the shutters broken into.'

Crevecoeur. In plain English that was his instruction. His order.

'And if I don't?'

His eyes had reappeared in their skull sockets. I remembered them now. They had a particular pale grey quality, of ice. Broken ice cubes.

'And if I don't?' I had repeated.

Or spit. The greyness of his eyes, I mean.

'Don't push me,' he'd replied, his voice hardly more than a whisper, as if his head was beside mine on the pillow.

I was boiling in the broken shade. Blood boiling, anger boiling. Yildirim was the threat, but Crevecoeur wasn't honest enough to say it straight out. Within him there is the morality of modern war. Not the great technological leaps in destruction and killing, but the terrorist's belief that everyone is in the front line. Babies are soldiers now, grandmothers can shake a stick at the enemy sky. If you are within range of the bombs you are worthy to be killed, to be sacrificed for victory. Crevecoeur fights an endless war against the enemies of France, even imaginary ones, and if you are at hand you are pressganged into service. Here, join my army, he says without the option. Ride point, he orders, draw their fire.

For relief from the boiling memories I watched the *mas* through my binoculars. Two men appeared, the pair who'd watched me at breakfast, got into their car and drove away. The gate rose as the car approached, sank back behind it. As they passed the police van outside, one of the men tipped a hand towards it. Maybe a dismissive wave. Or a greeting. Down to two press cars again. One of them started its engine, puff of exhaust smoke, and a cop from the van got out and crossed to it. He spoke through the driver's window and waited. What for? Vos *Papiers*, of course. The cop put his head on one side and inspected the identity card with the intensity of a customs officer leering at a porno video. He went over to his van, lifted out a radio microphone and spoke into it, reading from the card. He waited. He nodded. He returned to the journalist's car and handed the card back. The journalist drove off. Three minutes wasted while the first car disappeared.

It meant something.

That scene from contemporary French life meant something more than a cop flexing his muscles, but I couldn't work out what. My brain was boiling.

I had boiled over at Crevecoeur. 'If I don't work for you, to your orders, what happens? I insist you tell me.'

But my insistence had no spectacular effect. Crevecoeur simply lit another of his forbidden cigarettes, watched and waited. He knew that when the hooked fish is landed, it continues to thump and slap on the ground. The final convulsions are no threat; the fish is yours.

What would happen? While Crevecoeur kept silent, my imagination went to work. One of his men – perhaps Jean-Louis, he looked as if he'd blend into the *milieu* – would spend an evening in the bars of the 10th *arrondissement*. Most likely he was known to be a security cop, but this time he wasn't after information, he would be giving it.

Another whisky, he'd say. And one for yourself, Jo-Jo. Make them doubles, been a stinking day. How's business? Doesn't look too crowded tonight. Everyone off on holiday? Still, we get swamped with tourists, should balance out your trade. Used to be Yanks, now it's Germans and Japanese. Even Turks come to Paris these days. I heard Bayezit was in town. Seen him around? You know, Yildirim.

And Jean-Louis would knock back his Scotch while Jo-Jo or Mario or Jules or whatever the barman was called would give nothing away with his eyes.

I suspect Yildirim will want a woman while he's here, Jean-Louis would drop in a confidential tone. Sure, you know what these Turks are like. Here's an address of someone very special. Cody is the name, if Yildirim should happen to ask. Hot stuff, so they say. She lives on the top floor, close to the angels.

Every hit-man has his style. Yildirim likes to use a rifle from long range. It makes his get-away easier. Once or twice he's gone right the other way and used his bare hands. He could be waiting in the dark at the top of the stairs and his hands would be round my throat and his lips whispering in my ear, so that I realized before I died who my executioner was.

Crevecoeur knew my mind would be working. That's why he said nothing.

Nice guy, Monsieur Crevecoeur.

When I'm a little old lady and I see Crevecoeur come to help me across the road, I'll hobble straight out and take my chances among the forty-tonners. More of a hope with them.

I had to put Yildirim out of my head. Stop brooding. I had a job to do and Yildirim would simply get in the way.

I lifted the binoculars again and got to work. Trees, shrubs, floodlight poles, known camera positions, angles of vision, plotting a route.

So who was I working for?

The day was dying and I was watching the colours fade, the shadows intensify. Before I went in I thought it over one last time. Call it psyching myself up.

Ledru wanted to hire me.

The *American Journal* said they would publish me.

Crevecoeur thought he was using me.

None of these. My motive was the only worthwhile one: helping the missing girl. That was clear in my mind and I was determined.

The floodlights in the garden snapped on.

Discouraged, the last of the reporters had left in search of dinner. I doubted they'd be back tomorrow. There was no story here.

Two cars had driven away from the house. Ledru and Max were in one. Another three men I didn't recognize were in the second. The two cars flashed their lights at the police van and were gone. Restaurant? With Agnès dead maybe there was no one to do the cooking. Or business? Crevecoeur hadn't told me what the Gabizzi *clan* were diversifying into. He just shook his head. When I pressed him he'd said: "It's nothing you need to know."

One light shone out of a window in the middle section of the house. I saw it come on, but no one walked in front of the blazing window or closed the curtains or the shutters. I thought of one of those automatic timers to deter burglars, but I wasn't going to bet on it. Avoid that area of the farmhouse. By contrast no chinks of light showed round the edges of the shutters on the other windows.

'Why can't one of your men do this?' I'd asked.

'Oh, we were planning to,' he said, 'until you came along and volunteered.' He gave me a smile, the one that shows his teeth. What he meant was: I was a freelance, if I tripped and fell I was deniable. I was a foreigner: if I was shot down by a Gabizzi bullet, there would be no tearful French widow to console.

I had to make a wide circuit, the length of the olive terrace, the track down the hill, across the *garigue,* across a piece of cropped grass, until I approached the fence at the south-east corner because this was my best chance. During the afternoon wait I'd made a recce to a higher level of the terracing where I had a view of the culvert that the sewer rat had used yesterday. Yes, glint of fresh barbed wire. So it was Plan B.

Plan B is not necessarily second best. That was the wisdom of the strategists from Langley. Plan B is the one that the opposition doesn't think you can do, so it always has a crack you can wriggle through.

Why can't I march in through the gate? Say I've come to see Ledru and I'll damn well wait until he returns. That was my Plan A.

Because the police will stop you and send you packing, just as Inspector Gaudet had threatened.

Why don't *you* go through the gate? Flash your Sûreté card at the police?

Crevecoeur had given me his teeth again.

Yesterday I hadn't known about the cameras and thought I could go over the wire. Today I was wise and spotted the one that kept this stretch of wire under its glass eye. The fence was nearly three metres high at this point, topped by four strands of barbed wire plus floodlighting and surveillance cameras – this was Ledru's line of defence against… whatever he felt he needed defending against.

No friendly branch overhung the fence but a line of cypresses, the veterans of some ancient peasant boundary, stopped just short of the wire. To the last tree I went and, on the side away from the house and the floodlights, I got to work. The cypress is a dirty tree to climb, full of dust, spiders' webs, tiny dried leaves if you can call them that, like insect scales. Its branches are slender, upright and close to the trunk. I made mucky progress.

A dead branch gave with a crack. There'd been no microphones, had there? I swung by one arm, listening for the sound of cavalry. Nothing. No mikes.

I was a monkey the higher I climbed. Halfway up, above the level of the barbed wire and floodlights and camera, I changed to the side of the trunk nearest the house. Up, up. The tree was swaying now, not in view of the camera, God grant me, just on top. A cypress is slow-growing, made of hard wood. It wasn't about to snap under my weight. That's what this monkey told herself and clambered higher.

Pause, look, listen.

The trunk was thinning out, my hands encompassed it. And it was bending to my weight. Higher, using my knees to clamp the trunk. Haul with my arms, clamp with my knees. Again. Again. Sudden alarming dip like a rod with a big fish hooked. I was the fish. Further. Once more.

I looked down over my shoulder. The top of the cypress had bent nearly at right angles so I was now beyond the barbed wire. How far off the ground was I? The height of the fence plus my own height, plus a bit more. I relaxed my knees so that my legs hung free, feet dangling, lessening the drop. It was no more than jumping from a bedroom window. You'd do that if flames were licking at your tail.

I let go, dropped with my knees bent and rolled forward into the shelter of a solid bush. It was over in a second. Even if someone was glued to the monitor he'd blink: what was that? He'd rub his eyes and shake his head. I had vanished in a flash, like an angel falling to earth.

Let's hear it for the Plan Bs of this world.

I was standing by the back door, the one the gardener had come out of. All my senses had a fine edge to them, which is what happens when the talking is over. Also I had that feeling – not happiness, not satisfaction, more than that – that feeling of rightness from doing something. I could get over the fence where Crevecoeur couldn't. I was going to get into the house where Crevecoeur couldn't.

'It's for this,' he'd said.

'A bug?'

'One of the amazing advances in miniaturized radio transmitters,' he'd said like an announcer reading a commercial. Adding: 'A bug, yes.'

Crevecoeur and his boys had got the number plates of the cars, the long lens had captured close-ups of the visitors' faces, their identities were mostly known. Ledru's mail was second-hand by the time he got it. A tap had been put on the line but the telephone was proving a disappointment. People had nicknames. Someone was called *le faucheur*, daddy-long-legs, but with hints of darker meanings, of mowing down, the grim reaper. Other times they spoke in simple word codes, or maybe they hid from the truth. *More business for the florist* – murder, Crevecoeur interpreted, funeral wreaths. 'I need more,' Crevecoeur had said, 'I need inside information.'

I tried the handle of the back door just for form's sake. I spent two seconds on the lock to confirm it wasn't one of those that American Express cards do nicely. Windows on either side were locked and I didn't want to break the glass. I wanted to be in and out and no one ever the wiser. So it was back to the door, which had a half-light above it. I brought up the big plastic bin for garbage and clambered on to that.

Crevecoeur had held the bug out to me. 'Made in Taiwan,' he said, 'but under licence from the Japanese.' He wanted to reassure me of its pedigree, that the risk I was taking was worth it. 'Put it in that room with the shutters permanently closed, that's where they talk business. Gabizzi's villa at La Ciotat and that shuttered room.' Crevecoeur had turned from me, his fist clenched round the bug, staring down the hill at the farmhouse and its secret room.

I carried my burglar's tool with me, a nailfile. A woman has a right to carry a nailfile; it makes no one suspicious. Balancing on the dustbin, I probed between the half-light and the frame. They had installed all the modern security toys but the building still kept some of the original features. The wood had shrunk as it dried and, to stop it rattling when the mistral blew, it could have been nailed down. Instead it had a simple hook. I probed and caught the hook and forced it out of its eye. The half-light opened inwards, as French windows do. I hauled myself up and wiggled and squirmed through as far as my hips, and reaching downwards and outwards I could just grasp the window handle. It had a security lock with the key still in it. Great security. The window opened and the house was mine.

One last preliminary: tote the outsize dustbin back to its corner. You want to be a housebreaker, you must also be a housemaid. Who said that? Surprisingly I think it was Duraine, the no-shit bastard I'd run into at Langley, who'd tricked me in Istanbul and who now worked out of the US embassy in Paris. You've got to clean up behind you, Duraine said, brush over your tracks. Also – he swung round and jabbed a finger at me – no perfume because it hangs around, not even in bed for the big seduction scene, because it's like your fingerprints on the guy's skin. Is it okay if I clean my teeth, I'd asked? Duraine had stared and stared. You could see his thought processes: One day I'll get that sassy bitch, one way or another I'll get her.

The hell with Duraine. He should marry Crevecoeur. The hell with Crevecoeur too. Was he watching through nightglasses? Could he see me scramble over the sill?

I was in a scullery. A smell of bleach and dampness. What ever happened to the old French farmhouse smells? Where was the heady incense of garlic, herbs, pungent cheeses and *daubes*? I could make out a deep freeze, a washing machine, a drier.

Grandma would have put her hands on her hips and bawled them out of her domain.

My ears reached further than my eyes and they caught no hint of danger. The open door to the right led to the kitchen. I walked past it to the corridor that ran the length of this side of the building. To one side a pale line of light showed at the bottom of a door. Whoever kept watch over the property, scanned the monitors, drank a bottle of beer, that was his lair. I turned the other way into coal-mine blackness, trailing my hand against the wall to keep in touch with the real world. I walked blind.

At each step the bug I'd jammed into a pocket pressed into my leg. 'Transmit what secrets?' I'd asked Crevecoeur. But his frown tightened and he shook his head. I wasn't family, I wasn't to know. I was an outsider to be used and thrown away. 'Your boys have been on this hilltop for a week,' I probed again, 'so you must think it's reached a critical phase.' He nodded at that. Also, they must have witnessed the handover of the orphan to the Ledrus. One of Crevecoeur's boys gave a grunt and scratched his chest. 'Sure, but we could see it was a private visit, if you like, a man and a woman with a kid, so we weren't interested.' How did they get here? *'Un vieux tacot,'* he said, an old banger, 'all dust and rust.' You've been taking down licence numbers. 'Ah,' the chest-scratcher said, 'we couldn't make out anything because the number plate was covered in shit.' Then Crevecoeur had headed me off. 'Get your mind away from that orphan, get it on to putting that bug into that room.'

In the darkness I plotted my progress. The first window had been unshuttered, so the first door would be into the wrong room. I felt the frame of the second door and put my ear to the panel. No sound from the room, no voices, no machinery, no creak of a chair, nothing. My fingers found the door handle.

Get it over with, I scolded.

It can't be this easy or one of Crevecoeur's boys would have done it. But perhaps they wouldn't have found it easy. The French have fallen in love with America, embracing it all, McDonald's, tomato ketchup, Levi's, Hollywood, but particularly technology. They'd have had to whistle up a helicopter to lift them over the wire. They are forgetting human sweat.

With that smug thought I turned the handle, went through the door and knew at once I'd made a wrong move.

I stopped. Too late. I tried to isolate what had alerted me. Nothing so crude as an alarm bell. Nothing I could hear or see. Nothing conscious. Nothing I could define, no threat I could defuse. But I sensed something – a change in atmospheric ions or human brain waves – and felt a tingle through my nerve endings.

Knowing no better, we call it intuition. Laugh at intuition and you'll end up crying.

Now the light value coming through the door had changed. I had walked through an infra-red detector, stepped on a pressure pad, tripped some alarm signal and the security man down the corridor had got his bum off his seat and was coming to investigate. It was too late for me to go back.

Enough of the garden floodlighting leaked in round the shutters to show the outline of the desk and some chairs ranged round a low table. No, too much attention was focused on those areas. Something tall and spiky rose out of the shadows. Leaves. Called mother-in-law's tongue. Ripping the backing off the adhesive strip, I went to the big wooden planter and clamped the bug on its inside.

Scuff of a foot in the corridor, close, almost too close. I had time to get back and shut the door but only just. A closed door is a weapon. It sets up uncertainty. He is going to hesitate, asking himself what's on the other side. Man with a machine gun? Woman with a nailfile? He has to open the door and commit himself against the unknown.

I pressed myself against the wall on the hinge side of the door.

I don't think he anticipated the darkness. If there was an intruder, a burglar, a policeman, a rival, what would he be doing in the dark? The door swung open, the man came in. I saw him in profile, outlined by the pale glow from the passage behind, a hand outstretched holding a pistol.

Now, before he reaches for the light switch.

'Stop,' I ordered. 'Don't move. Don't even think of shooting. I've got you covered.'

He stopped dead. It was uncanny how he looked like a statue. I could see the outline of his frame, turned to stone, leaning forward, hastening to get to grips with whatever danger had lain ahead. I was to his side, four steps away, in shadow.

'Good. I don't want to shoot you,' I assured him. 'This is what you've got to do: drop your gun on the floor, then turn your back on me.'

He was too stunned to do what I said. Or he was working out his own move.

'Grow up. I can see you but you can't see me. I could drop you before you even finished turning. You'd make a mess all over Ledru's carpet and he wouldn't thank you for that.'

By degrees he straightened his back, losing that gung-ho forward thrust.

'Your gun. Let it fall on the floor. Then we can all rest easy and be pals.'

I used the word *potes*. The little bit of slang relaxed him, as if we were from the same bowl of stew. His hand drooped and the pistol made a soft landing.

'Turn away from me.' He did that. 'Take one step forward. Just one. Don't try to make a break for it.' He did that too.

I crept forward. I took my time about scooping up his pistol, for he might judge this was the moment to launch his attack. My clothing made a sound as I bent and his body stiffened. It wasn't to jump me; it was because his power was being taken from him. I stood back, fumbling with his pistol, before moving to close the door and switch on the light.

'Okay,' I said, 'let's see...' But I got no further.

He was swivelling round to confront me then, fury in his eyes. It was Inspector Gaudet.

CHAPTER EIGHT

'I told you to get back to Paris,' Inspector Gaudet said.

'I don't think you have the right to order me to go anywhere.' I was a little formal, a little cautious, because a French cop believes he has the right to order you to do anything he pleases at any time, and don't you ever forget it.

'I've had enough of you. You're under arrest.'

'What for?'

'Burglary.'

'I've taken nothing. Look.' I held my arms away from my body, empty hands angled towards him.

'Breaking and entering.'

'I've broken nothing.'

'Illegal entry.'

'Ledru invited me to return.'

'Hindering a policeman in the exercise of his duty.'

'I removed a weapon from an unknown man who was threatening my life. You didn't declare yourself a policeman, so I wasn't hindering.'

'Illegal possession of a firearm.'

'Here, take it back.'

I tossed it to Gaudet. He couldn't catch it one-handed and it landed at his feet. Stooping, he snatched at it, then came upright with the pistol pointed at my chest.

'You're a bitch,' he said, 'an interfering bitch sticking your nose into other people's affairs.'

Interfering? The word nagged at me.

'You pretended to me you were a journalist. You pretended to Ledru you were some sort of private investigator. You deny you work for Crevecoeur, and maybe I believe you and maybe I don't. Maybe you and Crevecoeur both work for someone else. The computer says you were trained in America. The CIA moulded you. I have discovered that Crevecoeur too was in America, in Washington. The French embassy is forty-five minutes' drive from the CIA headquarters in Langley. I think you are both spies.'

He dropped his eyes to the pistol pointing at my chest.

'Spies? *Spies?* You've made up your mind I'm a spy and you're pointing that thing at me? You can't use it. You're a police officer and I'm a private individual, guilty of nothing. Gaudet, do you understand what I'm saying?' I don't know. Maybe he couldn't even hear me, he was too worked up. 'What am I supposed to be spying on? Something in this room? So what's an ordinary cop doing, making himself at home here?'

He didn't like that, what I said or the tone of voice. I wasn't showing respect. All the questions I'd thrown at him, and the answer I got was this: he closed one eye and sighted with the other down the barrel. His trigger finger began to take up the tension.

'Gaudet? Inspector Gaudet? You are making a very terrible mistake. Put the gun down.'

I was to be taught a lesson, a great big lesson. He was paying no attention to anything I said. In his mind he was away somewhere else. He was thinking about giving more work to the good Dr Fignon. He was thinking how to explain my corpse away. I wouldn't be a spy, I would be a petty thief who had forced a way in, unwittingly alerting that ever-vigilant protector of the people Inspector Gaudet. France is lucky to have such men. Even though a *mutilé* from a previous police action, Inspector Gaudet came to challenge the intruder. When I jumped to attack him, he was forced to shoot me. And if, at this precise moment, I flinched and turned my back, then I would have been shot while trying to escape arrest.

Gaudet's face had clamped shut. He was giving me a hard stare along the pistol barrel. His open eye was judging me, the black eye of the pistol ready to carry out the judgement. Mesmerized, I stared back. Of all the stupid places…

His knuckle whitened.

Was I supposed to plead for my life? Please, don't shoot, I beg you. I'll do whatever you want, just spare my life.

I've never pleaded with anyone. It's never got that bad.

The trigger finger was squeezing. I could see the angle of the nail changing, the knuckle shining. I said nothing. I would not give him the satisfaction of hearing me beg. At the last second, the last micro-second, the pistol shifted a degree or two away from my heart so the shot would ring out and the bullet would bury itself in the wall. It would pass so close I would feel its wind.

I heard the click as the trigger hammered home. Gaudet twitched. He'd been expecting an altogether louder noise. He squeezed the trigger again. The third time he squeezed the trigger his mouth sagged open and he jerked in a breath.

'Thought you'd scare me,' I said, 'send me running back to Paris. I've got the bullets. I took them out.'

He hadn't seen me because I'd done it at the moment I picked his gun up, as I was moving to the light switch. I don't like guns. Their noise is too loud, their effect on people too permanent. His ammunition was snug against my thigh, in the pocket where I'd carried Crevecoeur's bug. I had a brief vision of Crevecoeur up on the hill, dragging on a forbidden cigarette, frowning as he listened to the conversation in this room.

'Give them to me. Those bullets are state property.'

'Oh sure,' I said. 'If they end up in my body do they become my property?'

Gaudet slipped the pistol away in the holster under his jacket.

'How did you get into the *mas*?'

'Does it matter?'

'Why didn't you use the front gate?'

I chose my words with care. There were relationships here which were not clear. 'There's a police van there. Its job is to keep people out.'

'You said Ledru invited you.'

'Well then, put it down to my desire to show off a little. But tell me, Inspector Gaudet, I'm fascinated to learn why you are here.'

'Official business.'

'The double crime?'

'I said, official business. That's enough for you to know.' His voice hardened. Some men take naturally to being a hard cop. For Gaudet it was a routine that had slipped and he was doing his best to claw it back.

'But Ledru isn't here for you either.'

'He was here, but he was called away on some urgent business matter. I said it would save time all round if I waited for his return. He appreciated the courtesy. He asked me to make myself comfortable in what he calls his video games room. Very security-conscious is Monsieur Ledru.'

'Did he ask you to shoot any intruders? Or was that your idea?'

'Don't be absurd.'

'Which question are you answering?'

'I don't have to answer any of your questions.'

'Why is he so security-conscious?'

'You're nothing but questions. Ask the man yourself.'

The edges of the shutters lightened, then darkened, as car headlights swung round on to the gravelled parking area.

Ledru stopped just inside the door, taking in Gaudet and me standing rigid like village-hall actors when the curtain rises. Behind him were faces, of which I recognized Max's.

'What's happened?'

'She managed to get in somehow or other.'

Ledru went on smoothly. 'So you arrested her. Very correct.'

'In fact,' I said, 'I think I arrested Inspector Gaudet.'

Gaudet was furious and seemed about to dispute this, but Ledru was smiling. He said to the men at the door, 'Lads, why don't you get yourselves a beer. Use the video games room. See if any more like her are getting in. Inspector Gaudet, I wonder if I could ask you to wait with them a few minutes while I talk to the lady.'

I thought Gaudet was going to refuse, I thought he was going to drag me with him for questioning, I thought he was going to demand his ammunition back again. He hesitated, gave a curt nod to Ledru, nothing to me, and left.

Ledru went to sit behind his desk, a black-stained pine model for the thrusting modern executive, ahead of the trend back in 1975. 'How did you get in?' He settled himself in his chair then looked up at me. 'I asked how you got in.' When I didn't answer a second time he muttered, *Nom de Dieu,* at least sit down, won't you?'

I took a chair where I could see both Ledru and the door. At the edge of my vision was a wooden planter with the sword leaves of mother-in-law's tongue, but I had no interest in that.

I asked my question. 'Why do you have so much security here?'

'To keep out undesirables. Though in your case you are not undesirable.'

There are men who will never stop trying. I know that from experience. The really persistent kind will reach out of his coffin to goose you if you get too close. It's in their nature. Ledru was giving me a grin now to show he was just kidding and we were pals. He let out a breath and gave a little shake of his head. Wasn't life just too crazy for words – that was the signal I was supposed to pick up.

I said, 'Tell me – if it's not too much to ask – what's going on?'

Ledru gave me another grin. Someone must have told him once that his grin was rugged and honest and appealing, and he'd practised it in front of the mirror along with that rueful little shake of the head.

I went on, 'Remember yesterday? You wanted to hire me to find out Agnès's killer. You have Inspector Gaudet doing it the official way, but you were interested in a private initiative.'

'Private initiative,' Ledru said. 'I like the sound of that.'

'I can't do the job without facts and you're an elusive man. I telephone here and you're not at home. I telephone your office and you're not there. So I decided to wait here for you to come back.'

Ledru gave a little nod of his head. I see, I understand, I believe you, or I want to believe you, or I think you're lying in your teeth but we're both engaged in bluff and double-bluff games. I've seen that nod in other men. They're thinking, they're deciding which way to jump.

'And to come in through the front gate is too ordinary for you.'

'There's a police presence there. They're stopping anyone getting in. That's normal police procedure, protecting the family of a victim. And in normal circumstances I could state my business to the police and they'd let me in, no problem.'

'So what is the problem?'

Now we were down to the tricky part. I was as open as I could be because Ledru must already know.

'The police would look at my ID, check on the radio, find I was an undesirable – according to them – and throw me in the can overnight. Inspector Gaudet doesn't like me. Well, that's hardly news, you saw how he was. He didn't like me the first time he saw me. Or the second time. As for the third time ... '

I thought I could leave it like that. But Ledru just ran his fingers through his tousled hair and waited.

'He thinks I work for the Sûrete Nationale and he doesn't like the idea of them muscling in. I haven't asked him why he thinks the Sûreté should be interested in your domestic tragedy. Nor does he explain why the Sûreté might employ a foreign citizen. But then tonight he came out with a wilder theory: the Americans are actually controlling me and the Sûreté. You want my opinion, he is a little deranged.'

Ledru still wanted more and now I was scraping the barrel.

'His very bad experience with this,' – I held up my left arm with the hand bent at the wrist – 'well, it's enough to make anyone bitter. He blames the Sûreté for the explosion. He's desperate to be a hero, but he has trouble picking his target. In the nineties heroes are out of fashion.' I had run out of things to say. 'So what progress has Gaudet made?'

Ledru got up and walked round the desk. His home office had nothing so vulgar as metal filing cabinets, though a pair of black wood cupboards might store papers. A workbench against a wall had two computer terminals complete with screens and a laser printer, a telephone with a Minitel, a fax machine, an intercom. Ledru walked towards me and I tensed. He walked past me towards the planter and I was constructing a story – in case he called Inspector Gaudet in to print me – about why my fingerprints should be on that miniaturized radio transmitter. But he stopped at a trolley with bottles and glasses and a vacuum ice bucket. He picked up the Macallan single malt and tilted the bottle at me. I shook my head.

'You don't think much of Gaudet.'

'Well, like I said, he's not as great as he thinks he is.'

'He tells me he saw you last night.'

'Warned me to go home to Paris.'

'Before that. He says he saw you having dinner with a journalist.'

'Oh, Lucien Pelletier. He's come here with some hunch, sees it as a great human-interest story. I know journalists in Paris. Lulu is one, we ran into each other so we had dinner.'

'Now, you see, Gaudet says Paris journalists are all in bed with Paris cops. You understand, he's got this fixation about the Sûreté Nationale. That's why, for all the organization behind him, Gaudet won't find the killer.'

Ledru stood before me, swirling whisky in a squat tumbler. I don't know what the Macallan people think of ice in their Scotch, but the cubes made a seductive tinkle.

'Which is why I need you,' Ledru said.

'Can you show me the advertisement?' I asked.

'I can't find it. I've looked all over. Agnès cut it out of the paper and maybe she threw it away. I thought she might have kept it for sentimental reasons, but she wasn't all that sentimental.'

Or marriage to Ledru had squeezed it out of her. We'd finally got down to details of the adoption.

'What did the ad say?'

'*Romanian orphans need good homes.* Those were the exact words, but when I got to meet the man he had just this one left.'

I swear Ledru said this, like he was discussing getting the runt from a litter. He opened a drawer in his desk and brought out a Polaroid photo of a little girl, taken here on the terrace. She was one of Ceausescu's orphans and looked it. Not that she was skinny. A lot of the orphans had picked up AIDS from infected needles, but little Ecaterina looked healthy enough. It was just that she was tight within herself, as if she hadn't received any love. She seemed self-sufficient when she was barely more than a toddler. She glared at the camera lens with suspicion.

'Who took the photo?'

'I did. Here's another.'

He dealt me a photo with Agnès in it as well. She was good-looking, blonde or sandy hair, kept her figure trim as the years had begun mounting up. She looked as if she swam forty lengths every morning and played tennis with the club pro. She was squatting down to be on a level with Rina. The orphan had no smile for the adoptive mother, no frown and no fear either. Life was accepted, hope was extinguished. That had been Ceausescu's way. She wore a pretty yellow sundress with white polka dots and held a small doll at her side. She didn't even hug the doll.

'When did you take the picture?'

'Day she came. In the photo album it was going to be labelled Day One. We wanted to chart her progress.'

'Pretty dress.'

He shrugged. 'Sure, nice dress. That's where Agnès was going when she was killed, to buy more dresses and stuff for the kid.'

Ledru drank and, finding his glass empty, went for a refill.

'How old is she?'

'Is? She's dead. She was thirty-two last birthday.'

'Ecaterina.'

'Rina? She was three, three and a bit. Somewhere round there. So he said.'

'You have her birth certificate?'

The birth certificate seemed to have gone the way of the advertisement. He took a mouthful of whisky, held it a moment before swallowing.

'No birth certificate, no official papers of any kind, a private initiative, to use your phrase. Not even a receipt for the money I paid. Fifty thousand in cash. The man said—'

'Has a name, has he?'

'Doicescu? I think I've got it right.'

'Perhaps I'll have that whisky after all.' I needed something to steady me. This great executive of a thrusting French company had given fifty thousand francs to a stranger whose name he wasn't even sure of, for a child with no legal documents. Of course Crevecoeur would say that legality wasn't a clear concept to a member of the Gabizzi *clan*. Ledru handed me the drink. Here's looking at you, Macallan.

'Doicescu said that with an orphan in Romania there usually were no papers. That was to hide who the real parents were. The parents could have been political dissidents who had disappeared. Or sometimes the opposite – the illegitimate child of one of the political top dogs. Ceausescu's son was reputed to have quite a few bastards scattered round the country. In either case, safer for the child not to know.'

True. In Ceausescu's Romania a little knowledge had been a dangerous thing. But Ecaterina had been born after Ceausescu had been executed.

'He insisted on cash? And when he called you happened to have fifty thousand on hand?'

Ledru kept weighing me up yesterday and again tonight – was I tough, was I impressionable, was I an easy lay, was I out to cheat him? I was a constant puzzle. He said, 'As it happened I did have the cash available. I'd been in business in the Far East and when I came back to France I put some of my money into property and some into the bank and some under the mattress, so to speak. In other words, I behaved like a typical peasant who doesn't like to have what he's worth known to all the world. So I, André Ledru, reassured this Romanian I could give him cash. Doicescu had insisted on cash because he said in Romania people had faith in dollars and Deutschmarks and francs, but nobody had faith in banks. It just sounded a more extreme version of what I feel. So agreeing was no problem for me.'

How much else did he keep under the mattress? It gave a reason for the elaborate security.

'Doicescu came out here?'

'First contact was by telephone. His advertisement had a box number at the newspaper and I replied giving my phone number. He called me and we arranged a meeting in town, in Nîmes, just him and me. He wanted it in the Buffet at the station. I didn't ask why.'

Came by train? But he had his dirty old banger of a car. Or there's a lot of coming and going at a station so they'd be part of a crowd. Or somebody in the crowd was a look-out.

'Do you have a picture of him?'

'Are you kidding? Why should I take a picture of some Romanian I do a bit of business with?'

'I need to know what he looks like.'

'What are you going to do – show his picture round the Buffet? They get hundreds of people in there every day.'

'Do you want me to call in at Systel tomorrow and tell you how to do your job?' I stared at him, his tousled hair, the cheeks that were getting fleshy. I pictured him with a gold medallion nestling among the chest hairs. The medallion would be his star sign. He'd say, I'm Aries, I'm a ram. Or, I'm Taurus, a bull between the sheets. Or, I'm Virgo, but don't you believe it. His familiar grin would be cuddling up.

'Listen,' Ledru said, 'he's very distinctive. You don't need a photo. There are some good-looking dark Latin types in Romania. Then there are others, chubbier, not so handsome. Got some Slav blood in them. He was one of those. Heavy build, like a boxer who's stopped training. In his thirties somewhere. Nothing special at a distance until you see his face. One whole side of his face is frozen, doesn't seem to move. The eye is dead, you know, I think blind. He sits with that side of his face turned slightly away, as if he wants to focus his good eye on you. You wonder whether he's had a massive stroke but he walks and talks all right.'

'He could have had an accident that injured the central nervous system.'

'There was no scar I could see.'

'Some accidents don't leave visible scars.' The other cause that came to mind was chemical and that implied an injection. It was deliberate and sadistic, but in Ceausescu's time that had been a matter of policy.

Ledru eyed me again, looking for hidden meanings, then nodded. 'Doicescu told me at the station he only had the one orphan left and he wanted a second meeting out here to make sure the house was *assez confortable,* as he put it. Jesus Christ, after Romania a dog kennel would be a palace. So I told him: "Bring the girl so we can see her and if both sides are content we'll do the business right then." All right, never mind the argument we had over that, he drove out here with a woman and the little girl. I thought the girl was a sullen little piece, though maybe just traumatized. But Agnès said: *"Ah ma pauvre,"* and scooped her up and gave her a kiss and stroked her hair, so the matter seemed pretty well settled. I brought Doicescu in here and asked him: "Comfortable enough for your taste?" He was gaping round at everything, the computer stuff, the air-conditioner, the furniture, the lighting, the carpet, and he gave me a sheepish sort of a grin. Well, half a grin. The women were out on the terrace and it was just the two of us in here. "Nice place," he said, "but a bit isolated." I knew what he was getting at. I said: "Don't worry, I've got good security." "No dogs?" "No dogs," I told him. "My wife has a problem with dogs, but maybe I should get one of those anti-burglar devices with a recording of an Alsatian barking." Half a grin again. "Don't worry that anyone can get in and harm the girl," I said, "I've got lights and barbed wire and video cameras, and if that's not enough I've got a gun." He nodded. Then it was down to business. I had the money ready and made him count it. Then we had a drink to seal the bargain. Then away they drove. That was it. Informal, which I appreciate.'

'You've had no ransom demand?'

'Nothing. The police are tapping my phone – actually Gaudet warned me they would. Also I think they're opening my mail. Well, they're out of luck. Nothing.'

'No note tucked under your windscreen wiper?'

'I told you, nothing.'

'I thought maybe that was why Inspector Gaudet was here tonight, he had news.'

Ledru drank and considered answering, but found nothing useful to say.

Ledru was topping up his glass again. If he took three paces to the left he'd be standing right over the bug. What did you think of the second act, Crevecoeur? Got some questions you'd like me to put? I had some questions of my own that I kept to myself. Such as: Why was Inspector Gaudet so keen to pack me off to Paris? Such as: Why did Ledru put men to watch me? No, I could guess that one. Such as—

Ledru interrupted my thoughts. 'How do you plan to track down the killer?'

'The police have the manpower to go round asking questions. They can stop and search cars. They can do all the lab tests and other forensic work. We have to do what the police can't do better.'

'Which is?'

'If there's no ransom note, you have to advertise a reward for the return of the little girl. You've got to draw him out.'

Abruptly he squatted on his haunches so he was level with me and spoke into my face.

'Listen, the return of the girl...' He made a dismissive gesture with his hand, waving her out of the way. 'It's the killer of my wife I'm hiring you to find, and when you have tracked him down you are to inform me.'

'The killer and the kidnapper are the same person. But to focus on the kidnapping aspect is the way in. I don't know his motive. Maybe he's a pervert. Maybe he's someone you've crossed in the past making you suffer. But just maybe he's waiting for you to make the approach. Simply because he knows the police are hovering to pounce if he does.'

'All right.' Ledru stood up and moved away. 'Okay, makes sense.'

'I suggest an ad in the paper. Say one hundred thousand francs reward for the return of Ecaterina. Address in Paris for the reply.'

'Paris?'

'Otherwise the local police will intercept it. We'll phrase it like the *American Journal* is offering the reward, but I'll pick up on any reply and check it out.'

'I want—'

I knew what he wanted: The killer of Agnès Ledru in his sights. But the intercom buzzed. Ledru pressed a switch.

'What is it?'

'It's Jacques. He's out doing a patrol and he's seen something.'

There was a click and then a faint haze of static from a personal radio. 'André, I'm out by the track beyond the olives.'

Ledru turned towards the windows, closed and shuttered. In his mind he was pin-pointing the position.

'What is it?'

'I noticed fresh tyre marks in the dirt which I thought I should find out about.'

Mine. Leading to trouble.

'And?'

'The track goes up towards the goat shelter. So I'm looking up there when I catch a flare of light, faint but it's there. You know, like someone putting a match to a cigarette. Then it's gone, darkness.'

Crevecoeur, giving up smoking.

'Sure you're not hallucinating?'

'I know what I saw. Could be a shepherd, gypsies, a couple screwing. But I don't know. Could be someone else.'

'Go up and check. What are you carrying?'

'A .38.'

'Okay. Let us know if you need help.' Ledru flicked up the switch. He said to me, 'Maybe it's him, the killer. Don't they sometimes return to the scene of the crime?'

'The crime was down the road.'

'Close enough.'

'If he's a weak personality, wanting to feel important...'

'Could be I'll save a hundred thousand francs and won't have to hire you.' He undid a button of his shirt, slid his hand inside and scratched his chest. 'Hey, don't worry, you won't lose out.'

Ledru crossed to the door to turn out the lights. In the darkness he barked his shins and muttered *Merde* as he went back across the room. He opened one of the windows then pushed the shutters wide. Night smells drifted in from the garden, the hot summer smells of the Midi, fennel and cypress and dust and jasmine. I went to stand beside Ledru and we stared at the low hill outlined against a starry sky. I could hear crickets but nothing else.

I thought, Crevecoeur's up there, and his sidekick from Paris, and the ones who've been staked out for a week. And Jacques is going to creep up on the blind side while they're all peering down here. Then I thought: No, Crevecoeur's been listening to every word that's been said.

From the hillside came the sound of a shot, clean and sharp.

'Jacques?' Ledru muttered, puzzled. 'That was no .38, that was a rifle.'

He crossed to the intercom and pressed down the switch. 'Jacques? Jacques?'

CHAPTER NINE

'Jacques! Jacques!'
    Ledru's voice was its own echo, only harder and louder. It was night out there but not inky black. The sky was jewelled with stars and a quarter moon had bumped up above the horizon.
'Jacques! Jacques!'
'Listen,' I said.
'What is it? What have you heard?'
'Nothing. You're drowning it.'
We listened. What we heard were footsteps clattering down the corridor. Ledru angled his head as the door opened, but his eyes were fixed on the hillside.
'They got Jacques,' Max said.
'I heard,' Ledru said.
'The bastards.'
There were other figures crowding into the door, but it was Max I watched. He was carrying a big pistol, not the little .38 of yesterday that fitted snugly in the Naf Naf bag round his waist. This had a hefty barrel, more like a Colt .45, drop a horse at a kilometre, give an elephant a headache.
'Look,' Max said.
We all stared, Ledru, me, Max, two other men, I think that was all. We concentrated on the shelter at the crest of the hill. We caught a flicker, a torch most likely, appearing in chinks between the stones of the wall.
'Think they're getting away with it.'

Max raised the .45, rested the barrel across his left forearm, aimed up the hill, squeezed off a deafening shot. The pistol jerked, he aimed, fired again, and again.

'Max, what the hell are you doing?'

'Bastards are getting away with murder.'

He fired a fourth time.

'Name of God, will you stop it.'

'They can't do that. They've got to be taught a lesson.'

'You trying to hit the moon?'

'They've got to learn respect.'

'What are you aiming at?'

'The lights.'

'You think someone's standing behind each gap flashing a torch as a signal? Max, you're just catching a beam as they move about.'

'It's our honour that's been stained.'

Jacques, who'd been shot down, had ceased to exist. He wasn't flesh and blood, he'd become a symbol.

Max rested the barrel on his forearm again. Ledru turned round. 'Alain, Marius, where's Gaudet?' The .45 boomed. 'Will you stop that a moment. Where did Gaudet go?'

Alain and Marius were gang members, soldiers, streetfighting soldiers but not street-smart. After a pause for thought one said, 'Went to the gate. He's going to get the van to drive up there.'

'The police van?'

'What else?'

'Stop him. Marius, run like hell and stop him. This isn't police business. Max is right, this is *our* business.'

Max looked at him. 'Then why do you keep jumping on me?'

'Because you're wasting lead shooting from here.'

There was a brief silence. Nobody talked of Jacques.

'What are you suggesting?'

'It's no suggestion. I'm telling you what we're going to do. We're going up there. We'll teach them respect.'

Max took a deep breath. 'Go up there, right?'

'You shoot at them from down here, they'll think you're scared. Is that any way to teach them respect?'

Thoughts of Jacques were way in the past. They had moved on to a different plane. They were gangsters but they were French gangsters. Talk and violence came in equal proportions.

'I've got my .45. What've you got, Browning Automatic, right? Alain has his .38. Marius – where's Marius got to?'

'To stop Gaudet going up there.'

'Right,' Max said, 'Gaudet could lie down in the back of the van and one of the cops take the steering wheel and get popped. That's not the way to teach respect.' Max took another deep breath. 'If we go up that hill now they'll be above us, pick us off one by one.'

'If we had a road grader,' Alain said, 'put its scoop up as a shield.'

'But we don't have a bloody road grader. Maybe we should get help. Call up Akli *le beur*. He's got a pal with a mortar. If that doesn't teach them respect, nothing will.'

'Where do you think you're going?' Ledru asked.

I stopped halfway to the door. 'There's a man shot on the hillside. Jacques is *your* man. Why don't you go to help him?'

'What do you think we're talking about?'

'Sounds like a revenge raid. Jacques doesn't enter into it. He's been shot but that doesn't mean he's dead. I'm going out to him.'

'They'll shoot you down too.'

'Look.'

They turned to see where I was pointing up at the animal shelter. Headlight beams made a huge arc against the night sky as they swung round. There was the roar of an engine being raced in first gear. The lights bounced across the uneven track and disappeared over the far side of the hill. The engine noise faded to silence. Then we could make out a man's voice, thinned by distance, calling for help.

Ledru and Gaudet had torches, the rest stumbled in the wash of light they threw. We went through a padlocked gate in the fence, across the *garigue,* following a path up through the olive terraces. As we got closer, Jacques guided us. Sometimes there were theatrical groans, sometimes shouts, *'Je suis crevé.'* He had propped himself against a trunk. In the torchlight a stain darkened his trousers halfway between his knee and his hip.

'Okay, Jacques, we're here,' Ledru said. 'Does it hurt?'

'Con, do you think I always sing like this?'

'What happened?'

'What does it bloody look like? I was bloody shot. One minute I am walking up that path, the next my leg is kicked from under me and I fall over the edge to this terrace. Must have hit my head against a bloody stone, knocked myself silly.'

I pushed through the men and knelt by Jacques. 'Give me a torch, someone,' I said. The bullet wound seemed flesh only, through and out. 'Can you move the leg?'

'I'm not bloody running anywhere.'

'Can you move it?'

He bent his knee, drawing in a sharp breath.

There was no bone broken. My father had been a doctor and I had the basics from him. The Agency had added their own imperatives: how to bind wounds, how to expel a bullet, how to splint your own arm. We used to debate what would come next: how to be your own blood donor? I shone the torch up on his face. His left cheek had a graze with a smear of blood. I tilted the torch so it lit my face. 'Can you see me?'

'Course I bloody can.'

'Two heads? One and a half?'

He took his time. 'One head, bit muzzy, slips sideways and jerks back.'

'Apart from the leg and the head, how do you feel?'

'Sick in my stomach.'

I felt his cheek, then his forehead. There was a bump there, nothing too serious. 'Mild concussion.'

'Bloody hell,' he said.

'What are you in your spare time,' Gaudet asked, 'some kind of great brain surgeon?'

I stood up to face him. 'Bad news, Gaudet.' I waited until I had his full attention. 'There's not a thing I can do for you.'

I took Jacques' torch but I didn't need it. My night vision adapted to the moon and starlight. *You want to know how to develop night vision?* Erica Fawcett had asked once. I'd been blinking at one of the male nudes she does. *I'll tell you. By staring at men's faces on the pillow in the dark and trying to work out what the lying ratbags are really thinking.* Erica would use a man a time or two and then go back to women. They were her night vision.

I'm going alone.

When I'd said that Ledru and his soldiers and Inspector Gaudet and the wounded Jacques had stared at me.

You'd sound like an army, I'd explained, *and I'm trained not to sound like anything.*

They're waiting for you.

They're gone, I'd said. *We saw them drive away.*

That was a trick.

I shook my head. No, that was no trick. Crevecoeur knew from the bug in Ledru's office that a war party was coming. He'd got out.

They could have rigged a booby trap.

Let her go.

That had been Gaudet. He'd waved me away up the hill. It was his left arm he used, with a hand missing from an earlier booby trap.

Trees, rocks, into shadow. I stopped and lifted my face up when it wouldn't catch the moonlight. There were no flickers of light glimpsed through the stone wall of the animal shelter. They'd been packing up their Renault Espace with the tents, the camping furniture, all the surveillance gear, the crate of beer. They wouldn't have left any nasty little box of surprises because it might be the goatherd who picked it up. But Gaudet could always dream.

I slipped through the gap in the wall and stopped. To one side was a pile of dead branches, used for blocking the entrance when the goats were inside. It was cover of a kind but no one was there. My eyes probed every pool of darkness for the flash of white teeth in a smile that meant nothing. *Couldn't wait to see me again, Cody.* As if he was my destiny. There was nothing left of the stake-out. I went to the wall where Crevecoeur had been watching the house. From the butts on the ground I saw he'd given up smoking ten or twelve times.

Standing by the wall I confirmed what I had come up for: my car was out of sight. Let them think it was hidden just off the road. That was okay. But to be abandoned halfway up to this hide-out, that would suggest possibilities to Ledru and Gaudet.

I aimed the torch downhill and gave three short flashes. Two long flashes in return. Oh, we were playing at spies tonight.

A small procession set out to return to the farmhouse. Gaudet led the way with a torch, Jacques hobbled with his arms round the shoulders of two soldiers, Max brought up the rear. And Ledru, he climbed the track towards me, his torch picking out the way, then swinging to left or right to stab out into the darkness. That's right, Ledru, it's the jungle out there, an ambush behind every boulder. And if you keep that torch going, they'll know precisely where to aim.

When Ledru entered the animal shelter he searched me out with the torch, then came to stand beside me. Snap, we were in darkness more complete than before. I waited for my night vision to come so I could study the face of this lying ratbag.

'*Bon Dieu,* you can see everything from here, the house, the fence, every visitor. I should keep a guard up here.'

'They won't come back now they know this place has been discovered.'

'You think so? You believe people who shoot down a defenceless man in the dark just give up and tiptoe away?'

No, not Crevecoeur, not any of the kind of people Ledru was involved with. Where would Crevecoeur go to ground now? How far did the little bug I'd placed transmit?

'Wish I'd brought a bottle.' Ledru looked at the ground with Crevecoeur's stubs crushed out. None of Crevecoeur's men had smoked while I was with them, which was un-French. 'They can't have been here long before we spotted them.' He seemed cheered.

'Who was it?' I asked. 'Do you have any idea?'

'The man who killed Agnès. Who else could it be?'

'What does he want?'

Ledru lit a cigarette to give himself time.

'It's a business matter,' he said.

'Systel's competitors do business with guns?'

'And the little girl has been taken as a hostage. Business rivals, yes.' He drew on the cigarette. 'I'm a businessman, sure. But I have diverse interests, you understand, not just Systel. There's more than me, more than the men you've met. We're part of a group, very profitable, and expanding. And there you have it.' He jabbed a finger at the cigarette butts. 'Some of our rivals are looking at us with greedy eyes.'

'Your rivals do business with rifles,' I said, 'while you only run to pistols.'

He took a fierce pull on his cigarette.

'We can get rifles. We can get machine guns. Helicopter? Personnel carrier? We can get whatever it needs. If there is to be war, we are ready. But first we have to know who the enemy is. You understand? We have asked questions everywhere and people shake their heads. They say they respect us and our business. And yet – my wife is killed, the girl is snatched, my house is under surveillance, one of our best men is gunned down without warning. All right, we go on asking questions, we have good police co-operation, but we also try a different approach – you.'

For a few moments we were both silent, looking down to the farmhouse. The little procession was making its way along the fence, through the padlocked gate, across the garden. Despite the floodlighting, Gaudet still had his torch on. Once he stopped and flashed the beam up the hill at us, on-off-on. It could have been a signal or a bit of useless action. They vanished inside. When the door closed and we were alone up on the hill, it seemed to be the prompt that Ledru needed to get going again.

'Cody, I have a proposition for you.'

'The answer is no.'

'I'm talking business. Though doing business with you would be a pleasure. You have looks, you have style—'

But no patience. 'What is the business proposition?'

He took a moment longer before committing himself.

'You've got half the deal already: catching the rat who killed Agnès. That is a short-term contract. Shorter the better. I want him very badly. You find out who it is and then it's good-night.'

He took another pull on his cigarette, dropped it among Crevecoeur's butts and stamped it to death.

'Then there is the longer-term contract that I have in mind, with our organization.'

'What's the nature of the business? Apart from Systel.'

'Come *on*,' he said, 'you've been around.'

'I don't know I've been around your kind of business.'

'I have contacts in Paris. I don't mean Al Richards, he's a pal from a different time of my life. You remember going to see Fonza?'

My past was catching up with me. Lulu Pelletier knew me from that time too. Fonza had been head of the Corsicos, a big man with a hairline moustache and a stare. The second most important man in Paris, I had been told. Maybe the President was the most important. Though Fonza's importance hadn't been magic armour against a bullet.

'I telephoned one or two of the Corsicos I know, who said: "Cody, sure we remember Cody. Very cool, very strong-willed, no connection with any firm. At one time had a boyfriend who was an undercover cop, so undercover she didn't even realize it. She made a mistake there, but an honest mistake. The boyfriend was blown away and Cody went right after the killers, nailed them. The cops didn't do it for one of their own, Cody did it." '

It seemed different when Ledru told it. Or I remembered other things. There had been a girl kidnapped, as now, but Ledru didn't mention that.

He turned to lean against the wall, casual, open, able to observe me more closely under the starlight.

'I've noted how you got into the *mas,* not once but twice, pissing all over the security systems. I've noted you insisted on coming up here first and alone. That impressed me. And see, I told myself, she's done it because she wants me to be impressed. She's saying: See what class I've got, better than anyone you've got, more skill, more brains, more guts. I've taken the message on board. So I'm making you this offer of joining us.'

I didn't breathe a word.

'Le grand patron – the head of our organization – will want to see you first. It's a commitment we make, you see, to look after each other, so the big boss has to satisfy himself you take the commitment seriously.'

'Who is he?'

'I don't—' Ledru took a deep breath and realigned his thoughts. 'A man by the name of Gabizzi. You'll win him. He likes toughness. He likes style.' Ledru considered this meeting, picturing me in his mind being tough and stylish with Gabizzi, and nodded. 'What else should I say? You'll need somewhere to live. You can move in here. There's plenty of room.'

'Move into the *mas*?' I gave it some consideration. Or Ledru must have thought so because he leant towards me. There was an animal smell about him, a male smell. 'If I moved in I might give in to my baser instincts.'

I could make out the beginnings of a grin, his lips parting. 'And then?'

'Kick you in the balls.'

He moved back, the grin vanishing. He took a moment then laughed and shook his head. 'That's good, very good. You've got spirit. I admire that more than anything. I bet you can be a real tigress, biting and scratching.'

He meant between the sheets.

I watched Ledru going down the hill, torch punching left and right.

What are you going to do?

Sit here a while thinking about what you suggested.

Come down afterwards. Tell me what your thoughts are. Have a drink. What have you got to rush back to Nîmes for? Stay the night. I can drive you in the morning.

I've got my car.

Where? I haven't seen it.

I'd impressed him again.

Ledru lurched and almost fell where Jacques had taken his tumble. He should have kept his eyes on the path the whole time. The sound of his shoes scraping pebbles faded. There was absolutely nothing I needed to consider in his proposition, but I sat a while anyway. I imagined I could hear a voice singing, very faintly, from a radio somewhere. Then it was the alarm call of a bird disturbed in the night, echoed by a squeal from the hinge of the gate through the fence. Finally, as Ledru passed into the house, there was the sound of soft clapping from a jumble of rocks hard against the wall outside the animal shelter.

'Bravo, Cody, wonderful. You'll be working right on the inside.'

'One fine night,' I said, 'someone is going to take a shot at those rocks thinking there's a rat in there, vermin of some kind.'

Crevecoeur rose, rubbing the small of his back. The smug smile I'd heard in his voice had gone from his face.

'Tigress, did he call you? Stylish pussy of some kind. You plan to purr in his bed, that's your business. Scratch and bite all you like. So long as you find out why Gabizzi's *clan* has hacked into certain computer networks, because that's my business.'

So there we had it, the first crack of light as Crevecoeur eased open the door on what he was concerned with. Computer crime. But he would say no more.

Close on midnight, the traffic in Nîmes no more than a growl, still people on the streets. It was all the usual suspects, tourists full of wine, lovers getting to bed in slow stages, solitary men hunched into blousons, eyes turning, a cough, a hiss. At my hotel I was handed an envelope. I read the note inside right there by the reception desk.

Cody, salutations. Journalists of the world unite. You have nothing to loose but your scoops. Come and see me soonest.

It was in English, printed in careful capitals, one spelling mistake, which gave it the flavour of being written after a serious dinner. It wasn't anonymous exactly but had what I thought was a tick; then I thought it was an X, somewhat scrawled, its bottom half cut off, a drunken kiss to sign off a love note. Hey, it's Al Richards come panting from Berlin. My mind leapt to that like lightning. El Al having fun. Or wanting to. But he'd chosen the wrong night. I was too whacked.

But I closed my eyes and thought: What the hell. I could use a friend. His hotel wasn't far. He'd even given me the room number. Ten minutes later I walked boldly in and swept past reception like any *poule de luxe* who'd received an urgent summons. At room 281 paused before knocking. What was I getting into? Middle of the night, Al's room. To me he was a friend, but he saw other possibilities. There was no need for night vision: you could see what he was thinking shining out of his face.

So I paused, but then I knocked. A hug would do me good. I needed the human touch. A kiss wouldn't do any harm. Maybe a second one. Isn't that how we all jump on the merry-go-round?

I knocked again.

There was no answering shout. I could hear the sound of a television set. El Al was getting himself in the mood with a Canal Plus steamy special. I tried the handle, the door was unlocked, I pushed it open.

'Journalists of the world ignite,' I began.

He was sitting in a hard-backed chair in front of the television. They'd used a bath towel round his waist to tie him to the chair. His feet were bare. They'd stuffed his own socks in his mouth to gag his screams.

There were voices in the corridor and I had to come right inside and shut the door. I listened to the voices come closer, one male, one female, and then pass.

I took another step so I could see into the bathroom. Empty. And another step so I could see beyond the end of the bed. Nobody crouching. His jacket lay on the floor.

The room hadn't been tossed. His suitcase hadn't been dumped, nor the lining of his coat slit. Whatever they'd come for, they hadn't had to search hard to find. He'd told them, fast. Another step and I could see why. His shirt was ripped open and someone had slashed his chest right across a nipple. He'd told them, then they'd killed him, a single shot in the temple.

It wasn't Al Richards. It was Lulu Pelletier. He'd gone for the big story he knew was there and found it, and they'd come and taken it right back from him.

CHAPTER TEN

Around her neck she wore a chain of golden bells that gave her the look of a houri in some rich man's fantasy. She had almond eyes and lustrous hair piled high like a helmet. Her head turned to the left at the sound of a male voice, then to the right as a reply came. The bells tinkled prettily. The first man said, 'As you know, I offered ten thousand dollars.' The second man asked, 'US or Hong Kong?' Perhaps she was a slave girl up for auction. She sat in the middle of a billiards table. She was naked, of course.

I stared at the television screen because I didn't want to look again at what they'd done to Lulu Pelletier. I would have to in a moment because his corpse screamed for attention. See how rough they play, it shouted. Can you get inside the mind of a torturer who could do a thing like that? He longed to tell me who they were, but couldn't get the words out.

There was a gust of laughter from the screen. The camera pulled back to show two men at the billiards table, unknown actors, studs when the scene came where they stripped off their Brooks Brothers suits. Which was the goodie, which was the baddie? I decided they were both villains. The naked girl got my sympathy vote. She squatted on her haunches with her knees well apart.

I crossed to the window and peeped between the parting in the curtains. A street lamp shone through the branches of a tree. There was no balcony with an unpleasant surprise. The bathroom, when I stood at the door, shrank to a hand towel tossed carelessly on the floor. A red smear showed what the hand towel had been used for. And so by a circular route I came back to Pelletier, tied with the bath towel.

The hole in his temple was small, purple-bruised, black-scorched, red-streaked. Not much blood, neat, professional. The television wouldn't have drowned the sound of a normal shot so they would have used a silencer. His body was plump from expense-account living. *Camels in Clermont-Ferrand, 12,000 francs*, I thought. *Sewer rat cheaper.* He'd enjoyed life. There'd been no fun in his death, none at all.

A click. I whirled into a crouch but it was only the television. A billiard ball had cannoned and was rebounding off a cushion near the girl's knees. It came to rest on the cushions of her thighs. She was part of the game – that was the excuse for a naked woman on the table.

I continued my tour of the room, touching nothing, an ear cocked for voices or footsteps in the corridor. Lulu was from the generation before computer terminals and modems, and a battered old typewriter stood on the dressing-table. A box of paper and some sheets of carbon lay beside it. The carbons were unused, the paper blank, the waste basket empty. His notebook was gone. On the night table by the bed was the only piece of used paper in the room. It was a napkin with the logo of the Pizz' Ritz. On it Lulu had scribbled my name and hotel.

There was the sound of breaking glass. On the television the nude woman had picked up the billiard balls and was lobbing them at bottles behind a bar, a huge gilt-framed mirror, a chandelier. Enraged, one of the men pinned the woman to the green baize with his cue across her throat. Her body writhed as if from an unbelievable sexual climax, but her face showed nothing. I thought there was big trouble looming in her future. Mine too.

From the street I caught the soft clunk of a car door. Peeping between the curtains, I saw three men crossing the road towards the hotel entrance. Though they wore plain clothes, they had the determined stride of men acting on a tip-off.

I'm sorry, Lulu, you don't know how sorry I am to leave you like this.

In the corridor there was a sign of a stick figure running towards emergency stairs with tongues of flame licking at his back. I know the feeling, fella. I followed the arrow.

In boulevard Victor Hugo I chose a bench with a newspaper kiosk on one side and a plane tree on the other. I was suddenly shy about showing my face. In my pocket was the napkin that advertised both the Pizz' Ritz and me.

Lulu had found his big story and it wasn't just about who killed Agnès and kidnapped the girl. It was about Ledru, the girl, the Far East, the Gabizzi *clan,* drugs, corruption, the computer hacking that Crevecoeur was so intense about, any or all of that. Only trouble was, he'd kicked over a wasps' nest and the wasps had come and stung him to death. They'd removed any story he'd written and his notes, but they'd left the napkin with my name and then rung the police. Ledru might want me but his associates didn't share his lust. Inspector Gaudet would lick his lips at the prospect of interrogating me. My ear ached with the sound of one hand clapping against it. I had a more immediate worry: returning to my hotel. Who would be waiting in my room?

After twenty minutes' hard thought and disappointing two men in leather blousons, I went in search of a telephone. I called the hotel and gave my name and asked if there'd been any callers.

'Monsieur Richards. You've just missed him.'

'He called from Berlin?'

'Berlin? No. I mean missed him at the reception desk. He registered here five minutes ago, two minutes ago. He's on his way upstairs. He's taken the room next to yours, madame.'

I found my face was smiling. El Al for real this time, hotfoot from the Berlin conference. The smile vanished.

'The room next to mine?'

'Yes.'

First thing he'd knock at my door. Who would open it? A man with a silencer on his gun?

'Connect me to his room.'

'One moment, please.'

Silence. I was in some café or other, don't ask me what, an undrunk coffee on the bar counter. Staring out of the window, I saw four or five cars come past in a pack, then nothing. It was late and the barman was starting to sweep up.

'He doesn't answer.'

'Keep trying. He's not reached his room yet.'

Two minutes, the clerk said. Mentally I paced myself up two flights of stairs and along a short corridor and stopped at the door next to mine. It would take two minutes. So why wasn't he answering his phone? Because he'd wanted to surprise me straight off and hadn't even gone into his room but gone to mine.

'Hello.'

Al.

'Thank God,' I said.

'Cody.' He gave my name in a shout of delight. 'I was out in the corridor and just about to knock on your door. Are you psychic? I'll be round in five seconds.'

'Listen to me, Al, I'm not in my room. Do not knock at my door. Do you understand?'

The silence ran a few seconds before he spoke, his voice dropping low. 'Co, what the hell have you got into?'

We sat in the car, tense and a million miles apart. I'd thought of asking Richards to drive because he knew where we were going, but he looked too angry to be behind the wheel.

'Why didn't you get back to Paris when I told you to?'

It was my turn to be angry. He was appointing himself my protector.

'I seem to remember,' I said, sniffy as hell, 'you proposed a deal. If I found out about the murder and kidnapping, the *American Journal* would run the story. You made it like a challenge so that I couldn't refuse.'

'The deal's off. No challenge.'

We were headed due west out through the suburbs, long line of small villas, closed cafés, deserted workshops, billboards advertising Kléber tyres, Crédit Agricole, a brand of pasta.

'Don't sulk, Co. It's not your style.'

I'd lifted my head and Richards thought I was being pettish. It was the big poster advertising pasta that had drawn me and I watched it grow smaller in the mirror. The brand name was Lulu, and it echoed in my brain.

'Lulu was tortured and killed because of something he'd found out. My name and hotel were written on a piece of paper in his room. I'm not sulking, I'm looking to see who's hiding in the shadows.'

Or who was on the road that night. In the mirror I watched a car some way behind us.

'Did you telephone the police?'

'No.'

'Why not?'

A light turned against us and we stopped. We sat staring through the windscreen and not speaking. I checked the mirror. The car was closer, slowing right down. The light turned green and we got going again.

'Why not?'

'Perhaps it was the police who did it.'

'Ah, come on. That was a gang thing.'

I'd given Al Richards a bare outline of the facts in the street outside the hotel, with the Sexy Show flashing at my back. *Lulu?* he'd said. He looked sickened because he knew Lulu Pelletier. *What the hell had he got his nose into?* Then he'd said, *Co, we sure ought to get away from here. I know a friend's place.*

I said, 'Al, I've met an inspector in the local police who's in the pocket of a gang. He was with me at Ledru's house tonight. The timing is tight, but he could have got to Lulu's hotel before I did.'

'Jesus. What's the name of this beauty?'

'Inspector Gaudet. Ledru orders him around like the hired help. He was even left alone to look after the house while they all went off earlier in the evening. That's why I say it could be the police.'

'Or I guess André could have done it. I mean been there. A knife, I can't see André wielding the knife. But he could have given the word.'

'Ledru knows I had dinner with Lulu last night, but that's not a reason for murdering him. Lulu had found out some dirt on the Gabizzi *clan* and some part of the mob killed him. Not Ledru. He would have behaved differently with me. It wouldn't have been something he could keep to himself.'

Another red light. In the mirror I watched the car draw closer. It was a dark Renault, blue or black, unmarked, but the uniforms inside were unmistakable.

'What are you staring at?'

'Don't look round, but in the car behind there is a pair of cops. They've been sniffing our exhaust, sometimes close up, sometimes far back.'

'Where did they pick us up? In the car park?'

'I don't know. I noticed them a couple of kilometres back.'

You only ever know when you first noticed the tail. The light changed to green and I accelerated away. The police dropped back but then hung on as if they were on a rubber band.

'If we were both men they would have stopped us,' Richards suggested. He pulled down the sun visor and peered into the little vanity mirror.

Vos papiers.

'Well, a man and a woman together at this time of night'

He didn't finish, and in a few moments I understood why. Al directed me off the highway on to a private road. I had to slow right down and we could both see the car with the police pass on down the highway. I took a breath.

It was one of those nights when the most ordinary events can seem scary.

We passed through an open gate and followed a curving drive between shrubs and gnarled old trees to the main building. It was constructed like a rich man's hacienda in Mexico, the overhanging tiles, the columns, the arches smothered in bougainvillaea, the fountain in the courtyard. The moon turned the flowering jasmine into a silver cascade. Its perfume was heady in the air. I caught a snatch of a woman's laughter, or imagined I did.

'Oh boy,' I said. 'Wow, this is some place for a little old farmer's boy like you to know.'

I flipped off the ignition and we sat a moment listening to the splash of the fountain. Now it was a snatch of piano I imagined I heard.

I didn't look at him when I spoke again. 'Remind me what it is they call you at the office. El Rat?'

A tasteful sign on the wall by the office door announced this, in English, as the Love Hotel.

It was a tart's boudoir, frilly lamps casting a peachy-pink glow, an urn with silk flowers, a carpet of white fleece you could lose your toes in, a mirror angled in the ceiling, a circular bed.

'My mother warned me about men taking me to places like this,' I said. 'So where is your friend?'

'Henri told me how to get here, I didn't say he'd be greeting us. He's not the manager, he's the owner. He's planning a chain throughout France and then Germany, just outside cities. Henri got the idea from the Love Hotels in Japan. A couple needs somewhere to go, a Love Hotel is the solution.'

For couples who weren't married, or couples who were married but not to each other. Forget the hotel by the railway station, a room with a stained rug on the boards, a bidet half-hidden by a screen, a bed that's heard a thousand sighs not of desire but of despair. A Love Hotel embraces and caresses the couple. I continued my tour: a bowl of apples to tempt the old Adam, a fridge with liquids to stimulate the imagination, a video camera to record the happy event.

'That's where you met him?' I said. 'In Tokyo, after Bangkok and Vietnam on your sex tour of the Far East? Hooray, Henri.'

I went into the bathroom and shut the door. There was a shelf of perfumes to match every mood. The tub was big enough for two, even three or four, provided you were very close friends. I splashed water to cool my face because I knew I'd been over-reacting.

Richards had flopped on the bed with an arm across his eyes. He didn't want to look at me. 'I should have stayed in Berlin.'

'*Fräuleins* kind to you?'

'What the hell is it, Cody? In Paris you're not like this.'

In Paris I didn't have days like this. Not too often. I wasn't threatened by two different lots of police, wasn't coopted to work for two opposing sides, didn't discover my dinner date of the night before tortured and killed, didn't turn round to discover pistols and rifles pointing at me, didn't run for my life and end up in a sex hotel. It had been a hard two days. I had a sudden thought: I was slowing down. I was too old to keep up the pace any more. But not, it seemed, too old for Al Richards.

I sat down on a *chaise-longue.* Al had the bed and he'd be happy to share it with me. But no amount of peach and pink could alter the mood. A couple of hours before I'd hesitated outside a hotel bedroom, thinking Al was inside, hesitated and then gone in. What might have been couldn't be now. The mutilated corpse of Lulu Pelletier got in the way.

Richards let out a deep breath. 'Let's all have a drink.' He went to the refrigerated mini-bar and peered inside. 'Well basically, you can have anything you want so long as it's champagne.'

I love the pop of a champagne cork. Up fizz memories of celebrations, good times, hopes. Tonight it sounded like a gunshot.

He poured the wine and gave me a glass. He squatted by the *chaise-longue* and raised his glass.

'Lulu,' he said. His eyes over the rim of the glass were the colour of caramel.

'Lulu.'

We drank. The toast to the memory of the murdered friend switched our mood. We were on the same side again.

'Are you going to tell me now?'

He meant what had happened over the past two days. I'd delayed until we'd got clear of Nîmes, put distance between ourselves and the murder.

'It'll take a long time.'

'We've got all night.' He went to the bed and stretched out. He lay on his side so he could watch my face while I talked.

I told him about his old hell-raising chum, who wanted revenge and thought he'd hired me – I didn't say yes and I didn't say no – and who had taken on some important role in the expansion of a Marseille gang. I told him Ledru was convinced the murder of his wife, the kidnapping of the child, the observation of his house from up the hill and the shooting of one of his soldiers were the work of a rival. I told him about Inspector Gaudet, who hated the Sûreté Nationale and the whole of Paris and was sure Pelletier had been a Sûreté informer, and possibly me as well. As if that wasn't enough, Crevecoeur was active.

Al knew about Crevecoeur because I'd told him in the past. He knew that with the Sûreté involved the whole tone of a crime changes. It is out of the realm of the personal and petty. It may still be grubby, but it has the security of the state involved. In this case, computer crime of some kind. It would not just be planting a virus that thumbed its nose and shouted *Poisson d'avril* on April Fool's Day. It would be hacking into something important, stealing information, stealing names, stealing secrets.

'But what?' My mind had been on a domestic tragedy. Now the murder of a friend added a new dimension. 'Crevecoeur wouldn't—' I broke off.

When I mentioned Crevecoeur again, Richards stiffened. I waited for the outburst, but it wasn't that. He held up his hand and cocked his head towards the door. He'd picked up a sound outside the *cabaña*. I'd missed it, too intent on talking. The urge had been building inside me for two days and Al was a friend and I needn't hold back. Now I was silent, staring at the door.

I saw the handle turn.

It was unnerving, knowing someone was outside and trying to steal inside, thinking this was the Love Hotel and we'd be too occupied with each other to notice a thing like a door opening, or maybe we'd be dozing, exhausted after our frenzy.

Al Richards looked at me, eyebrows raised. I shook my head. No idea.

Perhaps a sneak thief. Go away and try another door. Perhaps.

I hated that doorknob turning. Bad manners. It was the bad manners of people who lean on their horn when you get in the way of their car, or slit open a man's nipple to make him talk. Or a woman's. I could almost feel it, flinching from pain that hadn't been inflicted.

There was a rat-tat-tat at the door, seven or eight impatient knocks. Al swung his legs off the bed and got up. I went to the window to check outside, see whether there was a car, or if the manager stood in the door to the reception office. I parted the thick velours curtains and found there was no window. The curtains were draped in front of a blank wall. Who needed a window in this place? Their eyes would be on themselves. Logical, but logic was no comfort. We were caught in a trap.

I turned to speak to Al, to say: Don't open it, but it was no good. The knock was repeated, with fists this time. If we didn't answer, they would smash the door down. They were that type. There was no escape from here so I did the only thing I could. As Al reached the door I switched on the video recorder and angled the camera away from the bed and towards the door.

A final thumping. Next time it would be a shoulder or a boot by the lock. But at least whoever came in would have their faces recorded on video tape.

Al opened the door and there were two of them. Cops. And I thought: The ones from the car who observed where we peeled off the main road, giving us time to get locked in each other's arms. Buttons gleaming on their uniforms, caps just right, eyes darting from Richards to me and back to Richards.

There was no warning. They didn't introduce themselves. They simply came in on the attack. As he'd opened the door, Al had had to take two steps back and the first cop came forward with his gun waving all over the place. Most likely they'd decided Al would be naked and planned their moves accordingly and didn't change their minds. The cop spread his arms to get his balance and aimed his shoe as if he was going to kick Al's balls into touch.

I'd been in the gym fighting Al just days before and I'd needed to use guile. I'd had to outsmart him because he was stronger and heavier than me. He was as fit as a journalist is ever likely to be. Plus he was acquiring skills in martial arts. The last way to attack Al Richards is to take your pistol off his chest and put your trust in brute force.

Al didn't have time to think. His reaction was so swift it had to be pure instinct. He swivelled sideways, deflecting the shoe, and grabbed the ankle so that the cop was hopping on one foot. Al spun him like a top and the pistol went skittering under the *chaise-longue* as the cop fought to keep his balance. Al stepped in and caught him with a two-handed chop to the throat and the cop ended up at my feet gasping for air.

There are times when too much is happening, you have no time to think, and afterwards you can barely recall each event. I was looking at the man on the floor, I was looking towards Al, my brain was sorting out each danger.

'Al!'

The second cop had been following the action with his pistol raised, not being able to risk a shot. With his colleague out of the firing line he now had Richards in his sights. I was too far away, no help. But Al did a backwards kick, as high as I've seen a man of his size do, and struck the gun hand. There was a cry, a shot went wild. Al was on him, overpowering him, crashing him to the floor. Al was a man in a fury, slamming him again and again on the floor.

'Al, you'll kill him. Al!'

He looked at me as if he didn't know me, anger clouding his vision. Another time I would think twice before accepting a challenge from Al Richards. He'd been in Vietnam and Beirut and Afghanistan, and he'd volunteered for those assignments. Had the violence he'd witnessed affected him? Or had he volunteered because there was a side to his personality that hungered for the experience?

'Okay?' He was taking deep breaths, his body hungry for oxygen after the action.

'Me or him?'

I had put a neck-lock on the man at my feet. He went suddenly limp as the blood was cut off from his brain and I had to loosen the pressure. I had no call to kill him. That may have been their intent, but that was the difference between their kind and normal humans.

'I'm going to get on to Henri,' Al said.

'Tell him he needs better security.'

'Tell him ...' He broke off for another deep breath. 'Tell him his room service is lousy.'

That was the old Al I knew and almost loved. The deep breathing had brought him calmness. His wide-eyed stare had died and was replaced by a frown. 'Co, are we ever in deep shit! Have you any idea how many years you get in the slammer for beating up a French cop?'

Suddenly he was hungry for air again, as if these were his last breaths.

He stood naked before me.

'*Filez*,' he said, waving the two men away. Max wore the Naf Naf gun pouch today. The other man was a newcomer, a replacement for the wounded Jacques. Behind Ledru the swimming pool shimmered, ripples rebounding off the sides, splintering the sides. Water glistened among his chest hairs and ran like slug-trails down his belly.

'You think there's something wrong with me?' Ledru demanded. I'd said nothing, never questioned why they had decided to adopt. Ledru was not a morning person, on edge, snappish. 'You think I can't perform? Look, it's all there.'

He jabbed a finger down at his male tackle. I kept my eyes on his face. You can perform, I could have told him, but still shoot blanks. Then I got it. He wasn't concerned about why they'd adopted, but why I'd refused his offer of moving in. At the edge of my vision his penis lay quiet among a tangle of brown hairs, shrunken and wrinkled from his swim. Good morning, prune, don't stand up on my account.

He picked up a plain white towel, rubbed his face, then wrapped it round his middle. He sat on a moulded plastic chair and gave his attention to a cup of coffee and a cigarette. So the thrusting executive begins his day.

'You wanted to see me early,' he said, 'you must have something important.'

Sometimes he wanted to avenge Agnès. Sometimes he seemed to hate her. The psychology of the man was beyond me. Or perhaps it was just the psychology of any man in relation to a woman.

'The journalist Pelletier was killed last night.'

I was watching his face for a flicker of something, a hint he knew and was involved in the murder. All I saw was one eyebrow twitch up.

'So?'

'I think whoever killed him went to wait for me in my hotel. I think they followed my car out of the city. I think they came with the intention of killing me while I tried to escape.'

That was what Al Richards and I had decided while we huddled in my car for the rest of the night: that they'd heard his shout of 'Cody' on the telephone and trailed him out of the hotel. The assumption was that Lulu had found out something about the computer hacking and a link to the Gabizzi *clan* and they were taking no chances that he might have told me. It was a theory which fitted such facts as we knew.

'They didn't succeed,' he said. 'You're a survivor. Why are you telling me?'

'You know the Love Hotel?'

He nodded. My hunch was that he knew it very well.

'You'll find two men locked up in *cabaña* number eight. You might like to send someone to check them out. They're dressed in police uniform, if that means a damn. Any film studio can rent you a dozen cops' uniforms, more or less genuine. I don't think they're anything to do with the murder of Agnès. You've got enemies who don't like your trying to hire me. Maybe ... even in your own organization.'

I didn't believe that. I believed whoever murdered Lulu thought I was hand in glove with him, and that could be anyone.

Ledru was frowning but it wasn't my warning that concerned him. He stubbed out his cigarette.

'The Love Hotel, huh?'

'Yes.'

'You weren't alone?'

'No.'

He looked at me and I looked at him. He reached out a hand for another cigarette and thought better of it. The muscles along the line of his jaw clenched, then relaxed so he could speak. 'Of course not.' He gave me his grin, rugged and boyish, sharing our little secret, no hard feelings.

'You know that photo you showed me of your wife and the little girl,' I said. 'I need it.'

Ledru shouted for Max to bring the photo.

'Still no ransom note?' I asked.

'No.'

'No telephone call?'

'No.'

'Inspector Gaudet uncovered any more Sûreté plots?'

'No.'

'Do you happen to know Doicescu's first name?'

'No, no, no and no again. Ask me a question I can say yes to.' He gave me the roguish grin again. He ran a hand through the hairs on his chest, massaging a nipple. 'Hey,' he said, his face brightening, 'I do know his name after all. The woman he came with called him Dimitru. What's my reward for remembering?'

Max brought the photo. I studied it again, marvelling at my own slow-wittedness. Ledru was watching my face, waiting for my questions. I went about it carefully.

'Was she a natural blonde? Agnès, I mean.'

His face darkened. He was about to explode.

'What difference does it make?'

'Someone might have known her when she looked different.'

He took the cigarette now, lit it and blew out a lot of smoke. 'She got a little help from a bottle. Why the hell not? Some women have their boobs made bigger. Some have their faces tightened up. Some think blondes have more fun.'

Somehow I didn't think Agnès had had more fun.

'Ecaterina.' I gave the girl's name in full. 'Nice dress.' I'd noticed it before, yellow with white polka dots. 'I wouldn't have thought they dressed their kids so stylishly in Romania.'

'Hell no,' he said. 'We threw out what she came in straight off and bought her new stuff. She could have had lice in her old clothes, diseases, anything.'

Al Richards drove me to the airport to catch the after-lunch flight to Paris. He was staying to ask questions about Lulu's murder and try to uncover what Lulu had found out. I had my own agenda.

'I wish you'd tell me what you're planning.'

'Stop fussing.'

'People are getting hurt.'

'That's down here.'

'Co, people are getting hurt where you are. I don't want you to turn into another statistic.'

Al kissed me goodbye. It wasn't a Kama Sutra clinch, but it wasn't a peck on each cheek for Tante Marie either. The kiss was on the mouth, light, not pressing.

'You take care now,' he said. 'You take damn good care.' Because I'd told him I knew who'd killed Agnès and snatched the girl, and Paris was the place to start searching.

CHAPTER ELEVEN

I don't like Paris, I love Paris, and that's another thing. Paris, however, is not a constant lover.

Leave Paris for a couple of days and it's turned itself inside out, put on a different face, gone out in search of someone new. Paris reinvents itself each day as if it was preening in front of a mirror. Paris tries on a new colour, a new style, turns one cheek, then the other cheek. Paris hoists its skirts and shows you a third cheek. Paris basks in the sun, sulks in the rain. Paris never waits for you. Paris is deaf when you cry, throws its arms round you when you laugh. Paris adores having a good time with you, spending your money.

In high summer Parisians take their revenge and abandon the city to the poor and the tourists. Paris seems stunned by this betrayal as much as by the heat.

Also, Paris inspires overblown language.

Walking down rue St-André-des-Arts I felt the heat pressing in on my body. It was like the hot breath of a man all over me. I lifted my face to the afternoon sun, scanning upper windows and the jagged line of roofs.

'Have you returned, Mademoiselle Cody?'

'It appears so, Madame Boyer.'

She'd seen me through her spyhole and caught me before I reached the stairs. She can scuttle fast, like a crab, when she wants to. She's got a hide as hard as a crab's shell too. She held out my mail in one of her claws.

'Have I had any callers?' I asked.

'You mean men?'

I was looking at my mail. Some developer offered me the investment opportunity of a chalet in Isola 2000. Jacques Girault had scribbled a note apologising if his party had kept me awake last night. When Monsieur Roussy died, Jacques took the apartment under mine. He must have a rich *papa* to pay the rent.

'Madame Boyer, I asked if there were any callers. Women can call as well as men.'

'She's a woman, I suppose. That one.'

She meant Erica Fawcett. I looked at Jacques's note a little longer. He was desolated if the music had disturbed me and offered me a drink to compensate. He'd signed it simply 'J', a large swooping letter. He looks on me as the older woman. He hopes I'll share my experience with him. I can see it in his eyes and parted lips.

'But no men?'

I looked at her now, studied her face, her frown. Were her hands clenching, her throat swallowing? Was she lying? Was she hiding something?

'No,' she answered.

I needed to know if Yildirim had found out this address, bought his way in and was waiting for me. I decided she was telling the truth. I know when she's lying to me because she smiles. No men had been asking for me and I went upstairs. Peeping from the window by my desk I saw no one loitering in a doorway. I sat down to make my phone calls.

Soraya at the *American Journal*. Another piece of info. 'Oh no,' she wailed.

Erica Fawcett, who wanted to meet for a drink. 'I'm already going for a drink,' I said. 'Something in trousers?' 'Correct,' I said. 'Let's make it a sandwich,' she said. 'Have him in the middle, make the lying ratbag beg for mercy.'

At seven I rang Al who'd checked into the Imperator, like any journalist spending someone else's money.

He said, 'It's hot here, Co.'

I said, 'I'm hot too.'

We broke off while we each had our own thoughts. Was this the weather we were discussing?

He said, 'Your hunch was right. Those two comedians who broke into our room weren't the genuine article. Like honest French citizens they carried their ID with them. Didier Lasalle, born Besançon October 25th, 1962. Claims to be a salesman. He just has a variation on the foot in the door. Maurice Giofreddo, born June—'

'You went and took notes?'

'Like three-star chefs, we journalists never reveal our sources. Freddy's day job is supposed to be carpenter.'

'Are they being charged with impersonating police?'

'You want to go to the Love Hotel, dress up as cops, indulge in a little bondage, where's the harm? It's most likely enshrined in the constitution.'

'Who are they?'

'A little whisper that they are a rival outfit to Gabizzi's Marseille mob, of which my old pal André Ledru is an outpost. I think we're seeing the outbreak of a territorial war here. Whatever Ledru is into, the pickings are looking rich enough to attract competition.'

'Nothing to do with the murder and kidnapping?'

'I can't see it. With the murder of Lulu, yes. It looks like Ledru's being whacked twice. First in his private life. Next in his business life.'

'And going to be whacked a third time,' I said, 'by the Sûreté.'

Until that moment Crevecoeur had gone clean out of my mind. What was he doing?

'Co?'

'Yes, Al?'

He hesitated and then all he said was, 'Hurry back soonest.'

I'd been to two of the addresses Soraya had dug out for me, both off the place de la République. I'd spent time in each, asking questions of the bartender and the men having a drink at the counter. Now I was a the third place across the other side of the city in the 15th *arrondissement*.

No London brasserie manages a French atmosphere. No Paris pub could be mistaken for the genuine article, no matter how many Beefeaters and pictures of the Queen on a horse they put up. Was this bar like a watering hole in old Bucharest? It was called Dunare and it was sombre with wood panelling. There were framed photos of sports stars of yesteryear, Comaneci, Nastase, Popescu. A rugby team had posed in front of an empty stadium and signatures floated above their heads like wheeling crows. There were no portraits of politicians or pretenders to the throne. There were photos of snow-covered mountains, which never provoke arguments. But at some time there'd been a row here, a violent one, and the evidence was in the panelling: two holes. A frame had been put round them as if to make a picture. The holes were gouged and splintered in the way that bullets make. What had been a scene of violence had been turned into a work of art. It even had a title card: 25/12/1989.

I was staring at this, wondering at its significance: was it kitsch, a joke, serious, a tourist attraction, a warning, evidence, history, what? A voice at my shoulder said: 'That was the day Nicolae and Elena Ceausescu were tried and shot.'

It was the man behind the counter who spoke, the owner or barman. He was a little older than me, strongly built but running to flesh. Professional sportsmen who have stopped playing go that way. Maybe he was a footballer who had slipped the leash back in the bad old days.

'Those are bullet holes,' I said.

'That's right.'

'The Ceausescus weren't shot here.'

'A television set used to stand on the shelf. When the corpses were shown on the screen, one of the customers pulled out a pistol and emptied it. The set took the worst of it. Two shots ended up in the wall. You know, the insurance company wouldn't pay up for a new set. They said this bar was an extension of the revolutionary situation in Romania and was therefore not covered. Those insurance bastards can find an exclusion clause in a comma.'

Had the customer been shooting at the Ceausescus for revenge? Or shooting at the TV for daring to show the riddled bodies of the *Conducator* and his wife? There were ambiguities in the Dunare bar and it was necessary to tread warily.

I was here because of the information Soraya had given me. Tell me, I'd asked, the names of bars where Romanians go in Paris. What? she'd wailed. Such as – I'd said – places where there was uproar when the Romanian revolution reached its climax. Any newspaper worth its name would have sent a reporter to check émigré reaction, even if it had been on December 25th. The execution of the Ceausescus had been a Christmas present to the Romanian people.

'Are you taking something?'

'A glass of wine.'

'Red? Or white?'

He made it two distinct questions. There were eight or nine men in the room and all of them seemed to be waiting for my answer. This was a very political bar.

'Have you got anything to eat?' He pointed to a cardboard sign pinned to the wall: MITITEI. 'I'll have a glass of white. What is *mititei*?'

But he was already turning to pour the wine. One of the men standing at the bar slouched in my direction.

'She asks: "What is *mititei*?" The lady has the eyes and hair of our nation but not the soul. *Mititei* is what we eat to have a mouthful of the motherland. Some poets say the word is derived from mit, which means of course a myth. Others – rogues – say it has the same root as *mitocan,* which means cad. Yet others,' and he paused to refresh himself from his glass, 'cynics, men of the world, realists, they maintain it is derived from *mita,* which means a bribe.'

'It's bloody meatballs,' the man next down the counter growled. 'Cads, for God's sake, bribes. Waffling about the soul of the nation. He's drunk. Pay no attention to him.'

'The French have *foie gras,* the Ivans have caviar, the Americans have steaks as big as Texas, we have *mititei.* We used to have caviar too but now we have meatballs. That is the measure of our achievements.'

A plate was put in front of me. It had four sausage shapes with some sauce and a pickled cucumber. I ate because I'd had nothing for nine hours. What would Al have said? Was Lulu's spirit shuddering in some high corner of the room?

'Minced beef,' my neighbour told me, 'spices, a kiss of garlic.'

'Kiss of garlic,' the next man snorted. 'Don't listen to him. He's out of his mind. He's deranged.'

I was the only woman. It was a sombre place where men came to drink and argue about another country. Ceausescu was long dead but he'd left behind a land in ruins. Romania had violence in its past and violence to come, and the shadow of it lay across this room.

'What brings you here?'

The drunken man had moved off and it was his neighbour who spoke. It was a reasonable question, since the place was more like a private club than a Paris bar. I had taken a mouthful of food and delayed speaking for a moment.

I know who killed Agnès Ledru, I'd told Al Richards.

Co, who? Lawks amercy, woman – his black-mammy parody – *why you hiding de truth?*

Because, I'd said. Which infuriated him.

Because I was worried for the safety of the little girl.

Because I understood the trick that had been used and was afraid others were going to be hurt by it.

Because I was going to run the criminals down and I didn't want any media circus stampeding at my heels.

I swallowed. The decision was made.

'I am looking for Dimitru Doicescu,' I said. 'I was told he came in here.'

In the first two bars used by Romanian émigrés I'd asked for Doicescu and drawn a blank. Tomorrow, if it was third time unlucky, I'd think of another approach. But this stranger darted his eyes to each side, checking if anyone was close enough to eavesdrop. He lowered his voice.

'Who told you?'

I stared at him. I pointed a finger at his chest. 'What's your name?'

He hesitated. 'Ion.'

Half a name. Nobody I would ever be able to trace.

'Well, Ion, I don't know you from the Pope's nose. Why are you setting out to question me?'

He frowned. 'Asking for Dimitru like that.'

It was my turn to hesitate.

I didn't like the Dunare. The dark panelling gave it a wartime blackout feeling, and the customers intensified it. Exiles depress me. Escaping from a dictatorship, they bring their sense of persecution with them. They huddle together, conspire together, get drunk together. No one was openly listening to our talk; but they had antennae that picked up the alien vibrations I brought.

'I've never met Monsieur Doicescu,' I said. 'Obviously he's a friend of yours. Have you seen him recently? I mean, in the last couple of days?'

'Why do you want him?'

Sometimes the temptation to gamble is overwhelming. The roulette wheel is spinning and you stake your whole fortune on red to win. I sensed that this bar and this man were the way to reach my goal and so I took the plunge.

'I'm looking for a child to adopt. I heard Monsieur Doicescu is in that line. I heard he has orphans who need good homes in France.'

I stopped. Instinct told me I'd said enough to this man. I had Ion's unswerving attention. Eyes as dark as the wood panelling were riveted on my face. His voice dropped further, so low now it was barely above a whisper.

'Where did you hear this?'

I put some money on the counter. I didn't know how much the *mititei* were. Fifty francs should cover the exiled soul of Romania.

'If you see Doicescu, tell him what I said.'

'What's your name? Who shall I tell him is asking?'

'Cody.'

'Who told you about him? Where are you going?' I sidestepped his hand. 'How can he get in touch with you?'

'Tell him I'll come back here tomorrow night.'

I took a few steps from the Bar Dunare and stopped.

The evening was heavy, the air still and sultry, the light sinking deeper into dusk, even the sounds of the traffic seemed weighed down. I stood at the kerb and craned my neck in the hope of spotting a taxi. Taxis don't cruise in Paris like they do in London, but still I looked one way, looked the other, waiting and hoping. I had heard the bar door open and close after me. Steps approached but I didn't turn round.

'Madame ... Madame Cody ... '

He didn't raise his voice and it was more like the hiss of a loiterer in a doorway as a girl passes.

'It was difficult to talk in there.'

I turned now to face Ion.

'We talked,' I replied. 'I said what I wanted to say.'

I wasn't making it easy for him. He frowned. 'I mean *really* talk.'

It occurred to me that my visits to the first two émigré bars might not have been wasted after all. Once I'd left, a telephone call could have been made and Ion been told: Wait in the Dunare, if she's doing the rounds she might call there. Certainly he couldn't have been there all evening or he'd have been drunk like all the rest.

He could have been told: Find out who she is, find out why she wants Doicescu. Don't alarm her, simply find out what her game is, who she works for.

Because I knew that Doicescu had killed Agnès. I'd been so slow in fitting it together when the pathologist Dr Fignon and Ledru had given me the pointers. It was Dr Fignon's casually dropped remark about fibres under her fingernails that roused my curiosity. But by the next day analysis had shown they were low-grade Romanian polyester, such as Agnès would have picked up from hugging the child. My mind switched off at a conscious level, so that when I saw the photo of little Rina wearing a smart outfit I didn't make the deduction. It was only this morning that I got confirmation from Ledru: Rina's Romanian clothes had been thrown out. The girl was wearing a new French dress. The fibres under Agnès's fingernails had come from another source. Suppose she struggled with her attacker and clawed away a scarf masking his face. She got the fibres that way, recognized the man who'd brought little Rina and was now stealing her back. That was why Agnès had to be killed.

'Perhaps I can help you,' he said, peering over my shoulder and then back in my face. 'If I can be certain everything is ... you know.'

He raised a hand and teetered it between us. It takes a criminal mind to assume he's being cheated. I softened my stance a little.

'That's good of you.'

'But there are precautions, madame, necessary precautions one must take. Don't be offended. I must say you don't look like someone who would take offence at the first hint of…' He cleared his throat. 'Or should I say, you seem to understand that what life offers is to be accepted only if…' Again he couldn't quite commit himself. I didn't help him and after giving a little puff of breath he came out with: 'I need to know how you heard of him.'

'There was an advertisement in a newspaper down south.'

'You saw it?'

'A friend in Nîmes told me.'

'Yes?'

'She met Dimitru Doicescu and did – you know – the business.'

'Yes?'

For the second time in half an hour I plunged and put my fortune on red.

'She said he was returning to Paris but she had no address for him. So tonight I've been asking around for him. That's all.'

I finished with that curt wave the French use to dismiss a problem. Ion caught my wrist and with his other hand spread my fingers.

'But you are not married. No ring.'

'A stable relationship.'

'Where is he tonight? Something so vital to your lives, he should accompany you.'

'He works shifts at Charles de Gaulle airport.'

'Does he?' Ion still had hold of my wrist. He said, 'Come with me. I'll take you to Dimitru.'

He began to pull me and I resisted. 'Just give me his address.'

'It's better if I take you. He'll trust me not to bring someone…' Again that teetering with his hand. 'You know… someone undesirable. What you want from Dimitru is not one hundred per cent legal.'

'Where does he live?'

'Out towards Vincennes. You know that area?'

'The woods.'

'You can see trees from his windows. Yes, certainly. Tall trees.'

In that instant I stopped believing him. Ion was nodding, to reassure me, to convince himself. But he wasn't driving me to Doicescu's apartment. A man like Ion doesn't remember the view from someone else's window.

The last of the daylight was dying in the west as we took the slip-road on to the Périphérique and headed east. I had no means of knowing how long we would keep on this route, but if his luck held there would be no stopping, no chance for me to slip out of the car. On Saturday nights there can be traffic jams as the *banlieusards* try to get somewhere, car windows open, music playing, people laughing. It can be a party in itself, except you don't get to mingle. But Paris was emptying for the summer and the traffic had thinned.

What was in Ion's mind? We always want to know what an enemy is planning so we can prepare a counter. A passing car illuminated his face and he was frowning, working out his move. He had to brake suddenly as some idiot cut across in front, and I thought we would stop and I could jump clear. Looking out of the side window I saw the car that had darted in front take a slip-road exit. The driver flashed his lights at a woman standing there and she began to move. The police have tried to stop it but they always come back. They do their business in campervans parked fifty metres off the Périphérique.

'Stop the car,' I shouted. 'It's urgent I get out.'

A jab in the side made me swing round. Ion was accelerating now the road was clear. He steered with his left hand and gripped a pistol in his right. He sneaked a look at me to see I'd taken in the gun. How could I miss it? It was pressed so hard into my ribs, just below my left breast, that if he didn't shoot me he could stab me to death. I couldn't move away. I couldn't hit the gun aside.

He said, 'Open your door.'

I didn't stir. I hardly dared breathe.

He repeated in a flat tone, 'Open your door.'

This time each word was emphasized with a deeper dig in the ribs.

'Why?'

I knew why. I was being invited to stage my own suicide. Each step would be a small one, until the last. Somewhere along the progress to my death I had to find the chink through which I could escape and live.

'Because the gun is loaded and I order you to.'

I had the nailfile. Against the gun, forget it.

'You said you were taking me to see your friend Doicescu.'

'And you were lying. Your friend in Nîmes told you nothing because she's dead.'

'Before she was killed.'

'And she didn't tell you Dimitru was returning to Paris. You are a police spy. Open the door or I'll shoot you.'

'I'm going to have to move. Careful with that thing.'

The pressure on my ribs eased and I turned away. I wound down the window. I felt a series of furious jabs.

'I don't want bloody fresh air. Open the door.'

I said, 'It's you who was lying. I don't think Doicescu is even in Paris.'

'He's moved on. Toulouse, Carcasonne, somewhere round there. All this fuss in the press means he has to lie low for a bit. The door.' Series of renewed prods. 'I'm counting to three.'

'Doicescu's pulled this trick before? Why wasn't there any newspaper coverage?'

'Because people were breaking the law. You can't simply buy a child like it was a puppy. They couldn't go crying to the cops when he took it back. One.'

A car was overtaking on the inside. I looked out at it and the driver glanced at me. 'Au *secours*,' I mouthed. He blew me a kiss, lifted a hand to smooth the hair at the back of his head and swept ahead.

'Two.'

I looked at Ion again. The glow from the lights had turned his face the colour of uncooked pork. Beyond him, through the window, I could see other cars. But not enough at this time of night to cause a nice friendly jam.

'I'm moving again. Don't shoot.'

I gripped the door catch, pulled it towards me and put gentle pressure on the panel of the door with my knee to ease it open. Tyre noise increased a few decibels. The car wasn't going much above sixty or sixty-five kilometres, but wind pressure kept the door from flying open. I had completed the first small step to my suicide.

He said, 'Undo your seatbelt.'

That was the next small step.

'It's against the law. Do you want the police to—'

'Undo it.' A reminder in the ribs.

Snap of metal against metal as the bayonet came free of its housing.

Tail lights popped on in front and Ion had to brake. Impetus made the door swing wide, acceleration slammed it shut.

'Slide to the edge of the seat by the door. Open the door again.'

It had come, each small step leading to this point. Ion was going to invite me to jump under the wheels of the cars surging past. Or he would lean across and give me a shove. I doubted that, because he'd either have to put the pistol down or risk my making a grab for it when he was fully extended and trying to keep his eyes on the road. Or he'd give a violent twist to the steering wheel and hope centrifugal force would throw me out. Or, if none of these courses worked, in half a minute he'd pump two or three bullets into me, shove my body out into the traffic and hope to get clear in the mayhem that followed.

'Push the door wide open.'

The last seconds of my life were ticking away and I did the only thing I could.

'What does that man want?' I shouted.

I jerked my chin at Ion's window and in the moment he was distracted I half-stood and pushed the door open enough to get my head out and up. I got a foot on the sill of the window I'd opened and pushed up, feeling the door swing wide and the road gaping underneath, and the wind-rush pressing it back. Push up again, more, until I got my chest on to the roof, feeling the airstream start to slide me backwards. The radio aerial was centrally positioned and I made a grab and missed it, and grabbed again because it was my last chance and hooked a hand round it. I felt the rod bite into my flesh and ignored the pain. I hauled myself fully out of the car and swivelled my legs up behind me on to the roof.

There was a shout from Ion, a roar, anger and frustration together.

I lay flattened, one hand gripping the aerial, the other bearing down on the roof, fingers splayed to brace me against the car's movement. My head was tucked in to keep the wind out of my eyes. Lights streamed past, headlights, road lights, the lights of buildings. Faces in cars were pressed towards me, mouths open. A small boy waved. *Bonsoir, jeune homme.* Just taking the evening air. Get more of a lungful up here.

Ion's hand appeared above the line of the roof. He tilted the pistol in my direction and pulled the trigger. The explosion was part of the cacophony of engines, horns, tyre thrum, wind, radios. Where did the bullet end up? Through someone's bedroom window? He'd angled too high. Realizing the error, he tried to lay the pistol flat on the roof. He would hit some part of me, sure to. I hauled myself forward so it wouldn't be my chest that took the bullet, but my upper leg.

My shoulders were beyond the aerial now. I bent over, peering through the windscreen. His face lit with surprise, with a measure of panic. He was so startled he snatched the pistol inside and aimed it at my nose. Jesus, he couldn't be so crazy as to shoot out his own windscreen. Why not? His madness only matched mine. I jerked back out of sight.

Horn blaring, insistent, wouldn't stop. On my right a car kept pace with us. The driver was yelling something. He pointed up to his roof. Jump across? Did he think this was some circus stunt?

Over the Seine, dipping under a corner of the Bois de Vincennes in a series of tunnels, swinging up north. Flashing light of a police car going in the opposite direction.

Perhaps I could panic Ion into slowing down, give me a chance to jump.

I banged on the roof. Tin drum and he was inside. Thump, thump. Louder. Thump, thump, thump.

Muffled explosion.

A starburst had appeared in the metal close to my hand. I snatched my hand away.

A second starburst appeared close to my shoulder, I shifted as far as I could, to the edge of the roof furthest from Ion. A leg slipped loose and I scrabbled my way back.

Horns, screams, shrilling tyres.

Peeping back over my shoulder I saw the headlights of following cars. Get away, get back. I risked a hand to try to shoo them off. Worst case: Ion would wound me and I would slide back down over the tailgate and have to take my chance among those idiot drivers. They were no better than the charioteers in the Colosseum.

No more shots. Perhaps he could reach no further to his right.

Abruptly the car swerved across two lanes and I was flung to the other side. I grabbed at the aerial with my free hand as we swerved back. Bastard was determined to shake me loose and send me under the wheels of the cars behind.

There was the whoop of a police car now. It was behind us but closing.

Was Ion going to be caught on the Périphérique or would he take one of the exits?

I'll never know what was in his mind but he must have caught the police siren too. Was he aiming for an exit or still attempting to dislodge me?

He stamped on the brake pedal and hauled the wheel over. There was a shriek of rubber as the back end of the car broke away and swung to one side, hitting something, and my world tilted as I was flung back. The violent jerking snapped the aerial and I grabbed at the doorframe by the open window. Lights swinging, sound of screaming tyres, metal rending, glass shattering, juddering as we passed over something. Slowing, slowing, but not enough. Series of bumps, a final crash that wrenched me loose and I was flying. The world span, lights became tracer bullets and there was the wild music of percussion and brass and violins.

Flashed through my brain: This is the end.

Lights out.

Nothingness.

CHAPTER TWELVE

In the beginning was the worm. Wriggling. Up to the surface. In my brain.

Light, life, awareness.

Sounds of distant heel-taps and female voices, pungent smells, black tobacco and disinfectant, feelings of... feelings of...

Nothingness beckoned.

Another wave beached me into full awareness.

The feelings in my body. I could compose a dictionary of pain in its rich variety. Sharp stabs, aches, grazes, wrenches, stiffness, throbs, agonizing lightning, thirst, tremor, pricks, constrictions, nausea, hot sweats, bone-deep exhaustion.

'You're awake.'

'*Dukka,*' I whispered. Suffering.

I wanted the nothingness again. Nirvana. Bliss.

'You're a very lucky woman.'

'*Tham dii, dai dii,*' I told him. Do good and receive good.

'Is she hallucinating?'

'*Tham chua, dai chua,*' I explained. Do evil and receive evil. I opened my eyes and saw Crevecoeur. Next to him stood a woman doctor in a white coat, her hair pulled back into an austere bun. I knew she was a doctor and not a nurse. A nurse carries a thermometer, a doctor carries a stethoscope. Well done, brain. Head of the class. Head of the body.

'After-effects,' the doctor said. 'Short-lived.'

'Gibberish,' Crevecoeur reassured himself.

'Existence is suffering,' I explained to him. No dawn of understanding lit his face. Typical arrogance of his kind.

He frowned at me. 'Your existence was nearly terminated.'

'Great suffering.' I tried to remember more. 'Suffering is caused by desire. Eliminate desire and extinguish suffering.'

A Buddhist had tried to enlighten me. Wiry Thai. I learnt fast, especially that he was unsuccessful at eliminating desire. We shall eliminate desire by bodily contact, he murmured, and thus extinguish my suffering. Wily Thai.

Crevecoeur lit a cigarette.

'It is forbidden,' the doctor said.

'He has not eliminated the desire,' I told her. 'Extinguish the cigarette, extinguish suffering.'

I tried to shake my head, to unscramble my brains. I needed to be clear in my thinking. What had the doctor given me? Morphine plus what?

'How are you feeling?' the doctor asked.

'Alive,' I said. Existence is suffering.

Told them that already. Come *on*, Cody, get a grip.

'You are very fortunate to be alive,' Crevecoeur said.

'What's happened? Why am I here?' My awareness had expanded. From my pain to Crevecoeur and the doctor and now to my environment: hospital room.

'You don't remember?'

Brain protecting me from the agony of recall.

'On the Périphérique?' he said. 'On the roof of a car? The crash?'

Tracer-bullet lights, kaleidoscope world, Shostakovich music. Memories fell on me like assassins, hacking away at my armour of amnesia. I felt terror. I hadn't had time to be terrified while it was happening.

'He must have had an automatic car,' I blurted. This hadn't occurred to me at the time, too damn busy surviving, but some part of my brain must have worried away at the problem. 'He couldn't change gear, you see, because he held the pistol in one hand.'

Crevecoeur was watching intelligence return to my face. His eyes swivelled up to the doctor. 'You can leave us now. We have to talk.'

'No more than ten minutes with the patient.'

'Fifteen,' Crevecoeur said.

'And put out your cigarette.'

'I'd only light another when you've gone.'

'He's given up smoking,' I explained to the doctor. 'He enjoys giving up smoking so much he does it twenty or thirty times a day.'

'First she rambles,' Crevecoeur said, 'now she nags. Next she'll be asking for her lawyer to see who she can sue. Better keep out of her sight. I won't be more than twenty minutes.'

'Fifteen,' the doctor said.

Nobody consulted the patient's wishes.

It seemed it was the next morning, somewhere around ten. I'd lost nearly twelve hours from my life. Never mind that I would have been sleeping anyway, I still felt robbed.

'Where am I?'

'The Sisters of Little Mercy Hospital.'

'I don't think you have the name quite right.'

Crevecoeur waved away my objection. 'Why were you on the roof of the car?'

'Ion wanted to kill me, preferably making it look an accident.'

'A highly visible accident observed by about three thousand people on the Périphérique.'

'That wasn't how he planned it.'

'Why did he want to kill you?'

'Because I was asking about Dimitru Doicescu. You know about Doicescu?'

Crevecoeur was nodding. 'Yes. Tell me, why—'

'My turn. What happened to Ion?'

'He's resting,' Crevecoeur said, 'in the mortuary. A damn great Mercedes smashed into him. You came off the roof at the right time.'

Ion wouldn't be able to warn Doicescu about me. I registered that fact.

'What happened to me?'

'I wasn't one of the spectators, you understand. There are a dozen different versions. They mostly agree you lost your hold on the roof either just before or just after the final smash. You flew through the air a bit. When you hit the road you either did a somersault or a cartwheel or a dive or were like a sprinter lunging for the tape.'

'Most likely I was trying to run.' Training had taken over. The theory is that if you hit the ground while going through the motions of running, your leg action absorbs some of the forward momentum. Well, that's one theory. Then I must have taken a forward roll, forearms protecting the face, which would account for the abrasions and bruising from elbows to knuckles. There was an echo in my head now of shrilling tyres, of horns blaring and cutting short, the hammer blows of metal on metal. It was a miracle I'd got nothing worse than a knock on the back of my head. 'I've been under sedation since I was brought in?'

'I'm told you surfaced more than once and they put you under again. There were a lot of tests to do. One of the Merciful Sisters said it was through God's grace you'd survived.'

'It was CIA training,' I said.

'There are certain Americans who would ask what the difference was.'

Crevecoeur was so pleased with that he lit another Gitane.

I'd been moving my limbs one by one, testing for pulled muscles or ripped tendons. No bones broken. No internal bleeding or I'd have known all about it. Chest sore when I took a deep breath, but if a lung had been punctured I'd have screamed. I pulled back the sheet to look at my left leg, which felt on fire, and was somewhat surprised to find I was totally naked. I caught Crevecoeur inspecting my thigh. It wasn't the first visit he'd ever made to me in hospital. There'd been that time in Tunisia when I'd come stumbling out of the Sahara. To have me weakened and naked in bed gave him a certain shiver of pleasure. I believed that then and I believe it still.

He drew deeply on his cigarette. 'You're lucky it wasn't fatal.'

'You keep harping on luck. I don't see it as luck. That's what training is all—'

'I'm talking about going to that bar. The Dunare.'

'It seemed like a good idea at the time. They should be pleased to help nail a murderer.'

'It's the one place you can count on finding a murderer. Ex-Securitate.'

'Don't the rest of them care? Why do they go there?'

'Reminds them of home.'

'You know about Ion whatever-his-name was?'

'Ion Munteanu. Second Commercial Attaché. One-time Securitate. Well, they mostly were at the embassy. Lot of them still are under the skin.'

'What about Doicescu?' I asked. 'He's the one who supplied the orphan and the man who snatched her. He's also the man who murdered Agnès Ledru.'

Crevecoeur didn't leap to his feet crying: Eureka! Crevecoeur wasn't interested in routine police matters. To the Sûreté mind, Doicescu was just a heading on another file.

'Dimitru Doicescu, driver. Securitate thug. He left the embassy at the time of the revolution. Didn't fancy being sent home. Strictly speaking he's an illegal immigrant.'

'How about the little girl? Isn't she a Romanian orphan?'

'Romanian, I would say yes. Orphan, I really don't know. Could be his daughter. Or that woman's, the one who was with him, name of Maria Leonida. She was never on the official embassy list at all. God knows what she was. *Bedbug* most likely.'

We were speaking French. But he didn't say *punaise,* he used the English word.

Crevecoeur gave a narrow grin. 'On slow days when I was in Washington we used to invent our own American jargon. A *bedbug* is a woman who picks up pillow talk.'

Crevecoeur's eyes slid from mine to the pillow beside my face. Then dropped to the humps of my breasts, then down over the curve of my hip, down and down to my feet. I'd covered my nakedness with the sheet again, but I had the sensation he was calculating the space available beside me for another body.

'How did you know to come to Paris?' I asked.

'Tapped your phone. Heard the bars you were going to. Knew you were getting into deep shit.'

I was stunned by how much he knew, about me, about the people I'd met, about the people I was hunting. And it was repeated in such a flat speak-your-weight voice. Knowing so much, Crevecoeur and all the other Crevecoeurs in the world have the delusion they are God.

'Since you were spying on me, you might at least have warned me.'

'You're a big girl now, Cody.'

It was the old married couple act again. *Did you have a good day at the office, dear?* I wouldn't say good. *Boss playing up again?* He tried to murder me, if you call that playing.

'Talking of bugs,' Crevecoeur said and stopped. I thought he was fantasizing about my charms again, but he was speculating on how roadworthy my body was. 'That fool doctor says you need rest, you should be here for a week. Can you walk?'

I flexed the muscles in my legs. I didn't scream.

'I don't know until I try.'

'Well, try now.'

'I've got no clothes on.'

'I won't look.'

He didn't turn aside.

'It's just I've got to observe if you are able to walk.'

So that's how it was, me out of bed, the sheet around my body like a sarong, hobbling a few steps as the doctor came into the room.

'Your fifteen minutes are—' She stopped. 'What are you doing out of bed?'

'Seeing how well I can walk.'

'Get back this instant. Is this your doing, Monsieur Crevecoeur?'

'Chief Inspector Crevecoeur.'

'There are no ranks in here. We are one in the sight of God. The sick and the healers together. I must ask you to go.'

'Just another five minutes.'

'At once.'

'Or what? You'll say a prayer to make me?'

They were poker players outbidding each other in anger. White-faced, the doctor pointed at the door.

'Out.'

Crevecoeur got to his feet. He's not a big man but he seemed to puff up and up as he spoke, taking measured steps, bearing down on her. He kept his voice in check, the fury reined in, and it was the more terrible for that.

'You're a doctor and I've seen you order the nurses about – Nurse, do this; Nurse, fetch that – so don't tell me fairy-tales about no ranks in here. You just listen to what I have to say. I am a Chief Inspector in the Sûreté Nationale and I am not concerned with banal crimes like theft or murder, solely with matters affecting the security of France. There are people who do not appreciate what I do, and they are not all spies. Some of them pride themselves on being very upright citizens. Some are even very like you, pious and certain of their correctness. But all of them have this in common: they want to change the way we live and can be pretty damn careless how they set about it.'

The doctor had held her ground but as Crevecoeur went on relentlessly, she retreated step by step.

'The radical priests – I expect you're cosy with a few – and the green/red eco-communists, the muscular ex-paras of the National Front, the militant students who want the *Mouvement du 22 mars* of 1968 to be born again, Maoists with photos of an exhumed Chairman, Guevarists with placards shouting: Che Lives! Trots in six different flavours, all the *groupuscules* of the fissionary left, Castroites, Algerian Islamists, *Action Directe* bombers, Palestinian bombers, Mossad bombers, Ban the Bombers, punks in boots, Hell's Angels in boots and chains volunteering to break heads, anti-vivisectionists, Sandinistas, Colombian drug barons, racists, anti-racists, anarchists waving black flags. Even God cannot imagine what's to come – violent vegetarians, save the mosquitoes, the anti-Semites for a greater Israel, fundamentalists and rejectionists and haters and plotters and smugglers and crazies from all over the globe, the Gay Unicyclists Union, the Catholic Priests for Abortion, and now do you know who else? The Little Sisters of Mercy.'

He stopped.

The doctor had taken shelter in the open door, overwhelmed by this baroque tirade. Crevecoeur laid a courteous hand on her shoulder and propelled her out.

'Five more minutes.'

He shut the door.

Crevecoeur turned to me and I felt I'd caught hold of the tail end of a hurricane.

'A militant of some persuasion or other said to me, "You don't see cobbles in Paris any more because they've been tarred over. But one dark night we're going to steal some pickaxes and dig up the cobbles and then you lot had better start running."'

Crevecoeur took a deep breath and puffed it all out.

'*Alors,*' he said.

'Where's your bunch of flowers?'

'What bunch of flowers?' Crevecoeur gave me a sideways look full of suspicion.

'You visit someone in hospital, you take a bunch of carnations. Or irises. Not chrysanthemums, unless you think they won't get out on their own two feet. But you've come without flowers. So you're not just visiting.'

'Would you welcome a social call from me?'

When the silence threatened to become painfully long, I said, 'Only four and a half minutes left.'

'I'm here because of work, duty, the security of et cetera, et cetera.' Crevecoeur gave a vague wave of his hand but there was nothing vague in the way he was sizing me up. 'You are mobile, I think.'

'Hurts, but I can walk.'

'You'll make a swift recovery if you have to, because the work is not for me but for you.'

'You're not my boss. You don't employ me. The answer is no, whatever your suggestion is.'

'You must understand you are under an obligation—'

'No. N-O. Doesn't the word mean anything to you? You blackmailed me once, threatened to give my address to a Turkish killer who was out for revenge. So I broke into the farmhouse, planted the bug for you. I've paid your asking price, Crevecoeur. I'm not paying a second time.'

My watch had been taken from me along with my clothes. There was a wall-clock and I was watching the second hand go round. The doctor would be back in less than four minutes. She might come with a couple of burly kitchen porters this time. But Crevecoeur wasn't pleading. After half a minute's silence I had to look at him.

'The obligation,' he said, 'is to your friend.'

'What?' I was so indignant I sat up in bed, the sheet falling away. I pulled it up while Crevecoeur's lips twitched. It was a cynic's shadow of a smile. Did he seriously believe I was trying to seduce him with a flash of bare skin?

'He is listed as having known Ledru in the Far East. However, the indiscretions of our youth shouldn't be held against us. Let us discount all that. But now he is down in the Midi making all sorts of enquiries. If I've heard about this, how long will it be before the Gabizzi *clan* gets wind? It seems Richards is following the same trail as that other reporter was. You know, Lucien Pelletier who was tortured and shot in his hotel room.'

'Listen, I am not obligated to Richards. If it hadn't been for Richards I wouldn't be here right now. You warn him.'

'Cody, think a minute before you speak. It's not a question of warning him. First, he's a journalist and he's doing his job. He's got his nose after murder, corruption and industrial espionage.'

Industrial espionage? There it was again, the hint of where Crevecoeur's interest lay. Before he'd said 'hacking into certain computer networks', and would go no further. Now it had grown to industrial espionage.

'Second – or maybe it should be first – he is American and freedom of the press is guaranteed in the Constitution, along with the right to carry guns and drink Coca-Cola with hamburgers. And third, there is the nature of the man himself. Do you imagine a warning from me would do anything more than encourage him to go further?'

'At least we agree on that. Richards is a tough cookie.'

'He is one and they are many. He is strong but they are violent. He might just listen to you.'

Was I being uncaring about Al Richards? I think I was just angry at the whole world. Crevecoeur leant back in his chair a moment, reassessing, seeing what other pressure he could bring to bear. But it was only a moment.

'Yildirim,' he announced.

I waited.

'We have him in police custody.'

'Crevecoeur, pay attention. If you so much as hint you'll turn him loose and give him my address—'

He held up his hand. 'This is the deal. He will be put on a plane to Istanbul. I shall inform my contact in the Turkish Interior Ministry that Yildirim is being returned. He will be picked up at Yesilkoy airport and I doubt that anyone will ever see him again. You see, he killed two Turkish police when he escaped. He will never be a threat to you in the future. That is my side of the bargain.'

There was noise from the corridor. The five minutes had elapsed and the doctor was returning with fresh troops.

'Your side,' Crevecoeur said. 'Here is the problem. There is activity at Ledru's *mas* but we don't know what is happening. You see, the bug you planted has stopped transmitting.' He spread his hands wide. 'These things happen. Ah, the wonders of modern technology.' Voices were just outside now. Crevecoeur hurried on. 'What we need is for you to conceal a new bug that works. That's all there is to it. Then I'll know what's being planned, arrangements can be made, the dangers to both you and your friend will be removed.'

He snapped his fingers. Just like that. So simple.

The door opened. The doctor came in. Behind her there seemed to be a bunch of snowmen, five or six Little Sisters dressed in white habits. Heaven's Angels, I thought. The holy mob.

'It's all right, doctor,' Crevecoeur said. 'Just leaving.' He looked at me. 'Aren't we?'

CHAPTER THIRTEEN

This is how I see Crevecoeur: the president of some pocket republic. He has his palace, a château north of Paris where guests can be invited to make a voluntary statement. He has his praetorian guard with their gun-slit eyes, a disdain for more conventional forms of authority, a face pinched by cares of state, an air of limitless resources to be called up at the snap of his fingers. I don't know where he fits in the hierarchy of the Sûreté, but he must have a boss. Yet he acts like a free agent beyond anyone's control, answerable only to himself, or possibly to God, if they are on speaking terms that week. I don't know whether he has a link to President Chirac, but I know that he used to undertake tasks on the direct orders of Mitterand. How do I know? Only because Crevecoeur told me.

So it was that Crevecoeur ordered out a French Air Force troop transport for the journey south, much as the company chairman might wave his cigar and the Rolls would glide to the front door.

I'd been twenty-four hours in Paris. It felt the longest and toughest year of my life. Most of the damage to my body didn't show. The jolting and jarring were like the background music in a film, something I couldn't switch off, an irritation, finally ignored. I'd been tortured by experts, I decided, who didn't leave a mark visible. Only my knuckles showed red, as if I'd rubbed them over a cheese grater. Crevecoeur had taken me to rue St-André-des-Arts and waited in his car in the pedestrianized street while I limped up to my apartment. I had new clothes now, an Indonesian shirt, sky blue with a white *garuda* design. It had long sleeves that hid the abrasions on my arms. Plain dark slacks covered the bruises on my legs.

There were questions I wanted to put to Crevecoeur but he spent the entire flight in consultation with two men. These were not like his agents in the field who stared with a self-confident openness. These were ministry officials or lawyers or policy makers with the Sûreté. They were going to the hot south but still wore dark suits. They were accompanied by briefcases. I could imagine them, after their own weddings, going to the honeymoon suite and carrying their briefcases over the threshold.

At Nîmes these two got out first and I had a few minutes alone with Crevecoeur.

'You can tell the person in the field too much,' I said. 'You can also underbrief him. Or, in this case, her. I need some indication of the "industrial espionage" you talked of.'

'Did I?'

'You know damn well you did.'

Crevecoeur was stooping to peer through a window. He straightened up and inspected me.

'The doctor had a point. You do need some rest in a quiet room. I think you're going to have to be satisfied with what I told you: industrial espionage. The essence of all spying is that it is secret. The same is true of the counter-measures. Ah, here we are.'

A Citroën, grey and anonymous, had pulled up by the exit steps. For me there was a taxi.

'This evening, then,' Crevecoeur said before trotting down the steps to the car. I had a glimpse of his face turned in my direction as he was driven away. A hand was raised in a wave as lazy as royalty's.

Once Crevecoeur was out of sight, I was allowed down the aircraft steps. I sat in the back of the taxi and was driven into the city. The arrangement was to drop me at the railway station where no one pays particular attention to anyone arriving by taxi.

'How much?' I asked.

The driver waved aside the question of payment. 'You tell me how much,' I said, 'for the benefit of anyone watching.' Because the one way of drawing attention to yourself leaving a taxi is not to pay.

'Two hundred then,' the driver said. 'Here,' I said. After he'd taken the money I added another fifty.

'What's this?'

'Your tip.'

As he drove away, he spat out of the window. Perfect.

To go into the church I bought a red and blue scarf. It covered my head in piety. It covered half my face in disguise. I imagined enemies everywhere – Ledru's toughs, Gaudet's corrupt cops, Doicescu's Securitate pals, Crevecoeur's undercover men. How about that stooped old woman in black lighting a candle? Say a prayer for my deliverance.

The church was small and old, and the weight of centuries of prayer and incense and priests' droning weighed down on me. It was hot and airless and I could feel the scarf sticking against my cheeks. Some functionary must have oiled the door at the back because the hinges didn't protest. But I knew someone had come in because the traffic noise grew louder and was muffled again. I didn't turn. I waited and finally he sat down in the chair next to me. He let out a breath.

'It's still hot here.'

'Paris was hot too,' I said. Different kind of heat.

'I like that design.' Al Richards was looking at my shirt. 'Blue looks great on you.'

The old woman who'd lit the candle was something to do with the upkeep of the church. Or she was ultra-pious. She'd found a broom and dustpan and was sweeping the stone floor under the pulpit. Al and I watched for a few moments. She stooped with arthritic slowness to the pan, manoeuvring imaginary dirt into it.

'I've placed the ad,' Al said. 'Papers from Marseille as far west as Toulouse.'

While I was changing clothes in Paris I'd telephoned the Imperator Hotel and been lucky enough to catch Al in his room. 'Just writing up my notes,' he'd said. 'Tell me later,' I'd cut in, because though Crevecoeur was waiting downstairs in the car he would sooner or later get a transcript of this call or hear a tape. We arranged a meeting place and I told him of the advertisement I wanted placed, now that I knew Doicescu had gone to ground somewhere in the Midi.

'How did you word it?'

'Desperately seeking to adopt a little girl,' Al recited. 'We'll give a loving home to a refugee from the former Communist dictatorships. Please help us. Apply to box number whatever.'

'Desperately. Nice touch.'

'What happens if there is no response?'

'Is it prominent?'

'Front page, bottom right-hand corner in *Midi Libre* and *Dépêche du Midi*. Best position I could negotiate in the rest. Costing a fortune.'

'Doicescu will see it. He'll be poring over the papers to follow the police reports. It'll hit him smack in the eye. They're lying low, but when Doicescu sees bait like that, he'll bite.'

'How can you be sure?'

I wasn't. I was whistling in the dark and the tune sounded thin to my ears, but did Al have a better idea?

'He's vicious and stupid, but above all he needs money. He's an illegal immigrant, wanted by the police for murder, and he's on the run. He can't get a job because he daren't show his papers. He sees his francs trickling away. Greed will win out.'

'You sound,' said Al, 'as if you're trying to convince yourself.'

I shook my head, though Al had got close to the truth. 'Doicescu will see the ad, brood on it, count his francs again, and finally persuade himself it will be like taking candy from a baby.'

'Some baby,' he said.

He lurched towards me, possibly with the idea of planting a comradely kiss on my cheek. The old woman dropped the broom with a clatter. When we looked over she was scowling, at us or the offending broom or at her arthritis as she bent double.

'My opinion is that you are seriously crazy. On top of the car like a conquering general riding into the city.' The concern on Al's face had grown and grown as I recounted my twenty-four hours in Paris, until he looked appalled. On the telephone I'd told him the brute fact that Doicescu was the murderer and kidnapper and that I'd had an encounter with a friend or former colleague of his. *Rather hairy* was how I'd described it. A scrap of old-fashioned slang. Understated. Terribly British.

The door opened and we both turned to see who came in. It was a young man dressed in jeans and trainers and a T-shirt. He was the right age to be a scout for Ledru or Gaudet or Crevecoeur. How had I acquired so many enemies in such a short time? He didn't look at us. Not a flicker. Man and woman deep in animated conversation in a church must be worth a glance, but he betrayed not a scrap of curiosity. He walked down the nave to light a candle and stuck it in the sand-tray in front of a painting of the BVM. He knelt on a cushion to pray. The old woman hissed, then stacked her broom and pan at the side of a stand with missionary tracts and shuffled away. It was no good my telling myself she was just a widow doing some spiritual housecleaning and that the young man was asking help to sort out a mess in his love life. It was a textbook example of one watcher leaving as another fell into place.

I could feel the tautness in Al. It was like a sexual tension waiting for a thunderclap to break its hold.

'We're paranoid,' I said softly. He looked in my face and said nothing. Possibly he was remembering Crevecoeur's warning, which I'd repeated: that his life was at great risk. He didn't think he was being paranoid at all. He took my hand, for comfort or solidarity, and for the first time saw the grazes.

'Co!' It was a stage whisper that must have broken into the young man's prayers. Al pushed up the sleeve to see how far the damage went, then he began eyeing the front of my shirt with its line of buttons running down between my breasts.

'When you were a teenager in the boondocks,' I murmured, 'wasn't this known as getting fresh?'

He closed his eyes for a moment and let out a 'huh' of breath. His lips twitched. Some of his tension eased and we sat and watched. The young man finished his supplication, walked down past us, and left.

'Normally,' Al said when we were alone, 'I'm as cool as the next guy. It's just that every day someone gets cut up or killed and we haven't had today's ration yet.'

We got up together as if the thought had come to both of us at the same moment. We needed to stretch our muscles, needed movement, to get the kinks out of our nerves. He was watching each step I took.

'It was his paleness I didn't like,' Al said, nodding his head back towards the door. 'Got unhealthy habits. Begs favours from virgins. Believes her story about finding the baby in the hay.' A bit of the El Al grin came and went. 'How badly were you hurt?'

'It's okay,' I said. 'The bits are all still there.'

He touched the headscarf. 'What are you covering up?'

'Scarface Cody scares off the fellers. I'm okay, I tell you. Shake, rattle and roll, that's all. Nothing permanent.'

We walked to the painting of the Madonna and child. She looked spotlessly clean and well-fed and not in the least puzzled about where the baby had come from. Al lit a candle and dropped ten francs in the box, 'Insurance for Cody – are you listening up there?' We inspected a plaque on the wall commemorating Marcel Merilhou, patriot, shot in this place by the Germans in 1944.

'In the church? Can't have been,' Al muttered. 'A church is a place of refuge.'

He seemed to have forgotten his jitters of five minutes before.

At length we settled side by side again and Al talked. As always when Crevecoeur has stepped into the frame, there was the ritual of denouncing him.

'That creep thinks God put the safety of France in his hands. Or he believes he's God himself. Knows everything.'

'I didn't think you were so well acquainted.'

'I know him. Oh yes. What's he doing telling you I've got to take care? Since when have you run errands for Crevecoeur?'

I shot him a foul look and he veered away from the subject.

'I'm not Lulu. I'm not going down the same road he took. That poor guy. Such an appetite for life. When we get back to Paris we'll have a meal in his honour. A celebration of the man. He wouldn't want us in mourning. Have you been to Jamin yet? Their *Lièvre à la royale* ...' He kissed the tips of his fingers. 'No. July isn't the season for hare. I'll think of something special. You had dinner with him here? What did you eat? I want the whole menu from soup to nuts.'

'Pizza.'

'Pizza? Lulu? Nothing else?'

'It had tinned pineapple on top, which Lulu said was the beginning of the end of French civilization. I ate his.'

Al shook his head over these confessions. I shook my head too. Five minutes before he'd sat tense because he felt his life was under threat. Now his mind was focusing on food. And men say they don't understand how women's minds work.

'I don't know how far Lulu got in nosing out secrets,' Al said. 'Maybe he'd hit on the truth.'

'The note he left me had the air of someone who'd already begun celebrating.'

'So, a victim of his own success. In Paris his speciality was the criminal *milieu* and he had snitches who fed him titbits. He would have tried the same approach here, but his contacts weren't so good. Some of the local bad guys got upset and finished him off.' Al's head dropped on his chest a moment. The freedom of the press is a lofty abstract. The murder of a reporter you know is a chilling fact. 'Poor guy. I wasn't going to repeat his mistake by homing in on the *clans*, trying to buy information. Crevecoeur-thinking is the clue. What has concentrated his attention down here? Why is the bastard mounting a full-scale alert? How is his smoking, by the way?'

'Back to a pack a day and rising.'

'So what is driving him?'

'Industrial espionage, he said.'

Al was cheered. 'Not terrorists, not assassination plots against some political skunk, not laundering the drugs billions, not arms-for-Allah deals, not kidnap threats against the President, not a coup in some African slum. Industrial spying? Crevecoeur? Jesus, those must be some secrets they're stealing.'

He wrestled with his chair trying to get comfortable. Trouble was, the chairs were designed for the locals while Al is an all-American boy raised on steaks and milk.

'Crevecoeur-thinking begins with the fact that my old chum André is heading up Systel, and that he has the backing of the Mob. Or part of the Mob. So there must be mega-francs there for the milking. Systel is hunkered down in that business/science development they are pleased to call the Poly Parc. I mean, who thinks up a name like that? Some kind of great marketing hero?' Al reined in his critical instincts and got back to his story. 'So where's the pay-off? The old protection racket? How about the new protection racket – give us the dough or we'll put a virus in your computer. No, because Crevecoeur-thinking says that is not important enough. Same objection to the idea that Systel has access to the other companies' bank accounts. Sure, I bet they could hack their way in and transfer a hundred big ones, but any loss would be noticed in a matter of days. Crevecoeur-thinking says it has to be a silent rip-off and a long-term investment. It's got to be worth millions, which won't be uncovered for years, by which time it's too late to hammer the guilty, and which touches on the security of France.'

The damn chair was too constricting for Al. He thrust himself out of it, made a few steps towards the altar and came back.

'Crevecoeur-thinking is the key. I got hold of a list of tenants in the Poly Parc and weeded out the duds. Duds are ones Crevecoeur wouldn't waste two minutes worrying about. There's a glass-etching laboratory, the subscription division of a magazine publisher, there's the numbercrunching department of a market research company. What else? The artificial-flavour division of a chemical company. Crevecoeur-thinking says strike them all out. So what are we left with?'

He squatted in front of me. He dropped his voice.

'These are the prize winners. There's a company that has done research on the guidance system for the Ariane rocket, you know, puts satellites in orbit. There is a company that is developing a pulse-coding system for a battlefield radio. Another company is subcontracted to do work on the fly-by-wire system for the Airbus. Another is researching beefed-up lasers they believe can slice steel girders – sounds far-fetched – and if that application can work in shipyards, why can't it be stretched to slice through ships at sea? Even more far-fetched. Another is trying to solve the problem of curved gun barrels – shoot round corners. Another is working on the technology of sending telephone, television, the Internet, you name it, down the same cable as electricity. Another is trying to create virtual zero-friction alloys. Altogether, maybe ten companies at the sharp end of French technology. A couple of handfuls, Co, but handfuls of gold.'

Al, squatting down, held his hands out towards me. And that is how the priest saw us when he came in: a woman with her head covered in a pious scarf, a man on bent knees in front of her, hands imploring her to be his wife, or perhaps something less permanent.

The old woman had glared at us, the young man had denied we existed, the priest nodded at us and went about his business. His lips were pursed: affairs of our nature should not be conducted in church. He was at an awkward age for a priest: too old to be one of the radicals Crevecoeur had railed at, not yet old enough to have serenity. Al watched him fiddling with pamphlets, then rattling the collection box and disappearing with it through a door into a side office.

'Listen,' Al began.

'I've been listening.'

'Well, listen some more. I'm going to outline what a French intellectual would call my thesis. Back home a small-town mid-Westerner would say it was a hunch. It's my best bit of Crevecoeur-thinking. Here we have the Poly Parc in its beautiful landscaped grounds. The buildings are the very hottest of post-post-modernist design. Everything works by solar power. The lawns are mowed by robots. People commute by helicopter. Here the computer is king, and Systel acts as royal courtier. These days designs and algebra and hypotheses aren't scribbled on paper, they're worked and stored by computer. And the computer systems have all been installed by Systel, who are right there on the spot. My dirty mind whispers to me that at the end of the day, when the eggheads press the Save key on their computers, a copy goes along the wire that Systel installed right on to Systel's own hard disk.'

The priest reappeared with the collection box. Al stretched up to his full height.

'Do you think I should go and drop something more in his box? You know, like rent?'

'Sit down,' I said.

Al sat beside me.

'I buy your thesis,' I said, 'almost buy it. But why hasn't Crevecoeur closed Systel down? Burnt it down? He's not concerned with a court of law and rules of evidence and examining magistrates. Blow the place up and anyone in it.'

'Maybe he's under orders to collect evidence. I don't know. Or is assessing the damage. But real Crevecoeur-thinking would be to go for a much bigger coup. A lot of companies in the Third World would pay hefty sums to acquire hi-tech secrets like these and save themselves years of research. Crevecoeur-thinking says: Let's get the end-users too, let's smash the system internationally. My old pal André, after he enjoyed a night out in Bangkok or Manila, I bet the morning after he visited an electronics company or defence manufacturer and began collecting orders. Crevecoeur wants names. He doesn't want names and telephone numbers out of André's little black book. He wants all the morning-after names.'

I could see the attraction for the Gabizzi *clan.* Computer crime is clean. Computer crime can pay huge sums. Computer crime is safe. With computer crime you don't risk your getaway car being shot up by the cops.

'I haven't done the leg-work yet,' Al said. 'I've been a bad reporter. I've got the theory before the facts. Truth is I need your help with my story.'

'A few days ago, Al, it was my story.'

'That was the kid, the murder. This is different. Spying, hi-tech, the international dimension. This is the kind of thing I'm good at. It should have been Lulu's story, but now it's mine and I'm going to say to people: That's why Lulu died, that's the scam he was exposing. See, it's sort of a monument. Only trouble is, André knows me. If he sees me, if he hears I'm at the Poly Parc, he'll start to wonder. But you can dig a little.'

'So who's going to help with *my* story?'

'The missing girl? That's a personal crusade.'

'Not significant enough for the readers of the *American Journal*.'

'Goddamit, I placed the ad, didn't I?'

'And when a reply comes, you'll drop everything and come and help me?'

Well, he would or he wouldn't. He made no reply. He'd got tired of the confines of the church and we'd moved outside. The end of the street was blocked off by a view of the Arena.

'No built-in obsolescence there,' Al said to switch the subject. 'Let that be an inspiration to General Motors. You know, the Romans used to flood the Arena and then pit swimming gladiators against crocodiles. A bit like Crevecoeur and André, though I'm not certain which is which.'

'Have you seen Crevecoeur when he smiles?' I asked. 'Have you seen his teeth?'

CHAPTER FOURTEEN

The late afternoon sun caught one of the windowpanes. The *mas* was winking at me. Come on in, join the party, have a cream bun. Beyond the house was the terraced hill topped with the stone walls used for corralling animals. The shelter was called a *borie* and generations long dead had used it before it became a home to goats and sheep. Where were Crevecoeur's men now?

Why was I toying with the idea they were no-hopers? Resentment. I hated carrying the new bug in my shoulderbag.

I'd got my 205 back from Al Richards and coasted the last stretch to the gate. The reporters had grown bored and gone to find livelier doorsteps, and with no press to hound, the police van had disappeared too. Or had been ordered to leave.

'Who is it?'

'Cody,' I said into the entryphone.

'Wait there.'

Well, I wasn't going to drive away. And I was too tired to burrow under the wire or pole-vault over it. I was going to sail in like a princess. I climbed back behind the wheel and leant an elbow on the open window. Voices lifted over the house, chattering, high-pitched, monkey-like, a school playground heard across a field. A buzz jolted me out of the reverie, the gate rose, I drove through, the gate fell.

The gravel under my tyres rattled like hail against a window. I parked beside three other cars. A familiar figure bustled out of the front door and I searched for his name.

'What's the news of Jacques?' I asked. 'Did they keep him in hospital?'

The Little Sisters of Mercy may have twittered about me, but gunshot wounds drive a hospital into a paroxysm. Here is visible evidence that a crime has been committed. Failure to report this to the police is in itself a crime. Yet a doctor's sole consideration should be for his patient.

'He's inside.' Max jerked his head back at the house. 'He sits in a chair all day and drinks whisky. He says his honour has been compromised. Twenty-five centimetres higher,' Max laid a hand on his thigh, 'it would have been more than his honour that had been compromised.'

He gave me a look to see I'd got his meaning. A grin built on his face. Max was about my age, with a thick torso, a nose that had been realigned, and a white scar like a wood chip on one cheek. He was the kind of man you'd step aside for on the pavement. I grinned back.

'Come on,' he said.

In Max's eyes I was as good as in the *clan* now. I was one of the lads but with interesting biological differences. I'd been seen round the place often enough, I was Ledru's choice, I came and went in mysterious ways, I'd given the gunned-down Jacques a bit of medical attention. Max was moving towards the house as I got out of the car. Closing the door, a sixth sense made me look up. By the third car a man had appeared. Through the double thickness of glass windows a uniform showed dully. He wasn't tall and only his head cleared the roof. He had the utter stillness of the professional watcher. I raced through a shortlist of possible officials until I settled on the obvious. It was the proprietorial way a hand came to rest on the roof. He was the chauffeur for someone important and had the training to spot trouble, accelerate away from it, or run it down.

'*Alors*,' Max said.

I caught up with him.

'Who's the big guy who's come?' I asked.

'Big guy?'

'Well, too important to drive himself.'

'Big guy.' Max guffawed. It was a chesty laugh from a man whose idea of a joke is someone being upended on an icy pavement. 'That's good. You know, that's really good. Come.'

The *mas* was an old farmhouse with bedrooms jammed into the converted attic. Two wings had been created by joining on the former stable and barn. The shape was an E without the central bar. A passage ran the length of the long side, and I'd fumbled my way down half this passage in the dark. At this end near the front door were french windows that gave on to the terrace and swimming pool. That was where I'd sat at a table when Ledru had first tried to hire me.

Now Max led me to the french windows. He leant an elbow on my shoulder so that he could raise his hand and I could pick out the man he was pointing at.

'There he is, your big guy.'

He was, of course, a small man, not as tall as me. He had short, steely grey hair that lay flat on his head. He was dressed in a dark suit and his body looked trim. Some people are gaunt, as if their nerves are burning up every scrap of fat on their frames. This man looked as if he had eaten and drunk modestly all his life. You would say he had no vices. Except power. He looked as if he gave orders in a quiet voice and never had to check if they had been obeyed. It was the lift of his head and his calculating gaze that spoke of that kind of unquestioned authority which is so corrupting.

On this side of him were two of Ledru's men I had met briefly. I had to trawl for their names. Alain? Yes. Julius? No, Marius. On the far side of the important man was someone else in a suit, a darker person. Could be Arab or Turk or southern Italian. But of the group standing there, there was no mistaking the one whose word was law.

'Have a name, does he?'

'He's the big boss, Gabizzi.'

There was a lot of activity at the pool which the group of men was watching. But for the moment I kept my eyes on them.

'What do you call him?'

'*Patron.*'

'Doesn't he have a nickname?'

'A long time ago I've heard he was known as *Mezzaro*.'

I shook my head.

'In Corsica,' Max explained, 'a *mezzaro* is the black scarf of mourning that women wear on their heads. But the people who called him that have mostly gone to their rest. André calls him *le petit caporal*, but not to his face. His size, you see, also because he comes from Corsica, you understand, as Napoleon did. André did once let *le petit caporal* slip out and the *patron* looked as cold as iron. Naturally he sees himself as a general...a field marshal. You can see he is a serious man. Even now. Even with that.'

Max shifted his stance to point at the pool, which all the other men had been staring at with unwavering attention. It was curious that the noises from the pool had lifted over the house so that I'd picked them up at the gate. Here the sounds were muted. The windows were double-glazed and close-fitting, and life on the terrace took on the unreal quality of a dream.

First I saw Ledru, climbing out of the pool. The hairs on his chest were licked down into rat's tails. He wore swimming trunks today in an unbecoming tartan design. The French, when they believe they are rising in the world, take to tartan. Maybe it was the Gabizzi *clan* tartan. I would have thought trunks were not Ledru's style and he should have been wearing the briefest *cache-sexe*. In truth, the trunks did a poor job of hiding his sex. He was half-roused and, as Ledru would put it, you could see it was all there.

The cause was just behind him. A slim arm entwined itself round one leg, a second arm gripped the other leg. With a shout

Ledru disappeared backwards into the pool. Water rose like an explosion. A woman's shriek penetrated the double-glazing.

Now I took in there was a second man in the pool, and a woman's arms were round his neck. I couldn't see her face, just her glistening titian-red curls. The man's hands were out of sight under the water but not performing any swimming stroke I'd ever learnt.

The girl who pulled Ledru back into the pool began to clamber out. She had blonde hair and was topless. She made a big fuss about climbing the steps, flicking hair out of her eyes and glancing back to see if Ledru was in pursuit. She gave a shriek of delighted alarm and came all the way out, and it turned out she was bottomless too. Ledru was climbing the steps and she flicked drops of water from her fingers into his face, and frolicked away a few steps, then dithered until he caught up with her. Putting her arms round his back, she pulled him close and rubbed her body against his.

'Holy Mother,' Max murmured, 'doesn't it give you ideas?'

'I'm sure when André has finished with her...'

At that moment Ledru looked towards Gabizzi. Well, he was an old man and of moderate appetites, so one shouldn't have expected Max's fervent mutter. But Gabizzi appeared as unmoved as if he'd been observing cans of peas on a factory production line. Then Ledru's eyes flicked further and he caught sight of me standing behind the french windows and he frowned.

'I thought you were in Paris.'

'I was in Paris. As you can see, I'm not in Paris now.'

There was something about Ledru's self-importance that brought out the schoolkid in me, wanting to cheek him. And if I wasn't being so smart I would have picked up the coldness in his tone. But even if I had, I might have put it down to my catching him sporting with the naked blonde.

'All right, you've come back. I've got eyes in my head, I can see that perfectly well. You've come back a success or you've come back a failure. You've found out who the murderer is?'

'I know who the murderer is.' So would Ledru, if he put his mind to it. Also Inspector Gaudet must know. So why hadn't he told Ledru? Or kick-started the kind of manhunt that so thrills the French, with TV appeals, newspaper interviews, roadblocks with a slalom between barrels and a concertina of spikes to drag across the road for anyone who wouldn't stop.

'Who?'

Ledru had been watching me and now he thrust his neck forward like any bully sticking his face into yours.

'Not yet,' I said, 'because I don't know where he is.'

'I thought you were going to Paris to put an advertisement in the press and intercept any replies.'

'Slight change of emphasis. I am advertising, but it takes time to get results. Not long, if my hunch is correct. The way things turned out, he should have a feeling of desperation. Say, a couple of days more, three maybe.'

Ledru moved until he was crowding me. His face had flattened, his lips squeezed into a lipless line.

'I don't like this,' he said. I watched his eyes to see if they would signal a sudden attack. He was right on the edge of losing control. It had to be more than what I'd just said. The situation with Gabizzi and the other men and the naked girls had made him tense: this was an extra turn of the screw. 'You're not giving me what I hired you for. Maybe in that pretty head of yours is the idea that later on you'll touch me for a killing: a big wad, or you won't tell me who he is. In our organization we have ways of dealing with people who get the urge to go freelance.'

I waited until he'd finished, then said, 'You haven't hired me.'

His eyebrows shot up.

'We have no contract, no verbal agreement. You've given me no money. I've paid my own expenses. We never settled a fee, nothing I said yes to.'

The eyebrows lowered themselves into a frown.

'So why are you here?'

'To discuss the money now.'

Ledru relaxed a fraction. Talk of money made him happier. It was a motive he understood. We'd come into his office to be away from the distractions on the terrace. A door or window must have been open somewhere and girlish laughter followed a booming male suggestion.

'So,' he said. 'All right then.'

'Who are they?' I asked, nodding towards the sound of laughter.

'Girls,' He answered shortly. Then he seemed to size me up. 'You are a woman and they're just girls. That's all they are.' He gave the smallest wave of his hand. The girls weren't worth more.

'And the men?'

He looked at me and frowned. 'Business associates,' he said and looked away. There was a tightening of the muscles in my stomach. These weren't any old business associates. These were Gabizzi and henchmen. Ledru had wanted to take me to Gabizzi, have the *patron* inspect me, get his approval. Now he wouldn't even introduce me. Why? That and the coldness in his voice sent all sorts of panic signals through me.

'So, money.'

Ledru had a method of negotiation he must have picked up when he was a youngster, poor and easily mesmerized by the sight of a fat wallet. He went to the wall-safe, glanced in my direction to be certain I wasn't on tiptoe to look over his shoulder, and turned the combination lock. He opened the safe and came out with two piles of notes, held together by jumbo paperclips. 'Twenty thousand.'

I didn't move or speak.

'Plus another ten on delivery.'

I still made no sign. From the pool came the sound of a male voice whooping like a war cry. Both girls were screaming, not frightened screaming, all good dirty-fun screaming.

'Okay, make it another twenty thousand on delivery of where the rat is holed up. That's final.'

I'm not up to date with the going rate for fingering somebody for the Mob in the south of France. I was doing work he was incapable of, and which for whatever reason he wouldn't entrust to his own thugs. What he offered didn't seem over-generous. I put that down to the fact that I was a woman, only one up from being a girl.

'When I was in Paris,' I said, 'I did some asking around, as you or your associates could do if you weren't so occupied here. I didn't track down the person I was looking for, but I did find a friend of his. He fed me a fairy story about taking me to his pal's apartment, and then tried to kill me.' I held up an arm and pulled down the sleeve to show the abrasions. 'I ended up in hospital for the night.'

'What's the bastard's name? I'll get someone to go and see him.'

'Don't bother. He's dead.'

Ledru laid the money on the desk. He got out a cigarette and stuck it in his mouth. He'd put on a towelling wrap when he left the pool and now he patted the pockets for a lighter or matchbox. Nothing. He stood there with the unlit cigarette between his lips. It jiggled when he talked.

'I only have your word for this.'

'Do you want to see the scraping down my legs? The bruising along my ribs? You want a medical certificate?'

'How much then?'

'Fifty thousand.'

He stared at me with poker eyes.

I went on, 'Only it's not for me.'

'Not for you?' Ledru's gaze remained steady but his nostrils flared. Here was something he didn't understand. Someone who wasn't out for everything she could take was not to be trusted. 'How do you mean?'

'You find an orphans' fund or an orphanage in Romania and donate the money to them.'

'You work for nothing?' Was it disbelief in his voice? Even contempt?

'Money to orphans? I don't call that working for nothing.'

He patted his pockets again as if a lighter would suddenly have appeared. 'Excuse me a minute.'

He disappeared through the door. *Now,* I told myself, be quick. Before I could move he'd returned. He scooped up the money from the desk, put it in the safe and pushed the door shut.

'It's not you I don't trust' he said. 'It's Gustave. He might get it into his head to rise from the dead and go for a walk.'

Gustave was Eiffel, he of the tower. He was engraved on the two hundred franc note. After Ledru's second exit I hesitated a moment or two, listening. Now, really now, I ordered – move it. I crossed to the jardinière, already groping in my shoulderbag. I could hear Ledru's espadrilles slapping away down the corridor. I was alert to every sound, a distant splash, a muffled shriek. *Girls,* I thought, *they're just girls.* Why are they here? Rest and relaxation? The troops are readying for war and the girls are provided to get the kinks out of their nerves? And Gabizzi? Why wouldn't Ledru introduce me? There Gabizzi was, in his undertaker's suit, staring, unsmiling, unaroused – and Ledru kept mum. Why?

My brain, sparking, ran through these half-thoughts as I crossed to the wooden planter. I could hear Ledru's voice out on the terrace. *Fifi,* he said. Good, I had time. I reached down to the mother-in-law's tongue. Hold on, I thought, girls aren't called Fifi any more. If they ever were. Maybe poodles. More likely he shouted, *C'est fini.* And yes, it had definitely grown quieter out there. I parted the leaves.

This was the spot I'd put it in.

I was sure of it. Positive.

I hadn't put it on the other side of the planter. A fleshy round-leaved plant grew there. Here, where the mother-in-law's tongue flourished.

I did. I know I did. My heartbeat was speeding up. The thump was painful in my chest.

I bent close to look under the rim. I looked round all four sides. For good measure I used my fingers until I chanced on it: a small area of tackiness where the adhesive had been. I searched the compost under the leaves in case the bug had become dislodged and fallen. No. It had been found and removed. Crevecoeur could listen and listen but he'd never hear anything.

I used to wonder about the idea that your blood ran cold. Now I knew it was the truth. I felt a chill right down my spine. It could have been a cold breath from an open grave. Ledru had found the bug and was searching for the culprit.

Dear God, I thought, no wonder he kept me away from Gabizzi.

My legs had gone stiff, the muscles withered. Get back, get across the room before Ledru returns, but you'd think I was dragging myself to the gallows. That damned shoulderbag kept banging against my side as I moved. Ledru would come in, take one look and say: That bag is bloody heavy from the look of it, what are you hiding? I could hear the espadrilles approaching, each footfall like a backhand smacking across my cheek.

What Ledru said when he looked at me was, 'Why don't you sit down? We'll have a drink.'

Smoking the cigarette had calmed him down. I should have one. My nerves were stretched like an elastic band before it snaps. Every look he gave, everything he did or said, seemed loaded with suspicion.

'Some other time.'

'Fifty thousand is agreed, right? No need to have anything in writing. We trust each other. Do you have an address for these orphans?'

'Get in touch with the International Red Cross.'

He nodded.

'Sure you won't change your mind? Drop of Scotch would bring the colour back to your cheeks.'

'I have things to do.'

'When do you expect to have the rat cornered?'

'Couple of days, like I said. He's got to be under considerable pressure because of the police activity. He's holed up and doesn't know where to turn. If he rings Paris and finds his colleague is dead, there'll be a measure of panic. Above all, he needs money. But in a sense it's up to him now. He's the one who has to respond.'

My voice sounded unreal in my ears, too loud, too high-pitched. I couldn't stop babbling, anything to fill the time it took me to walk to the door. My elbow pressed the shoulderbag tight against my side. Ledru was staring at it. Then his eyes switched to my hips, and up the buttons of my shirt, up to the open V at the top. Thank God for male hormones.

He swallowed. 'Fifty thousand, it's agreed.' Forgetting we'd agreed it just two minutes ago.

'Yes,' I said.

But I don't think the orphans ever got it. I don't think Ledru had time.

Public telephones I have known: in a place full of noise and bustle where any cruising listener can pass close enough to pick up a snatch of your talk; in an empty hall like an echo chamber; in a hotel room with a bored switchboard girl sharing your secrets.

I stopped at a bar on the outskirts of the city. A group of men were drinking Ricard and I got plenty of looks. I stood at the rear of the room, waiting until they went back to discussing the national humiliation caused by an American wearing the yellow jersey in the Tour de France.

I rang the number I'd been given and said, 'Cody.'

There was something of a pause. I suppose he was considering my tone of voice.

'Well?'

'I couldn't do it.'

'Couldn't? You couldn't do it? What do you mean? You have actually been in—'

'Couldn't. Do you want me to spell it? I couldn't do it because the last bug was discovered and removed. If whoever did that went for another look and found a replacement, he'd know it was me who placed it. That's why I couldn't do it. Satisfied?'

In Corsica, I remembered, *a mezzaro is the black scarf of mourning that women wear on their heads.* Would anyone wear a *mezzaro* for me? He was turning over in his mind what I'd just said and the edginess in my voice. 'Who found it? Any theories?'

'I suspect...'

'Yes.'

'The whole damn world.'

The hell with Crevecoeur.

CHAPTER FIFTEEN

Another night, another hotel. Each twist drove me to a new place as if I could make a fresh start, rest in peace.

Les Platanes was one of those narrow-shouldered French hotels squeezed half to death between grander apartment blocks. There was a reception counter in the hall and a manager who limped out from behind a bead curtain. A bullfighting poster on the wall gave the place class. A room? The manager's charmless gaze took in my lack of a suitcase, the dark shadows under my eyes, the abrasions on my knuckles as if I'd been in a fight, my woozy air of someone who's just surfaced from a drug trip. He took all that in and gave me a room. But I would pay in advance. I would even produce some ID, which showed he must be really worried.

I could hear the tinny sounds of a TV from beyond the bead curtain and a long hacking cough. The air was dead in the reception hall, killed by the day's lingering heat and the smell of mutton and couscous.

'Room eight,' he said, handing me a key from the rack. 'Second floor. The front door is locked at eleven. No guests in the room.'

I climbed narrow twisting stairs past half a dozen different floral-patterned walls. Room number eight had dog roses. Lying on the bed, my eyes searched among the leaves for a face peeping at me. The roses repeated themselves and my eyes climbed towards the ceiling until I was dizzied by the pattern. Resisting sleep, I got the Imperator on the telephone and asked for Monsieur Richards. Well, try the restaurant.

'I've just been served my fillet of sea bass.' Would I call that a peevish edge to Al's voice? There was a puff of breath just loud enough for me to hear. Yes, peevish. 'What did you dig out?'

'How's it been cooked?'

'What? Oh, grilled over charcoal. What dirt did you, get on the Poly Parc?'

'What sauce?'

'Sort of a hollandaise flavoured with fennel. And I'm drinking a chilled Lirac rosé, since you're writing up the social notes.'

'Good, is it?'

'The Lirac was an experiment. Not wholly successful. Lacks the acidity to cut through the richness of the hollandaise.' There was a pause. I found a face peering down from the roses. With the phone clamped against my ear, I got to my feet to inspect it more closely and it turned out to be a mosquito hammered flat against the wallpaper. 'You're not telling me anything, Co. Which tells me everything.'

'You might at least be pleased I got out of this one with a whole skin.'

'What happened?'

'Oh, just your usual Saturday afternoon orgy, booze, guns, gangsters, scads of used banknotes, naked girls. I didn't have to dig for any dirt. It was lying all round me. As for the Poly Parc, if you think that was the right moment to start on the big probe ... Oh, forget it.'

Suddenly I was sick of men: Al Richards concerned about his stomach and his scoop, Crevecoeur, Ledru, Gabizzi, whose activities put mourning scarves on women's heads, Inspector Gaudet, Max and all the chorus of minor players I hardly knew but who all knew me. And Doicescu, a dark presence hovering in the wings.

'Where are you?' Al asked. 'Have you got a hotel?'

'A mosquito pit called the Platanes. I'm not having you hammering on the door. No guests allowed in the rooms.'

'Meet me for a drink.'

'I'm exhausted, Al. I'm aching, I'm drained. Go back to your fish. Tell the head waiter my voice curdled the sauce.'

I hung up.

Two minutes later I regretted snapping, but that was two minutes too late. I stripped and lay on the bed and searched among the flowers and leaves and thorns for a spy. Even a leering voyeur would do. Human contact was all.

I was hallucinating. The roses changed to yuccas and palms and pots of geraniums. Gabizzi was motionless on the patio, staring at the men at play with the naked girls. Gabizzi wasn't about to throw off his dark suit and join in the frolic. He was intent on something else.

All I could come up with was checking girls to be sent abroad. Some big shot in the Middle East. The white slavery of Victorian whispers.

I didn't think I could help the girls. They seemed to be racing towards their fate with their legs wide open.

I wondered what Crevecoeur would do about the bug.

I searched for Crevecoeur among the dog roses. There he was, his face among the leaves, the smear of blood that had been a mosquito.

My brain was closing down in a chaos of doubts. I switched off the light.

I was naked when they came. Nudity is a powerful weapon against a man because it triggers conflicting desires in him. His urge is to mate with the naked female presented to him, not to fight and risk destroying her.

But the room was in darkness so that advantage was lost to me. I hadn't heard footsteps outside, nor the handle rattle. I was too exhausted, too deep in the sleep pattern. Not an excuse, a reason. The lock had obviously presented no problem. They were in the room before I was even awake. Sleep was falling away from me fast but I had one twisted idea: I was being kidnapped and taken to join the two naked girls in the swimming pool.

The bed was jammed against the wall at the head and at one side, so I slipped down to the end of the bed, which was when I discovered there was more than one intruder. I bumped into knees, drew back at once and slid over the side, feeling on the floor for my shoes, for something to throw and make a clatter in the corner of the room. A distraction, anything that gave me a chance of reaching the stairs. What I grabbed was a trouser leg, the slippery coarseness of jeans. I tugged to overbalance him and got a smack across the top of my head for my pains. I dived sideways and rolled over my shoes and made enough noise to wake the whole hotel. I was on my feet and making for the one bright point in the room: the luminous light switch which showed where the door was. The man stepped in behind me and reached under one of my arms. He grunted, possibly at the unexpectedness of naked skin. I stamped back at his instep and met a sturdy shoe. I turned my head down and bit, but it was a leather sleeve. I jerked my head back, but only met the top of his chest. I twisted and tried to lunge backwards to get him in the groin, but he was tight against me. Then both hands were behind my neck, the knuckles locked, my head forced forward. He tugged me in closer and leant his full weight on me. I was a trussed chicken. I couldn't budge.

It was now in the deep breathing darkness, in long seconds of stillness while I flexed my muscles and stretched my limbs and could make no space for a move, that I knew these weren't sneak thieves or rapists. There was a deeper purpose in their coming.

Satisfied I was immobilized, the one from the foot of the bed moved to the door and switched on the light. He had an eyeful of my nakedness now, when it did me no good. He held a pistol in one hand but it drooped, forgotten, pointing at the moth-eaten rug.

He said, 'Do we have to go straight away?' I suppose it was his little joke.

The man with the neck-lock on me replied, 'He'll be waiting.'

His colleague left the door, picked up the bolster and jammed the pistol into it. It made a primitive silencer. The man behind me squeezed his elbows into my sides to sharpen my attention.

'I'm letting go of you. If you try to get away, he'll shoot. If you try to fight, he'll shoot. If you shout for help, he'll shoot. If you try any tricks at all, he'll shoot and ask questions afterwards. Do you understand?'

Yes, or he would shoot.

'Get dressed.'

Les Platanes didn't run to private bathrooms. I didn't bother to turn aside. They'd seen all there was anyway. The one with the gun was younger and he watched me with close attention.

'Okay, let's move.' At the door the man in the leather jacket paused to check the room. 'Bring her shoulderbag.' At the top of the stairs he said, 'I'll go first. You're in the middle. If you try to make a dash for freedom, he'll shoot.'

Down the stairs, into the reception hall. It was empty, holding its breath as our little procession went on its way. From beyond the bead curtain I heard the hacking cough.

Thanks, *mon brave,* for bringing the dogs on me.

Outside was a van with corrugated metal sides of the kind you see delivering meat in rural France. It was unmarked.

'Where are you taking me?'

I was bundled into the back and the door locked. I beat my hands on the metal side-panels but the noise would hardly sound above the wheezing engine.

Where was I driven? I couldn't tell. Not too far, so somewhere in the outer suburbs. The van waited at red lights like any law-abiding citizen. We took a couple of right turns, a left, and stopped while a gate was opened and clanged shut behind. The van tilted nose-down, the engine growled in an echo, then the noise died away. The back of the van was unlocked and I was invited to get out by a hand hauling my ankle. We were in an underground garage, but the door behind us had already swung shut so I saw nothing outside.

I was taken up an inside staircase to a hallway, then through a kitchen. Outside in the garden we walked a short distance along a concrete path to a solid brick cabin. The walk gave me a chance to look around. This was what estate agents are pleased to call une *villa de grand standing,* complete with cemented garden walls and trees beyond that masked the street lights. Isolated. Then I was pushed into the cabin and the door locked.

It was something past midnight when I was shut in. It was after one o'clock before anyone came to see me. This is the softening-up period when you swear you'll be strong and can feel the determination leak away. You run over your sins and your knowledge of others' sins and vow that you'll clam up. But your vow counts for nothing because all these things you know have gathered right there at the front of your brain, eager to slip out.

I used the time to assess what I'd picked up: the institutional green paint in the hall, the pinboard on a wall, rumble of male voices, strangled music from a radio, a kitchen where no serious cooking was done, the absence of furniture in the cabin except for a mattress on the floor (foam rubber because you could always get at a spring and use it to scratch someone's eye out), the lack of ceremony of the men who'd brought me. Part of an organization, I said to myself, but apart from it. Official, but unofficial. Men who are accustomed to the physical side of what they do but who aren't basically vicious. I also remembered men who expected to be obeyed or 'he'll shoot'. So it was hardly a surprise when the door was unlocked and Inspector Gaudet came in.

I wanted to be so cool. Gaudet, I think, came to preen a little, possibly to explain, certainly not to apologize or give anything away. But it was like pouring two chemicals into a retort, and when the smoke clears you find yourself on the floor with the science lab in ruins around you.

I was squatting cross-legged on the mattress. It was a position that took the tension out of my stomach and shoulder muscles. Also I was at less of a disadvantage than I would be lying down. Gaudet stood a moment with his hand resting on the door, trying to measure my mood, also measuring the distance I was from him.

'Cody, you've brought this on yourself.'

I said nothing.

'Everything you are has got you in this position. Everything you have been. Everything you pretend to be, everything you deny. Cody, ace reporter. Cody, high-class tart. Cody, super spy. Cody, keen-eyed investigator. Cody, moral high-wire artist. Cody, poodle for the Sûreté.'

He'd got the bones of it from the computer in rue des Saussaies. But the rhetoric, I remembered all those flourishes from another night-time encounter.

He came away from the door and took half a dozen paces to the window. His shoes squeaked on the linoleum. He perched on the window-sill with his back jammed against the bars. I could feel pressure inside my chest. I took slow breaths, wanting to stay calm. I said nothing.

'I warned you and you paid no attention. I told you to stop and you kept putting your nose in.'

He got out a cigarette. Unlike Ledru, he had a lighter and had no need to leave me alone. He lit the cigarette and inhaled deeply. The pressure inside me grew. It seemed to have spread from my chest to the pit of my belly, my heart, my throat. Say nothing, I warned myself. Not one word.

'So now here you are, out of harm's way, lost to the public eye. You can't get out and nobody will free you, because nobody knows you are here. This cabin is a back room that has no official existence – like you, in fact. Nobody is going to pass by, nobody will show any curiosity. You're in the grounds of the Club des Sports of the Nîmes police.'

If he'd just shut up and gone away, I'd have let him. But perched there, giving me his little lecture. running on about my hopeless position ... The pressure grew too great.

'This is where the sport takes place, right in here,' I spat out. I couldn't stop. More boiled up. 'Window barred and shuttered. Soundproofed walls. No furniture except this –' I banged a hand and sent dust flying from the mattress, '– in case a female prisoner decides to co-operate in a sporting fashion.'

'You're not a prisoner.'

'What am I then?'

'You're not charged with anything. You're not being held for interrogation.'

'What am I?'

'You're being kept out of circulation.'

'If I'm not a prisoner, what the hell am I?'

'Let's say a guest.'

'Then this guest wants to check out. Call me a taxi and I'll get out of your hair.'

There was no ashtray. Gaudet flicked ash at the floor and his casual gesture turned into disdain in my mind and I let rip.

'I was at the *mas* this afternoon, yesterday afternoon I should say. I gatecrashed a party: Ledru, his henchmen, others including the great Gabizzi himself, a couple of young women. The women were naked. No law against an orgy, you'll say. But if you were any kind of a cop you'd say there was a prima-facie case that Ledru and Gabizzi were involved in prostitution. You'd mount a big raid, tear the place apart for evidence, seize papers that might show payments not declared for the purposes of income tax. And at the same time you'd uncover what the hell Ledru is really up to.'

'Raid the *mas*? My God, I couldn't do that.'

'Of course you couldn't, because you're in on it.'

I was standing in front of Gaudet. I didn't remember getting to my feet but there I was, a step away from him. He'd dropped the cigarette on the floor and stood with his arm floating in front of his solar plexus. It was the reflex of a man who thought that when words ran out, war was swift to follow. He was alert but not worried. Why should he be? He'd have a friend or two outside the door.

'Sit down,' Gaudet said. 'Relax.'

'You know what's going on and—'

'And you don't. Don't be a bore. Sit down.' He waved his hand at me. 'Make yourself comfortable. This is your home for the next...' The hand flipped over, fingers spread, as if appealing for something. My understanding, my indulgence. 'I don't know how long. Today, maybe several days. As long as it takes. It's not the Ritz, but you'll have room service. Meals, wine. What else do you want? Books? A video? What's your taste? Westerns? Existentialist thrillers?'

I stared and stared. I couldn't believe this was happening. Then Gaudet strode boldly into the land of the grotesque.

'I can't offer you a man. I've seen you with Pelletier and Ledru. If I sent you, say, Bernard to help pass the time, I think you'd twist him round your little finger after one night.'

'Gaudet, you can't do this. I'm an ordinary private individual—'

'No.'

He cut me short. Stealthily, a pickpocket, he dipped his hand inside his jacket. His eyes held my eyes, locking on to my expression and how it would change. He drew his hand out clenched, then unfolded it like a flower to show in his palm the bug, the miracle of Japanese radio miniaturization, that Crevecoeur had forced on me.

'Ledru left me alone in his office in the *mas*. I was going to help myself to a whisky but having, you see, only the one hand, I went to stub out my cigarette in the earth of a big plant pot. I saw this. Neat, yes? We don't have any use for these ourselves in the police in a provincial city like Nîmes. I didn't put it there, I couldn't see why Ledru should bug himself, and I didn't think a business rival would have had the opportunity. But then I remembered there was someone who'd broken in, got right into Ledru's office. So I took the bug. I had it dusted for fingerprints and then I sent them by fax to Paris, the Big Boss computer. No record, came the answer. So I sent further instructions. Try the foreign register and back came the answer: Cody. Plus the warning: No executive action with or against this individual without consulting Chief Inspector Crevecoeur, Sûreté Nationale.'

He slipped the bug into his pocket. He seemed to wait to see what I had to say. But I could think of nothing useful except: Damn you, Crevecoeur. And that wasn't particularly useful.

'That must have been Crevecoeur listening up on the hill, correct? Well, I thought, he's not going to interfere any more. But I underestimated his stubbornness. I heard you were back from Paris, I heard you had visited the *mas,* then I heard where you were staying.'

Gaudet had heard so much and I was reeling with doubts and queries: how he'd heard, who'd told him, what his relationship with Ledru was?

'I had you picked up, and look what was found in your shoulderbag.'

He dipped his hand inside his jacket a second time and pulled out the identical twin of the bug.

'Care to tell me again you're not working for the Sûreté?'

'What are you doing?' I whispered. 'What do you want?'

'I want you out of the way. I want the Sûreté out of the way.'

Gaudet left me. He knocked three light taps on the door, it was opened and under a lamp on a small terrace outside I saw the older man in the leather jacket who'd had the neck-lock on me at the hotel. Then the door was closed and I heard the lock click.

Gaudet had said – his only form of goodbye – that I could sleep or spend the rest of the night thinking or praying. I could shout at the top of my voice but there were no neighbours. If I wanted a little action I could go to hell and chat up the devil, play strip poker, watch the flames rise higher up his legs. Some more of his fancy rhetoric along those lines. He was a little mad and I supposed I had driven him that way.

The Inspector had a deep-rooted anger against the Sûreté, against Crevecoeur and by extension against me. That was why I was here, locked away in a police safe-house. I lay on the mattress and dozed fitfully, and in the wakeful moments in between I puzzled over Ledru's relationship with Gaudet. Gaudet was Ledru's creature, a bent cop. Had he shown him the bug? But if he knew my fingerprints were on it, why didn't he warn Ledru?

Exhaustion was washing over me. I couldn't work out the answers. As my brain was slipping over the border into sleep it played one final silly trick: I thought of Gaudet as a one-armed bandit, you scored three cherries and out spewed a cascade of bugs.

I smiled a half-wit's smile. The smile stuck on my face because I was too tired to wipe it off. No, tired is too pale a word for how I felt. I felt too worn out to fight life's battles. I felt old, old. I could struggle no more. I died. And when I woke up from a dreamless sleep, he was walking through the door.

He'd shaved and put on clean clothes. How much he'd slept I don't know. Not much, I guessed. The rings of blackness under his eyes had become heavier, his eyelids stained dark too. The younger man was on guard outside now. He handed in a tray, which Gaudet carried over to the mattress where I lay.

'Breakfast,' he announced. 'It's late, but you weren't clamouring for it so they didn't disturb you.'

'Is that Bernard?'

'Now, don't go getting ideas about him.'

I checked my watch and it was approaching ten. A good prison this. Considerate of its inmates. They thought of everything – for instance, I was given two croissants rather than rolls and butter. Butter demands a knife to spread it and even a plastic knife can be a weapon.

Gaudet turned his back on me and went to the window. It was a sash window because bars would stop a casement window being opened. On the outside there were metal shutters that I'd been unable to push open. Twisting his head, Gaudet was able to look up through a gap at the top at the sky. If I was kept here much longer that is what I'd be doing, gazing up at the blue sky like any prisoner.

'It's come very much closer,' he said.

'What has?'

'That's why I'm here. To ask you Crevecoeur's intention.'

'I don't know.'

'But you're working for him. Two miniature radio transmitters. Access to Ledru. You're not just some cheap—'

He swung round to face me as I moved. I hated this cell. There were no chairs, no table, no furniture of any kind, no rug over the linoleum, no pictures or calendar, no lamps. I leant against a wall, arms folded.

'I didn't know what Crevecoeur was like at first,' Gaudet said. 'I've seen him now, watched him while he sat in a car and listened to one of his men report. He's got a thin face, all squeezed up, like the spine of a book.'

'Is there a title on the spine of the book?'

Gaudet raised his eyebrows at the unexpected question. He pursed his lips while he thought. 'I would say *La Peste*. You know Camus? Set in Oran, Algeria, when Algeria was French. Rats spread the plague. Terror, indifference, tragedy, death. I see Crevecoeur in those terms. For me he is a true citizen of Oran.'

I took a deep breath and another. Well, this was France. The bent cop who kidnaps you is an intellectual. I thought of the very first meeting with him at police headquarters when he'd had me picked up after my visit to the morgue. His rage against the Sûreté had been like a fire lighting him from inside. Crevecoeur was his rat, just as Doicescu was Ledru's.

'Crevecoeur blackmailed me,' I said. 'Usual carrot and stick. First time it was straight stick: break in and leave the bug, or else. Second time I was offered a carrot as well: a threat to my life would be removed for ever. With the bug in place, Crevecoeur would know in advance what Ledru planned. Of course,' I paused, listening to the cooing of doves outside, '*you* could provide advance warning just like that.' I snapped my fingers.

Gaudet's look narrowed until it was fixed between my eyes. His face was taut as if he was holding something in check. Again I hesitated. He was about to explode in anger, hoot with laughter, rock back in dumb disbelief, who could tell? He was waiting for more.

I had to go on. 'Seeing as you are so chummy with Ledru.'

The expression on his face changed, like a light being snapped on. Even as he began speaking, piling on his supposed crimes, an entirely different truth dawned on me: how I had misread Gaudet's relationship with Ledru, just as he mistook mine with Crevecoeur.

'Well now,' he said. He hauled one of his haunches up so that he was perched on the window-sill. 'So I'm in Monsieur Ledru's pocket, eh? I'm his tame cop, fix his parking tickets, fix his girls, fix any snoop who comes down from Paris, fix the Sûreté, look the other way while he stashes away the loot. That's us in bed together,' he poked forward his hand with two fingers crossed, 'deciding whose turn it is to be on top. And nobody will notice. Not my colleagues. Not my bosses. Maybe we're all in on it.'

He fished out his cigarettes and lighter and went through the business of getting smoke into his lungs. 'So,' he said as if he was announcing a judgement. I very much wanted to claw back the words I'd said. 'Are you sure you don't know what Crevecoeur has in mind?'

I shook my head. He studied me for some time, trying to decide how good a liar I was. What to believe? The evidence of the fingerprints? Or my explanation that I was blackmailed? I don't know if he really decided or if in the end he was too weary, as I had been before I slept, too weary to continue on his lonely path.

'You know what I am?' he asked. He jerked his thumb at his chest. 'I'm a *pied noir*.' He took another pull on his cigarette, then eased himself back on the windowsill, as anyone might settle for a lengthy journey. 'And my parents were *pieds noirs*. And *their* parents... Do you know why we were called *pieds noirs*? Not because we ran barefoot across the burning sand. Because the early settlers in Algeria came from Alsace, where people wore black boots. My family had been four generations in Algeria. It was home. We weren't like your English colonials, live ten years in Hong Kong, make their fortune, run back to Mummy. We *belonged*. And then suddenly we no longer belonged. We had to get out, a million of us, some to Corsica, some to Marseille, some to Hérault or Tarn. Some had contacts in Paris. Others finished up around Nîmes.'

With his hand trailing smoke, he'd distributed the *pieds noirs* around him. He put the cigarette to his lips, frowning, before deciding to go further.

'I was six when we came here. My father got a smallholding. Apricots and peaches. He worked hard. Worked himself to death, you might say. All the *pieds noirs* worked hard, worked their way to acceptance, or at least tolerance. And sometimes not even succeeding in finding tolerance. That was something I observed.'

He'd slowed right down. Now he stopped. If you don't want to tell me, don't. Words would hardly come. Like trying to milk a donkey, someone once said to me. With an effort he got going.

'I became a cop. If you want to get all psychological, you'd say it was my way of making certain I was treated with... No, forget it. Now others – boys I was at school with, second cousins, people who'd been taunted too much – well, they took quite another route. Drifted into the *milieu*. I know them. They know me. They don't rob the very rich, because that causes trouble. They don't rob the very poor, because what's the point. The big soft underbelly in the middle is their target. Nobody gets hurt much because they're all insured. But more important, the *milieu* is a supplier: drugs, prostitution, gambling. These are things people want. The *milieu* is meeting a need.'

He was looking at me to see I was following where he was leading.

'I know them and they know me,' he said again. 'It's a balance, a form of coexistence. They don't go too far, they don't touch the daughters of the rich, and they don't carve up plain tax-paying citizens around here. Or not too often, and then we fall hard on them. The ordinary Frenchman doesn't appreciate being approached by a man waving a knife. He thinks it's degenerate. Sicilian or Spanish or Arab. Or Corsican. Which is why—'

He broke off again, dropping his cigarette butt, grinding it out of existence under his heel, looking back at me to give full force to what he was saying.

'Which is why I will not tolerate the spread of Gabizzi's influence to Nîmes, Ledru and his henchmen.'

Another pause. He was letting me think back over meeting him at the *mas* and Ledru's careless assumption that the cop was thoroughly bought. My mind was struggling to adjust to the new Inspector Gaudet. Not a bent cop, nothing so simple, a cynical cop maybe, or a realistic cop with – to use the jargon – damage limitation his priority. Or he saw himself a downbeat hero, a civilized cop; and if he was bent it was only in the sense of bending to accommodate human foibles.

'Do you understand? My priority is the big *coup* against Ledru, a grand-slam operation that wipes him and his colleagues right off the map.'

'But that's what Crevecoeur wants. You're in competition to do the same thing.'

'I cannot stomach the Sûreté in here. Cannot and will not. They think they are the guardians of morality and will clean up Ledru's gang and, while they're about it all the other little gangs as well. That's what happens when they muscle in. They haven't liaised with us. They take over. They become a law unto themselves, obeying only their own orders. They're an occupying army and God help you if you get in their way.'

He held up the stump of his left arm as evidence.

I was in a foetal position on the mattress. Inspector Gaudet had left me with my mind in turmoil. I kept trying to get a new fix on him. Was he a shining beacon in a sea of corruption? Or trying to con me? Or lying to protect Ledru? Or the opposite – about to betray Ledru to the local *milieu*? Was Ledru part of the 'big soft underbelly'? How did any of it fit with Crevecoeur's industrial espionage?

It was a jigsaw where I couldn't make the pieces fit because I hadn't seen the whole picture.

How about the torture and murder of Lulu Pelletier? Inspector Gaudet would retort: See what I mean about cutting people up being unacceptable.

How about the police van guarding Ledru's gate? Ledru only *thought* it was guarding his gate. Really it was taking note of his visitors.

How about the two bogus cops who came to the Love Hotel? The local *milieu* trying to scare you off because you were working for Ledru. Or Crevecoeur. Or both.

How about the murder of Ledru's wife and the abduction of little Rina? That was a different matter, entirely divorced from the matter in hand.

Well, how about Gabizzi's visit to the farmhouse and the naked girls disporting themselves? I think, if pressed to answer,

Gaudet would have said that also was a private matter and that not everything that happens during the course of a week is part of the same pattern.

I think that is what Gaudet would have answered. But I don't think it was the right answer. I witnessed the scene. The nakedness and abandon of the young women were in such contrast to the strictness of Gabizzi. There had been a purpose to his presence.

Gaudet said before he left me: 'I wonder if I can make it more fun for you here.' He seemed to be considering again his bizarre offer to send me a lover, then shook his head. 'I'll get you some books. I can't let you out because Crevecoeur would only make use of you again. And you're sure you don't know what he's planning?'

'It's soon,' I said, 'whatever it is.'

Once there was the sound of someone walking by quite close to the cabin, whistling. I almost shouted out and then gave it up as pointless. It's only men who whistle while they walk, and he'd just assume I was locked up for some piece of police business.

The cicadas got going as the heat built. A small bathroom had been tacked on the side of the cabin and I took a cold shower and lay down again. Through the shutters drifted the sound of a distant car horn and raised voices. A man, closer, shouted something I couldn't catch. More voices, arguing, angry, in conflict. I heard the chair outside scrape as the guard moved off.

I didn't know what was going on but it seemed to me that maybe – just maybe – this could be my chance to get out.

There was silence for a minute or two, then the sound of a soft footfall outside. Five swift steps and I was by the door. I took the hinge side because I would be hidden. Nothing, silence, waiting, the scratch of a key in the lock. Pause. The door was being pushed cautiously open as I took hold of the handle and jerked as hard as I could. The door swung wide and a man was pulled in, off balance, stumbling and recovering, his pistol twisting towards me.

CHAPTER SIXTEEN

I should have slammed the door in his face instead. Broken his nose, blinded him for a few seconds. How could I know he had a gun? When a door opens, even in a police cell, you don't expect a man with a gun.

He was steady on his feet now, the pistol pointing not at my chest but at my face. My eyes were focused on the black hole at the muzzle end. Nothing else existed in the whole world. The thing would come out propelled by a force of gas, spinning, punching its way through the air towards me. My eyes would pick up the moving object. That is to say, my optical nerves would isolate it and transmit the data to the brain. Would my brain 'see' it as a bullet? Would it register the fact before the brain itself ceased to function? I suppose I held my breath. That's the animal instinct in humans. As if by not breathing you won't provoke an attack. Animal instinct also wanted me to bolt, wanted it badly. It was the jungle in here and instincts had to be suppressed and the brain take over.

Make for the open door. I couldn't. I was on the hinge side which had been the right position before and was the wrong position now.

Dive to the floor and go in a roll towards him. He was close but not quite close enough, and I was too big a target and he couldn't miss.

Drop like a stone and hook a foot round an ankle and up-end him. Again, he was close but just too far to reach.

Fling up an arm and shout. Break his concentration. Assume he'll look up and his aim will follow his movement. Assume you can move faster than he can correct his aim.

That's a lot of assuming.

One second, two seconds, the possibilities came into my mind and I threw them out. Three seconds and I was focusing on a finger folded round the trigger. Watch for the knuckle going white. But the knuckle was white to begin with.

Stare into the face beyond, into the eyes, for a warning flicker. The eyes stared back. Both eyes wide open, not narrowed and concentrating on the aim. Eyes staring, a glitter to them. He was observing me. He wanted to see my reaction. He wanted to see fear. He wanted to dominate me. It was Crevecoeur.

Once upon a time I had taken Crevecoeur's gun away from him. Not a fairy-tale. It had been in East Berlin when there was still a Wall to cross to get back to safety. Crevecoeur's intention had been to toss me to the wolves in the Stasi and in return they'd let him fly out. So I took his pistol and got him and myself out and kept his pistol because I believed it had murdered a reporter. It's still in a strongbox in the Kredietbank in Luxembourg, but I can't use it to blackmail Crevecoeur any more. The forensic details of the dead reporter have disappeared along with the Stasi and the Wall and the whole of East Germany.

I kept staring at him and saw the urgency fade from his face. The eyes still looked furious but no longer dangerous. He took a deep breath and the gun dropped away. He turned aside, inspecting the room.

'Why didn't you get out?'

I shrugged. Reasons, explanations, I owed him nothing. He owed me. It was his smart Japanese-designed miniaturized radio transmitters that had landed me here.

'I thought you could get out of anywhere. That was your boast. So why didn't you escape from here?'

'I don't boast.'

He went to the window. Like Inspector Gaudet he twisted his head to squint between the slats of the metal shutters. He could see the sky but not the layout of the grounds. He put an ear to the bars and stayed very still, identifying sounds from outside: muffled traffic, sparrow talk, breeze through leaves, klaxon of a distant truck, pop-pop-pop of a tennis match.

'Let's go,' he said.

'How about Gaudet and his men? What happened to Bernard outside?'

'Want his telephone number?'

Crevecoeur was at the door and I hadn't moved.

'We're wasting time.' He looked at me for a few seconds. 'You're so stubborn, Cody. They're under... Let's say they're in protective custody.'

'The police nab the police. Great. What for?'

'Hindering the Sûreté in carrying out its duties.'

'How?'

'Removing the bug you planted. Preventing you planting a replacement.'

'But you wouldn't know Gaudet had removed the bug until after you'd searched him.'

'He was getting in the light. I wanted him out of it.' Which is what Gaudet had said about Crevecoeur. The difference was, Crevecoeur got his way.

'How did you—'

'Stopped him after he'd come through the gate.' Crevecoeur couldn't wait for me to finish. 'Jean-Louis and Pierre took Gaudet. A pussycat with a paw missing. Then they dodged in while the gate was open and called the man who was waiting outside. Your Bernard.'

I got to ask my question. 'How did you know I was here?'

'Bloody questions,' he said. 'Are you coming? Shall I lock you in?'

It was my rented Peugeot 205 parked a hundred metres from the gate with Al Richards behind the wheel. I like a smile to light up a man's face when he sees me. Al was scowling as we drew close.

My clothes were grubby, I wore no lipstick, my hair was messed, but didn't the essential Cody blaze through these blemishes?

Crevecoeur sat in the back and I chose to sit next to Al. He turned to me. 'What kept you?'

Crevecoeur answered before I could open my mouth. 'She was being difficult.'

'If I wanted to be difficult I could always tell you to get the hell out of my car and walk.'

'Attagirl,' Al said. 'Don't take any more shit from the fucker.'

Al's French is functional, but to express his finer feelings he'd switched to English. *Les anglo-saxons* united in the face of French trickery. The sun was high and sitting in this oven of a car hadn't improved Al's temper. Trickling sweat left trails down his cheeks like tears. A police car drove slowly by and two men eyed us. It continued up the road and headed into the Club des Sports. Al turned the key in the ignition and eased away from the kerb. He took two right turns so that we were heading back towards the city centre. We passed a rash of new houses, then a patch of vineyard some stubborn old peasant wouldn't sell, then a villa in a large overgrown garden. The stucco on the house was coming off in patches and a shutter hung loose. A sign by the gate said *A vendre*. Al pulled the car into the entrance and stopped. We could be prospective buyers and would not draw the attention of passing police.

Crevecoeur leant forward and spoke over my shoulder. 'He's in a bad mood because he went to your hotel this morning and found you weren't in your bed and had to come to me for help.'

Al gripped the wheel and spoke, staring straight ahead. 'I went to your hotel and they said guests weren't allowed up to the rooms, so I had to change their minds.' Al had an ugly look on his face and I could see that creep at the reception desk being hasty in changing his mind when invited to. 'Place is run by a couple of ageing fairies, and the constitution may promise you can be as gay as a knickerbocker glory, but a fairy is still a fairy and here's one farmer's boy who's not taking orders from one. I suppose it was your room they sent me to, but there was nothing of yours in it, the mattress was cold and the towel was dry. So down to the desk again. I invited them to make a voluntary statement about where you were and they suddenly remembered you'd left in the night in the company of two men. What kind of men? Thugs? Cops? This old fruitfly shrugs – who can tell the difference? Got a point.'

This came out in a great torrent. Al rested and took a few breaths. With talking his tension had eased.

'So then I pulled the journalist thing. *Les Platanes,* I wrote in big letters in my reporter's notebook. *Proprietors,* got their names off the tariff sheet pinned on the wall above the desk. Start writing notes right there on the desktop. I had them both out, staring, and they ask what I'm doing. "It's a story for the newspapers," I say, and flash them my press card. I go on writing. "What's it about?" "Safety of tourists in French hotels," I say, "being hauled out of bed by thugs in the middle of the night while the management holds hands behind the bead curtain. Raymond will be along later to take the photos." Et cetera, et cetera.'

Al favoured me with a little smile and stretched his big shoulders.

'So, after five minutes they say they're from North Africa, came over in the big exodus in '62, pals with old man Gaudet, whose son is now an inspector. Naturally the old Algeria hands keep together. They do each other favours, such as passing on names when dubious characters register – recognize yourself, Co? And turning deaf when Gaudet's men mount a little raid. "So how does Inspector Gaudet repay his debts to you?" I asked. "Send down his boys in leather blousons and boots, handcuff you naked and tickle you with their *bidules*?" '

'He's being subtle as only an American knows how,' Crevecoeur said. He was smoking and seemed to have got a scrap of tobacco on his tongue. He wound down the window to spit outside.

'You want to tell the lady the next part,' Al said, 'or you want to pass?'

I was the lady. No name. An excuse for them to clash again.

'What he did was unforgivable—' Crevecoeur began.

'By *he*,' Al cut in, 'he means *me*.'

There was movement outside the car and a truce was declared while we all looked out. A woman in widow's weeds was walking a poodle on a leash. The woman reminded me of Madame Boyer, the same habit of tilting her head back so she could look down her nose. She could smell a sin before you'd had time to commit it. While the poodle cocked a leg against a tree trunk, she glanced from the car to the For Sale sign outside the rotting house. She jerked on the leash to hurry the dog. She looked at us again and her nose wrinkled. Huh, you could see her thinking, perverts looking for a love nest to set up a *menage à trois*. With these two? They'd be at each other's throats twenty-four hours a day and I'd never get a look-in. No wonder the English never bothered to translate the phrase from the French.

When the woman had stomped on her way Crevecoeur said, 'Your American friend phoned Paris, the Sûreté Nationale. Since it's Sunday he got the duty officer, an unfortunate who'll soon be looking for a job sweeping the streets. Richards said he was in Nîmes and had urgent information for Chief Inspector Crevecoeur and needed to contact him within the next thirty minutes. I mean, I've heard the tape of the phone call, got the fool in Paris to play it for me. There Richards is, speaking French with a foul American accent—'

'Come on,' Al said, big grin now, good humour restored, 'you should hear French spoken with a Bronx accent.'

'Now the duty officer is a sick man. He's got a July fever, his wife's gone to visit her mother, his mistress has gone to Saint-Tropez, whatever. Instead of fancy footwork, he comes straight out and asks if it's to do with today's operation and Richards says "Yes" and the fool believes him. Yes,' Crevecoeur finished, with a private look to his eyes, 'that duty officer's health could be permanently impaired.'

I turned from Crevecoeur to Al. 'You knew there was—'

'No, I did not,' he cut me short. 'You want to grow up into a big strong girl reporter, Co, you got to learn to box clever.'

I can lie as well as the next man when it's needed. Richards had that touch of smugness as if only he knew the black arts. El Al.

Crevecoeur said, 'The duty officer told him to go to the Poly Parc. He even told him which office building.'

'I stood in the car park, hands cupped to my mouth,' Al said, action matching his words, 'and yelled, "Crevecoeur, come out, I've got news for you." You've never seen anyone come out so fast in all your born days.'

That was the early-morning heroics. Al had suggested that Crevecoeur get moving, unless he wanted a story about Sûreté bumbling plastered over next day's *AJ*. Crevecoeur used a source inside Nîmes police to find out where Gaudet's men had taken me. And Crevecoeur was in a hideous mood.

'I've no more time,' he said. 'I've got to get to the Poly Parc.'

'He's expecting a party there,' Al said. 'About lunch-time. Could be someone flying in, that's my hunch. I thought we'd drop the Chief Inspector off at the Poly Parc and then sort of hang out at the airport to see who flies in. Unless, of course, you would like to share the secret with us newshounds. Strictly unattributably.'

Crevecoeur looked at his watch. Was it the second or third time?

'Get going,' he said.

The French don't trust a politician who smiles a lot. If he smiles like that, what's he trying to put over the voters? That's why Chirac lost out to Mitterand. Now Chirac is President you don't see him smile at all. If Crevecoeur had been running for President that day, he'd have won by a landslide. His face was closed up in fury. He was barely able to force a cigarette between his lips. We drove in silence for five minutes while he glared out of the window. Al had turned on to boulevard Président Allende then turned off again. We crossed a bridge over the *autoroute* and Crevecoeur frowned at the traffic heading towards Avignon. The Poly Parc was some ten kilometres in that direction. There was no slip-road to join the *autoroute* and Al showed no intention of finding one.

'You said you were taking me to the Poly Parc.'

'Change of plan,' Al said. 'We're going direct to the airport. You can always pick up a taxi there. You've got people staked out at the airport? Leaning against walls, smoking cigarettes, hiding behind newspapers? Suave French guys in designer leather blousons? Not like us American hicks. Well, we'll just fool about and watch them watching the incoming passengers, and when we see them wiggle their ears we'll know who your Mr Big is. Not that we know why he's here, because you won't tell us. Perhaps I might just get out my reporter's pad and pen and interview him. Excuse me, sir, have you come for the bullfights or to chase the girls or maybe catch up on the latest French technological advances? You know us newshounds, always a nose for a story.'

Reporters ask questions. Al didn't. He was talking and not letting Crevecoeur get a word in. It was like keeping the lid on a pressure cooker.

Al knew that.

'Pull in over there.'

Al stopped the car where Crevecoeur had pointed. It was the entrance to a garden centre with piles of terracotta urns by the gate. Beyond the fence were rows of the young pine trees that the French plant in the middle of the lawn, because it turns their *jardin* into a *pare*.

'You can't use this story,' Crevecoeur began.

It would have been fatal to show triumph because Crevecoeur might just have got out and walked away. Al Richards must have understood that, because he went right the other way. He hunched round in his seat. 'Are you threatening me?'

'I'm telling you. If you print this you'll be thrown out of France. Not by me. The politicians will do it. I couldn't prevent it even if I wanted to. You might not even make it to the plane alive. You'd be got at. Again, not by me. You could always ask for police protection if you thought your life was threatened, but after today how much protection do you think the police would give you?'

Al squared up to challenge Crevecoeur and decided against it.

Crevecoeur said, 'The information comes from the Air France reservations computer. That's how we knew he was coming to France.'

Crevecoeur was busy with his cigarettes and lighter again. Al glanced at me and I shook my head: no, I didn't know who Crevecoeur was talking about; no, don't interrupt, let him tell it his way.

'Let's call him the Man. He comes from a certain foreign power... No, you can't know which country. I'm not telling you every secret the Sûreté possesses. Richards, I'm only indulging you because if I don't you'll get in the way, which could be fatal.'

Again Crevecoeur paused, drew on his cigarette, flicked a look at me. And perhaps he's speaking because there's a bit of guilt there. I wouldn't have thought Crevecoeur had a conscience, but there was a definite reluctance to meet my eyes. He'd used me and I'd ended up in a cell, so now he was making amends by drawing one or two veils aside and showing a glimpse of what lay underneath.

'Let's say the Man comes from Libya. Or it could be Syria. Maybe the Yemen, maybe Iraq. If you saw him you'd think he could even be Armenian or an Azeri or a Kurd. Somewhere in there.'

Another glance at me. Take your pick, he was saying, there are a lot of wolves roaming the forest.

'The computer told us the Man was flying to Paris via Rome. He was careful not to travel Air France but, where the traffic is shared with certain death-rattle airlines from Third World countries, it's the Air France computer system that all passenger names get put into. That's how we got on to him. His is one of the names that is automatically flashed to the Sûreté when he books a flight. The next indicator we got was that his embassy had booked for the following day, that is today,' and Crevecoeur studied his watch, 'a flight from Paris to Nîmes on Air Inter for someone of a different name. That name does not appear on their diplomatic list, so we assumed it was our man. But we didn't know why he was coming. Our first alert was sixteen days ago and for three days we scratched our heads.

'Then chance or luck or God gave us the next clue. One of the companies in the Poly Parc let out a scream for help. Their mainframe crashed and the IBM engineer who came to fix it said: "Hey, why is it wired up to the telephone system?" It wasn't the telephone link-up that had caused the trouble, that was just the chance thing I talked of. Now that is a company doing very sensitive work affecting the security of France. Someone came down from Paris to have a look, then thought to check other businesses in the Poly Parc and found no fewer than eight had the same hook-up. All the systems had been installed by Systel, or in the case of the IBM mainframe, Systel had been called in for advice on compatibility with micros. Systel was funded through finance houses, a bank out in the Dutch Antilles and nominees and all the other camouflage of international big money. But ultimately – our enquiries turned up – ultimately it was owned by a Marseille gangster and Ledru was the man in charge on the spot. You know about the surveillance on Ledru's house. Thanks to the bug you put in place,' Crevecoeur gave me a nod, 'we found out which company the Man was interested in. Then, unfortunately, the bug was discovered and made inoperative.'

'That was Inspector Gaudet,' I said. 'Gaudet says he wanted to be the one to break the gang.'

'You fell for that? You don't know the scale of this thing. It's out of Gaudet's league. All he'd do was squeeze Ledru for a few hundred thousand francs. I know his type.'

I thought of Gaudet wanting to keep Gabizzi's mob out to make the city safe for the small-time crooks he knew. It didn't seem worth while riding out in his defence.

'Let's go,' Crevecoeur said to Al.

'You haven't finished.'

'I have to check certain arrangements at the Poly Parc.'

Al sat tight. 'What's the company?'

'You see they chose a Sunday,' Crevecoeur said, answering a different question. 'Place is deserted. They can show the Man how they got a copy of the computer file, show him it's genuine and worth the asking price.'

'What is it? Guidance system for the Ariane? Pulsecoding for the battlefield radio? Places you mentioned are hungry for stuff like that.'

'I'll tell you while you're driving.'

Al got the engine going, waited for a gap in the traffic and swung out.

'What the Man is interested in is RP Chimie.'

Al braked to a sudden halt. 'Don't give me that crap. RP Chimie has a lab where they cook up artificial flavours for ice-cream and drinks.'

I was watching Crevecoeur and saw the hint of a smile. 'Relieved to hear it. In my world, Richards, that's known as good cover.'

Al was watching Crevecoeur in the mirror. Without a word he got the car moving again.

'France has no chemical weapons, of course, but what it does have is anti-chemical weapons research. For research purposes very small amounts, strictly limited, of chemical weapons have to be produced.'

I said, 'They keep all that stuff well away from population centres.'

Now he turned his attention to me. His feeling of guilt at having used me had been purged.

'Manufacture and full testing indeed take place in restricted rural areas,' he said. 'But research and small-scale laboratory tests are carried out at the Poly Parc. The research is at a very advanced stage. It is to do with combating the semi-persistent nerve agents sarin and soman and the persistent nerve agent VX. Currently there are certain antidotes that can be injected at the time of the attack. You have eight seconds to make the injection or you are dead. What RP Chimie are developing is the chemical equivalent of a vaccine for the three common nerve gases. The Americans have a similar programme, but the RP Chimie product gives ten weeks' protection. No need for stinking hot suits or grabbing your needle, if there is an attack, or second inoculations. No side-effects either, they claim, no Gulf War syndrome. It's worth a fortune, as well as rendering certain weapons of mass destruction obsolete.'

'Jesus,' Al whispered. He wiped the back of a hand across his forehead.

You can work out in the gym until your muscles scream and the sweat is like tropical rain drenching your body. You can practise all kinds of fancy martial arts. You can fight shoulder-to-shoulder with the mujaheddin in the mountain passes and show no fear. But mention chemical weapons and the strongest man gets an attack of the shakes. It's more than fear. It's dread. The unseen enemy is going to invade your body while you twist and turn in agony before dying. And there's not a thing you can do.

'So you're going to wait in the bushes and spring out on Ledru and the Man?' I asked.

'More sophisticated than that, but yes. Because of the nature of the danger – they keep small stocks of the nerve agents at the lab – I've had to call on certain elements of the 11th Shock Regiment—'

'Just a moment,' I cut him short. 'Stocks of the nerve agents and the inoculation are actually kept at the lab?'

'Limited quantities for research and testing.'

'What time is the Man's flight?'

'11.10 departure from Orly.'

A terrible idea was forming in my mind.

'Al, find us a telephone. Hurry.'

Crevecoeur looked as if he was on the brink of a heart attack. His pallor was unearthly.

'The Man was a no-show for the 11.10,' he said, leaning in through the car window. 'But someone who fits his description caught the 9.10. Bought a ticket at the airport. Paid cash.'

'More,' I said. 'Give.'

'No activity at the Poly Parc. He hasn't gone there. He's vanished.'

I closed my eyes. Crevecoeur was a solitary, taking all the responsibility on his shoulders, never sharing. In this case he'd had to post men in the field to watch the *mas*. He was an opportunist so he'd made use of me to place the bug. Finally he'd called in the cloak-and-dagger elements of the 11th Shock, but only because he had to. At heart he was a loner, but if he'd used his organization properly, posted agents, had the Man followed, liaised with Gaudet rather than fighting him, covered all the important sectors, well, he wouldn't be in this mess now.

I said, 'Who were the two men who flew down with you yesterday? Come on, you've told us everything else.'

He said, 'From the Quai d'Orsay.'

The Man was so politically sensitive it needed Foreign Ministry clearance to arrest him. But the Man was lost. Crevecoeur had posted a single field agent at Nîmes airport, but the Man had already landed by the time he was in position.

I said, '*You* think they chose a Sunday because the Poly Parc would be deserted. I think Ledru chose a Sunday because his gang could break in on Saturday night to steal the nerve gases and the inoculation antidote and no one would find out until Monday, and by then the Man could be anywhere.'

'There are sophisticated alarm systems—'

'Crevecoeur, they've been going in and out fixing the computer installations. They've fixed the alarm system too. They're good at that kind of thing. They're a professional gang. If they wanted to draw money from a bank, they wouldn't wait until the bank opened its doors on Monday morning, they'd do it when the bank was deserted. They're experts.'

Crevecoeur took a long breath and got out his packet of Gitanes and lighter. We were in the forecourt of a Total station and a man shouted out to ask if he was blind, couldn't he read the sign? Crevecoeur got in the car. He was reordering events in his mind, working out what had to be done, who warned, what help he had to call on, even if it meant using Inspector Gaudet and roadblocks and helicopter searches.

I said, 'They haven't gone up in the hills and found a nice deserted field to talk business. I know what they're doing. I *know*.'

I knew it right there in my stomach where the muscles had tightened, and in my chest where there was no breath, and in my throat which had squeezed tight, and in the palms of my hands where the sweat sprang.

'More than just saying: Here's the formula?' Al said.

'More, much more.'

'I'll get someone to check inside the RP Chimie lab,' Crevecoeur said.

'You mean you had no guard inside overnight?'

'There are closed-circuit cameras and a check by a security patrol—'

'Whose timetable Systel well knows. Think of the closed-circuit cameras along the fence at the farmhouse. I got past those. There's always a way. I know what's being planned.'

Crevecoeur's mind was off somewhere else.

'Can you hear me? I know what they're going to do. Maybe it's already too late.'

At last, with great reluctance, he gave me his full attention. 'All right, what's your theory?'

CHAPTER SEVENTEEN

The sun's power had bleached the colour out of the sky, leaving it exhausted and empty. I stared up and then down at the road taking the curve up the final hill.

'You're going too fast.'

'No bloody time to lose,' Al said.

'It's the engine noise. We'll lose everything if the sound lifts over the hill and they hear.'

No, it wasn't empty after all. A bird circled. I'd seen that bird before. I couldn't remember which day, in a different lifetime. It wasn't a crow or a vulture, looking for carrion. It was a hawk or a kite and it wanted live meat. It was black against the aching sky, wheeling in great arcs, eyes searching the ground for movement, mouse, lizard, snake. As I watched it pulled up as if an unseen hand had clutched it, then wings folded and neck pulled in, it plunged down. It passed from sight beyond the rim of the hill and if there was a scream from its prey it didn't reach me.

We were almost at the top of the hill when Al pulled the car to the side of the road.

'What are you looking at?'

Not the bird any longer. 'Sun flashes off metal or glass,' I said. 'Looking for, not at.'

It was possible they had posted a man out here. The road was barely used and the odds were that any car coming down it had business at the *mas*. Today – if I was correct – they ought to be taking extra precautions. We searched the hillside and the horizon and saw nothing. I still believed I was correct, even if they hadn't posted a look-out. We stood outside the car in the full heat of the sun and double-checked. A look-out would need shade and so our eyes hunted through each olive tree, leaves, branches, trunk. Negative. Well then – consider Max, Ledru, Marius, all the others, consider the nature of such men. They would be engrossed in the girls, in their nakedness, their vulnerability, their behaviour. The outside world would no longer exist in their minds.

I touched Al's arm and gestured to him to leave the car doors open. We might need to leave fast. We headed for an outcrop of rocks. Crouching among them we had a view down to the *mas*. Two men guarded the gate. Five cars were parked in the yard. All the cars were black as if it was this year's fashion colour.

Just an edge of terrace jutted beyond the farmhouse. Nobody was in sight.

'Could be you're wrong,' Al murmured. 'Could be they're all inside having a little old Medellin-type get-together. Your nose candy, Mr Man, against our secret—'

'I'm right.'

'You're acting on a hunch, Co. You could—'

'I'm right.'

He sighed but otherwise he was quiet. His eyes took in the stubbornness of my face and returned to the cluster of cars and buildings.

'So what now? Knit socks? Wait for the cavalry?'

We'd left Crevecoeur hunched over the telephone, making calls to the Poly Parc, to his own operations centre, to a Colonel Paga in the 11th Shock Regiment. Crevecoeur had said, one hand over the mouthpiece: 'They were planning an ambush and now it's an assault. How quickly can the military mind adapt?'

I said, 'If we wait for Crevecoeur and whatever he puts together, we could be too late. The Man came in two hours early. There's a chance we're too late already, but I can't just sit back like … like …'

The parallel of the Roman arena in Nîmes was in my mind, but it was too fanciful to put to a farmer's boy from the Midwest. The idea of prisoners being thrust into the arena while the lions paced and the spectators edged forward on their seats...

I got to my feet and began to move.

'Co,' he said so loudly I thought the guards might hear. 'We can't do any good on our own.'

There was a sort of appeal in Al's voice. I thought of his horror when I'd laid out the scenario. I said, 'You can't come because Ledru knows you. You've got to stay here, for when the rescue team comes thundering along the road. Make them understand what's in there.'

It was a kindness, giving him a task outside.

I could hear their voices from the pool. They sounded so young, girlish laughter, all the teenage fun and games they'd missed.

Sweat was running down my neck from the sun, from dodging between rocks, from running bowed low round the back of the property, from the same dread that paralysed Al and turned Crevecoeur's face white.

I'm not too late – that's what the sound of voices and laughter meant to me. They're just girls – that's what it meant to Ledru.

'Give me your shirt,' I'd told Al. My voice must have been harsher than I meant. He didn't even ask why. Also I'd taken the jack from the car. Best I could do. I wasn't planning anything elaborate, none of those ornate exercises they carry out at training school with code names and passwords and blackboards with different-coloured chalks and contingency plans and fall-back positions. There could be no falling back.

I used the stormwater culvert I'd used the first time I'd visited the *mas,* when I was big-headed and wanted to show I could stroll into their guarded fortress. I'd thought the concrete tunnel would act like an echo chamber for the girls' voices, but all I heard was grit under my belly. At the end were the strands of barbed wire that had been added after my show-off entry. I squirmed along on my stomach, head knocking the concrete, pushing the jack in front of me. When the culvert came to an end I got to work. I had no wirecutters, but the jack would do the job. I forced it between two strands of wire and began cranking.

Memo to Peugeot: Have you ever tried using the jack from one of your 205 models while lying prone in a concrete tube? Do you realize how difficult, how bloody difficult it is to stop the jack from slipping clear of the strands of barbed wire before expansion takes up the slack?

I composed the blast in my head to take my mind off the silence that had come over the terrace area. The jack slipped once, shooting free of the wire on the wrong side, and I put a gash along my elbow retrieving it.

When the jack was fully expanded I studied the gap it had opened up and knew it was too small. I'd never make it. But I had to make it, because I couldn't go to the front gate and ring the bell. I wrapped Al's shirt round the lower set of barbs and wriggled. I could feel a parting dividing my hair, and then my own shirt snagging and ripping and then a prick and graze over my bum to add to all the other scrapes.

I was a miracle of speed but it still took half a minute and the silence from the terrace was unbroken.

It had been at this point on my first entry that I'd been confronted by shoes and had looked up into a pistol, but not today. I unwrapped the shirt and got to my feet and crossed in six swift steps to the tree with the camera covering this stretch of garden. The shirt covered the lens and the sleeves tied it up. I doubted anyone was hunched over the security monitors. Anyone on duty would be riveted by the naked play at the poolside. But he might give a quick check. To see a blacked-out screen meant that a fuse had blown. To see me creeping up the slope towards the house was something else.

I used what cover there was, yuccas, oleanders, a stone pine. I had to get close because if I was seen at a distance one of the gang – Marius, Max, Alain – would be ordered to deal with me. If I succeeded in getting close, it was Ledru I would speak to. But as I stepped out from behind a drift of sweet jasmine I knew I was too late.

There was a path of smooth paving slabs leading towards the pool, which from this angle seemed to have the shape of Australia. The house was where the Great Barrier Reef would be and the waterfall drenched Melbourne. I knew I was seeing everything out of scale. I was flying high, scared. The house could have been an ocean liner with all its portholes battened down against a storm. Those double-glazed doors and windows were tight shut and the faces, ten or a dozen, stared out. They were all male, but they showed none of the eagerness of men gathered to watch a scene from a porno movie.

And I knew I was being proved right. I'd said to Crevecoeur that I knew what was being planned. We'd been sitting in the car in the Total forecourt and he was desolated because he'd lost track of the Man. I looked along the faces at the windows and thought I could pick him out, two away from Gabizzi, dark features, dark hair, dark suit, dark tie. A type more than an individual. You'd say he was a businessman here to conclude a deal and you'd be right. Except the deal had nothing to do with a blue film.

I'd had to say it more than once to get through to Crevecoeur: 'I know where they are. More important, I know what they're doing.'

Even then he'd just gawped at me. It was Al who had said, 'It's something very particular.' It was as if Al knew, had picked up my thought patterns.

'Yes,' I had said, 'you could say very particular.' At last Crevecoeur had given me his full attention, so I'd let him have it all. 'In order to win over the Man they're laying on a demonstration. Where they all are is the *mas*. To be one hundred per cent convincing it has to be a controlled experiment. Two guinea pigs – human guinea pigs. I'm not inventing all this,

I've seen them. Couple of girls. I don't know what story Ledru has fed them, but they are the kind of girls who are open to just about any kind of suggestion. I'll tell you what's going to happen. I haven't got the proof of it but I *know* – It's the logic of it all. One will be injected with something neutral. The other will be given the antidote. Then, in front of everybody, they'll be exposed to the nerve gases. One will die and one will live and the Man will be convinced. There is nothing more persuasive than the evidence of your own eyes. One living breathing girl, one corpse.'

There'd been a few seconds' silence in the car while Al's face grew sick and Crevecoeur's face shifted through amazement and rejection and settled into belief. The logic of it all, as I'd said. Then he went racing to the telephone.

I looked away from the faces at the windows to the waterfall. The girls stood naked. The titian-curled one was rubbing her forearm. The blonde one was looking down as a needle probed a vein. Ledru was beside them. He wore a fawn suit today in honour of his client. Beyond him a man had what looked like a clay-pigeon launcher set up by the house, hard by a door.

I heard the titian one say, 'Why are there so many, please?'

Ledru replied, 'They are all to do with the film. You see the one holding the video camera – he's inside to keep the sun out of the lens. There are technicians and the director and the writer who's going to polish the script. The man in the dark suit – not the little one, the other – he's the distributor who'll be responsible for the Middle East.'

'And who is she, please?' She lifted her arm to point.

Ledru turned and saw me.

It's human to forget the ugly times in life. The terrifying moments, the dangers, the shameful defeats, they're in our memory core, deep, buried away. But I'll never forget the venom in his expression and his voice.

'Who let you in? What do you want here?'

I tried the Cody smile. It turned out to win enemies and land me in the dirt. 'Looks like party time again.' The light touch.

'Want to join? Strip your clothes off and pile in.' Ledru made a visible effort to get control of himself. 'No, forget it. Why have you come?'

All I was trying to do was buy time. There was no question of my mounting a rescue mission for the girls. In any case, the kind of people who wanted to save them were the kind of people they were running away from. Nor could I attack Ledru or the man with the launcher, because there were a dozen men inside and probably a dozen guns. I had only one card in my hand so I played it.

'It's about the killer of Agnès.'

He stretched himself fully upright and came forward a step. 'Well?'

'I told you yesterday I had his name. Now I can give you the proof he did it and what you're really after – the place he's hiding.' Which was massaging the truth. I still didn't know where Doicescu was. There'd been no time to check if he'd taken the bait of the ad.

It was all I could do. I was putting my trust in Ledru's bruised male pride, wanting revenge on the man who'd taken his woman from him. I had to believe that was more powerful than his greed and his business with the girls and the nerve gas, if only for fifteen minutes. Then I saw I'd lost.

'I'm busy. Contact me later this afternoon. And make an appointment this time.'

'He might have moved on.'

'Then you go and watch him. That's your job.' He turned to the blonde girl.

I searched for more objections. 'It could be he's about to leave the country.'

I'd gone too far. Ledru's head lifted and he turned back to me. 'Where did you put your car?' His voice seemed to have grown angrier, rumbling at me.

'Out there.'

'Why didn't you come in the front gate? Why did you break in through the security fence? Why do you always come sneaking in? Who are you really?'

The rumble was more distinct and it wasn't in his voice. When he stopped speaking it grew louder. It could have been thunder, except the sky was still cloudless.

'Why don't you answer? What's your game?'

'I wasn't sneaking—'

I stopped.

They came low over the hill, hugging the contours, which is why the warning time had been so short. There were two of them, Alouette helicopters with camouflage markings. Their windows were of armoured glass and caught the sun and flashed urgent messages. Everyone stared at the sky and for several seconds there was no movement. This could be the army out on normal manoeuvres, or going to fight a forest fire, or chauffeuring the general to Sunday lunch. Then the helicopters stopped in midair, their tales swinging gently as if a tide had caught them, and began to drop. Both machines had their doors open and soldiers were bunched in the gaps. They wore chemical warfare suits, their faces were hidden by masks, they carried weapons like mechanics' tools. They looked nothing like your friendly *poilu*, more like invaders from an outer galaxy. They were men of the 11th Shock, who had the reputation of shooting first and if you asked questions shooting again.

'You bitch,' Ledru said. He swung back towards me, his hand snaking inside his jacket. His face showed a full understanding of betrayal, even if he didn't know how it had come about. 'You brought them.'

The french windows had been pulled open and the men inside had piled out, shouting. There were screams from the girls, who seemed suddenly conscious of being naked and were frightened by the soldiers' battledress. A full-scale war was in prospect until the man with the launcher decided to be a hero. He would send a projectile through the gaping door of one of the helicopters, no matter that the soldiers were in protective suits. Maybe the pilot wasn't. Instead it hit the side. I saw it bounce back to earth and burst open, fizzing. A cloud of gas like a drift of autumn mist was released into the air and was caught by the downdraught of the rotors. It swirled towards the swimming pool and the house and, as it spread, it became invisible so there was no telling where death was stealing. What had been chaos before, with men waving guns and running to shelter behind pillars, changed to panic. I had glimpses of running figures, bursts of automatic fire, windows shattering, pale shirts turning dark, of titian curls and blonde spikes and open mouths. There were screams of terror and pain.

The Israelis might win a seven-day war. This was over in sixty seconds.

I turned and sprinted to get the house between me and the lapping waves of unseen gas.

Crevecoeur only had time to say to me, 'Take her inside and find her some clothes.' Then he was gone because there were angry shouts and more trouble threatened and the 11th Shock weren't in the mood to be taking any prisoners if it came to a fight again.

Cut-off jeans and a T-shirt were in a pile by the french windows. I picked them up and handed them to her.

'These aren't mine.'

'You'll damn well put them on, unless you want the whole of the 11th Shock going through you.'

A little rough talk was the way to get inside her head. She got dressed, the girl with the blonde spiky hair. The clothes would have belonged to the girl with titian curls. No bra, no knickers. Only got in the way.

We went into Ledru's office with the closed shutters and the mother-in-law's tongue, where we'd be out of the way but available. I found the bottle and poured us both a good slug of the Macallan. The bottle chattered against the lip of the glass, but she had the calmness of the very young or the very stupid.

She told me her real name was Monique, but that wasn't chic enough so about the time she chopped her pony-tail off, she chopped her name and became Mini.

'Two little syllables that speak of today, yes?' She ran fingers through the spikes of her hair. 'Like mini-skirt. Hide the goal but show the way. More interesting, more sexy, don't you agree?'

Well, there was Minnie Mouse but I don't think even Mickey thought her specially sexy.

Also at the time she topped and tailed her name she became blonde. 'The women who attract men are all blonde. Haven't you noticed?'

I said I'd remember her advice.

She walked to the window and stared at the shutters as if she could see out to the terraced hillside where the olive trees grew and the sun shone. She wandered back and sat in a chair and closed her eyes. She thought she was hard and had seen life, but she suddenly began to shake.

'Tell me about it if you want.' Sometimes unburdening yourself to a stranger is a relief.

'Oh shit,' she said. She ran her fingers through her hair again and started to talk. Once started, she couldn't stop. 'The beginning, I suppose, was going to the Crow and Rick's Hole. I was almost fifteen. Rick's Hole used to be *the* place but of course it's dead now, old people, marrieds, soldiers, that sort.'

These were discos in Marseille, and I was asked about discos in Paris. I said I'd been to Le Palace but she'd have been more impressed if I'd said I'd been to prison.

'I met this *mec* there, and he had this scar on one cheek like those Nazi officers in old war films and it was really sexy. He asked how old I was and I said eighteen. You always say eighteen. I've been eighteen for three years now and I've decided I'm going to stay eighteen. I can imagine being twenty. Twenty-one, that sounds a whole different life. Anyway I lived with this *mec* and he didn't treat me bad, didn't knock me about or anything, except a couple of times. But he used to come home with these friends and he'd say: "You can do it with her if you like." And I'd say: "Hey, how about asking me? Doesn't my opinion count?" And he'd say: "Shut that little hole in your face, he's not interested in that one." He wasn't threatening, not really, just telling. Actually, I didn't think his friends were so terrific. Well, they weren't friends, not what you and I would call friends, just people he met. Some of them, well the things I could tell would make you laugh. One guy brought a lobster, I mean a *live* lobster. In your wildest dreams can you imagine doing it with a lobster? He said he would tie the claws, but I said no. I mean those eyes staring at me and those stalk things waving around when it got excited.'

The voices outside had stopped for the moment. Had they been taken away? Handcuffed? Gagged? It wasn't silent. The helicopters still made long, low passes overhead, their rotors dissipating any pockets of nerve gas that lingered.

Mini was grinning and then her face worked itself into a frown.

'I was so innocent then. I didn't even know these men were paying my *mec*. Then I found out and said I wanted a split, and he hit me with a hammer and I tried to protect myself, and he hit me on the hands and it really hurt. But he gave me a needle to stop it hurting and we went to bed and it was all right. Next day I went to hospital and he'd broken three fingers so I got out of his place.'

There were other men after that. But it was her first *mec* that was most vivid in her mind. The clubs changed and the men changed. Or the men stayed the same but their faces and names changed. Somewhere along the way the needle became more demanding and she had the scars on her arms to prove it. Mostly she wore long-sleeved things. But when it came to the swimming-pool scene, that was all right because she was completely naked.

'The men aren't interested in my arms. Real men aren't.' Mini said it as a simple truth. 'Fact. I've seen a postcard of that statue, Venus Milady Something, and she doesn't have arms but she's got on all right.'

And how did she get to be at Ledru's *mas*?

Mini was with her friend Annelise, the one with the titian curls. Annelise had got out from something in Hamburg and had passed through Liège and Lyon and beached at Marseille. They were in Sergeant Pepper's (discos had to have English names for added glamour) and got drinking with this man Marius. It was two nights ago. He'd said: How would they like to be in films? And Mini had said: Hey, come on, that's the oldest gag in the book. And Marius said: No, truly. Films for the export market, special films, adventurous films, but he guessed they were girls who wouldn't mind doing one or two adventurous things, especially if the money was okay. And Mini said, or maybe it was Annelise: What kind of things? And he said: Well, the kind of things you do every night, only this time with a camera behind a potted palm.

Which is how Mini and Annelise got to be at Ledru's *mas*, frolicking naked round the swimming pool.

'Excuse me a minute,' I said, 'I'll be right back.'

For my own sanity I had to look somewhere else than at Mini, her body that had been so used and abused, her voice that droned on, her opinions that were so destructive, her life that was racing down a one-way street with a brick wall at the end.

You see them in every city, their life's ambition being to beg the money for the next trip. They'll put their hand out and if that doesn't work they'll offer the rest of their body. They are without hope.

From the corridor I looked out at the terrace. No sign of Al. The soldiers had their masks off and underneath they wore camouflage paint. Perhaps that was from the time they were preparing an ambush at the Poly Parc. They were standing in a line at the end of the terrace, facing the house, weapons in their hands. A man – maybe an army doctor – was kneeling at the side of the pool, but I didn't stay to see more.

'Real turn-off is André,' Mini started straight off, the moment I returned, as if she'd been dying to tell me. 'See how fat he's getting round his gut? He's old too, and his breath smells. Have you kissed him? Like kissing an ashtray. His bedroom's got all his wife's things in. The closet and the dressing-table and the drawers. I had a look but there's nothing that suited me. It's all really mouldy stuff. Where's she gone anyway?'

'She died,' I said, 'a week ago.' About a week. The days were a blur.

'A week?' When she thought about things, a frown disturbed her smooth face. She primped her hair and recovered. 'Well, doing it after a week, in my opinion that's disgusting.'

I don't know if Mini would have thought it disgusting if the wife was alive.

'Anyway there was this film, you see. And we were perfect because Annelise was a carrot-top and I was a blondie and the film was for the Middle East. Those Arab men go crazy over girls like us because we look so exotic. We'd been paid something already, so they weren't just having a look for free. André explained the movie but I didn't really understand. He said it was like the Garden of Eden, only there were two Eves and the snake was Adam and he did the tempting. Or it was Adam's own snake that did the tempting. Something like that. André called that the concept. We were going to do a scene here for a test. There's this waterfall coming into the swimming pool, and Annelise and me would be in the spray soaping each other and doing stuff with a sponge. He said they would move branches and things round the waterfall so it looked like it was in the jungle where the real Garden of Eden had been. Also they'd fire off this smoke thing to give some artificial mist, make it more sexy. Then this man comes out of the leaves and he's wearing just a loincloth. Sort of like Tarzan. Only I don't think Tarzan ever gets to do it on the screen and that's what this guy does. There's a bit of chasing and we let ourselves be caught, then he whips off his loincloth and we go aaargh! I mean we've never seen anything like it in our lives. And we've got to look excited and frightened all at once, which is difficult because I was practising in the bathroom this morning. I tried it several times – aaargh! – because his *zob* is so huge it's going to split us open, well nearly.'

She ran her fingers through her hair again. She was one of those girls whose first thought when life grows tough is how they look. Touching her own body reassured her.

'Between you and me, I don't mind being hurt a teeny bit,' she said. 'Better than those men you can hardly see. Don't you think?'

'So you were going to have Tarzan today, but you had André last night?'

'You jealous or something? You're welcome to him. Anyway, he was the boss, he was paying. He said there'd be others watching this morning because that's how it was with a film test, to see how we acted in front of the camera. But they'd all be inside, behind closed doors, so they wouldn't make us nervous. Then he said…'

She took a drink of Scotch, which she hadn't touched until now.

'He said he thought we ought to have a little something to loosen us up, because he said a film camera often made people freeze, even natural fun types like us. What he wanted was for us to throw our inhibitions away with our clothes. So what he had were these two hypodermics, one for me and one for Annelise.'

And Mini came to a complete stop. She took another drink. She tried running her hand through her hair again and touching a cheek but this time it gave her no comfort. Other events, making a dirty movie, her own past, seemed hazy to her, as if these things had happened to a third person. Now she'd run smack into reality and couldn't cope.

'Oh God.'

She began to convulse in sobs, a hand knuckling tears from her eyes. I didn't reach out. I didn't pat her shoulder and murmur: There, there, it'll all be better soon. If she suffered and felt remorse, it offered a chance for her survival in the long run. She might escape from her long-drawn-out suicide.

She might.

But then I thought of seeing her as I stepped out from the jasmine, her body naked and abandoned to whoever wanted to see, her face avid for one more experience.

'Why have you left her?' Crevecoeur asked.

'She's sobbing her heart out. I'll go back when she's got most of it out of her system. She'll need someone then because she'll be so low. What's the news?'

'We got most of them,' Crevecoeur said. 'We caught the Man, who tried to claim diplomatic status but his government will say they've never heard of him. We got the gang boss who put up the money for Systel. And we landed some small fish.' You couldn't tell from his voice whether he was pleased.

Three he didn't get were at the edge of the pool. They could have been sunbathers who'd decided they'd had enough for the day. One was the titian-curled girl whose nakedness was covered by a towel. Then there was a man in a twisted position as if he'd doubled up in agony. A long cushion from one of the sun-loungers covered most of him. Another man must have been so messy from gunshot wounds he was already tied up in a body bag.

'Is that—' I began.

'No,' Crevecoeur said. 'Ledru got away.'

CHAPTER EIGHTEEN

A colonel from the Rangers gave a pep talk to us budding spies once. He addressed us all as 'gentlemen' and flicked hostile eyes at me. He was going to talk about 'low-intensity conflict'. Perhaps, I thought, he's delivering a warning against marriage. He spoke in a sort of military camouflage, using words to conceal meaning. What he meant was: a small war. And that's what we'd just had – a battle in miniature, helicopters, sub-machine guns, nerve gas, corpses.

Crevecoeur picked up a cigarette packet dropped on the terrace and I stopped him before he opened it.

'Didn't you say the nerve gases in that lab were persistent? What'll you be putting into your lungs?'

Crevecoeur let the packet fall. The helicopters had been used to flush the air clean but you never knew what might be trapped in a box. A pin-head is enough. In fact, the release of gas had been tiny and fully dispersed, but even the idea of poison gas preys on the nerves.

We could hear Al Richards coming, his voice lifting over the house, first in French, then in English, because saying it all twice meant he gained extra time and extra steps. They came round the corner of the house, a soldier with an assault rifle walking backwards as Al pressed him on the democratic rights of a free press. Then, spotting his target Crevecoeur, Al put on a passable Southern gentleman's drawl, dragging out the vowels until they were torture. 'And you, sir, I'll have you understand that the constitution of these United States guarantees its citizens life, liberty and the pursuit of women, so you stop pointing that thing at my balls, son.'

'Get him out,' Crevecoeur said.

'You're not thinking straight.' Al moved the soldier gently aside and spoke direct to Crevecoeur. 'You've had more than a police action here, you've had a military strike. In about thirty minutes from now you're going to have every reporter and stringer from Nîmes out here, and after lunch they'll be coming from Nice and Marseille, where they appreciate a good body count, and this evening from Paris. I'm the first of the many. And if you try to keep them all outside the gate and pretend nothing's happened – or, worse, that it's so damned secret even your own grandmother couldn't be trusted with it – why, they are going to make up wild, *wild* stories. So this is your only chance to deal with one reporter who knows the score and who you can hopefully point in the right direction. Because after me it's the ratpack.'

On. There was more. Al's style, I was beginning to appreciate, was to go centre stage and make a speech until the other person was bursting to talk. Al inspected the scene and got unattributable quotes, and was warned to keep the nature of RP Chimie's research out of the story.

'Straight industrial espionage,' Crevecoeur said.

'I've got to build it up. The 11th Shock doesn't get involved just because someone steals the formula for cherryade. A scheme to catch the Mr Big from the troubled sheikhdoms of the Middle East – that story runs and runs. Maybe this one's the Mr Big of all the Mr Bigs. Oil billions, arms shopping lists, bribery and corruption, boozing and whoring, all nipped in the bud under the ever-vigilant eye of—'

'And keep my name out of it,' Crevecoeur said.

Al drove back to Nîmes to write his story and be near a fax machine. I had to hang around because there was no other woman to chaperone Mini. Try chaperoning a hedgehog. After she'd cried on my shoulder a bit, she had no more time for me. She got a pout to her lips and her nose up in the air and she wandered out. She'd find one of the soldiers in warpaint to sniff round.

Alone in Ledru's office I pushed back the shutters and looked up the hill at the animal shelter where the Sûreté had staked out. The shutters had got me here. If they'd been open, the Sûreté team's electronic ears would have heard Ledru's plans. I wouldn't have had my arm twisted to plant the bug. I ran my fingers over the shutters. They were absolutely ordinary, see them on every house in France, keep the burglars out, stop the neighbours watching *monsieur* and *madame* in the bedroom.

'He's not up there.'

It was Crevecoeur at the door behind me.

'Helicopters went out and reported back. All they found were cigarette ends and beer-bottle caps, so the soldiers said the place was used for lovers' romps. Did they look at the ground? The rocks? It would puncture the woman's backside. Shitkickers, that's all they are.'

It was anger that had brought him in here. A mob of journalists was collecting at the gate, *gendarmes* had arrived in force, soldiers trampled down the flowers, helicopters blew up a dust storm, a dull-eyed girl wanted to sell her story to the highest bidder and would probably throw in service for nothing, the telephone screamed and screamed until Crevecoeur ordered it left off the hook, and the strain was showing.

In the chaos with the helicopters arriving and the nerve gas being loosed off, nobody had noticed Ledru slip away. The gate through the security fence in the rear was found open.

'I've told them to fetch a tracker dog. It's the end of the twentieth century and we've nothing more sophisticated than a dog's nose. We'll find the trail leading to the road over the hill and then nothing. He's stopped a car. By this evening he can be anywhere, because we can't block every crappy little road and farm track. He's got friends in Marseille and Paris. He can get away in a fishing boat or an executive jet. Or he can stroll across the border into Spain like the ETA terrorists do.'

Crevecoeur sat down at the desk and opened drawers, rummaged and closed them. It wasn't a methodical search for Ledru's little black address book. I think he hoped to come across a packet of Gitanes, even a loose cigarette.

'He's good at getting out of tight corners,' I said. I was thinking of what Crevecoeur had told me up on the hill, of Ledru slipping out of jail in Benin when the coup he was involved in fizzled out.

'Wherever he goes, he better choose his country damn carefully,' Crevecoeur said. 'One that doesn't owe France any favours.' He began counting on his fingers. 'Evasion of taxes, supplying drugs, computer fraud, theft of defence secrets, murder... We're not talking unpaid parking fines here.'

He said to come alone so I came alone. He said to go to the Maison Carrée and then to walk to the little square a block away on the west side, so I did that, exactly as he said, even though I was coming from the west anyway and had to retrace my tracks. He said to be there at 9.30, though it was a couple of minutes after because I'd had dinner with Al Richards, who was in an exuberant mood after filing his story. 'Got a kissogram from the Kid,' he said, 'that's good for a bottle of Romanée-Conti on expenses.' The Kid was the office name for his editor, a quiet Bostonian called Young. I had to skip the dessert trolley so I wouldn't be late.

All told, the instructions Inspector Gaudet had given me were so precise I assumed he was checking I came alone. Nobody followed me from the hotel, but that's not to say nobody was watching. Twice a Kawasaki motorbike passed me and it could have been the Pope under the helmet. Al and I had been having a pre-dinner drink when I was paged for the phone. Gaudet had tracked me down, I assumed, by calling all the hotels in town. Or, if he started at the top, simply by calling the Imperator.

I wondered if he often made rendezvous in this square. His instructions had been so simple and straight to the point, his voice tight under control. One side of the square was a sort of Gothic arcade with an antiquarian bookseller, a place selling sheet music, a hatseller, nothing to set the pulse racing. Another side was taken up by a brooding hulk of a building with a sun-blistered sign: *École Maternelle*. The other two sides looked to be taken up by small offices, notaries, accountants, staff bureaux. Without exception the windows in the square were dark. Street lamps clamped to the walls deepened the shadows.

In the centre was a fountain, the usual bare-breasted nymph balancing on one leg, one hand coyly clutching a sheet, the other hand holding up an improbably large stone shell from which water dribbled. I did a circuit of the fountain and it hid nobody. A fitful breeze blew spray to one side making the pavement blocks slippery, and I noted that in case I had to get away fast.

Two cars were parked in the square but nobody sat in either of them or crouched on the floor, and their bonnets were cool. Footsteps approached and swung into the arcade, two pairs, man and woman, out of step. I watched as the pillars and street lamps switched them on and off. They walked apart, not talking, and I thought an argument was brewing when they arrived wherever they were going. Gaudet came from the other direction as if he'd been waiting for the other two to clear the square. He wore a suit with the jacket buttoned up, though the night was warm, so I made the assumption: shoulder holster.

'Are you planning on running?' Gaudet asked.

I'd thrown away my dirty torn clothing and borrowed Al's jogging suit, about three sizes too big. I'd rolled it up round the ankles and pushed back the sleeves and undone the front zip, and then a bit more and then an extra bit for luck. I'd smiled at the head waiter at the Imperator as if this green-and-grey outfit was the sexiest new sensation in rue St-Honoré.

'Is that a question,' I asked, 'or a suggestion?'

'Exactly,' he said. That is just a French way of avoiding answering, but in my mind it was answer enough. That and the elaborate precautions for our meeting, and the anger that blocked his throat and raised the pitch of his voice. 'I warned you.'

His voice was another warning and I rubbed a shoe on the paving stone to test its grip and from the corner of my eye watched his one good hand, how the thumb could not keep still.

'I should have known when you first came to Nîmes,' he said.

He made a little pause here, but there was nothing I wanted to say.

'You said you were working for the Sûreté and the Chief Inspector in Paris denied it, so you had to change your story and deny it too. Obviously.'

'I merely used his name so I could—'

'You were, and are, working for the Sûreté.'

'That simply is not true.'

'They came to rescue you.'

'What? The American journalist forced—'

'Since when does the Sûreté take orders from journalists? Even American ones? Particularly American ones? I was arrested – no, I wasn't arrested because that implies a legal process. I was kidnapped, gun in my kidneys, *me*. By your friends.'

They're not my friends. I wanted to shout it loud enough to make the bare-breasted nymph tremble. How could I be friends with Crevecoeur? But instead of shouting I was watching his hand, how he flexed the fingers and then dug them into his palm and squeezed as if he was throttling someone.

'Do you know where I was taken?'

'Of course I don't.'

'They had a caravan out near the *mas* and I was driven there and left alone all day. The first time I ran into them, the Sûreté blew my hand off.' Now he held both arms forward. 'But they left me this one hand. This time they made use of their generosity and handcuffed the wrist to the ladder of the bunk-beds. Me! I am an inspector and they did this to me as if I was a criminal. Even a criminal has certain rights. An animal then, a dog chained to its kennel. For the rest of my life I shall remember this. Then at six o'clock one of them came back to release me and said the affair was cleared up. Except of course it isn't, they bungled it just as they did…' He held up his stump. 'Ledru slipped through their fingers. Plus there are others of his gang who were not present when the great assault took place. But I heard you were there, got in first, distracted everyone's attention at the crucial moment and were rescued when Ledru rumbled you.'

Voices had been growing louder and four men came into the square. They came to the fountain and one of them dipped in his hands and washed his face and then scooped up water at his friends. When the water fight began, Gaudet seemed at a loss. He couldn't deal with four young men, full of wine, on his own. Threatening them with a pistol was out of proportion. When the men moved off and Gaudet turned back to me, his anger seemed to have lost its thrust.

'Why are you telling me this story?' I asked.

'I want you out of here.'

'You always have. Why meet me like this to tell me?'

'You're a selfish woman. You never see things from anyone else's point of view. Ledru understands after today that you are working with the Sûreté. He couldn't see that before. All he could see were your tits. Like tonight, trying the same trick on me. He may not have proof, but in his guts Ledru will understand. He'll get together tonight or tomorrow with his friends and if they find you're still about they'll come for you. Your murder will bring more trouble.' He shook his head. 'Not because you're foreign and a tourist and bad for the city's image. But because it will bring Crevecoeur back and he'll be leading a crusade, cleaning up what he believes is corruption. That includes me.'

Gaudet drew his hand across his throat.

'I'm going to make you a happy man,' I said. 'I'll be leaving tomorrow morning with luck. There's nothing to keep me.'

'Paris?'

'No. To get the little orphan girl away from Doicescu. Doing what's really your job.'

'Doicescu.' He gave a little nod, though whether he knew Doicescu was the guilty person or just accepted what I said I don't know. 'Is he in Nîmes?'

'No. I'm told he's lying low somewhere else in the Midi.'

'If he's not in Nîmes, it's not my job.'

We stared at each other and there was nothing more to say. I was sick of him, his petty corruption, his bent morality, his indifference to the fate of Rina. He, equally, was sick of me because my presence here, dead or alive, threatened his security.

That's what I believed as I turned to leave him: that he was warning me to get out for his sake. I walked away from the fountain, slipping on the treacherous stones.

'He said Ledru still had pals in this city?'

'Yes.'

'And they'd be after your neck?'

'Yes.'

'So what did he propose to do, this cop, knowing a wanted criminal was on the run and after your blood? Is he going all-out to arrest the guy, mounting a big operation, searching his haunts, breathing down the necks of his known associates, tracking him down and holding him? Is that it? You know us farm boys, Co, brains the size of watermelons but full of pips. I'm just trying to get things all lined up in my mind. Is this Inspector Gaudet going to do his job? Or is he just going to hold his hand out and wait to see who drops ten thousand francs in it?'

I made the only answer I could, which was nothing. I'd been through the whole scene with Al Richards and he knew as much as I did. All he lacked was the *feeling* of Gaudet's hate for the Sûreté and anyone with a link to it. There was a word for it: obsession.

Al said, 'So what are our plans?'

'Tomorrow I'll move on to somewhere else, Montpellier perhaps, or Toulouse. Hopefully somewhere near where Doicescu is lying low.'

'Our plans. You help me, I help you. Didn't we have a bargain?'

I'd found Al in the garden of the Imperator, enjoying an Armagnac. I took his glass and had a sip and made a face.

'Don't you like it?'

'It's not that.' I remembered the last time I'd taken a drink out of a man's glass it was Ledru's. That was the first time I met him and I'd wanted his trust, I'd wanted to make a gesture allying the two of us, so I'd drunk from his glass.

'Listen, Gaudet is right about one thing,' Al said. 'It's not safe for you to be alone. There are bad *hombres* out there. You're a smart lady, but how will you outsmart someone who decides to shoot you in the back?'

Last night at the mosquito pit, Gaudet's men had forced their way in before I was awake. This night it could be Ledru.

Al had taken back his glass and was studying it as if it held the key to the universe. He tilted the glass to one side and watched the brandy drain down the slope. The little amber pool in the bottom held an image of one of the garden lanterns in miniature, a glow worm. He spoke without looking at me, as if a look could say too much.

'There's upstairs. I can offer you a bed,' he said. 'Half a bed.'

Then he looked at me.

He closed the door behind us but didn't turn on the light. The curtains were still drawn back and the shutters open, and my eyes adjusted to the illumination from the moon and street lamps. There were two mirrors in the room and I checked each in turn, not through vanity but because it is second nature to me now. You get a different perspective from a mirror, see things you'd miss, are alert to dangers. Lulu Pelletier came to mind.

In a mirror I saw Al move to stand behind me and then I felt his hands on my hips. He turned me round and his arms ranged up my back as he pulled me close. I laid my cheek on his chest and I clung tight. He wanted to turn my face up to kiss, but I just clung tighter. I needed the feel of him, the solidity, the warmth even on this July night.

'Co, what's wrong?'

I'd begun shivering, yes, even on this July night. It was a different kind of shaking, a bodily reaction. And the feel of him was a different kind of warmth. I clung harder, that was my answer.

'You've a bout of fever, that's just what it feels like.'

Malaria, DTs, stage fright, bite from a tarantula, could be anything. Or memories, an accumulation of bad things.

'Or it's because I'm so close. Could be that. Never had quite that effect before, though.'

That was the farm boy in him. For a moment more I was lost for words. Couldn't he understand how I felt? Maybe not, he'd missed the whole show. He hadn't seen Agnes's corpse, found Lulu's tortured body, held on by his fingernails to the roof of a car on the Périphérique, had guns pointed at him, gone under and over barbed wire, run from nerve gas, been threatened and blackmailed and made enemies of just about everyone.

'Do I rate a kissogram from you too?'

We kissed but it meant nothing to me and he could tell. I didn't kiss him so much as let it happen. He moved a hand and pulled down the zip in the jogging-suit top a fraction more. His hand slipped inside and a finger stroked my left breast. It wasn't a grope, it was gentle. The finger was saying: I'm here and I could kindle a flame.

'It's just that I've taken too much,' I managed finally. I found I could talk after all. 'Too many bodies. The stink of formaldehyde and Agnès shot just about where your finger is now. Lulu and what they did to him before they killed him. And the three corpses laid out by the pool today like someone's catch of fish. And I know you'll think this sounds dumb, but it all gets mixed up with that blonde, Mini, who survived. Well, she survived today at least. She's all dope and tits. She spent last night with Ledru and it meant nothing to her. Nothing. Just another little screw. That's wrong. It means something to me. That's why I can't. Al? Do you understand?'

He didn't say: *It's all right, it doesn't matter.* It damn well should matter. He was roused, and I could feel that and knew that he wanted me. I'm not like a soldier who comes out of battle and goes to find a woman – any woman, no matter who – to get the taste of war out of his mouth and feel himself a man again and not a cog in a killing machine. To me it matters. I tried to explain it some more.

'I don't know if it would work for us, Al, but I know it would have no chance of working with all those other bodies sharing our bed.'

It did matter to him. I knew that because he hugged me very hard indeed, then his arms went slack and he took a step back.

'You know whose fault this is? I wish I'd never met that André, my old buddy. Bastard.'

He moved to the door to switch on the light while I stood at the window looking out.

'Don't do that.'

'What is it?'

Al came to stand beside me and I pointed across the street. 'Against that tree.'

'I can't see anything. What am I supposed to be looking for?'

'Someone standing there lit a cigarette. I saw the flare of his match before he cupped it.'

'A million people are lighting cigarettes at this very moment all over the world.'

In a moment we saw part of a face brighten in the glow of the cigarette. Then the man began walking along the pavement away from the hotel.

'There,' Al said. But he closed the shutters before he turned on the light. And while he was by the door I heard the rattle of the security chain. 'If I had to choose,' he went on, just making small talk to cover our own private little difficulty, 'I'd lay odds on Crevecoeur. He's got an unhealthy look to him. I think he likes to watch.'

CHAPTER NINETEEN

The first explosion should have woken me, but I was still running about a night and a half behind on sleep. It could have been the second or third explosion that I became fully aware of. I was isolating the sound, identifying it. Gun, powerful gun. Not pistol. Handguns were for boys who had never grown up, only grown bigger. This was a far-away crack, a rifle shot lifting over the hills.

It was Yildirim. Crevecoeur hadn't kept his word and Yildirim had tracked me down. The rattle of the shutters brought me fully awake. Fingers were tapping against the wood. Or it was splinters of metal or brick-dust. Then thunder crashed almost overhead while lightning flickered in the central gap of the shutters and I got off the settee. I pulled one of the shutters closed and stared out through the open half. When lightning came again it made the buildings stand like cut-outs and bleached the colour from the trees. The thunder cracked and drummed. I heard Al get out of bed and he came to stand beside me without turning on the light.

'When I was a little girl, I used to be frightened of thunderstorms.'

'You?'

'My father used to open the door and hold me in front of him and say that thunder was shouting at me and I had to shout back. So that's what I'd do. I'd go *Roar! Roar!*'

'And you're no longer scared?'

A wind gusted furiously down the street at the approach of the rain. I could hear big drops hitting car roofs and spattering on dry leaves in the gutter.

'I like thunderstorms. Look at the energy, the force. If we hold out long enough, the storm grumbles and goes away and we're still left standing. We've won.'

When the lightning came again, the trees seemed to jump out from the buildings. I suppose the hotel façade was also lit by the flash and that Al and I standing by the half-open shutter would also be visible. Just as the man standing by a tree-trunk became visible as, head ducked down against the sudden torrent from the sky, he ran for shelter. I no longer thought it was Yildirim.

'The thing is,' I said to Al, 'both times his face was hidden from me. First time he cupped his hands to shield his match. Second time his head was ducked down because of the rain.'

'You don't know. A guy lighting a cigarette...'

'I know.'

'Someone running to get out of the wet...'

'I know.'

We'd had this conversation before. There are things Al knows for his work and things I know for mine. He was driving and I was in the front passenger seat, with the door mirror angled so that I could watch the traffic behind. He'd parked the car overnight in a side-street well away from the hotel so it should have been secure. But I'd checked it first before we got in: under the wheel arches, the chassis, the exhaust. I'd opened the bonnet and checked the engine, checked the wiring. He watched me the whole while and each time I caught his face there was a different expression: embarrassed, exasperated, amused, or the El Al look of superiority. So in the end I chucked him the keys: You want to be a hero, you turn the ignition. He never hesitated, but all the damn fool expressions disappeared from his face. He became grave, even his driving style subdued. Take little streets, I'd said.

I watched the mirror, sometimes I hunched round for a direct look, and I thought we were clear. We hit avenue Jean Jaurès. It is a wide boulevard, which I like because the traffic sorts itself out and there are cars and motorbikes that overtake you and others that dawdle in a way no French driver ever naturally does. In particular there was an Alfa Romeo with local plates that was always two cars behind, closing up at traffic lights, falling back. But when we turned west on to the *autoroute* we lost it.

'Last night you were hot for me being careful,' I said. Or maybe he'd just been hot for me. 'Don't make a joke of it today simply because the sun's shining again.'

We overtook an open truck stacked with wooden trays of peaches. Gaudet's father had grown fruit around here. This was the Inspector's home territory and he'd have friends.

I said, 'I've been totting up enemies and the tally goes like this. Ledru heads the list, plus any of his men who weren't rounded up at the *mas*. Gabizzi would also be pushing for first place if his lawyer has got him out of custody. Plus all the boys from his *clan*. Gaudet hates me, and if you're with me he hates you too. The foreign buyer – the Man that Crevecoeur collared – he's got to have some tough associates. Crevecoeur isn't out to cut me down, but if I happened to get in the way that would be just too bad. And then of course there will be Doicescu. But not just yet. For the moment that Citroën about two hundred metres back is not Doicescu. Anybody else, could be.'

'Shall I lose him?'

'We can't outrun an XM.'

'So?'

'Slow down. Make him pass or show himself.'

The Citroën caught us up and hung on our tail. Some drivers like to use the car in front as a pacemaker. Or are too lazy to overtake. Or feel lonely out in front. Or use the other car to catch a police speed trap. Or …'

'Slower.'

Al gave me a lingering look. His natural instinct was to put his foot down and challenge the other driver to a duel. But he eased up on the accelerator and the Citroën swept past. Man driving, woman beside him. Al's eyes were on the fluffy blonde hair framed in the window. He seemed to relax, then frowned.

'One of Gabizzi's boys could always have brought his little piece of fun along to watch the action.'

'Why didn't she sneer at us as they passed?' Nothing seemed right to me this morning. 'We held them up. She should have given us a dirty look. Why is she deliberately turning her face away?'

'She's lighting him a cigarette,' Al said.

That's cover, don't you know a damn thing? I screamed at Al in my mind. Nerves were stretched today, because for me this was the final act, the meeting with Doicescu. But for others there was no doubt that I formed part of the final act. The harvest of corpses had grown by three yesterday. There were all those enemies out there who wanted to add my corpse to the harvest.

'Pull over to the side,' I said.

Again the lingering look from Al while the car drifted out of its lane. He looked forward again and corrected his steering.

'If we're to get to Toulouse—'

'Al, stop the car on the hard shoulder. Just do it.'

Nerves again. Or was it the old man-woman skirmishing? I took several slow, deep breaths as Al tucked the car in behind a truck with a giant cylinder marked Total Gaz and then on to the shoulder. He slowed and stopped. We sat silent and unmoving for a few moments, like a married couple having a spat and fearful that a wrong word would open up a breach. Al was gripping the wheel and staring after the vehicles passing us.

He said, 'Now what?'

The morning paper was squashed up on the seat between us. I could see part of the headline. *Le Wild West arrive* was all that was visible but I'd already read the story. It wasn't played for laughs exactly, but it was definitely a local story – gang warfare – and not the sale of a defence secret to a foreign national. I suspected the hidden hand of Crevecoeur, twitching a string here, pulling a lever there, to divert attention from what could be a mouthwatering scandal. There was no mention of the Man or of nerve gas.

'We wait,' I said, 'and we watch. Two minutes.'

I squirmed round in my seat so that I looked past Al's shoulder at the oncoming traffic. The *autoroute* was Monday-morning busy. The overnight storm had cleared away and my eyes flicked to each sunflash off glass or metal.

'Watching out for anyone special?'

'Questions,' I said. Al was a journalist and asking questions was in his nature, but sometimes there aren't any answers.

Earlier that morning Al had gone out to a payphone to make calls and returned to the room in the Imperator with a glint in his eye. We've struck oil, he'd shouted, he's made contact with the *Dépêche du Midi*. That paper was based in Toulouse, but where Doicescu was based was an open question. Doicescu hadn't written offering his Romanian orphan girl and giving a helpful return address. He'd telephoned the newspaper and said he would ring again at one o'clock, if we would be there. You can tell he's not French, Al said as he helped himself to another croissant from the breakfast tray, or he'd still be eating lunch at that time.

Reflections on the windows mostly hid the faces of the drivers, but if a side window was open I caught the passengers' features as they flashed past. A stopped car on the *autoroute* is something to look at and most faces were turned our way. A pair of motorbikes approached and the riders were helmeted and goggled so you couldn't make out even if they were human. Big BMW bikes they were, and as they cruised past I could make out *Gendarmerie* on the fuel tanks. They looked but they kept going. Dampness sprang from pores all over my body.

'Why didn't they stop? Why didn't they bully us, ask for our papers? We're just sitting in a car at the side of the *autoroute*. Why didn't they ask what we thought we were doing? Why didn't they boost their egos?'

That was me asking questions. There were no answers, or perhaps we guessed them already. Without a word, Al got the car moving again.

La Dépêche is not in the world league of newspapers. It carries regional news first, national news second, and world news if there is any white space that needs filling. It was not like *Le Monde* or *The Times* or the *American Journal*. Al sniffed, but that could just be the old warhorse in him smelling printer's ink and famous battles against edition deadlines. He didn't know the editor of the *Dépêche* but it turned out the man had been at some conference with Young, who was Al's boss.

'Co-operation,' explained Al after the two men had been closeted together. 'Which means that in return for the facilities they are giving us, they get first bite of any story.'

I was frowning.

'Favoursville, Co. Goddamit, nothing's for nothing. You know the wicked ways of the world. Don't push your Mother Teresa bit to impossible lengths.'

I thought of seeing Agnès's corpse in the mortuary, of the paint marks daubed on the road where she'd been murdered, my first meeting with Ledru when he was taking comfort from his bottle of Scotch. Somewhere along the way I'd decided my interest in the tragedy was exclusively rescuing a little orphan, what Al called my Mother Teresa bit. Everybody else had a different motive: revenge, a news story, national security, local corruption, justice. Correction, not justice. I could think of no one interested in that.

The facilities Al grandly talked of were the use of this room, a poky office that seemed to be a retirement home for old machinery. They must have got computerized because there were five hulking manual typewriters parked on the floor against one wall. There was a desk with rings from coffee cups or glasses and scorch marks from forgotten cigarettes. There was a telephone. Al was at the window looking down at the street and then away across the roofs.

'Bet you didn't know they've got a district out there called Les Cocus,' Al remarked. He had a breezy tone of voice, making conversation, wanting to smooth over the bumps between us. 'A whole suburb of them. They must go at it night and day to earn that name.'

The telephone rang.

We both looked at it and then our eyes met. We'd already agreed it would be better if I did the talking, but there was still the moment of hesitation.

The telephone rang.

Al's eyes held mine. There was a tension in the air, I could sense it, almost sexual. We were doing this together. Sometimes he would take the lead, sometimes I would. He licked his lips but said nothing. I had a flash-thought: his tongue finding its way between my lips last night, his finger exploring, staking a claim to a little territory.

The telephone rang.

There was just the one telephone in the room. There was no extension for Al. He would have to be content with my side of the conversation and let his imagination fill in the rest. Afterwards he could listen to the tape.

The telephone rang and I picked it up and said: 'Hello.'

'Who is that I'm speaking to?'

'The name is Cody.'

'Are you the advertiser?'

'Do you mean: Did we advertise in the *Dépêche du Midi* for a child to … give a home to? The answer is yes.'

'And are you—'

'One moment please,' I cut him short. 'Are you the person who telephoned early this morning? You wouldn't leave a name or a telephone number?'

'I have to take care. There are legal rules we may want to avoid. Both of us.'

'What is your name?'

Long pause. Don't hang up, keep talking to me, think of the money. I imagined I could hear his breathing. Or somebody listening in.

'Hello? Are you still there?'

'Why do you want to know?' His voice had tightened.

'I've got to call you something.'

I wished I could see him, his face, his body movements. He was a man on the run, wanted for murder, in need of cash. He'd be in a payphone somewhere, a slight sweat on his face, staring at the people walking by or waiting to use the phone. He could be here in Toulouse, in the suburb named after cuckolds. He could be anywhere in the circulation area of the *Dépêche*. I pictured his eyes, restless, flicking to each movement, fearful of some trap. Like giving his name.

'You can call me Patrick.'

Patrick! What made him choose Patrick? Because it could be French or English or Irish? He was Dimitru Doicescu and he spoke fluent French with a faint slurring accent and he traded in violence. Did he think there were no murderers called Patrick?

'Well, Monsieur Patrick, tell me about the child.'

'What?'

'Boy or girl?'

'Girl.'

'How old is she?'

'Three. Her fourth birthday is ... coming quite soon.'

'What nationality is she?'

A pause there, looking for traps. 'She is Romanian.'

'Poor thing.'

'What?'

'I said, Poor little girl. Victim of Ceausescu's regime. And she's an orphan?'

'Where's your husband?'

Thrown by the suddenness of the question I said, 'I can speak for both of us.'

'But where is he?'

'Out on business.'

'What's his business?'

'Commercial traveller. He sells chocolates.'

'Chocolates?' He sounded puzzled at the detail, as if a chocolate salesman couldn't be taken seriously. Or mightn't have the money for the black-market trade in orphans. 'Where do you live?'

'In Liège.'

'Liège?' Another silence and I let him think it over. People are always pleased when they've worked something out for themselves. 'That's in Belgium.'

'Yes. We're down here for a little business, a little holiday, and... well, for this. You see, we advertised in Belgium and the police visited us. We were doing something illegal. You understand?'

'The police are... It is necessary to be careful at all times.' Al was concentrating on me across the desk and I gave him a little nod. It was going as I had wanted: Doicescu's caution was being put to one side because we were allied against authority.

'Have you had trouble with them – the police, I mean?'

'What?'

I'd made an error. Trying to show more sympathy, trying to align ourselves against authority, I'd brought his suspicion right back.

'They're *salauds*,' I said. 'I was hurrying to get here to take your call and they stopped me. Cost me nine hundred francs. On the spot.'

'Cash?' he said.

'Yes. I had to count the notes right into his hand. How do I know his hand didn't put it in his pocket when I'd gone? He gave me a receipt. What's a receipt?'

'Tsk.'

Better. His mind was back on his primary need: money to get out of France and start anew somewhere else.

'What's her name?'

'What?'

'Her name – the little girl's.'

It's not that he was stupid, it's that his mind was focused on money. Anything else seemed an irrelevance.

'Ecaterina.'

'That's a pretty name. Is she pretty?'

'Oh yes, I think you'll find her pretty. She's suffering a bit from shock, you understand. These have not been easy times.'

'I understand.'

Another pause. This was a difficult conversation, neither of us quite certain how to go forward. I had to ask some of the questions a prospective parent would, but not so many as to make him suspicious. Out in the corridor in the newspaper building I could hear men's voices. Perhaps they'd been there all the time, or perhaps they'd just come back from lunch. Al and I had only had time for a sandwich in a bar and his look was hungry and intense.

'I'm dying to see her. Poor mite. Already I have a mother's feeling for her.'

In French it sounds better. But even in French, to my ears, it limped like an afternoon soap on TV. Perhaps to Doicescu too, for he was once again suspicious.

'To see her?'

'Yes.' I took a breath and closed my eyes to concentrate on getting the tone of voice right. 'Oh yes. You see we've been trying, Bert and me, for a family and the doctors finally admitted after all the tests that I could never hope … Well, for us, in our situation, a family means so very much and without it, I'm afraid … No, it is unfair to put the burden of our marriage on a stranger … But I'll let you in on a little secret. Bert – he's my husband – he's away on business down towards Pau and he said he was going to visit Lourdes specially to pray. Now this has come up and truly, Monsieur Patrick, it is like a miracle. We came down to the south of France prepared for such an eventuality. It is as if some higher power had been guiding us. I'm referring to the financial side, of course.'

'Money, you mean cash?'

'Yes. Bert and I discussed it often because we knew that such transactions as we are contemplating have to be done just right. I mean credit cards have no place. I mean …' I took another deep breath. Keep in there, keep the balls in the air. Mesmerize him with the prospect of the money. Reassure him that you're fluffy-headed. 'I mean with the credit-card voucher, where it says Nature of Services or Goods Supplied, what could you possibly write there? We had quite a laugh over that, though naturally we were shocked at ourselves afterwards. No, it had to be cash. We knew that. We were coming from Belgium, naturally, but we decided Belgian francs might not be the right currency in all situations. There might be certain foreign expenses, I don't know. I'm only a housewife, Monsieur Patrick, and soon I hope a mother. But there could be papers and lawyers and taxes and stamps.'

'No lawyers,' he said.

'That's a relief. Lawyers always demand so much money. Have you ever met a poor lawyer? Bert always says – No, let me get back to the point. We brought dollars. I have them with me now. I came to the newspaper office with them because I wanted to be prepared. I do hope it's enough. We haven't discussed the … er, the fee. Is that the right word?'

'How much do you have?'

Got you. In his voice I could at last hear eagerness. It only needed me to take a step back to draw him forward.

'Well... I haven't even seen the little girl yet. Ecaterina, you said. You said she was pretty and naturally I accept that. But the country she's come from... Pardon me, Monsieur Patrick, perhaps you are from Romania yourself. I can't tell from the way you speak. You sound French to me. Not from Liège, that's for sure. We have so many Flemish there... What was I saying? Oh yes, Romania has had such a terrible time recently, AIDS, starvation even...'

'But seeing her...'

'It could be today, this afternoon even, if you don't object to me coming by myself. Oh, do say yes. Just suppose when Bert returned tomorrow, I had Ecaterina. That would be the miracle he prayed for.'

'You'd come alone? Your husband wouldn't object?'

'Object? When he sees what's in my arms?'

'You would bring cash?'

'Is five thousand enough? Oh, do say it is. We can't afford any more.'

From the corridor there was a cry of *'Merde'*, followed by laughter. From the telephone there were four or five seconds of silence. I think he was trying to picture what so much money looked like.

'Dollars?' Doicescu said.

'Dollars,' I told him.

CHAPTER TWENTY

'Why chocolates?' Al asked. 'Of all the damn fool things to go round selling, why chocolates? Suppose he'd asked you the brand?'

He was tense, and I supposed partly from last night. Sorry I couldn't oblige. Just a woman's way, Al. The gallant knight gets all set to storm the castle and one day the gates are wide open and the flags flying in welcome, the next day the drawbridge is up and the portcullis is down.

'Bert, my husband, travels in chocolate novelties.' Talk him down, I decided. 'Coming from Belgium, a chocolate Mannekin Pis, naturally. Then there's the Venus de Milo with detachable arms – known to some as Venus Milady – sort of have your chocolate and eat it. He's off down to Lourdes selling the latest novelty – miracle-linked chocolates. A chockie leg or arm or breast, blessed by some venal bishop. You eat it and if your affected part gets better, you say it's the chocolate.'

'Your idea of a joke?'

'Please, Bert comes from Belgium.'

'And why the name Bert?'

'It just popped into my head.'

It was the other half of Al's name. I thought about that and couldn't decide if it meant anything. Freud would have made a meal of it.

Silence. Al was driving, fast. There were a hundred kilometres to cover and he wanted to do it quick-quick in case Doicescu changed his mind. We followed a river where canoeists in orange life-jackets braved rapids, crossed a bridge, climbed through a town and up into the *causse*. Rocks stuck out of the soil like broken bones through flesh and the fields were white with stones.

Driving fast tenses some people, relaxes others. Al seemed easier now.

'Yesterday.'

He flicked a look at me and back at the road again.

Certain he was no longer sulking I went on, 'Yesterday, before the Wild West circus at the *mas*, while we spying the land from up on the hill – remember?'

'Co, I was there. Me, my big hands, my big heart.'

'I looked up in the sky and saw something circling. Hawk, eagle, I don't know. Some bird of prey.'

'So?'

'Duck your head and look up.'

Al never slackened speed but hunched over and glanced up between the top of the steering wheel and the roof. He straightened up.

'Bird of prey,' I told him.

I was watching it again, single-engined plane, circling in the sky.

'Joyrider?' he suggested.

'You think?' Its circles seemed to overlap, keep us as the focus. 'Did the editor of *La Dépêche* listen in?'

'Part of the deal.'

'Would he tell someone else what he overheard? Say, someone in authority?'

'So what's authority? A police uniform is authority, a shotgun under your chin is authority. This is France, kiddo. You twist my arm, I scratch your back.'

Who was up in the sky? What could they do?

We'd passed through the village of Clugue. Go about a kilometre out, had been Monsieur Patrick's instruction, there's a chestnut wood with an unmarked dirt road beside it.

'Pull in under the trees.'

Al stopped the car and I got out, branches hiding me from the spy in the sky.

'Turn round here and go back to the village,' I said. 'Park the car outside the café. Make sure the plane is locked on to you. Listen for it, don't look up at it. Then saunter into the café as if you've lost the way and are asking directions. Ham it up. Peer round you, scratch your head.'

'Co, I don't like it.'

I could hear the little aircraft up there, buzzing around. To my overloaded imagination it sounded annoyed. You hear wasps like that. I leant in through the window and laid a fist softly against his jaw. I didn't tell him how I felt.

So what's the great plan? Al had asked while we were still at the newspaper office.

You want Plan A or Plan B?

Let's start with Plan A, Al had said, and when that sucks we'll move on to Plan B.

Plan A is that I knock on his door and when he opens it I flash him a big smile, show him a bit of leg and, while he's saucer-eyed, I grab the girl and run.

Yeah? Al had said. And if he's gay?

We move on to Plan B. You show a bit of leg.

But in Al's black mood this didn't get so much as a twitch of the lips.

Plan C was the feeblest of the lot, except for the others. I was offering Doicescu a swap: the girl against a chance for him to make a break for it. But he's a tough *hombre,* he's ex-Securitate, he's a killer. I didn't need Al to point out the shakiness of my position. I'll tell him I've got colleagues backing me up and he'll never get away unless they see me walking hand in hand with the girl. Co, it's a game of poker you're playing with this guy and suppose he calls your bluff. Suppose he takes out a gun and demands to see the money and, when you don't have it, he shoots you. I had no answer to that. Never in my life had I played poker with such a weak hand.

Now, listening to the drone of the little plane as it circled up above, I could at least jerk a thumb at the sky and say this was part of my back-up and they'd track Doicescu if he tried to make a get-away without trading.

It was thin. I thought again about calling in the police and letting them take Doicescu. But Doicescu, seeing the net closing, would go down shooting and there was no guarantee Ecaterina wouldn't be caught in the crossfire.

Jesus, Co, what's the female of Sir Galahad?

I started walking down the dirt road.

The chestnut trees formed a wood up the slope of a hill and at the top, where the land flattened out, the trees continued on one side of the track, fields on the other. I was no longer hidden by the canopy of leaves but was out in the open. There was maize that was waist-high and a meadow that had been cut for hay. Magpies fled in alarm when I appeared. One for sorrow, two for joy, three for a girl... There were more than three, but I stopped counting. A tractor had been gathering the hay into a big stack and had stopped with two bales still in its forklift. It disturbed me, that abandoned tractor. It was as if the farmer had been called away on urgent business and had never come back.

The dirt road had a kink in it following some ancient boundary. When I reached the bend I could see beyond the chestnut wood an abandoned farmhouse, a barn that looked bigger than the house, outhouses for chickens and rabbits. The buildings were in grey stone and the roof of the barn was subsiding into ruin. A large tangle of brambles partly concealed a car. It was dusty off-white, an old Renault 4, the kind of workhorse that goes on for ever.

I was walking more slowly now, dragging myself closer, conscious of the heat of the sun. Listening, I could hear the chatter of some birds and the buzz of insects. Something nagged at me and I listened harder and then I realized what it was: I could no longer hear the sound of the little plane. Was that significant? I tried to puzzle it out – flown away, landed, atmospheric trick blocking the sound – but had no hard evidence. Mostly I thought that my chance of claiming it as a back-up ally had gone. Plan C was already fraying at the edges.

An old walnut tree stood to one side of the barn and I thought of making for that. Shade. The sun was an enemy, I'd been walking without a hat and every pore in my body seemed to be open. The tree was dying from old age or neglect and the leaves were sparse, but any shade was better than none. I wondered if Ledru's *mas* had looked like this before it was restored. Somehow this place had the feel of always being more impoverished. There are a million abandoned farms in France where the land has been divided and subdivided with each generation until the living is too poor to hold the young. An empty place like this made a good hide-out, until someone turned up and asked what the hell you thought you were doing. Such as a farmer harvesting his hay.

The place had no electricity and no telephone. Doicescu would have driven into Clugue to buy food, seen the ad in the paper and used a payphone. The place would have no running water, either. I could see an outside latrine, a little grey hut with its door hanging by one hinge.

'Stop. Stay right there.'

I found the face in the window next to the front door. The shutters had been pushed out and the windows pulled open and there he stood, Doicescu, aka Monsieur Patrick, ex-Securitate, murderer, kidnapper, bogus supplier of orphans. There was no sign of the little girl.

'Who are you? What do you want?'

His face seemed to be half in shadow. Then I remembered what Ledru had said: one side of his face was frozen, had lost all movement as if struck by a nervous dysfunction.

'Is that you, Monsieur Patrick?'

I wanted to see him right out in the open. Half his face seemed in shadow because of its dead nerves, but the whole of it was obscure because the sun beating down was so bright and he stood a pace back in the dim room. I wanted to see how he behaved, how his eyes moved. I wanted to study him and be prepared, the same as you take the measure of a Doberman that's tensed to charge.

'Who are you?'

'Madame Cody. We spoke—'

'Where's your car?'

'I left it parked in the woods.'

'Why?'

'I wasn't certain if the track was suitable for an ordinary saloon car. I mean, without four-wheel drive. I see it is.' I nodded at the dirty old Renault 4.

'And you walked?'

'Yes.'

'With the money?'

'I've brought it.' I patted a pocket. Fifty hundred-dollar bills doesn't make a thick pile, not if they're unused. Two bills had volunteered from the back of Al's wallet and I'd cut paper to size and snapped on two broad elastic bands, so that it looked at first glance like a wad of money.

'You've walked all alone carrying that money?'

Doicescu was getting ideas that he could wander out and take the money off me. Would he tie me up and make his getaway? Or do something more in keeping with his violent history? I said, 'I asked them at the newspaper office and they said it was safe up here.'

'So you came on your own,' he said and disappeared from the window. The door opened and he came out into the full glare of the sunshine. He was a bulky man, a hard man going to flesh. He could have been a soldier at one time but of a particular kind.

There is the soldier who puts on clean underwear, shaves like it was his wedding day, then goes out and gets his balls shot off. And then there is the soldier who never shaves, is not a regular chap, uses every trick to make certain it's the first soldier's balls that get shot off. Doicescu hadn't shaved.

'I've come to see the girl,' I said, 'to see Ecaterina.'

'Without Monsieur Cody? Who is off selling chocolates to the priests?'

He was coming slowly towards me. His face looked like something from an old horror movie. The good side was animated, high-coloured, angry. The bad side was the wooden Indian on a totem pole. He spoke out of half of his mouth. How did he drink a cup of coffee? How did he kiss? Who would want to kiss him?

'I was in the village making the telephone call,' he said. 'I went off to the baker and then returned to the café to ring the newspaper office again. It must have been about twenty minutes later. I wanted to tell you to be sure the money was in old notes, not new notes with consecutive numbers. I said to the switchboard girl that I wanted to speak to the woman about the advertisement and she said: "Oh, you've just missed them, they've just left." They? They have just left? When you said you were alone? And his name turns out not even to be Cody but to be Richards.'

I said, 'No closer please, Doicescu.'

That stopped him. The colour drained from the angry side of his face until the two halves were matching pale.

'Doicescu?' he queried. 'What do you mean, Doicescu?' As if he was going to insist that he was Monsieur Patrick, the well-known Franco-Irish philanthropist. He really seemed to be about to dispute what I'd called him and the two halves of his face once again went their separate ways, one side icy and unemotional, the other side angry and wide-eyed. But I knew his real name and there was no point in pretending. He began moving towards me again.

'Stay where you are,' I said. 'I don't know what's on your mind but don't think you can play tough with me. I didn't come alone.'

He had stopped. Now he looked all round, at first sharp little glances at the corners of buildings and trunks of trees, finally a great sarcastic tour of the horizon and a sweeping gesture with one arm like a buffo opera star. The Romanians, I reminded myself, pride themselves on being Latin.

'I don't see your army.'

I could have done with that little plane buzzing up in the blue.

'If you're careful,' I said, 'you won't. I've come to offer you a deal and if you accept the terms you'll be left alone.'

'Deal?' He turned his head so that he gazed at me with the eye on the good side of his face. I suddenly had the feeling the other eye could be blind or glass. 'A woman such as you, lying to me on the telephone about a husband and chocolate, walking towards the farmhouse like a thief in the night, offering me a deal?'

Simply the fact of his standing there, talking rather than taking action, made me think he could be open to an offer. I said, 'This is the nature of the deal I propose. Ecaterina, the little girl you sold and stole back, is to be handed over to me. In exchange, you can get into your car and go, a free run. There are other refinements we can work on, safeguards on both sides, a little money perhaps, but in essence that's it.'

Free run to where, for God's sake? Into a police roadblock? Now I'd trotted it out, it sounded pathetic. But Doicescu wasn't even bothering to listen at the end. His attention had shifted to something over my shoulder. Turning, I saw Al at the bend in the road. He must have been spying out the land, but realizing he'd been spotted, he walked forward. No one spoke a word. There was silence apart from the calls of birds and the hum of insects and, at the very end, the crunch of Al's shoes on the dirt track. His chest was lifting and there was a glow to his face as if he'd been running from the village. He came up beside me and put an arm round my shoulders. There was a certain comfort in its strength, but not if I had to move fast. Gently I shrugged until the arm fell away.

'Part of your army?' Doicescu asked. 'Maybe the husband who sells chocolates?'

'I want to see the little girl,' I said. 'Ecaterina.'

'Ecaterina... I don't know. Maybe she's not here. In another place. Why do you think she's here?'

Behind Doicescu was the house, its shutters and door open. No one was visible and the house stayed silent, but the girl had to be in there. Ledru had mentioned a woman and she would be inside keeping the girl quiet.

Doicescu abandoned this line of argument. He said, 'This is a trap. I give up Ecaterina, I run for it, I get shot down. You are full of lies and tricks. Better I keep Ecaterina.'

Al wasn't the most patient of men. 'For God's sake, you make the kid sound like a magic suit of armour you put on to protect yourself.'

'That could be,' Doicescu agreed, but again his attention had wandered over my shoulder.

In the distance there'd been the sound of a heavy engine struggling into life.

'More of your army?'

'Sounds like a tractor,' I said. I looked at Al and he shrugged: none of his doing. 'That's the farmer back from lunch, unless you've got him tied up inside.'

The tractor came into view, following the same route I had taken, and Al after me, down the dirt track towards the house. The bales of hay skewered on the prongs in front hid the face of the driver. He must have seen to steer through a gap between the bales, but we never saw his face until the last minute. He swerved the tractor, cut its engine and jumped down. It was Ledru, and in his hand he held a pistol and in his eyes he held hatred. Doicescu had gone rigid, both halves of his face frozen, his body twisted awkwardly as if he'd been struck by a sudden muscular spasm and didn't dare move.

'Bastard,' Ledru said in a whisper. Then he gathered a huge breath and bellowed. 'You... you absolute filthy...' He ran out of steam. When he spoke again he'd found a middle level, almost conversational. 'There is no word dirty enough to describe you. You took my woman from me. You killed her, killed my woman.'

Doicescu's throat contracted. He could swallow but he seemed unable to move another muscle or to speak.

Ledru's eyes slid over to me. 'You found him. And in the end you led me to him. You should have told me where he was sooner.'

I said, 'I didn't know until this afternoon.'

'That's not what you said yesterday. Yesterday you told me you knew where this man was. I hired you to find him, and how you repaid me – you sneaked in under the fence and tried to get my attention, to distract me and let the army make its assault. We have a certain reckoning to make over that.'

I hadn't known where Doicescu was. I'd been buying time. What could I do to buy time now? And who was the greater danger?

Ledru's head turned another degree and he began to nod as he took the measure of Al's unsmiling face.

'And you, *copain*. In it together with the lady, *copain*. I don't see a reporter's notebook, *copain*. What I see is another betrayer, *copain*.'

The *copains* fell regularly, like the clapper of a cracked bell.

'Please be so good, *copain*, as—'

He never finished. Doicescu, seizing this moment of discord, made a lunge inside his blouson. Ledru was much faster. Doicescu only had the butt of a pistol showing when Ledru shot him. Doicescu's chest was a big target which Ledru couldn't miss. It was a single shot that plucked at the fabric of the blouson. Red droplets were splattered round the bullet hole and in an instant they were swallowed in a red flood. Doicescu staggered one step to the side, his knees folded and he keeled over. He could have been dead as he fell. He made no effort to stop his skull cracking on the hard ground. Ledru stared at the body, stared at it and shook his head. His anger still boiled up.

'Doicescu! Doicescu, I'm talking to you. Get up, God damn you.'

He aimed a kick at Doicescu's thigh. Then, appalled, he realized the truth.

'Bastard's dead. He's cheated me. He did it before and he's...' Ledru fixed furious eyes on me. 'You were to find him for me, tell me where he was. He had to suffer for my woman's death. You know what I'm talking about? I wanted him...' He broke off. His eyes narrowed and looked mad. 'You think I'm talking about revenge. He took something from me and had to pay. A bullet in his belly. He had to be on his knees, holding his guts from spilling out, screaming for mercy. What mercy did he show my woman? He wants an end to his agony? He wants deliverance? He wants a bullet in his brain? Let him wait until I've seen his suffering. Now he's gone and I can't reach him.'

He let out a breath. The anger was still in his eyes, unappeased. We had half a minute, at most a minute. Did Al understand that? Ledru didn't see himself as a simple executioner. He was the judge and the jury and the prosecutor. He had his big speech to make, not justifying but glorifying. He was his own public gallery as well. I was working out my move and wishing Al hadn't stood so close because we presented a single focus of attention for Ledru.

'But you two,' Ledru began. He ran his tongue round his lips. 'I've got friends who are going to thank me for this. They're going to say, "André, you did a good job getting rid of those rats." I've got as many friends as rats have fleas, believe me, and your progress has been monitored. Your love nest last night, the *autoroute,* the newspaper, up the valley. Like passing a baton in a race.

There they go, pick 'em up at the Toulouse exit, at the St Antonin bridge, whatever, expect the rats in ten minutes.'

For a moment he fell quiet. He wet his lips and let his eyes wander over my body. I've seen the signs before in men of his kind. He wanted to humiliate me, violate me. I was a challenge and there was something inside him that needed to defeat me. But first there was Al to consider. His eyes switched.

'Oh Albert, Albert, Albert, running after the ladies again. What's the matter? It should be the ladies running after you. But a lady only has to twitch her skirt and you twitch your nose.'

Al had gone rigid except for his hands. Or the one hand I could see from the corner of my eye. His arm hung straight down at his side and at the end of it were these fingers waving, as if they could catch something in the air.

'Albert ... Albert ... twitch your nose, Albert.'

Ledru flicked the end of his own nose with the barrel of his pistol. It was sudden and unexpected and I could take no advantage of the moment. The gun dropped back to its position between the two of us. I wanted the gun pointing straight at Al, because I was going to need that extra fraction of a second. Ledru was going to shoot Al first and deal with me second, and before that first shot rang out I was going to have to go into a diving somersault and come up swinging to knock the pistol out of his hand. I was going to have to do it just right and the odds looked poor. But do nothing and no one would give odds on our survival at all.

Ledru was speaking to me now and when he next switched his attention to Al I was going to have to move. Deep, steady breaths for oxygen intake. Anger to raise the adrenalin level. He was a murderer, a torturer, a sadist. He was a brute, a rapist. Straightforward rape would not satisfy him For me he would have refinements. Concentrate on that. Feel the blood in the muscles, the nerves taut, the energy waiting to explode. He was saying, 'You should have seen his nose twitch in Bangkok. You must think you're something special, but let me tell you this. There was a place there out on Pat Pong Road. All the names were English. This was called The Big O, real poetry, and—'

The shot came before I could make my move. And a second shot. And a third. But by then he was on the ground in a heap. It was the second shot that killed Ledru.

The little girl came out of the farmhouse first. She had been pushed out by unseen hands and was none too steady on her feet. It was my first sight of Ecaterina, presumed orphan, source of income to Doicescu, the reason for my being here. Seeing her at last, standing in the stained clothing which had been bright and new and full of hope when Agnès had bought it, seeing her sway ever so slightly in the harsh sunlight, I felt... I felt... Pity? Mother love? Desire to protect the helpless? I searched and found no emotion. I felt nothing. No. The fact was that I was too numbed by the rush of events and for a moment too confused. I'd been preparing for Ledru to shoot and instead he'd been shot in the back by an invisible person in the farmhouse.

Al was crouching by the body of his one-time pal Ledru, head to his chest to listen for a heartbeat, holding a limp wrist. You search the wrist for the pulse and when you can't find it you blame your own stupidity and search harder. Al's face was pale at the sight of blood. For a moment he seemed to hold on to the wrist for support and then he let it fall. Ledru's pistol had bounced to one side and he—

'No.'

The woman came out of the house, a gun in her hand. In all the confusion I'd had no time to consider her. I'd forgotten her name. Crevecoeur had called her something, but that had been in hospital when I was still groggy and I couldn't recall it. I knew nothing about her except she had been taught how to shoot with a pistol and had a good eye and a steady hand and no conscience about killing. I studied her now as she came forward. Thirty or so, dark hair in disarray, a body that looked used to physical work, clothes that were just clothes to cover her, without style or allure. I recalled the bit of mock jargon Crevecoeur had come out with – *bedbug* – but I doubted it. She wasn't seductive.

To me she was simply Doicescu's woman. Wife? I didn't know. Mother of Ecaterina? I didn't know. I didn't know the structure that the Securitate had had, whether they had taken married couples or whether simple liaisons had been the norm. I didn't know how they'd been living since Ceausescu had been toppled. Some might have brazened it out at the Paris embassy, others asked for political asylum, others gone underground. Many, when the Securitate had been disbanded, had simply parted their hair on the other side and gone straight back to work. All I knew for certain was that Ledru had killed her man, and she had searched for a gun and killed Ledru and now that gun was pointing at us.

The woman spoke and her voice sounded cracked or harsh, or I was hearing nothing right after the gunshots. There were no social preliminaries. She said, 'You have those dollars you talked about in your pocket? Put them down on the ground and then step back. Both of you step back from the money.'

She wasn't concerned with making speeches like Ledru. She knew what she wanted and acted. She had shot Ledru in the back for revenge or because he was in her way. So I took the money out, put it on the ground and stepped back. Al joined me.

She didn't have the pistol raised to her eye but it was covering us. She was too close to miss, too far to disarm. She pushed Ecaterina ahead of her as she walked and now she spoke to the little girl. Nothing happened and she spoke more sharply. The girl came forward uncertainly, not watching her feet across the rough ground, staring at Al, and then at another command tottering towards me. She had dark-ringed eyes. She had learnt young how to conceal her feelings.

'Pick her up.'

I picked Ecaterina up and held her against my chest. The little body was too stiff to hug.

'If you move, I shoot,' the woman said. 'If you try any tricks, I shoot. If you scream for help, I shoot. I am an excellent shot, I have won many medals. The girl gets the first bullet. You have her life in your hands. If the man moves, I shoot the girl first and then I shoot him and then I shoot you.'

Al let a breath hiss out through his teeth.

'You say something?' the woman said. 'You want to argue? You prefer me to shoot you now and get it over with?'

Al didn't speak.

'All right,' she said.

Keeping her eyes on us, the woman bent her knees and scooped up the money. She weighed it in her hand, rubbed it between thumb and fingers. Her brows grew together slightly. Something about the feel of it made her flip through the stack. The cut paper between the two hundred-dollar bills showed as a white blur. In a fury, her face distorted and looking suddenly old and embittered, she raised her arm so that she was looking along the length of the pistol aimed at Ecaterina. Behind her little body was my heart.

'No,' I said, 'don't.' I grabbed another breath and held on to it as if it was my last. When I had to let the breath out I said, 'She's done nothing to harm you.'

I could have pleaded but I don't think begging ever got anywhere with the Securitate.

I said, 'She has the whole of her life in front of her.'

She tilted her face a degree above the pistol and we looked into each other's eyes. We stayed like this for a time. I have no way of knowing how long. Some seconds, half a lifetime, long enough to communicate things in silence between us. Possibly she saw the strength of my determination, perhaps in the end I saw a glimmer of compassion in her.

She stripped off the two hundred-dollar bills and chucked away the waste paper. In a low voice she said, 'Take the girl. She's your responsibility now.'

I asked, 'Are you the mother?'

'What?' She lapsed into silence again. She was staring at Ecaterina and me as if something puzzled her. She ignored Al completely, but if he'd made any move the pistol would have jumped on him.

'You'll never understand,' she said, and her voice had that harshness again. 'What is motherhood in a country like Romania? A woman's privilege? No. A free choice? No. An expression of love? No again. If a woman did not get pregnant she had a medical examination. You can have no idea of the humiliations heaped on us. Pregnancy was an order that had to be obeyed. Don't ask me who the father was. Him, one of the others, I don't know. So many of them.'

What did she mean? I still don't know. Possibly she was a shared woman in the Paris embassy, part of the duties expected of a Securitate agent. Another possibility: she was traumatised by mass rape. Did she feel no love for her daughter? Was she rejecting what had been done to her? As she said, I had no idea what it had been like in Romania. She had the same eyes as the daughter she was leaving: they kept their secrets locked away.

Finally, with a jerk of the head, she said, 'Go in the barn. Take the girl and both of you go in the barn.'

There was no final hug. She was abandoning her daughter to a total stranger. A less harsh judgement was that she knew Ecaterina had a better chance this way.

The metal door slid shut. The padlock snapped. A minute or two later the old Renault wheezed and fired, then the sound faded in the distance.

High up in the barn were ventilation gaps in the stone walls that cast a dim light over a pile of rusting farm machinery. Al was already turning this heap over, searching for a metal strut or bar strong enough to use as a lever. I put the girl down and knelt to be her height.

'Ecaterina?'

I got less response than I would from a doll. There are dolls that say *Mama,* or close their eyes when you lay them down, or wet their pants. I remembered that Ledru had chopped her name in half.

'Rina? Are you all right?'

She looked at me and said nothing.

The barn was more modern than the house and in a better structural state. Al had gouged out some of the mortar and removed a couple of large stone blocks and torn his fingernails, when we heard the growl of a motor. We shared the gap in the wall, cheek to cheek, and at first could see nothing. Finally two vehicles came into view. In the lead was a jeep which halted abruptly when the two corpses were visible. Armed riot police ran in a crouch to find cover behind bushes and the trunk of the walnut tree.

A man shouted, 'This is the CRS. Give yourselves up. I repeat, this is the CRS. Give yourselves up.'

Al called out, 'Over here, in the barn.'

Suddenly every automatic rifle was aimed at us. We pulled our faces away from the gap. Figures had been approaching from the car behind the jeep. A voice called out, 'Who's in there?' It was Crevecoeur.

Al called out, 'Richards, Cody and the little Romanian girl. We're locked in.'

There was no key and the padlock had to be shot away. I held on to Rina's hand because of the shooting, but she didn't flinch or utter a sound. When we got outside we found the riot police going in and out of the ruined farmhouse, looking for an enemy, still crouched over.

Crevecoeur was standing, his hands thrust deep in his pockets, his head bowed, staring at Ledru. He glanced at me and then back at the corpse. 'We knew – that is to say, *I* knew – you'd lead us to him. Not that you were going to him, but that his pals were tracking you and he would follow.'

'Using me as bait.'

'We kept an eye on things.' He pointed at the sky, rotating his finger. '*Shit,* there were things I needed to ask him. How he'd made contact with the Man. The Man's connections. Important stuff.'

He looked at the bullet holes in Ledru's back and then at Doicescu.

I said, 'She killed him. Doicescu's woman.'

'Where is she?'

'She left twenty minutes ago, half an hour ago.'

'How?'

'An old Renault 4.'

'Colour?'

'White. Dirty white.'

'Armed?'

'I suppose she still has her pistol.'

Crevecoeur went to the jeep and slumped against the side holding a radio mike. He was talking into it while his eyes roamed, sometimes on the bodies, sometimes on Ecaterina, who squatted in the dirt and scratched her head, sometimes on Al and me. When he came back to us his hands were thrust deep in his pockets again, as if he didn't trust them out in the open.

He said, 'She'll resist arrest. That's what I expect.'

'Good God,' Al burst out, 'is that what you ordered? She's to be shot while resisting arrest?'

Crevecoeur wheeled on him, jabbing out a finger. 'You better be damned careful, Mr American Journalist, if you want to keep your residence card. I shall be reading every single word you write and if I think there's even a hint…'

He let the threat drift and turned to the farmhouse.

'Jean-Louis!' One of his men turned from the door and came over. I'd seen this man before, up on the hillside above Ledru's *mas*. 'Give me a cigarette.'

'You've given up.'

'Don't bloody nag. Give me a cigarette.'

'I don't have any because you said you'd finally given up. You said it was the end, no more.'

I said, 'Ledru smoked.'

Crevecoeur half-bent down and checked himself. Nobody had covered the bodies and Ledru's eyes stared vacantly.

'Corpses,' he exploded. 'All over the place. Richards, better watch out if you hang round Cody. Wherever she goes, that's what you can be sure of. Corpses. Death.'

That just about summed up my own feelings. Yes, that was it. I felt like a firm of undertakers. Death & Co. Murder a speciality. Corpses guaranteed.

I took hold of Rina's hand and began walking.

'By the way,' Crevecoeur began, cool, off-hand. 'Had a flash from Paris this morning that may interest you, Cody.' I was finished with Crevecoeur. I went on walking. 'Concerns Yildirim.'

I stopped.

'They were taking Yildirim to Charles de Gaulle airport when the police van was ambushed. In the shoot-out two cops were killed. Yildirim got away.'

I had no particular thoughts. I was too drained. Oh, just the usual little spurts of emotion. Never trust Crevecoeur to keep his side of a bargain. Was it safe to go back to Paris?

'Who is Yildirim?' I heard Al ask.

'Fellow who's chasing Cody,' I heard Crevecoeur answer.

I squeezed little Rina's hand and got walking again.

'Co?' Then Al's voice came again much firmer. 'Co!'

Printed in Great Britain
by Amazon